The Tige

The Tiger Killers

Part Two of
The Marshes of Mount Liang

A New Translation of
the *Shuihu Zhuan* or *Water Margin*
of Shi Nai'an and Luo Guanzhong

By

John and Alex Dent-Young

The Chinese University Press

© **The Chinese University of Hong Kong,** 1997

All Rights Reserved. No part of this publication may be reproduced or transmitted in any form or by any means, electronic or mechanical, including photocopying, recording, or any information storage and retrieval system, without permission in writing from The Chinese University of Hong Kong

ISBN 962–201–751–7

THE CHINESE UNIVERSITY PRESS
The Chinese University of Hong Kong
SHA TIN, N. T., HONG KONG
Fax: +852 2603 6692
+852 2603 7355
E-mail: cup@cuhk.edu.hk
Web-site: http://www.cuhk.edu.hk/cupress/w1.htm

Printed in Hong Kong

Contents

Acknowledgements	ix
Introduction	xi
Chapter 23	1
Chai Jin entertains his guests with class;	
Wu Song kills the tiger of Jingyang Pass!	
Chapter 24	19
Mrs. Wang does brisk trade in sin;	
The Young'un's miffed and barges in!	
Chapter 25	61
The old woman tells his Nibs the plan;	
The adulteress poisons her old man!	
Chapter 26	77
Uncle Ho attends the funeral and steals some bones;	
Wu Song makes an offering of some human heads!	
Chapter 27	101
On the Mengzhou road the Ogress sells meat pies;	
Wu Song meets the Gardener at Crossways Rise!	
Chapter 28	117
Wu Song cuts a dash in the Fortress of Peace;	
The Young Master's ousted from Happy Woods!	
Chapter 29	131
The Young Master reigns again on the Mengzhou road;	
Wu Song drinks his fill and beats the Door-God!	

Contents

Chapter 30 145
The Young Master makes three visits to Death Row;
Wu Song reaps havoc at Flying Clouds Quay!

Chapter 31 165
In Ducks and Drakes Tower the General's blood will spill;
The false pilgrim Wu Song comes to Centipede Hill!

Chapter 32 185
Wu Song gets drunk and beats Red Star;
The Dandy treats Song Jiang with honour!

Chapter 33 211
Song Jiang goes to see the lights;
Hua Rong with his colleague fights!

Chapter 34 229
On the Qingzhou road, the Tamer fights a battle;
Thunderclap comes to the field of desolation!

Chapter 35 251
Shi Yong delivers a letter at the inn;
The Tamer shoots a goose on the wing!

Chapter 36 271
The Professor speaks of the Magic Messenger;
Song Jiang meets the White Water Dragon!

Chapter 37 289
Song Jiang is chased by Mu Hong, the Unstoppable;
The Pilot acts up on the river at night!

Chapter 38 309
Song Jiang and the Magic Messenger get together;
Iron Ox and White Eel have a set-to in the river!

Chapter 39 333
Song Jiang writes a poem, he should have known better;
The Magic Messenger carries a forged letter!

Chapter 40 361
The heroes of Mount Liang raid the execution ground;
Twenty-nine leaders at White Dragon temple assemble!

Contents vii

Chapter 41 377
   Song Jiang plans the capture of Wuweijun;
   White Eel takes Bee Sting Huang alive!
Chapter 42 399
   The mystic books received in Dead-End Village;
   Song Jiang meets the Mystic Lady!
Chapter 43 419
   The false Li Kui robs travellers on the highway;
   Iron Ox kills four tigers on Yiling Heights!

Acknowledgements

As for Part One we are indebted to many people's help. In particular we should mention Zhu Zhiyu for further help with the verse, and the begetters of the project, John Minford, Joseph Lau and Sean Golden, for their continued support. We would also like to record thanks to Fung Wai-kit, our indefatigable editor at The Chinese University Press.

The illustrations are from two series of old engravings from the Ming Dynasty. One is known as the *Rong-yu-tang* 容與堂本, and the other as *Yang Dingjian* 楊定見序本. These illustrations have been published in two different volumes respectively entitled *Rong-yu-tang ben Shuihu Zhuan* 容與堂本水滸傳 (China: Shanghai Chinese Classics Publishing House, 1988), and *Shuihu quan zhuan* 水滸全傳 (China: Zhong Hua Book Co., 1961).

Introduction

We wish here only to reiterate that this translation is aimed at the general reader. We believe all translation is a compromise. In this version it may take the form of going a little more than halfway to meet the English reader. In terms of style, we have aimed at some degree of formality for the more ritual moments, and informality, a suggestion of dialect even, for much of the dialogue. One walks a knife-edge in such matters, as every translator knows. We can only hope that the inevitable anachronisms are not too obtrusive in the relatively fast and easy reading that we want to make possible. Once again we have been very free with the verse in the hope of recapturing some sense of how it might be a bonus, not an impediment, to the narrator and his audience.

English readers have suggested that some sort of guide to *pinyin* pronunciation might be helpful. The following note is meant only to allow the reader some way of sounding the names.

A Note on the Names

Chinese names, except for a few like Tao already well-known in English, are given here in the standard modern system of transliteration (known as *pinyin*). It is the system used nowadays in news reporting, but it presents a few major problems for the uninitiated, mainly with the use of consonants:

c = ts
z = dz
q = ch as in *cheap*
x = sh as in *sheep*
zh = j as in *judge*

If the reader should wonder about the reason for these outlandish spellings, it is basically because there are two different sets of consonants representing sounds that resemble the English *ch*, *sh* and *j*, so extra symbols are needed to distinguish them.

Vowels mostly resemble those in a European language like French or Spanish. Two vowels together represent a diphthong. But again the double set of consonants produces a problem:

Shi, Zhi, Chi = sh etc. followed by a sound like English r — approximately the first syllable in *Shirley*, spoken with an American or West of England accent

Zi, Ci = a similar vowel sound to the above

Xi, Ji, Qi = the sounds in *she*, *gee* and *chee(se)*

o (in Poxi) = the o in *for*, so that Poxi rhymes with *for she*

ü = the French sound in *tu*

Chapter 23

Chai Jin entertains his guests with class; Wu Song kills the tiger of Jingyang Pass!

Let me remind you now how Song Jiang, in order to miss a round of drinking at Chai Jin's manor where he was taking refuge after killing his mistress, had gone to wash his hands and, making a detour back to the gallery, had tripped over a shovel full of hot coals, greatly to the annoyance of a certain stranger, who leapt to his feet looking for a fight. And how his host came rushing to the rescue and how he happened to reveal Song Jiang's name, so that the stranger, hearing who he was, threw himself on his knees and refused to get up, saying: "Fool that I am, I couldn't see what was staring me in the face. I insulted you just now. Can you ever forgive me?" and then Song Jiang raised him up and asked: "But who are you? Won't you tell me your name?"

Chai Jin supplied the answer. "This gentleman is from Qinghe. His name is Wu Song, he is the second son in his family. He has been with us a year now."

"I have heard much talk of Mr. Wu among the rivers and lakes fraternity," said Song Jiang. "But I had no idea I was to meet him here today. What a pleasure this is!"

"It's a great thing when men of honour meet by chance like this," said Chai Jin. "We shall celebrate with a dinner, so we can have some talk."

Song Jiang was pleased to take Wu Song's hand and lead him into the inner hall. He called his younger brother Song Qing and introduced him to Wu Song. When Chai Jin invited Wu Song to sit down, Song Jiang immediately asked him to sit beside him in the place of honour. Wu Song naturally refused. This modest show of reluctance went on a long time until finally Wu Song was prevailed upon to take the third place. Chai Jin then ordered the cups filled again and invited them to drink deep. Song Jiang was now able by the light of the lamps to get a better look at his new friend:

> *His stature is awesome, his bearing deeply impressive; the eyes blaze like winter stars, the brows are an unbroken line drawn in lacquer; the chest so broad ten thousand foes could never throw him down, the speech forceful, evidence of a soaring ambition; the spirit so brave you'd think the lion which shakes heaven had descended from the clouds, the frame so powerful you'd imagine you were confronting the beast which shatters the world. Truly this seems a god walking the earth, a veritable Mars among men.*

Song Jiang liked what he saw exceedingly, and he asked Wu Song: "Tell me, pray, what is the reason for your staying here?"

"I got drunk one day, back in Qinghe, and had a fight with a confidential secretary," the other replied. "He really riled me. I only hit him the once, but I knocked him out cold. Well, I thought I'd killed him, so I cleared off and came here to Mr. Chai's, waiting for it to blow over. Since then I've heard the fellow isn't dead, they revived him. I was planning to go home to see my brother, but then I suddenly came down with malaria, so I couldn't travel. Just now I had a shivering fit and I was sitting over those coals in the gallery when you walked into them and gave me such a shock I broke out in a cold sweat, and now I think I'm cured!"

Song Jiang listened delightedly. That night the drinking went on till the small hours. Afterwards Song Jiang insisted that Wu Song go and sleep with them in the west wing. Next day Chai Jin organized a big banquet and had goats and pigs killed to feast Song Jiang. Of this no more.

After a few days Song Jiang took out some money for Wu Song to make himself a new set of clothes. When Chai Jin learnt of this, of course he would have none of it. He went to a chest and took out some pieces of fine silk, and commissioned his own tailor just outside the gates to supply all three of them with suits of clothes made to measure.

Incidentally, Chai Jin was displeased with Wu Song. Why so?

Chapter 23

Well, when Wu Song first arrived he had received a grand welcome. But later he was always getting drunk and owing to his impetuous temperament he was inclined to get a stick and beat the servants whenever their ministrations failed to meet his standards. Consequently there was not one of them who looked on him favourably. In fact they all hated him, and invented all kinds of stories to tell Chai Jin about him. So although Chai Jin did not turn Wu Song out, his behaviour towards him had grown much cooler. However, now when Song Jiang adopted Wu Song and made him his constant drinking companion, the latter mended his ways.

After Song Jiang had been with them about ten days, Wu Song felt the urge to return home to Qinghe to see his brother. Chai Jin and Song Jiang both urged him to stay on a while, but he said: "It's a long time now since I had news of my brother, I think I should go back and see him."

"If you really want to go," Song Jiang said, "we must not detain you. But if you have time later, do let us meet again."

Wu Song thanked Song Jiang and Chai Jin gave him some silver for which Wu Song thanked him, saying: "I am afraid, sir, I have given you a lot of trouble." Then he tied his bundle, took up his cudgel and was ready to depart. But first Chai Jin laid on a little send-off party. Wu Song was wearing a new robe of fine red silk and a white Fanyang hat. With his pack on his shoulders and carrying his cudgel he was finally on the point of leaving, when Song Jiang said: "Dear brother, wait one moment." He went to his room and got some silver and hurried back to the manor gate. "I shall accompany you on the first stage of your journey," he said to Wu Song.

Song Jiang and his younger brother waited while Wu Song said his last farewell to Chai Jin and then Song Jiang also told Chai Jin they would be back in a little and the three of them set off from Chai Jin's eastern manor together. After a couple of miles, Wu Song suggested it was time to part: "Dear friends, you should go back now. Chai Jin will be waiting."

"Just a little further, why not?" Song Jiang said.

They conversed as they went and without noticing it, they had covered another mile or so, when Wu Song stopped Song Jiang and said: "You really shouldn't accompany me any further. You know the saying, 'When you're seeing someone off, you may go with them a hundred miles, but still you have to say good-bye!'"

"Allow me to go just a little further," Song Jiang pleaded. "See that little inn on the highroad there, why don't we go in and drink a farewell cup together?"

They went in and Song Jiang seated himself at the head of the table. Wu Song laid down his cudgel and joined him, while Song Qing sat across the table from them. They told the waiter to bring wine and ordered some dishes and a variety of fruit and vegetables which were spread on the table before them. They drank some cups and watched the sun sinking in the west. "It's getting late," Wu Song said. "If you'll allow me, I want to prostrate myself four times so I can call myself your blood brother."

This pleased Song Jiang greatly. The ceremony completed, Song Jiang told his brother to take out ten taels of silver to give Wu Song. Wu Song refused it, naturally, saying: "When I was a guest at Mr. Chai's I received a generous allowance."

"Don't make a fuss about this, dear brother," Song Jiang said. "If you refuse I shall think you do not prize my friendship."

So Wu Song, after prostrating himself again, had to take the money, which he put away in his purse. Then, Song Jiang having paid for the wine with some loose change, Wu Song took up his cudgel and the three men left the inn. There at the inn door they said their farewells, Wu Song saluting with tears in his eyes before he departed. Song Jiang and his brother stood there at the door and watched him out of sight. Then they set off on the return journey. They had covered little more than a mile when they saw Chai Jin approaching on horseback, leading two riderless horses. It was a welcome sight. They rode back together to the manor. When they had dismounted, Chai Jin invited them to drink in an inner chamber. For the time being, Song Jiang and his brother stayed at Chai Jin's.

Here our story divides.

Wu Song, after parting from Song Jiang, spent the night at an inn. Next morning, having breakfasted and paid for his room, he

Chapter 23

tied his bundle, grasped his cudgel and took to the road. As he went along, he mused: "Among the rivers and lakes, they talk all the time about Song Jiang, the Opportune Rain. And what they say is no exaggeration. It's a real privilege to know a man like that!"

After following the road for several days, Wu Song had reached the district of Yanggu, but was still some way off the provincial capital. By noon that day, when he was feeling hungry and thirsty, he perceived in front of him a tavern, advertised by a sign with five characters, which read: "Three bowls, forget the pass!"

Wu Song walked in and sat down. He laid his cudgel down and called out: "Landlord! Quickly, some wine!"

The innkeeper came with three bowls, chopsticks and a dish, which he laid in front of Wu Song. He filled one of the bowls with wine. Wu Song picked it up and drained it in one gulp. "This wine's got a real kick!" he exclaimed. "Now then Landlord, how about something to line the stomach? I'll have something to go with this wine."

"Some boiled beef is all I've got," the man said.

"That'll do," said Wu Song. "Slice me two or three catties."

The innkeeper went in and cut two catties of beef and put it in a big dish which he then placed in front of Wu Song. Then he poured another big bowl of wine. Wu Song drank it off and said: "Now that's what I call good wine!"

One more bowl was poured. And that made exactly three Wu Song had drunk and the host wasn't going to pour any more.

Wu Song started to bang on the table. "Landlord!" he shouted. "Why don't you come and pour the wine?"

"Sir, more meat I'll bring you, if that be what you desire."

"I want more wine — but don't worry, you can cut me some more meat as well."

"If it's meat you want," the landlord repeated, "I'll bring it for you, but no more wine."

"What's all this?" Wu Song said to himself. To the innkeeper he said: "Why don't you want to sell me any more?"

"Lord, sir!" said the man. "You seen our sign, haven't you? Says it clear enough, don't it? 'Three bowls, forget the pass!'"

"But what's that supposed to mean, 'Three bowls, forget the pass'?"

"Well, 'tis a local brew, I know that, but this wine of ours has got more class than many a famous vintage. Everyone who comes to our inn here, they have just the three bowls and then they're drunk, see, they have to forget about climbing the pass up there! That's why we say, 'Three bowls, forget the pass!' All our guests, just three bowls you know, and after that they don't ask for no more."

Wu Song laughed and said: "Oh, so that's it! But I've had three bowls, how come I'm not drunk?"

The innkeeper said: "They calls her the Perfumed Glory, but they also calls her The Knockout. Slips down like mother's milk, she does, but she'll go off like a time bomb!"

"Balls!" said Wu Song. "Are you afraid I won't pay you? Bring me another three bowls."

Seeing that Wu Song was still entirely steady, the innkeeper brought him another three bowls.

Wu Song drank and said: "First-class wine. Landlord, whatever I drink, I'll pay for. Just keep me filled up!"

"Oh sir!" the man protested. "Don't go on drinking! When you're drunk on this wine there's no remedy."

"Enough of your bullshit! And if you're thinking of doctoring the wine, watch out, I've got a nose for that sort of thing!"

The innkeeper found it was no good arguing, so he poured another three bowls.

"Bring me another two catties of meat!" Wu Song shouted.

The innkeeper cut another two catties of beef, poured another three bowls of wine and for a long while Wu Song went on guzzling. Finally he took out some silver and called: "Landlord, come and count this silver, see if it's enough to pay for what I've drunk and eaten."

The innkeeper had a look and said: "More than enough, you'll get some change."

"I don't want your change, just give it to me in wine."

"But sir, if you want it in wine, that's another five or six bowls! I'll warrant you can't manage that."

Chapter 23

"I don't care if it's more than six bowls, just bring it!"

"You're such a big man," said the innkeeper, "if you pass out, how are we ever going to carry you?"

"If I needed the likes of you to carry me, I wouldn't call myself a man at all!"

But the innkeeper still didn't want to bring the wine.

Wu Song began to lose his temper. "It's not as if I'm not paying you for it. If you don't stop trying to provoke me, I'll smash the place up, I'll turn your bloody house upside down!"

"The bugger's drunk, I'd better humour him," the innkeeper said to himself. And he brought another six bowls, all of which Wu Song drank.

Having consumed altogether no less than eighteen bowls, Wu Song now grasped his cudgel, rose to his feet and saying: "Who says I'm drunk?", marched out of the door. "And you can forget all that stuff about 'Three bowls, forget the pass'," he shouted back.

So off he went, brandishing his cudgel.

But then the innkeeper was chasing after him, crying: "Sir, sir, where do you think you're a-going to?"

Wu Song halted and said: "What are you shouting about? I've paid for everything, haven't I? Why all this song and dance?"

"I'm only trying to help," the innkeeper said. "You'd better come back inside and read the government notice."

"What government notice?"

"There's been this big tiger, see, recently, a monster with bulging eyes and a white forehead, up there in the Jingyang Pass. He comes out to attack people at night. Done for twenty or thirty good men already, he has. The hunters are under orders to trap him, there's a deadline set by the government. And there's signs posted up in all the approaches to the pass, warning travellers to form groups if they want to cross, and only to go morning, noon or afternoon. It's forbidden to cross at any other time. And what's more, single travellers are supposed to wait till there's a group. 'Tis late now, it'll soon be night, and when I saw you walk off like that, without a word to anyone, I said to myself, 'he's just throwing his life away.' You'd much better spend the night here. Tomorrow you can wait till a sufficient number's gathered, and then you all cross the pass together."

Wu Song laughed this suggestion to scorn. "I'm from the region," he said, "and I've crossed this pass a score of times. Who ever heard of a tiger there? It's no good thinking you can frighten me with that sort of shit. Anyway, even if there is a tiger, I'm not afraid of it!"

"I'm telling you what's good for you! If you don't believe me, come inside and take a look at the government notice."

"Balls! I tell you, if there really is a tiger, it doesn't scare me. What you want is to get me to stay in your house so you can come in the middle of the night and rob me of my money and my life. That's why you're trying to intimidate me with some tale of a fucking tiger!"

"Well I never! Here's me, out of the kindness of my heart, trying to help him, and all he does is twist my words around to give them a bad meaning. All right, if you don't believe me, just go ahead!"

It was like this, you see:

Of those that went before, a thousand came to grief;
That the next will safely pass is surely beyond belief!
In pointing out the facts nothing but kindness is meant;
But the fool with his suspicions imagines an ill intent!

Shaking his head, the innkeeper stepped back inside.

Wu Song picked up his cudgel and strode off towards the Jingyang Pass. After little more than a mile, he arrived at the foot of the pass. Here he saw a big tree, with a white patch where the bark had been stripped off to make room for two lines of writing. Wu Song was a passable reader. He raised his eyes and read:

In view of the recent attacks by a tiger in the Jingyang Pass, travellers are advised to make the crossing only in the morning, at noon, or in the afternoon, and furthermore to organize themselves into groups for the said crossing. Ignore this advice at your peril!

Wu Song did not take it seriously. "It must be a trick by that scoundrel of an innkeeper to frighten travellers into staying at his

Chapter 23

inn. That sort of bullshit won't scare me!" he said, and with his cudgel at the slope he began to climb the pass.

By now the afternoon was drawing on and the sun's red disk was starting to sink behind the mountains. But Wu Song, spurred on by the wine he had drunk, was determined to conquer that pass. He had not gone more than a few hundred yards, however, when he came upon a tumbledown little temple dedicated to the spirits of the mountain. Approaching, he saw that there was a notice bearing an official seal fixed to the door. He paused to read it. It said:

> *Yanggu district office announces that due to the recent appearance of a fierce man-eating tiger and the fact that the local hunters commissioned to trap it have not yet succeeded in their objective, all merchants and travellers are accordingly advised not to attempt the crossing of the pass except between the hours of nine and three, and furthermore single travellers are not to attempt the journey alone, lest they perish in the process. Traveller take heed!*

After reading this, Wu Song realized that there was indeed a tiger. At first he thought of turning back and going to the inn, but then he said to himself: "If I go back there, I'll have to endure his mockery. It'll look as if I'm scared. So I can't very well turn back." He turned it over in his mind for a while and then concluded: "What the hell am I afraid of? I'll just go on and see what happens."

So on he went. And as the wine began to mount to his head, he took off his hat and strung it on his back, and tucked the cudgel under his arm. Step by step, he trudged on up the pass. Turning to look at the sun, he saw that it was slowly setting. This was real November weather, when the days are short and the nights long, and it's easy for nightfall to catch you unawares. "What's all this nonsense about a big tiger," Wu Song was muttering to himself. "People are scared of the mountain that's all, they don't have the guts to climb it."

He walked on a bit further and the wine began to make itself felt still more. He was feeling hot, so holding his cudgel in one hand he used the other to loosen his clothing and bare his chest.

He was swaying and stumbling as he advanced towards a dense thicket. There happened to be a smooth black boulder here, so he laid his cudgel aside and sank down to rest upon the boulder. He was just drifting off to sleep when there came a fierce gust of wind.

There's an old four-line verse which exactly describes this wind:

Formless and invisible, it strikes to a man's heart;
It comes in any season and it blows all things apart;
Sweeping through the autumn woods it strips the branches bare,
Whistling among mountain peaks, it fills with clouds the air.

For clouds, as we all know, originate with dragons, and wind is associated with tigers.

When the gust had passed, he heard something crashing through the trees and out sprang an enormous tiger, with bulging eyes and a white forehead. When Wu Song saw this a horrified "Aiya!" broke from his lips. He rolled off the boulder and grabbing his cudgel dodged behind it.

Now the tiger was ravenous. It struck the ground with two paws and sprang upwards, intending to land on its prey like a thunderbolt. Wu Song had such a shock that he felt all the wine start out of him in an icy sweat!

It's slow in the telling, but happens in a flash. When he saw the tiger spring, Wu Song leapt out of the way, ending up behind it. That's exactly what the tiger didn't like, to have a man at its back. Thrusting upward off its front paws, it flexed its back and twisted round to pounce again. But again Wu Song dodged to one side. Failing to grasp its prey, the tiger gave a roar like half the heavens exploding, a roar that seemed to shake the very mountains, and lashed out at Wu Song with its tail, rigid as a steel bar. Once more Wu Song leapt aside.

Now when the tiger attacks a man, it generally has these three strategies: the spring, the pounce and the tail-swipe. When all these three methods failed, this tiger's spirit was half broken. After failing to catch Wu Song with its tail it gave a loud roar and turned away. Seeing the tiger had turned its back on him, Wu Song

Chapter 23

grasped his cudgel in both hands and brought it down with all the strength of his body. There was a resounding crash.

But what he had done was demolish a whole tree, branches and all. He looked for the tiger. His staff had not even touched it. He'd rushed his stroke and all he'd achieved was to bring down a dead tree. Now his cudgel was broken in two and he was left with only the broken half in his hand.

The tiger roared, it was enraged, it turned and sprang at him again. Wu Song leapt back, covering ten paces in a single bound. The tiger reared up on its hind legs and came at him with all its claws out. Wu Song threw away his broken stick and suddenly grabbing the tiger's striped neck with his bare hands began forcing it down to the ground. The beast tried to struggle, but all Wu Song's strength was employed against it, not for a moment did he relax his grip. With his legs he delivered fearful kicks to its nose and eyes. The tiger roared furiously, and as it thrashed about under this onslaught its paws churned up two mounds of mud. Wu Song thrust the beast's head down into the mud and irresistibly its power began to ebb. Still gripping the striped coat tightly with his left hand, Wu Song managed to work his right hand free and began raining down blows with an iron fist, hammering the beast with all his might. He got in fifty or sixty blows, till from the tiger's eyes, mouth, nose and ears the red blood began to gush.

With all the power of the heroes of old, by the sheer force of his manly spirit, Wu Song was able easily to convert that savage monster into a senseless heap, for all the world like an embroidered bag. There's a traditional account of this:

> *On Jingyang Pass a sudden squall,*
> *Day hides its face in a thick black pall;*
> *Twilight cloaks the desolate wold,*
> *And a deadly chill pervades the world.*
> *A sound like thunder splits the ears*
> *As the king of beasts on the slope appears.*
> *He proudly bounds, teeth and claws on show,*
> *Filling the antlered tribe with woe.*

Chapter 23

The Qinghe hero, still half tight,
Waits alone, but ready to fight.
To watch that man-eater hunt a meal,
Crouch and spring ... it would make you squeal!
He falls on the man like an avalanche,
But the man's a cliff, he doesn't flinch;
He grips with the force of a missile crashing —
And the tiger's paws in the mud are thrashing,
Blows and kicks, a relentless flood,
Both hands soaked in the crimson blood.
Dreadful carnage! On the blood-soaked ground
Fur and whiskers are strewn around.
There it lies now, bright stripes fading,
Sprawled among weeds, the wild eyes clouding.

Now what Wu Song on the mountain provided for that savage tiger, in less time than it takes to eat a simple meal, was a surfeit of blows and kicks: he beat the beast senseless. For a moment it lay helpless, faintly panting. Then Wu Song let go and went to find the broken end of his cudgel. With this, fearing lest the tiger revive, he belaboured it a while longer, till the breath was quite gone out of it.

"I might as well drag the carcass down the mountain," he decided. But when he thrust his hands into the bleeding mass and started pulling, he could not shift it. All he did was exhaust himself, till his arms and legs began to fail. So he went back to the black boulder and sat down to rest for a while. Presently he said to himself: "It's getting quite dark now. If another tiger should appear, I don't think I'd be able to cope. I'd better try and get down off the pass. I can come back and deal with this thing in the morning." He picked up his hat, which had fallen beside the boulder, and skirting round the thickest part of the forest, set off at a steady pace down the mountain.

He had hardly gone half a mile when he saw, emerging from a thick patch of tall dry grass, two tigers! "Aiya!" he cried, "now I'm finished!" Then in the shadows the two tigers rose on their hind legs, and when Wu Song looked carefully, it was two men who had sewn themselves suits made out of tiger skins, fitting tightly to their bodies. They carried five-tined forks.

They were shocked to see Wu Song. "Have you the courage of a wild beast, a leopard's gall, a tiger's claws?" they said. "Have you a heart so big it won't fit in your body, that you dare, alone in the dark of night and unarmed, to cross the pass? Are you a man or a ghost?"

"Who are you?" Wu Song asked in return.

"We are the hunters," they replied.

"And why are you headed this way, up the mountain?"

They registered amazement. "Haven't you heard? There's a truly enormous tiger, right here in Jingyang Pass. Every night someone is attacked. Seven or eight of our fellows, hunters that is, have lost their lives already, and countless travellers, all devoured by this terrible monster. The Magistrate has made the local authorities and us hunters responsible for capturing it. But it's incredibly ferocious and dangerous to approach, no one dares get too near. We've had I don't know how many beatings on account of this, but we just can't catch him. It's our turn again tonight. We've got a few dozen villagers here to back us up. We've put down traps everywhere, loaded with poisoned darts. We had just finished setting our ambush. Imagine our surprise when we saw you strolling down the mountain. Who are you? Did you see the tiger?"

"I'm from Qinghe, my name is Wu and I'm the second in my family. Yes, I ran into the tiger, in a pretty wild part of the mountain too, and I've just beaten it to death."

The hunters' jaws fell open. "Are you joking?" they said.

"If you don't believe it, look at all the blood on me."

"But how did you kill it?"

Wu Song recounted his exploit with the tiger. The hunters were as relieved as they were astonished. They called the villagers, who now came crowding forward, a dozen or more of them, carrying steel-tined forks, foot-bows, knives and spears.

"Why didn't these troops go with you up the mountain?" Wu Song asked the hunters.

"Catch them going up there, with a ferocious beast like that on the loose!" the latter replied.

Chapter 23

When the hunters told the villagers that Wu Song had killed the tiger they didn't believe it.

"If you don't trust me, let's all go and have a look," Wu Song said. They had flints and tinder boxes with them, so they lit half a dozen torches and followed Wu Song back up the mountain. There was the dead tiger, sprawled in a heap. Immediately there was great rejoicing. One of the villagers was sent on ahead to inform the district authorities, while the others put a rope round the tiger and carried it down the mountain.

When they reached the bottom a crowd had already gathered. They proceeded on, the tiger going in front and Wu Song now being carried in a mountain palanquin, till they reached the house of a local bigwig. This personage, accompanied by the Magistrate, was waiting for them outside the gate. The tiger was carried to the main hall. Everyone of any standing in the district had come to see Wu Song, and so had all the local hunters, so there were twenty or thirty people all told.

"Won't you please tell us your name and where you come from?" they said to Wu Song.

"My name's Wu Song and I'm the second in my family. I was on my way home from Cangzhou. Last night I stayed at the inn on the other side of the pass and got rather drunk. When I climbed the pass there was this tiger." Once more he gave a detailed account of his pugilistic exploits with the tiger.

"My! This is a real hero!" the audience said.

Wu Song was now offered wine and the hunters produced dishes of game to go with it. Wu Song was exhausted from his fight with the tiger and the master of the house, after telling the servants to prepare a guest-room, urged him to go and lie down.

Next day at dawn the head of the household sent someone to the Magistracy with a report. A frame was constructed for carrying the tiger. As soon as it was fully light Wu Song got up and washed. The important people of the village brought a sheep and a barrel of wine, which was served in front of the main hall. Wu Song dressed and put on his hat and came out to meet everyone. They toasted him and said: "Heaven knows how many people this beast injured, or how many hunters suffered floggings because of it. Now at last a hero has appeared and rid us of the menace. What a relief, both for the people of this village and for all travellers, who can now complete their journey in safety! We really owe you a lot!"

"It is not through any merit of my own," said Wu Song modestly. "I must have acted in the shadow of your good fortune."

Everyone had come to congratulate him. When they had breakfasted and drunk wine the tiger was carried out and placed on the frame, while Wu Song was garlanded with a piece of red silk. Wu Song left his bundle and other things in the village, and they all departed through the gate. Immediately some police officers from Yanggu appeared, with orders to escort Wu Song. After some introductions, four servants were instructed to carry Wu Song in an open sedan, while the tiger was borne along in front, draped in red cloth. Thus they proceeded to Yanggu.

The people of Yanggu, having heard about a hero killing the tiger of the Jingyang Pass, all turned out to cheer. The whole district was in an uproar. From his sedan Wu Song saw them pushing and shoving, packing every street and alley, everyone eager for a glimpse of the tiger. The procession reached the government offices and stopped at the entrance to the court. The Magistrate was already in the courtroom, waiting to receive them. Wu Song alighted and the bearers set the tiger down on a raised walkway. The Magistrate, having observed Wu Song's manly aspect and seeing the tiger was such a magnificent specimen, said to himself: "Who but such a fellow could have finished off that enormous animal?" When Wu Song had saluted, the Magistrate said: "Come now, do tell us all about how you killed such a mighty beast."

So Wu Song told his story all over again, in the courtroom. Everyone present heard him with amazement. Toasts were drunk in his honour and he was presented with some money collected by the local dignitaries as a reward, a thousand strings of cash in all. But Wu Song modestly said: "I am simply enjoying the reflection of your good fortune, Your Excellency. I was just lucky to kill the tiger, it was not through any merit of my own. How can I accept this money? I have heard that the hunters here suffered sanctions on account of the tiger. Might we not divide the money and give it to them?"

"If that is your wish," the Magistrate said. "I leave it to you to arrange it."

Wu Song distributed the money among the hunters, and the Magistrate, impressed by Wu Song's open-handedness and humanity, decided he would like to secure his advancement. "Although you are from Qinghe," he said, "that's right next to us here at Yanggu. I would like to offer you a commission in our forces. What do you say?"

Wu Song knelt to thank him. "I shall be forever in your debt for this, Your Excellency," he said.

Accordingly, the Magistrate called the registrar and had him write out the order appointing Wu Song with immediate effect a captain of foot. All the important members of the community came to offer their congratulations and there were celebrations lasting several days. Wu Song thought to himself: "Really, it's amazing. I merely wanted to go home to see my brother, and now here I am, an officer in the Yanggu militia!" From that day on he was honoured by all and his fame spread throughout the district.

Several days had passed, and then one day as Wu Song left the government offices in search of amusement, he heard someone call out behind him: "Captain Wu, you've made your fortune now, is that why you don't come to see me?"

When Wu Song turned and saw who it was, he let out a cry: "Aiya! what are you doing here?"

Had Wu Song not met this person, things would have turned out very differently, and Yanggu would not have witnessed a scene of terrible carnage. As a result of the meeting,

Blades will whistle and heads will roll,
Bright swords be drawn and the hot blood flow.

But if you want to know who it was who called out to Wu Song, addressing him as Captain Wu, you must read the next chapter.

Chapter 24

Mrs. Wang does brisk trade in sin;
The Young'un's miffed and barges in!

Now when Wu Song turned round that day and saw who it was that had called him, he threw himself down in respectful greeting, because this person was none other than his elder brother, Wu Da.

So Wu Song prostrated himself and said: "I haven't seen you for over a year brother. What are you doing here?"

"You were gone so long," Wu Da said. "Why didn't you write to me? You know, I was furious with you, but I missed you!"

"What's that supposed to mean, you were furious with me but you missed me?" asked Wu Song.

"Well, you used to make me so angry in those days, always getting drunk, always getting into fights, always in trouble with the authorities and obliging me to go the court on your behalf. Never a moment's peace, always some headache because of you! That's why I was furious with you. But I missed you when I got spliced recently. People treated me dreadfully, there was no one to stand up for me. If only you'd been there we wouldn't have heard a fart out of them, you can bet your life on it. It got so I couldn't stand it any more, so I've had to move to this place and rent a house. That's why I missed you."

What you must know, friends, is that although Wu Song and Wu Da were born of the same mother, Wu Song was a tall, impressive figure of a man, immensely strong — of course, how else would he have killed the tiger? — but Wu Da was barely four foot and ugly as sin; his appearance provoked nothing but ridicule. The people of his town, on account of his dwarfish stature, had nicknamed him "The Three-Inch Poxy Midget."

Now in Qinghe there was a family who had a maid called Pan Jinlian, or Golden Lotus. At the age of twenty she was rather pretty. Because the master was trying to force his attentions upon her (and she unwilling to accede to his demands), she had gone to complain to her mistress. The master was furious, and after giving her a small trousseau, married her off to the Midget, free, gratis and for nothing. After Wu Da married the girl, certain cheating and dissolute young men of the town began to swarm round his house and disturb the peace. The girl herself, naturally enough in view of Wu Da's lack of inches and unimpressive character, was eager for something better and she made it her prime objective to find herself a lover, as the poem about her says:

> *She's not the kind to be passed over,*
> *With charms galore to please a lover.*
> *Just wait till a nice young man she meets;*
> *There'll soon be games between the sheets!*

Now once this girl had entered his home, the Midget, who was a timid conventional kind of man, was continually pestered by the shameless gang of good-for-nothings who camped at his gate, making lewd comments like: "What a juicy piece of mutton to fall into the mouth of a dog!" It became impossible for him to go on living in Qinghe, so he moved to Yanggu, where he rented a house in Redstone Road. Here he continued in his old trade, going out every day to sell bread on the street.

He had been carrying on his business outside the government offices on the morning he met Wu Song. "Well, brother," he said, "the other day the streets were buzzing with the news of a great tiger-killer named Wu, who'd eliminated the monster on Jingyang Pass and been appointed captain by the Magistrate. I wasn't sure but something told me it must be you. Anyway, now that I've found you, I'm going to knock off work and take you home with me."

"Where do you live?" Wu Song asked.

His brother pointed. "Just round the corner in Redstone Road."

Wu Song picked up his brother's carrying-pole, and the Midget guided him past several turnings till they reached Redstone Road.

Chapter 24

They continued down it and after rounding two more bends came to the house, adjoining the compound of a teahouse.

"Open the door, dear," the Midget called. The bamboo curtain was raised a little, and a woman's face appeared beneath it. "Why are you back so early?" she said.

"Your brother-in-law is here, I want you to meet him." He took his carrying-pole and deposited it inside. Then he came out again and said: "Come on in and meet your sister-in-law."

Wu Song parted the curtain and entered. He greeted the woman. The Midget said to her: "You heard about the person who killed the tiger, dear, on Jingyang Pass? And who was made a captain by the Magistrate? Well, it's my little brother!"

The woman crossed her hands and wished her brother-in-law a thousand happinesses. Wu Song said: "Please stay seated, sister-in-law," and made a most gracious obeisance. The woman darted forward to raise him up, saying: "Please, brother-in-law, this is too much."

Wu Song said: "I am your most humble servant, sister-in-law."

"I heard them saying that a very brave man who had killed a tiger was coming to town," she said. "I planned to go and see, but unfortunately I got there late and missed my chance. I never got to see him, but now, well, so it's you! Do please come upstairs and sit down."

Here's what Wu Song saw when he looked at his sister-in-law:

> *Brows like willow-leaves in early spring, but oft-times clouded with the sadness of showers; a face like third month peach blossoms, hinting at romantic desires and amorous thoughts; a slender figure, full of indolent grace and feminine allure; lips red enough to tantalize the bees and butterflies; bewitching beauty, arousing every sense with its soft fragrance.*

She now told the Midget to take his brother upstairs to the sitting-room. When they were all seated she gave the Midget a look and said: "I will take care of your brother. You go and order food and wine for him."

"All right," the Midget said. "You sit here brother; I'll be back in a moment."

When the Midget was gone, the woman covertly examined Wu Song. "They're brothers with the same mother, but how well-built this one is!" she was thinking. "If only I'd married this one instead, life would really seem worth living! There's absolutely no comparison with my Three-Inch Poxy Midget, who's only three parts man and seven parts ghost! Oh, how unlucky I am! Judging by the way he killed the tiger, Wu Song must be terrifically strong. Apparently he isn't married yet, so why not get him to come and live here? Surely it's fate that brought him to me!"

Smiling her most winning smile, she asked Wu Song: "How long have you been here, brother-in-law?"

"About ten days," he answered.

"And where are you staying?"

"I doss down at the government offices."

"That doesn't sound very comfortable."

"I'm on my own. I don't need much. And I've got the soldiers of the militia to serve me."

"Soldiers? How can they look after you properly? Why don't you come and live here? Then whenever you wanted something to eat or drink I'd prepare it for you with my own hands. You wouldn't have to depend on dirty people like that. I'd give you some nice soup for instance, and you'd know it was safe to eat."

"That's very kind of you."

"Or perhaps you have a wife somewhere? You could bring her here to look after you."

"I'm not married."

"Can I ask how old you are?"

"I'm twenty-five."

"That's just three years older than me. Where were you before you came here?"

"I was in Cangzhou for just over a year. I thought my brother was in Qinghe, I didn't know he had moved here."

"Well, you can't imagine the trouble there's been since I married your brother! He's too good you see. People were horrible to him and we couldn't stand to live in Qinghe any more, so we came here. Of course, if you'd been around, a hero like you, no one would have dared to say a word, that's for sure!"

Chapter 24

"My brother has always been very correct. He never went around getting into scrapes like me."

"How can you say that? You're twisting things around. Have you forgotten the proverb, 'If you can't stand up for yourself, you'll never live in peace'? Personally, I always like to speak my mind, I can't bear the kind who, you know, ask 'em three times and still they won't tell you what they think!"

"You ought to be thankful my brother keeps out of trouble."

They were still talking when the Midget returned with the meat and fish and fruit and nuts he'd bought. "Come down and cook the meal, dear," he called out as he was coming upstairs.

"What a fool you are!" the girl said. "You're asking me to go downstairs and leave my brother-in-law here all alone?"

"There's no need to worry about me," Wu Song said.

"Why don't you go and get old Mother Wang next door to come and cook for us? Can't you ever organize anything properly?"

So the Midget went and got their neighbour, Mrs. Wang, to prepare and cook the food, which he then brought upstairs and arranged on the table. There was no lack of fish and meat dishes, and of course all kinds of fruit and vegetables, and it was not long before the wine was warmed and brought up too. The Midget made his wife sit in the host's place whilst his brother sat opposite and he himself on one side. He then poured wine for each of them. Taking her cup the woman said: "Please drink, brother-in-law, and pardon us for not providing you with better fare."

"Nonsense, sister-in-law. This is a feast," said Wu Song.

The Midget busied himself warming the wine and filling the cups and paid no attention to anything else. Jinlian smiled her most dazzling smile and said: "Why aren't you eating, brother-in-law? You must try a little fish. And some meat." She chose the best pieces and put them in his bowl.

Wu Song was a straightforward fellow and he simply put her attentiveness down to the fact that he was one of the family. But she had been in service and knew how to make the most of these little attentions. The Midget, on the other hand, was a good but ineffectual man, unskilled in the art of entertaining.

After several cups of wine, the woman could no longer take her eyes off Wu Song's body. Wu Song grew embarrassed and lowered his head, no longer liking to look at her. After some twenty cups, he rose to his feet.

"Have some more," the Midget said.

"I've had enough," he replied. "I'll come and see you another day."

They both went downstairs with him and Jinlian said: "You really ought to move in with us, brother-in-law. Otherwise people will laugh at us, they'll say you prefer strangers to your own brother. Husband, why don't you prepare a room and ask him to come and live here? If you don't the neighbours will start making up stories."

"You're quite right," said the Midget. "You must come and live with us, brother, and give us face."

"If that's what you both want, I'll go and get my luggage and bring it here tonight."

"Don't forget," the woman said. "I shall be expecting you."

The woman's interest was decidedly engaged. It was like this:

A brother's wife, that's a taboo relation,
Though mutual help is an obligation.
The hero thinks only of family ties,
But the wanton sees him in lustier guise.

When Wu Song left his brother's in Redstone Road and went back to the government offices, he found the Magistrate was in session, so he went straight in and made his request: "I have a brother, sir, who's come to live here in Redstone Road. I'd like to move in with him. Naturally I'd always be here for the morning and evening sessions. But I thought I should ask you first. May I have your permission?"

"It's only natural you should want to be with your brother," the Magistrate replied. "Of course I've no objection. It needn't prevent you coming in to work each day."

Wu Song thanked him and went to get his luggage and bedroll. There was also the new suit of clothes and the other things he'd been given with the reward. He found an orderly to carry all this, and they made their way to his brother's house. When the woman saw him coming she was as pleased as someone who's stumbled on a treasure trove. She couldn't hide her delight. The Midget got a carpenter to come and put up partitions upstairs and make a bed. A table was also put in there, with two chairs and a stove. Wu Song unpacked his things and sent the orderly away. That night he slept at his brother's.

Next morning he was up at dawn. The woman quickly got up too, to heat water for washing and provide him with water to rinse his mouth. When he had completed his toilet, he put on his cap and was ready to report back to work. As he went out, she called after him: "When you finish work, be sure to come straight back here to eat, don't go and eat somewhere else."

"I'll come straight back," he promised.

After the morning's work at the office he returned to the house. Jinlian had washed and manicured her hands and dressed herself up. She served the food and the three of them sat down to eat. But when she offered Wu Song a bowl of tea with her own hands, he protested: "Sister-in-law, it's too much trouble for you. I feel embarrassed about staying here and eating with you. I must get one of the soldiers to come and serve you."

She said quickly: "You're one of the family, you shouldn't treat me like an outsider. With one's own flesh and blood it's not at all the same as serving other people. If you give one of your soldiers charge of the pots and the stove nothing will ever be clean. I just can't stomach those kind of people."

"But really, I must be giving you too much trouble," said Wu Song.

Well, enough of all that. After he came to live with them, Wu Song gave his brother money to buy cakes and pancakes, and tea and fruit, to invite the neighbours for tea. The neighbours got together to return the compliment, and after that the Midget organized another party for them. We say no more of this.

A few days later, Wu Song gave his sister-in-law a fine piece of coloured silk to make a dress. She was delighted with the gift. "You really shouldn't have," she said. "But since it's from you I can't very well refuse, can I? I'll have to accept it."

So now Wu Song was established in his brother's house, and his brother went out every day as usual to sell his bread on the street. Wu Song went every day to the office, where he performed a variety of tasks. When he returned, early or late, it made no difference, his sister-in-law had soup and rice ready for him, and counted herself happy to be able to serve him. He was sometimes embarrassed by it. Sometimes, moreover, she made suggestive remarks. But Wu Song was of an innocent, straightforward nature, and he saw nothing in them.

Well, let's concentrate on what's important, and pass over the time when nothing happened. Imperceptibly a month or more had slipped by. It was mid-winter weather: for days a bitter wind had been blowing and reddish clouds filled the sky. Then the snow began to fall, a myriad whirling, dancing flakes.

It went on snowing till evening, by which time it was a world of white, a universe of powdered jade. The next day, Wu Song went to work early, and had not returned by midday. Jinlian pushed her husband out of the house to pursue his trade and then sent the neighbour, Mrs. Wang, off to buy wine and meat. She herself, meanwhile, installed a charcoal stove in Wu Song's room. "Today's my chance," she was thinking, "to get him excited. I really don't believe I can fail to have an effect on him."

So there she stood by the curtain all alone, waiting composedly till the moment she saw Wu Song striding home, crunching through the jade-like snow. She raised the curtain and said, with her most captivating smile: "You must be frozen!"

"Thank you for your concern," he replied politely. Entering, he removed his hat, which she took with both hands. "Please don't trouble," he protested, taking it back and brushing off the snow, before hanging it on the wall. Then he took off his belt and his parrot-green robe, which he put away in his room.

"I waited for you all morning," she said, "why didn't you come back for lunch?"

"A colleague at the office invited me," he answered. "And then just now someone else wanted me to go and drink with him, but I preferred to come straight home."

"Well, then, come closer to the fire," she said.

Chapter 24

"Good," he said. He took off his oiled boots and changed his socks and put on warm slippers. Then he moved a chair up to the fire and sat down. She went to fasten the front door, and then the back door, and then fetched some fruit and vegetables to accompany the wine, all of which she took into Wu Song's room and put down on the table.

"Where's my brother?" Wu Song asked. "Why isn't he back?"

"He always goes out to sell his stuff at this time," she said. "You and I are going to enjoy a cup or two together."

"We may as well wait till he comes back and all drink together."

"Why ever should we wait for him? I don't intend to wait!" Before she even finished speaking she had begun to warm the wine.

"You sit down and let me do it," Wu Song said. "I know how to warm it properly."

"If you say so," she said. She moved a chair up and sat down beside the fire. The cups and dishes were laid out on a table near the fire. She took a cup of wine, held it out and looking directly at Wu Song, said: "Drink this cup, brother-in-law."

He took it from her and emptied it. She filled another and said: "It's such a cold day, you should drink this one too, to make a pair."

"If you say so," he answered, taking the second cup and emptying it. Then he filled a cup and handed it to her. She drank, then took the jug and poured again and placed the cup in front of him.

There she was, her bosom half revealed, her raven tresses in partial disarray, wearing the sweetest of smiles. She said: "I have heard some gossip about you. They say you keep a singer, somewhere behind the government offices. Can it be true?"

"You shouldn't believe such rubbish," he replied. "I'm not at all that kind of person."

"How can I trust you? Maybe your heart and your words don't tally!"

"If you don't believe me, ask my brother."

"What would he know about it? If he had any knowledge of the world he'd be doing something better than selling bread. Come on, have another cup."

Another three or four cups were poured and drunk. With three cups of wine inside her, lustful thoughts began to surface, she simply couldn't repress them. Her talk grew more and more suggestive. Wu Song, who could more or less see what she was getting at, dared not even raise his head.

When she went to warm more wine, Wu Song picked up the tongs and began to poke the fire. When she came back with the warmed wine, carrying the carafe in one hand, she rested the other hand on his shoulder. She rubbed the cloth between her finger and thumb and said: "Aren't you cold, with such thin clothes?"

Wu Song, desperately embarrassed, gave no answer. Seeing that he remained silent, she took her hand away. She seized the tongs and said: "You don't know how to make up a fire. I shall poke it for you. We want it to be as hot as a brazier."

Wu Song, now thoroughly alarmed, still remained silent. But she was burning with desire and she didn't notice Wu Song's repugnance. She put down the tongs and poured another cup of wine. She took a sip and then, looking Wu Song straight in the eyes, she held out the cup to him and said: "If your heart responds, drink the rest."

Wu Song seized the cup and dashed it to the ground. "Don't be so shameless!" he said, giving her a push that almost knocked her down. Glaring ferociously, he said: "I am a man of honour, not a wild animal. I don't go in for that kind of disgusting stuff, that's fit only for pigs or dogs. Don't ever dare behave in that disgusting manner again, or start any of that business. If there's the least breath of suspicion, even just enough to stir the grass, I swear to you this: even though my eyes tell me you're my sister-in-law, my fists won't care. So don't ever let that happen again!"

She blushed scarlet. Collecting up the cups and plates, she said: "I was only joking, why do you have to take it so seriously? You really are uncouth!" Carrying the things she took herself off to the kitchen.

The poem says:

Drink's a bawd to goad desire;

Chapter 24

Lust emboldened knows no shame.
Aiming to kindle passion's fire
All she gets is bitter blame.

So Jinlian failed to seduce Wu Song and earned herself a scolding instead, while Wu Song remained in his room, fuming.

It was still early, only mid-afternoon, when the Midget returned with his carrying-pole. As he pushed the door, his wife hurried to open it. He came in and put down the carrying-pole. Then he went into the kitchen. Noticing that Jinlian's eyes were red from crying, he asked her: "Have you been quarrelling with someone?"

"It's all your fault," she said. "You're so weak, you allow people to insult me."

"Who's had the nerve to insult you?"

"Who do you think? Who else could it be but that brother of yours? I went to all the trouble of getting him some wine to drink when he came home, because it was snowing so hard, and then because there was no one else around he tried to make a pass at me."

"My brother's not like that. He's the most honourable person. Anyway, keep your voice down or the neighbours will laugh at us!"

The Midget abandoned his wife and went to Wu Song's room. "You haven't eaten yet, have you brother?" he said. "Come and eat with me."

Wu Song was silent. After hesitating for a long time, he finally took off his slippers and put on his oiled boots again, his coat and his hat, and started for the door.

"Where are you going?" his brother shouted after him, but Wu Song went out still without answering.

The Midget went back into the kitchen. "He didn't answer when I called him," he said. "He just went off in the direction of the government offices. I really don't understand what's going on."

"You stupid idiot!" Jinlian said. "Can't you see? He's too ashamed of himself. He daren't look you in the face so he's left!

I bet he's sending someone to move his luggage. He won't want to live here any more."

"If he does that the neighbours will laugh at us," the Midget complained.

"You stuffed dumpling! If he stays here and seduces me the neighbours will laugh even more. You can live with him if you like, but I'm not going to put up with that kind of thing. Or you can write me out a divorce, if that's what you want, then you can keep him here."

The Midget didn't dare open his mouth again.

At this point Wu Song returned, accompanied by a soldier equipped with a carrying-pole. They went straight to the room, collected Wu Song's things, and came out again. The Midget chased after them. "Why are you moving out, brother?" he asked.

"Don't ask me that. Best to let sleeping dogs lie. Just let me go, it'll be best."

The Midget didn't dare ask again or try to prevent his brother from leaving. All the time the woman was muttering to herself within: "That's nice, that's fine! Everyone thinks you're so lucky if your brother's made up to captain. They think he'll help you. When all he does is go and stab you in the back! Well, like they say, 'Don't judge a crab-apple by its looks!' Thank heaven he's gone. Good riddance to bad rubbish!"

The Midget heard her cursing but he didn't know what to do. This business had unsettled him and he couldn't get it out of his mind. However, he continued to go out each day to sell his bread in the street, after his brother had moved back to the government offices. At first he wanted to go and look for his brother, but his wife ordered him not to with such fierce insistence that he dared not. So the two brothers did not see each other.

Time passed in a flash and imperceptibly the snow had melted away. One day — it was about ten days later — the Magistrate, who had been at his post for over two and a half years and had amassed quite a fortune, decided he wanted to send some of his funds back to a relative in the Eastern Capital for safekeeping, and also to buy him a promotion. But he was afraid it might get stolen *en route*. He needed a capable and trustworthy person to send with it. He bethought himself of Wu Song. "Of course, he's the one to send! He's absolutely fearless!"

He summoned Wu Song that very day. "I've got a relative in the Eastern Capital," he told him. "I want to send a load of gifts to him and a letter. But here's the problem. The roads are dangerous and it needs someone with your strength and courage to bring this mission off. Would you be prepared to render me this service, regardless of any difficulty or hardship? You can be sure I will reward you handsomely when you return."

"Your Excellency, I owe my position to you," said Wu Song, "so of course I shall do whatever you tell me, I couldn't possibly refuse. If it is your wish, I shall go. I have never been to the Eastern Capital and it will be a good chance to see the sights. I shall leave straight away tomorrow, if you will have the things ready."

The Magistrate was most satisfied with this answer and offered Wu Song wine. Of this no more.

Having received his instructions from the Magistrate, Wu Song went back to his room, got some silver, and sent an orderly off to buy a bottle of wine, some fish and meat and some dried fruit. With these provisions they went to the Midget's in Redstone Road. About this time the Midget returned after selling his bread and saw Wu Song sitting outside his gate. The orderly was sent into the kitchen to prepare the food. When Jinlian, who secretly still had a soft spot for Wu Song, saw him coming with wine and food, she said to herself: "Can it be he's still thinking of me? Is that why he's come back? Anyway, it looks as if he knows he can't get the better of me. I'll sound him out, but I'd better tread carefully."

She went upstairs, powdered her face with care, rearranged her raven tresses and changed into her most glamorous dress. Then she went downstairs again to receive him. "I can't think what we've done wrong, brother-in-law," she said. "You haven't been to see us for days. I really wondered what was going on. Every day I told your brother to go and see you at the office, but he always came back and said he couldn't find you. I'm so glad you've come now. Only what's the reason for all this extravagance?"

"There's something I want to say to both of you," Wu Song said. "That's why I've come."

"In that case we'd better go upstairs and sit down," she said.

They went upstairs to the sitting-room. Wu Song made them sit in the place of honour, while he pulled up a chair and sat down to one side. The orderly brought up more wine and meat and laid them on the table. Wu Song urged his brother and sister-in-law to drink. Jinlian did not take her eyes off Wu Song, but he just drank his wine and seemed not to notice. Five cups were drunk in rapid succession. Then Wu Song told the orderly to pour another cup. He took it in his hands and looking fixedly at his brother, said: "Hear what I have to say. I have been entrusted by the Magistrate with a mission to the Eastern Capital. I am leaving tomorrow. It could take two months and won't be less than forty days. Here's what I came to say to you: you've never been a strong kind of man and I'm afraid other people may try to make trouble for you while I'm gone. Now then, let's suppose you usually sell ten baskets of bread a day; from tomorrow on, I want you to sell only five. Start late and come back early. Don't stay out drinking with anyone. Lower the blind as soon as you get home, and bolt the door as early as possible. That way you'll avoid trouble. If anyone tries to provoke you, don't get into a fight, just wait till I come and I'll deal with them. To show you accept my advice now, please drink this cup."

The Midget took the cup and said: "You're absolutely right, I'll do just as you say." And he emptied the cup.

Wu Song poured another two cups of wine and turned to his sister-in-law. "You're a clever woman," he said, "so I don't need many words. My brother's always honest and straightforward with people so he needs you to look after him. A strong character is worth more than muscles, so they say. If you keep the house well, there's no reason why he should have any trouble. You know the old proverb, 'If the fences are strong, the dogs can't get in'."

These words, this lecture from Wu Song, made Jinlian blush from ear to ear. Scarlet with mortification, she pointed at the Midget and screamed: "You stupid idiot! What sort of rumours have you picked up in the street and brought back to persecute

Chapter 24

me with? I tell you, I may look like a woman, but I've a man's spirit! I'm not some useless flibbertigibbet! You could stand firm on this fist, you could race horses up this arm, do you hear? I can hold up my head anywhere. I'm not that kind of woman! Since I married you not so much as an ant has got into this house, so what's all this about bad fences and dogs sneaking in? You've got your facts wrong! You ought to find out what's what before you start flinging accusations!"

Wu Song laughed and said: "Good, I'm glad you've got such confidence. But make sure your heart and your words agree. I shall remember what you say. And now I ask you to drink this cup as a pledge of faith."

She brushed the cup aside and ran to the stairs. Halfway down she paused to shout: "You're so clever, but haven't you heard that an elder brother's wife is like a mother? When I got married nobody told me anything about a younger brother. Why should you turn up here to order us all around, even if you are one of the family? It's just my bloody luck to get caught in a mess like this!" And with that she burst into tears and ran downstairs. As the poem says:

> *For good advice she doesn't give a rap;*
>   *Her smiles and tears are all on tap.*
> *She knows what she wants,*
>   *These are just tricks to get it.*
> *If you think she's tragic or feels shame,*
>   *Forget it!*

Of course it was all pretence, she was just putting it on!

The two brothers remained there drinking for a while, and then Wu Song said he had to leave. "Take care," said his brother, "and come back as quickly as possible!" As he spoke the tears sprang to his eyes. When he saw this, Wu Song said: "I really think it would be best if you stop work completely and stay home. I can send you money."

The Midget accompanied his brother downstairs. Just before he went out, Wu Song said: "Don't forget what I told you, brother."

Wu Song and the orderly returned to the government offices to prepare his luggage. Next day he rose early, tied his bundle, and went to see the Magistrate. The latter had already commandeered a wagon and had it loaded with boxes and cases. Two sturdy soldiers had been appointed as escort and two trusted servants from his own staff. They all assembled in front of the government offices to bid farewell. Then Wu Song strapped on his armour and took up his pike and together with the cart and its escort left Yanggu and took the road to the Eastern Capital.

Now our story divides in two again. After his brother left, the Midget had to put up with three or four days of recriminations. He bore it in silence. He just let her scold and concentrated on following his brother's advice, only going out to sell half the usual amount of bread each day and coming home early. As soon as he had put down his carrying-pole he would lower the blind and lock the door. Then he would sit down. This infuriated Jinlian. Waving her finger in his face, she would say: "You imbecile! You moron! What do you want to lock the flaming door for when the sun isn't halfway across the sky? The neighbours are going to think we're afraid of our own shadows or something. I know, you have to listen to that blessed brother of yours. You don't care if everyone's laughing at you!"

"Let them. My brother's advice was good. It'll keep us out of disputes."

"Bah! You moron! Can't you decide anything for yourself, do you always have to follow someone else's instructions?"

The Midget merely waved his hand and said: "I don't care what anyone says. My brother's advice is golden."

For the first ten days after Wu Song left, the Midget continued to go out late and return early, locking the door as soon as he got home. His wife kept on reviling him, but he got used to it and paid no attention. Finally she herself would go and lower the blind, around the time of his return, and lock the front door. This greatly pleased the Midget. "Now things are really going well!" he said to himself.

Two or three days later — winter was nearly over and the weather was beginning to warm up again — Jinlian went to lower

Chapter 24

the blind with the forked pole, as it was now her custom to do, just before the Midget's return, and it just so happened that a man walked past. There's an old proverb which says: "It's chance that keeps the story going." She was not holding the pole securely enough: it slipped from her hands and fell, as luck would have it, precisely on top of the man's headdress. He stopped in his tracks, intending to kick up a tremendous fuss. But when he turned to see who was responsible, and saw that it was a devilishly pretty young woman, his heart was softened at once and his anger fled to the Isle of Java, as they say. A smile spread right across his face.

When she saw he was not complaining, Jinlian crossed her hands, curtsied profoundly, and said: "It was an accident. Please forgive me."

The man rearranged his headdress, bowed and said graciously: "It's nothing. Think no more of it."

Now all this was seen by the neighbour, Mrs. Wang, who had been standing in the doorway of her teashop. Mrs. Wang laughed and said: "Who told you to walk so close to the house, anyway? It was a direct hit!"

The man smiled too and said: "Yes, really, it was my own fault. Now I have inconvenienced a lady. I beg you to forgive me!"

Jinlian also smiled and said: "All the same, I'm afraid you must blame me."

He gave the deepest of bows and replied: "How could I do that?" All this time his eyes were devouring her. He made as if to depart. But six or seven times he turned back to look at her. Eventually he swaggered off, stepping jauntily for her benefit.

She collected the pole and put it by the door, and finished lowering the blind. Then she shut the front door and waited for the Midget. As the poem says:

The fence is broken, the dog sneaks in;
That blind afforded the chance to be seen.
To seduction's course Mrs. Wang gives a prod;
The pole you might say was a fishing-rod.

Now just who exactly was that man? And where did he live? Well, he was the scion of an impoverished gentleman's family of

Yanggu, who had set up a medicinal herbs shop opposite the government offices. From his childhood days he'd always been a bit of a crook, good with his fists and with the staff. Recently he'd suddenly become rich. He had good connections in the government and went around brow-beating ordinary people. For a fee, though, he would help them with applications, just like a government official, so everyone in the town kowtowed to him. He had the double surname of Xi-men and his given name was simply Qing. He was a first son and people called him his Nibs. Recently since he'd made his name and fortune they'd taken to calling him Your Honour, as if he was a real government official.

Well it wasn't more than a few moments before his Nibs, Mr. Xi-men Qing, appeared in Mrs. Wang's teahouse and sat himself down beside the entrance curtain.

"That was a fine greeting you gave just now," Mrs. Wang said with a grin.

"Come over here, old woman," he replied, also smiling. "Tell me, that young woman next door, who's her husband?"

"She's the King of Hell's younger sister and daughter of the God of Calamities! Why do you want to know?"

"I'm serious, so stop teasing."

"Then how come you don't know? Her old man's outside the government offices every day, selling something to eat."

"She's not married to Third Brother Xu, is she, the one who sells date cakes?"

Mrs. Wang shook her head. "No, if it was him they wouldn't make such a bad pair. Guess again."

"Is she the wife of Second Brother Li, the silver carrier?"

Mrs. Wang shook her head again. "No, that wouldn't be such a bad match either."

"Then I suppose it must be young Lu, with the tattooed arms?"

Mrs. Wang laughed. "No, it's not. If it were him they'd make a pair. Have another go."

"Mother Wang, I give up."

Mrs. Wang was laughing her head off. "This is going to kill you," she said. "Her old man's the one who sells bread. He's Wu Da, the Midget!"

Chapter 24

His Nibs almost fell over laughing. "You don't mean the one they call the Three-Inch Poxy Midget?" he said. "Not that Wu Da?"

"That's the one," she said.

"Well!" he exclaimed, as the horror of it dawned on him. "What a juicy piece of mutton to fall into the mouth of a dog!"

"That's about the size of it," she said. "Like they always say, 'a lovely woman in the hands of a stupid oaf, that's like a sensitive horse ridden by a clumsy rider.' What was the God of Marriages thinking of when he coupled those two?"

"How much do I owe you for the tea, Mother Wang?" his Nibs asked.

"It's hardly anything," she said. "Leave it, we can settle up another time."

"By the way, who's your son with at the moment?"

"I can't tell you. He went off with someone to the River Huai and since then I've not had a word, not so much as to say if he's dead or alive."

"Why don't you send him along to me?"

"If Your Honour would take him, I'd really like that."

"Wait till he comes back and we can talk about it again."

After some more idle talk of this kind he said good-bye and left.

In something less than an hour he was back at Mrs. Wang's teahouse, sitting by the entrance curtain where he could watch the Midget's front door. Mrs. Wang left him alone for a moment, and then went over and said: "How about some plum soup, Your Honour?"

"All right," he said. "But don't make it too sweet."

Mrs. Wang prepared the bowl of plum soup and gave it to his Nibs with both hands.

His Nibs drank slowly and then put the bowl down on the table. "Excellent," he said, "Mrs. Wang you can certainly pick your plums. Do you have a good supply?"

"A good supply? With all the years I've been in business, I think I can supply any need you might have!"

"I ask you about plum soup and you answer about supplying my needs — are we at cross-purposes?"

"You asked about a supply of plums. I'm just telling you I've got plenty," she said.

"Mother Wang, I know you can move mountains. Suppose I should want you to arrange a little affair for me, a little personal affair? I should certainly know how to show my gratitude."

"And supposing, Your Honour, the lady of your house should get to hear of it, wouldn't I run the risk of getting my face slapped?"

"My wife's a kind and accommodating sort of woman. I've already got several companions at home, the trouble is not one of them exactly suits my taste. If you had the right sort of thing and could arrange it all for me, there wouldn't be any problem — even a widow would do, so long as she was to my taste."

"Well, now, something did turn up just the other day. But I'm not quite sure you'd want her."

"If she's the right thing and you can arrange it for me, I should be most grateful."

"I'd give this one ten plus, except there's a little problem with her age."

"A year or two more or less doesn't make a lot of difference. How old is she, actually?"

"Well, her birth year is the Tiger, so come the new year she'll be just ninety-three."

His Nibs burst out laughing. "Just listen to the woman, she's mad! One just can't have a serious conversation with her!" Still laughing, he got up and left.

As it was getting dark, when Mrs. Wang had just lit the lamp and was about to lock up, the door opened and in walked his Nibs again. He sat down in the same seat beside the door and fixed his gaze on the Midget's front door.

"What do you want to drink, Your Honour?" the old woman cried. "Some wedding soup?"

"All right," he replied. "But make it sweet, Mother Wang."

She prepared a bowl of soup and gave it to him.

After sitting there all evening, he rose and said: "Put it down on my account, Mother Wang, and I'll pay it all together tomorrow."

"That's all right," she said. "Just go and have a good night's rest

Chapter 24

and tomorrow I hope you'll honour me with another visit." He left with a smile on his face and nothing further occurred that night. Early next morning when Mrs. Wang opened up the teahouse and went to look outside, there was his Nibs pacing up and down in front of the door. "Well, now," she said to herself, "this fellow's properly worked up. I'm going to put something sweet in front of his nose, just where his tongue won't reach. The pig thinks he can get the better of everyone in this town, but wait till I get a hold on him, he won't wriggle out of that!"

Indeed there was more to this Mrs. Wang, this teashop owner, than you might suppose. As the poem says:

> *She'd deceive a politician when she speaks; her words would defeat the cunningest statesman. Two lone phoenixes, male and female, she'd have them pairing on the spot; a widow and a single man, with just a word she'd get them mating. Always scheming, she'd make a Lohan embrace a mendicant nun; a little calculation, and she'd have Lord Li make love to a she-devil. With sweet words and flattery, she'd win over the most resolute of men; with soft speech and cooing tones she'd arouse the purest of girls. She could move the Weaver Maid to lustful longings or provoke the Moon Goddess to copulation.*

Now as we were saying, Mrs. Wang had just opened up and got the fire going and arranged the tea things and there was his Nibs already at this early hour hanging about in front of the door. He now rushed inside and took up his customary position by the entrance, gazing at the Midget's front door. Mrs. Wang pretended not to see him and instead of going over to ask what tea he wanted, busied herself blowing up the fire.

"Mother Wang!" he called. "Bring me two bowls of tea."

"Oh, it's you, Your Honour!" she replied. "What a long time since we saw you!" She made two bowls of good strong tea and put them on the table.

"Come and drink a bowl of tea with me, Mother Wang," he said.

She cackled. "I'm not your secret lover," she said.

He smiled briefly, then said: "What do they sell next door?"

"All kinds of sweet and delicious stuff, that's what they sell, all hot and spicy it is!"

"There you are, I said you were mad!" he said, laughing.

"I'm not mad," she said. "There's only one thing in her house, and that's a husband."

"Mother Wang, let's be serious now. I've heard that they make delicious rolls there, and I'd like to order thirty or forty of them. I just wonder if there'd be anyone at home?"

"If you want to buy rolls, just wait a bit and you can buy them from him in the street on his way back. What call is there to go to the house?"

"No doubt you're right." He drank his tea, sat there a little longer and then got up to go, saying: "Put it all down, Mother Wang."

"Don't worry," she said, as he went out, "I keep good accounts."

Observing dispassionately from the teahouse Mrs. Wang saw his Nibs pass in front of the door, going first one way and then the other, looking around him this way and that. When this had occurred six or seven times, he wandered back into the teahouse.

"What a surprise, Your Honour," she said. "Haven't seen you in ages!"

Smiling sheepishly, he sat down and took out a tael of silver, which he handed to her, saying: "Here's something to settle the account, Mother Wang."

"That's much more than what's needed," she said.

"Just take it," he said.

Secretly she was delighted. "That's it," she thought to herself. "Now I've got him!" She put the silver away carefully and said: "I can see you're thirsty, Your Honour. I expect you'd like some sort of fresh young brew, is that it?"

"How did you guess?"

"Easy. You know the saying, 'When you enter the room, don't ask how things are going, just look at the faces.' You've no idea what kinds of weird and wonderful things I can guess!"

"Well, I've got something in my mind, and if you can guess what it is I'll give you five taels of silver."

"Well, I don't need any clues. From the merest hint I can tell it all. Approach your ear, Your Honour. You keep dashing about, these last few days, like a cat on hot bricks, and I warrant it's all to do with a certain young person next door. Right or wrong?"

"Mother Wang, you're a witch. You'd be a match for the finest and subtlest of statesmen! I'll be honest with you. I don't know how it is, but ever since that day she dropped the pole on me and I first saw her face, it's as if I'd surrendered my three souls and seven spirits. The problem is, I just can't think of any pretext to get in there. Do you think you can help me?"

The old woman set up a gleeful cackling. Then she said: "I'll be honest with you too. This teahouse of mine is a front, the kind of place they call 'The Devil strikes the hours.' Three years ago, the day it snowed in early June, I sold a cup of tea, but I've hardly had a regular customer since. No, what I rely on to make my living by is 'mixed trade'."

"What do you mean by 'mixed trade'?" he asked.

"Well, to start with, matchmaking and dealing. Then there's pregnancies, I assist with those, and even deliveries. And I can help with affairs of the heart, or simply fix you up with a woman."

"If you can really arrange this business of mine, I'll give you ten taels of silver. You'll have enough to buy yourself a coffin!"

"Listen to me then," she said. "These seduction cases are generally the most difficult. In order to succeed there's five things you must possess: number one, looks like Pan An's; two, a tool as big as a donkey's; three, the wealth of Deng Tong; four, youth, together with all the patience of a needle sewing silk; five, plenty of leisure. If you've got all five of those — call them for short Pan, donkey, Deng, youth and leisure — then you've a hope of succeeding."

His Nibs answered confidently: "I can honestly say that I'm pretty well equipped with all five. For the first one, I may not be Pan An but I'm not bad-looking; for the second, even as a child I had a bloody big prick; for the third, I've no shortage of ready cash, and even if I'm not quite the equal of Deng Tong, there's certainly enough to go on with; for the fourth, I can put up with anything — if she were to hit me a hundred times I wouldn't retaliate; for the fifth, I've more than enough time, as you can see with your own eyes from the fact that I'm round here so often. So Mother Wang, please help me. If you can set it up, you can be sure I shall reward you handsomely."

"Even if you've got the five basic requirements, Your Honour, there's still one big obstacle that's hard to overcome."

"What is it? Tell me quickly!"

"All right, but don't blame me for being frank. Generally the tough part in a seduction is this: if you're serious, you've got to be prepared to part with your money or you won't get anywhere. Now as far as I know you've a tendency to be tight-fisted, you don't like throwing money around. That's the problem."

"That's easy to remedy. I shall simply follow your instructions."

"Well, if you're prepared to spend, I've got a plan which will secure you a tête-à-tête with the young person in question. But are you really willing to do as I say?"

"I'll do anything you tell me to, no matter what. What's your plan?"

"It's a bit late now. You'd better go home first. You come back in a few months' time and we'll talk it over then."

His Nibs went down on his knees. "Mother Wang stop fooling and just help me," he implored.

"My, you are in a hurry!" she said, laughing. "My plan's a brilliant one. It may not be exactly something you'd put in the temple of Prince Wucheng, but it's worthy of Sun-zi and his Amazons. It's ninety-nine percent sure. Now, listen, here's your instructions. This girl was once a servant in a rich man's house in Qinghe and she's a very good hand at sewing. So you're going to go and buy a piece of white silk, a length of blue silk, a piece of white gauze and ten ounces of good silk floss and have them delivered to me here. I will go and see her and invite her to take tea, and then I'll say to her, 'There's this rich official, he's given me the materials for a set of burial clothes, I wanted to borrow a calendar from you and ask you to choose an auspicious day for me to invite a tailor here to make the clothes up.' Now, if she hears me out and says nothing, then we'll have to forget your affair. But

Chapter 24

if she says, 'I'll do it for you,' and won't let me call a tailor, well, that's the first step towards your objective.

"Next thing, I shall invite her to come to my house to sew. If she refuses and says, 'No, we'll go to my house,' we may as well give up. But if she's tickled pink and says, 'I'll come and cut them for you and sew them,' then that's the second step completed.

"If she comes to my house, I shall arrange some wine and things to eat. But mind you don't come here, not the first day. The second day, if she says it's not right and she wants to work in her own house, then the whole thing's no good. But if she comes to my house again, that's the third step. Only again, you must keep away.

"On the third day, round about noon, you appear, all dressed up to kill. You give a cough, first, to warn me. Then you call out, 'Mrs. Wang, why haven't I seen you around lately?' I'll come out and invite you in, see. Now, if when she sees you enter she jumps up and rushes off home, there's nothing we can do to stop her. In that case, it's all over. But if she doesn't move, then that's the fourth step.

"After we've sat down, I shall say, 'This is the generous provider of the material. Oh, how grateful I am to him!' I shall praise you in all sorts of ways and you must admire her needlework. If she's not moved to reply, then we're not going to get anywhere. But if she's drawn into a conversation, then that's the fifth step.

"Then I say, 'I just don't know how I'd manage if I didn't have this young lady to help me with the work. Really, I'm so grateful to both of you. One's so generous with his money, the other with her labour. I don't want to sound like a beggar, Your Honour, but since she's taking so much trouble, don't you think you should treat us? I mean, cough up the necessary for a little refreshment?' Then you fork out some money and tell me to go and buy things. If she gets up and leaves, we can't stop her, we have to give up. But if she stays put, things are looking good, we've accomplished the sixth step.

"I take the money, and as I go out I say to her, 'Do you mind keeping the gentleman company for a few minutes?' If she then gets up and goes home, I can't do anything, it's all over. But if she stays, that's great, that's the seventh step.

"When I come back with the food, I'll lay it on the table and say, 'Put away your work, dear, and come and have a cup of this wine that the gentleman has so kindly provided.' If she refuses to sit down at the table with you and goes home, forget it. But if she only says she ought to go, and actually doesn't move, then everything's all right, we've got through the eighth step.

"When we're well into the wine and the conversation is warming up, I'll say there's no wine left and ask you if you'll pay for more. You send me off for more wine. As I go out I bolt the door, with you two inside. If she's upset and tries to run away, then you must give the business up. But if she hears me bolt the door and doesn't protest, then that's the ninth step and we're only one step away from success. But this last step may prove the most difficult!

"Now, you're alone with her in the room and you've got to start off with some very sweet words. On no account must you be violent or hasty. You've got to control your hands and feet. If you're rough with her in any way, I won't answer for the consequences. First you pretend to brush the table accidentally with your sleeves so that a pair of bracelets fall out. As you bend down to pick them up, touch her feet gently. If she starts to scream, I shall come to the rescue straight away. Don't try to push the matter any further, you won't get anywhere. But if she keeps quiet, you know the tenth step is over, she's all for it, your success is assured.

"Well, how do you like my plan?"

"I don't know if it would get your portrait hung in the Emperor's hall, but it's brilliant," his Nibs cried ecstatically.

"Don't forget to give me the money," the old woman said.

"No one forgets Lake Dongting after tasting its wares," he replied. "When can the plan go into operation?"

"I'll answer that this evening," she said. "I'll take the opportunity while the Midget is still out to go and show her the bait. Meanwhile, you'd better get someone to bring me the material."

"Right you are," he said. "If you can bring this thing off, Mother Wang, I assure you I shall not forget my promise." After leaving

Chapter 24

Mrs. Wang he went straight to a haberdasher's in the market where he bought all the necessary goods. Arriving home, he told a servant to pack them carefully and take them round to the teahouse, together with five taels of loose change. Mrs. Wang received all this and sent the servant away.

How can lechery's course be stayed?
The trap is set, the ambush laid.
When the ten-step seduction scheme's applied,
Into the pit she'll blindly slide.

Mrs. Wang now popped out of her back door and went over to the Midget's. Jinlian welcomed her and invited her upstairs to sit down. "Why haven't you been round to see me?" the old woman asked.

"I haven't been feeling very well lately," the girl answered. "I just didn't have the energy."

"Do you by any chance have a calendar you could lend me? I want to find an auspicious day to ask a tailor to come in."

"What clothes are you making, Mother?"

"Well, the fact is at my age there's always something wrong with one, and I've this feeling there may be serious health problems ahead for me. That's why I've been wanting to have some burial clothes made up, so as to be prepared, you know. I was lucky because a rich man I know heard me say this and he provided me with the materials — some fine silk and gauze and plenty of good floss for padding. It's all been sitting around for over a year because I can't manage to do it myself. But I really feel my health is going downhill this year and as we've got two extra days this month I thought I'd take the opportunity to have it done. Only now the tailor's trying to blackmail me, he says he hasn't got time. All this trouble, it's just what I don't need!"

"Well, I don't know if I could do it as well as you want," she said, "but if you'd let me, I'd do the sewing for you."

The old woman's face lit up. "If you'd do it for me," she said, "I know I'd die happy! I've always heard how beautifully you sew, only I just didn't like to ask you myself."

"Then there's no problem. If you agree, I'll be happy to do the work for you. As soon as you've got someone to name an auspicious day, I'll start at once."

"If you're going to do it, that's sure to bring me luck anyway. We needn't worry about the day. Actually I got hold of someone the other day and he said tomorrow is a lucky day for me. I wasn't paying a lot of attention, because I didn't really think it mattered all that much, just for making up some clothes."

"Of course you should have a lucky day for making up burial clothes! What's the point of choosing any other day?"

"If you're going to be kind enough to do it for me, do you think you could start tomorrow? I'd like to invite you to my house."

"You don't have to do that. Why don't I do it here?"

"I'd like to be able to watch you. I can't leave the house because there's no one to look after things there."

"In that case I'll come round after breakfast tomorrow."

With many expressions of gratitude the old woman left. When his Nibs returned that evening, she told him everything had been arranged to start the next day. Nothing else happened that night.

First thing in the morning, Mrs. Wang cleaned and tidied her house. She brought the thread, prepared the water for tea and sat down to wait.

As soon as the Midget had had breakfast, sorted out his wares and taken himself off to start trading, Jinlian hung up the curtain and went round to Mrs. Wang's, leaving by the back door. The old woman greeted her effusively and took her into the sitting-room. She made her a good cup of tea and offered her pine-seeds and walnuts. Then she carefully wiped the table and brought out the material. Jinlian measured and cut it, and started sewing. The old woman was lavish with her praises. "My, what wonderful work! I've lived over sixty years, but never have I seen such fine needlework!"

Jinlian went on sewing till midday, when the old woman produced some wine and a catty of noodles and invited her to eat. She continued afterwards until it began to get late, when she tidied up her work and went home. She was just in time to open the door to the Midget, returning with an empty load, and to lower

Chapter 24

the blind. Noticing that his wife was a little flushed, the Midget asked: "Have you been drinking?"

"It's the neighbour, Mrs. Wang," she explained. "She asked me to go over to make some burial clothes for her, and she invited me to lunch."

The Midget was a little shocked. "Aiya! You shouldn't be eating her food, we ought to invite her. If she asks you to go over and do some work for her you should come back here to eat, you shouldn't go bothering her. If you go there again tomorrow, take some money with you; you can buy the wine and food to return the courtesy. 'A close neighbour's more useful than a distant relative' as the saying is. You don't want to make yourself unpopular. If she won't let you pay, better bring the work back home and give it to her when you've finished."

Jinlian said nothing. As the poem says:

Her schemes are deep, layer upon layer;
What lies beneath, the poor man doesn't see.
Forking out money to benefit your betrayer!
That's just giving your life away for free!

Well, the plan was working, she'd lured the girl to her home! Next morning after breakfast when the Midget had left, Mrs. Wang went round and invited Jinlian back. Arriving at Mrs. Wang's, Jinlian got out her work and started sewing. Mrs. Wang made some tea for them. The morning passed uneventfully.

At midday the girl took out some silver and gave it to the old woman, saying: "Here you are, Mrs. Wang, this is to buy wine and food."

Mrs. Wang protested: "Aiya! Why should you give me this? I asked you here to do the work for me, how can I possibly let you spend your money as well?"

"It's my husband's orders. He said if you don't agree I must do the work at home and give it to you when I've finished."

Mrs. Wang quickly said: "What a stickler your husband is! Well, if you say so, this time I'll have to accept." Apprehensive for her plan, the old woman added some money of her own and went out and bought some particularly good wine and food, and some rare fruits, in order to entertain Jinlian royally. No doubt you've heard, friends, that women are like this: these small attentions, if they're thorough enough, will always get a response, nine out of ten will fall into the trap. Anyway, Mrs. Wang arranged the things on the table and invited Jinlian to eat and drink. Afterwards the sewing continued, and in the evening, after many protestations of mutual gratitude, the girl went home.

Well, to speed things up, on the third day after breakfast Mrs. Wang waited till she had seen the Midget leave and then went to his back door and called out: "Excuse me, my dear ..."

Jinlian ran downstairs. "I was just coming," she said. The two of them went back to Mrs. Wang's. Jinlian sat down, got out the work and started sewing. Mrs. Wang made some tea, which they drank.

It was nearly noon. At this point his Nibs, who had scarcely been able to contain himself till this day dawned, put on new headgear and his smartest clothes and with a good supply of loose change in his pocket betook himself to Redstone Road. Arriving at the teahouse door, he coughed and called out: "Mrs. Wang, are you all right? I haven't see you lately."

Mrs. Wang heard the signal and said: "Who is it?"

"It's me," he answered.

She got up and hurried to the door. She smiled when she saw him: "Well, so it's you, Your Honour! I was wondering who it could be. You're just at the right time, I want you to come in and take a look." She caught him by the sleeve and pulled him into the room. "Look who it is," she said to Jinlian. "It's my benefactor! You know, the one who gave me the materials."

His Nibs greeted the girl ceremoniously. She quickly stood up and returned the courtesy.

"You know all that cloth you were so kind as to give me?" the old woman said to his Nibs. "I've had it a year and haven't managed to get it made up yet. But now this young lady has most generously offered to do it for me. Her stitching is a miracle, like tapestry it's so close and even, truly it's a wonder to behold! Come and look."

His Nibs went and looked. Then he sipped his tea and said:

Chapter 24

王婆貪賄說風情

"The young lady's work is miraculous, you'd think it the work of a fairy's hand!"

Jinlian smiled and said: "Don't make fun of me, Your Honour!"

"Dare I ask whose house the young lady is mistress of?" he asked Mrs. Wang.

"Why don't you try and guess?" she said.

"I just can't," he replied.

Mrs. Wong laughed happily. "Well, she's the wife of my neighbour, Mr. Wu," she said. "Don't you remember? The other day she dropped the pole on your head — without hurting you of course."

Jinlian blushed scarlet. "It just slipped out of my hands, it was an accident. Please forgive me."

"It was nothing at all," he said.

Mrs. Wang carefully added: "This gentleman never gets angry, he never bears anyone a grudge. He's the kindest of souls."

"I didn't know who you were then," his Nibs said. "I had no idea you were Mr. Wu's wife. I know Mr. Wu as a man who works honourably for his living. I believe he sells something in the street. One who goes simply about his business, giving offence to no man, and who has a good character. Such men are hard to find."

The old woman seconded this: "You're absolutely right. Ever since she was married this young lady has been kept busy all the time observing all his instructions."

"My husband is a feeble useless person, don't laugh at me, please," Jinlian said.

"You're quite wrong," his Nibs said. "Don't you know the proverb, 'He who gives way will live in peace, he who is stubborn will court disaster'? One can say of people like your husband, who always show restraint, that they 'make the most of every drop of water, even in times of flood'."

"That's so true," said Mrs. Wang approvingly.

His Nibs continued to sing the Midget's praises for a moment, and then sat down opposite the girl.

"Do you know what they say about His Honour?" the old woman asked her.

"No," she said.

Chapter 24

"He's one of the richest men in the district, you know. He's a friend of the Governor. People call him 'Your Honour,' just like an official. He's got millions. He runs a little medicine shop opposite the Magistracy. Yes, he's got more money than there are stars in the Milky Way! There's more rice in his storeroom than he'd use in a month of Sundays! Gold, silver, pearls, jewels, you name it, he's got it. And other treasures too, rhinoceros horns, elephant tusks ...!" On and on she went, lauding his Nibs to the skies, with her deceitful intent. Jinlian only kept her eyes on her sewing. His Nibs studied the girl avidly, impatient to be alone with her. Mrs. Wang went and fetched two bowls of tea, handing one to his Nibs and the other to the girl, saying: "Drink this dear, and keep His Honour company."

After they'd drunk the tea the girl seemed, by the faintest quivering of her eyebrows, to betray some feeling. When Mrs. Wang saw this, she gave his Nibs a purposeful look and touched her face. He understood this signal as meaning that he was half-way there.

"If Your Honour hadn't come," the old woman said to him, "I wouldn't have had the courage to go to your house and invite you. So it must be fate, especially since you came just at the right time. But as the proverb says, 'A guest shouldn't ask two hosts for favours at the same time.' Now, since you've contributed the money and the young lady's giving me her skill, well, I was wondering, not wanting of course to seem presumptuous, but seeing as the young lady here is so good to me, I was just wondering if I could ask you to play the host? What I mean is, do you think you might offer her a little extra something on my behalf?"

"I'm so sorry I didn't think of it before. Here's some money," he said, taking out his purse and giving it to the old woman for her to buy more food and wine.

"Please don't trouble yourself," Jinlian said. But she did not move. Mrs. Wang took the money and started to leave. Still Jinlian did not stir. As the old woman went out of the door, she said: "May I ask you to sit with Mr. Xi-men, dear?"

"Please, no," the girl said. But she still did not move. Maybe it was fate. But they were both now aware of what was going on. His Nibs, the bastard, was devouring her with his eyes! And she in turn was giving him little covert glances. Most likely in the presence of such a personage she was already more than half won over. However, she lowered her eyes and continued her work.

Mrs. Wang was soon back with some cooked food — plump goose, roast meat, choice fruits — which she put onto dishes and brought upstairs and laid on the table. Then she looked at Jinlian and said: "Put your work away dear, and come and take some wine and food."

"You go ahead, Mrs. Wang. You can serve Mr. Xi-men. It's not for me to do so." But she still made no attempt to leave.

"But this is specially for you," Mrs. Wang said. "You can't refuse!" She arranged the dishes on the table carefully and all three of them sat down. The wine was poured. His Nibs took a cup and said to Jinlian: "Madam, please do me the honour of emptying this cup."

"You are too kind, sir," said the girl.

"I know you can drink wine," Mrs. Wang said to her. "So please drink up and enjoy yourself."

There's a poem which says:

Eating together, dangerous habit.
What can follow but lechery and sin?
She didn't remember the Captain's warning;
The dog's at the fence, about to get in.

Jinlian took the wine and his Nibs picked up his chopsticks and said: "Mother Wang, please ask the young lady to try some of these dishes."

Mrs. Wang chose some of the best pieces and put them on Jinlian's plate. After three rounds of wine, Mrs. Wang went and warmed more.

"May I make so bold as to inquire how old you are, madam?" his Nibs asked Jinlian.

"I am twenty-three sir," she said.

"Then I am just five years older than you," he said.

"The comparison is unworthy," she said.

Chapter 24

Mrs. Wang butted in: "Such an accomplished young lady she is, sir. Not only is she a beautiful seamstress but she also knows the hundred philosophers."

"Where could you find her equal?" he said. "Truly Mr. Wu is a lucky man!"

"I don't want to sound critical," the old woman said, "but for all the women in your household, I'll wager you haven't one to equal her."

"Well, that's a long story," he said. "But it's true I have not been blessed. I have never found a good one!"

"Surely your first wife must have been good?" Mrs. Wang said.

"Ah, don't talk of her! If she was still alive, then my house would not be in the mess it's in now. The three or four concubines I have seem to do nothing well except eat, they can't organize a thing."

"How long is it since you lost your first wife sir?" Jinlian asked.

"Oh, that's a sad story," he replied. "My first wife was a wonderful and clever woman, though she came from a very humble background. She managed everything for me. It's three years since I was unlucky enough to lose her, and my household's going to the dogs. Why do you think I go out so much? I can't stand being at home."

"Forgive me for saying this, Your Honour," said the old woman, "but your first wife couldn't match Mrs. Wu for needlework."

"Nor for beauty, I have to admit it."

The old woman laughed. "But you keep a mistress in East Street, don't you? Why haven't you invited me to go and take tea with her?"

"You mean Xixi Zhang, the singer? She's just a common soubrette. I think nothing of her!"

"Haven't you also been with Jojo Li for a long time?"

"Yes, she's living with me now. If she were cleverer at running the household I'd have made her my wife long ago."

"If you did find someone like this young lady, I mean someone who really suited your taste, would there be any problems?"

"Who would object? My parents are both dead, I'm my own master!"

"I'm only joking. I don't suppose there's anyone who would satisfy you."

"Why shouldn't there be? It's just that I never have any luck in these matters. I just haven't met the right one."

These exchanges continued for a while and then the old woman exclaimed: "We've finished all the wine, there isn't any left! What do you say, Your Honour, shall I go and get some more?"

His Nibs said: "I think I've got four or five taels in my purse. Here, take the lot. Spend whatever you like on drink and keep the rest."

She thanked him and stood up. First she cast her eye over the young woman, noting how she had grown quite excited with all the wine she had drunk. The two were now totally absorbed in one another and it looked as if they would not be long in coming to an understanding. The girl kept her head lowered and gave no sign of wanting to leave.

"I'm going to get more wine and then we can continue," the old woman said, grinning happily. "You stay here, my dear, and look after His Honour. Let's just see if there's any more wine left in the pot. Yes, just enough for another two cups for you and His Honour to drink. I'm off to the shop in front of the government offices. They've good wine there. I'll go and get a bottle. It may take me a little while though."

"You don't need to," the girl said, but she made no move.

The old woman went out. She tied a string across the door and then went to sit in the street.

Within the house, meanwhile, his Nibs was pouring wine and inviting the lady to drink. Soon his sleeve brushed across the table and the two trinkets rolled out and fell on the floor. Whether by destiny or lucky chance, they came to rest right beside the girl's feet. His Nibs immediately went down on his hands and knees to pick them up. What should he see but those sweet tiny feet, gracefully poised beside the trinkets! Instead of picking up what he had dropped, he gently pinched the tiny brocade shoe. The girl

Chapter 24

began to giggle. "Heavens, sir, what are you doing?" she said. "Surely you don't mean to seduce me?" On his knees before her, he said: "Madam, have pity on me, I beg you!" She took him in her arms and raised him up. And then, right there in Mrs. Wang's parlour, they both removed their clothes and went to it with a will:

> Ducks in their pairs bill and coo in the water; the phoenixes stroll through the flowers. The trees that interlace their branches are filled with the joy of life; hearts that are at one are joined in sweet concord. Vermilion lips are closely pressed, face lies by powdered face. Gauze stockings are thrown in the air; a slip of crescent moon is glimpsed over his shoulders. Gold hairpins fall to the floor, beside the pillow a cloud of raven tresses floats. A sea of vows, a mountain of promises, provoke a thousand flutterings. A bashful cloud and shameful rain are imminent, as a million secret charms are crushed together in the hand. The quiet oriole's call carries no further than the adjacent ear; in the moist mouth the tongue half advances, half retreats. The willowy waist welcomes spring's bounty; the cherry lips whisperingly exhale. The starry eyes cloud over, a fine dew perfumes the jade kernel. The soft breast ripples, a bubbling spring waters the heart of the peony. Such bliss in union is the end of all things; such stolen moments are indeed the sweetest of delights.

The climax over, they were just arranging their clothes when Mrs. Wang pushed open the door and marched in. "Well!" she exclaimed, with feigned indignation, "You two certainly don't waste any time!"

The pair looked thoroughly startled.

"Here's a fine thing," the old woman went on, "I asked you here to do some sewing for me, not to have it off with a man! If Mr. Wu finds out, what's he going to think of me? Maybe I'd better go and tell him before he does." She turned round and started to leave. But the girl caught hold of her sleeve and said: "Mrs. Wang, please forgive us." And his Nibs said: "Mother Wang, please lower your voice."

The old woman grinned. "If you want me to let you off," she said, "you've to promise me one thing."

"Not just one," the girl said, "ten if you wish."

"Starting from today, you are to keep everything hidden from the Midget and come here every day without fail to see His Honour, Mr. Xi-men. If you miss a single day I shall tell the Midget."

"I'll do exactly as you say," the girl said.

"As for you," the old woman said, turning to his Nibs, "there's no need for me to tell you. This business is successfully concluded, so don't forget what you promised. If you go back on anything, I shall tell all to the Midget."

"Don't worry, Mother Wang, I shall keep my promise."

Then they all drank more wine. But it was afternoon already, and soon Jinlian stood up and said: "My idiot of a husband will be coming home, I'd better go."

She slipped into her house through the back door and was just lowering the curtain when the Midget came in.

Meanwhile Mrs. Wang looked at His Nibs and said: "Nice work, eh?"

"I owe it all to you," he said. "I'll go home now and send you a silver ingot. And of course I won't forget everything else I promised you."

"All right then, I shall, as they say, 'watch for the banners and await good news.' But I hope I won't be like the paid mourners, trying to collect their money too late, after the coffin's in the ground!"

His Nibs was laughing as he went out of the door.

From that day on Jinlian went every day to Mrs. Wang's for her rendezvous with his Nibs. They stuck together close as lacquer, clasped each other tight as rubber. But as the saying has it, 'Good things remain secret, evil will always out.' In less than a fortnight the whole neighbourhood knew about it and only the Midget remained in the dark. As the poem says:

What's the good of all those charms?
Their taste is greatly overrated.
When she fills the house with rude alarms
He'll rue the day she was instated.

Chapter 24

Here we must digress because our story divides in two. There happened to be in that place a young man of fifteen or sixteen by the name of Qiao. His father was a soldier serving in Yunzhou when he was born, and the boy was generally referred to as the Young'un. He lived at home with his old father. He was a lively, quick-witted lad and he was generally to be seen around the local inns selling whatever fruit was in season. Xi-men Qing had often helped him out with funds. Well, on this occasion he had just got hold of a basket of crystal pears, which he was toting about the streets in search of Mr. Xi-men, when some busybody said to him: "If it's his Nibs you're wanting, I can tell you where to look."

"All right, Mr. Know-all, tell me where, 'cos I need to earn a spot of cash for the sake of my old pa."

"His Nibs is having it off with the wife of the Midget, the one that sells bread. Every day he's round at old Mother Wang's in Redstone Road. You'll most likely find him there now. Just go right in, it won't matter since you're only a kid."

The Young'un thanked the man for the information. Next thing, the young monkey picked up his basket and headed straight for Redstone Road. He barged into the teahouse where he found Mrs. Wang sitting on a stool, sewing.

"Greetings, Mother Wang," he said, putting down his basket and looking straight at her.

"What have you come for, Young'un?" she asked.

"I want to see His Honour, 'cos I need a spot of cash to buy food for my old pa."

"His Honour? Who do you mean?"

"I mean the one you know I mean, who else would I mean?"

"If he's that important he has a name, I suppose!"

"Course 'e does, a double-barrelled one too."

"What do you mean, double-barrelled?"

"Oh, come off it! I want to talk to 'is Nibs, Mr. Xi-men." And with this he headed for the inner room. But Mrs. Wang grabbed him first. "Hey! where do you think you're going to, you young jackanapes? You can't just invade people's privacy like this!"

"I'm going inside, 'cos he's there and I want to see him."

鄆哥不念
鬧茶肆

Chapter 24

"You bloody little ape, how do you expect to find Mr. Xi-men in my parlour?"

"Don't be such a dog-in-the-manger! Why can't I have some of the gravy too? D'you think I don't know what's going on?"

The old woman was furious. She began to shout: "What do you bloody well know, then, you little bastard?"

"I know you want to keep it all to yourself because you're an old meany. All right then, suppose I talk. Let's see how the bread-man takes it!"

This indication that he had cottoned on to the truth made the old woman see red. "You bloody ape!" she screamed. "Who asked you to come farting round here, stinking the place out?"

"If I'm a bloody ape, you're a filthy old tart!" he replied.

She took a firmer grip on him and boxed his ears.

"Ow! Why are you hitting me?" he yelled.

"Shut your noise, you fucking monkey, or I'll beat you all down the street!"

"You ugly old bloodsucker, yer've no right!"

Maintaining her grip with one hand and slapping him with the other, she pushed him out into the street. The basket of pears followed, the pears spilling and rolling in all directions. Recognizing he was no match for this ferocious old woman, the boy took himself off, cursing and crying simultaneously, picking up pears as he went down the street and pointing his finger at the teahouse and shouting: "You filthy parasite, you'll be sorry for this! I'll tell him, I'll tell him everything, just see if I don't!" And when he'd picked up his basket, he went straight off to find the person he had in mind.

Well, in truth, once an affair's under way, the troubles come all in a bunch:

> *The den is discovered, the burrow found,*
> *The paired ducks taken where they sleep on the sand.*

But if you want to know who the Young'un was going off to see, read the next chapter.

Chapter 25

❧

The old woman tells his Nibs the plan;
The adulteress poisons her old man!

Now the Young'un, filled with fruitless rage against Mrs. Wang for the beating she had given him, gathered up his pears and dashed off to look for the Midget. He traversed two streets, turned a corner, and there, coming towards him down the street with his carrying-pole and his load of bread, was the Midget.

The Young'un stopped in his tracks and said to the Midget: "I ain't seen yer lately. How come yer gettin' so fat?"

The Midget put down his carrying-pole and said: "I'm the same as I always was, who says I'm getting fat?"

"I wanted some poultry feed the other day an' I couldn't find none. They told me you'd 'ave some."

"Why would I have poultry feed? I don't keep ducks or geese!"

"Oh, yer don't keep geese, doncha? But yer a fat goose yerself and if they hung yer up by the heels in the pot, yer 'd cook lovely!"

"Hey, you watch your tongue, you little twerp! My wife hasn't got a lover, why d'you call me a goose?"

"If yer wife hasn't got a lover, it must be the lover what's got her!"

The Midget grabbed the boy. "Who is it?" he shouted.

The Young'un said: "That's a laugh. Pull me about, go on, but it won't do no injury to what he's got between 'is legs."

"Listen, lad," said the Midget, changing his tone. "If you tell me who it is I'll let you have ten rolls."

"Bugger yer rolls! But if you treated me to three cups of wine I'd tell yer."

"So you drink wine, do you?" said the Midget. "All right, come with me, then."

The Midget picked up the carrying-pole and took the Young'un off to a little wineshop. When he'd put his pole down he took out several rolls, bought some meat and ordered a bottle of wine. He told the boy to help himself.

"The wine'll do, don't need no more," the boy said, "but yer can order an extra helping of meat."

"Come on, lad," the Midget said. "You'd better tell me what you know."

"Don't rush me," the boy said. "I'll tell yer when I've eaten. And if yer keep yer 'ead, I'll help yer to nab 'im."

The Midget watched the boy eat and drink. Then he said: "Now are you going to tell me?"

"If yer so interested, just feel these lumps I got on me 'ead!"

"Hm, how did you get them?"

"I'll tell yer. I 'ad this basket of pears, see, and I were looking for 'is Nibs, Mr. Xi-men, to try and get some money out of 'im, but I couldn't find 'im nowhere. Then I met someone in the street who said, 'He's at Mrs. Wang's teahouse. He's got something going with the Midget's wife, they meet there every day.' Well, I were hoping to earn meself a spot of cash, see, so I went down there, but that old bitch, Mrs. Wang, wouldn't let me go in to 'im. She started beating me up. That's why I been looking for yer. I only spoke to yer like I did just now in order to get yer worked up, I thought it were the best way to get yer to start asking me about it."

"Is all this true?" the Midget asked.

"There yer go again! I always said you was an idiot. I tell yer, them two's 'aving a great old time. They just wait till you go out, and then they get together at Mrs. Wang's. And all yer do is sit here asking if it's true or not!"

The Midget thought and said: "All right, lad, I'll tell you what. My wife does go off every day to Mrs. Wang's to make clothes. And she is a bit flushed always when she gets home, and, yes, I was beginning to wonder! That must be it! I'm going to get rid of this load and then I'll go and catch them at it, how about that?"

"Yer supposed to be a grown-up, how come yer 'aven't got more sense! Yer must know what a crafty devil that old woman is! If yer get into her clutches yer'll never escape. Anyway, they must

Chapter 25

'ave a signal. When they see yer coming, yer wife'll hide. And 'is Nibs ain't no pushover, he could take care of twenty like you! Yer won't catch them and yer'll get yerself a good beating into the bargain. Besides, 'e's got all that money and influence, 'e'll make an accusation and yer'll wind up in court. And don't expect no one to speak up for yer. Yer'll lose your life for nothing!"

"You're dead right," said the Midget despondently. "How am I ever going to get even?"

"That old bitch beat me up, so I owe her one. I'll tell yer what: go 'ome a bit later than usual tonight and don't let on that yer know anything. Don't go shooting yer mouth off, mind. Just do like yer always do. Tomorrow morning, don't take so much bread out to sell. I'll wait for yer down the end of the road, and if I sees 'is Nibs go in I'll come and fetch yer. What yer do then is, yer wait with yer stuff near the teahouse, on the left, and I'll go in first and get the old bitch angry. She's bound to start hitting me. When I chuck my basket out into the street, you rush in. I'll hold her up, somehow, while yer barge straight in, shouting that yer bein' cuckolded. 'Ow about that?"

"Well, if it works, I shall be in your debt, lad. But wait, here's some silver you can have to go and buy rice. You come early, then, tomorrow, and wait for me on the corner of Redstone Road."

The Young'un picked up the silver and some rolls and departed. As for the Midget, after paying the bill he took up the carrying-pole and went off to do one more round before going home.

Now we have to relate that Jinlian, although she was in the habit of yelling at the Midget and bullying him in a hundred ways, had recently become very attentive towards him, because she felt herself at fault, and had taken to offering him all manner of little comforts. As the poem says:

Though the trollop feigns when home she steals,
Soft words to hide what she really feels,
On her next door beau he's not a patch;
The evil plan begins to hatch.

When the Midget came home with his pole that evening it was

just like any other day; he said nothing. Jinlian asked him: "Shall I go and get some wine, dear?"

"No," he answered, "I've just had a few cups with a merchant." After that she gave him his dinner, and nothing else happened that evening.

Next day, after breakfast, he made only two or three baskets of bread, which he loaded onto his carrying-pole. His wife's thoughts were full of her lover, so she wasn't going to notice if he made a little more or less. Finally he left. Jinlian, who could hardly wait for him to go, went straight off to Mrs. Wang's to await her lover.

Meanwhile the Midget had arrived with his carrying-pole at the entrance to Redstone Road, where he met the Young'un, who was waiting for him there, equipped with a basket.

"Well?" the Midget said.

"It's too early," the Young'un said. "Go and sell some bread first. But I'm pretty sure 'e'll come, so stick around."

The Midget shot off to do a quick round and was back in no time.

"Remember, wait till I throw out my basket and then rush in," the Young'un reminded him.

The Midget put down his carrying-pole — but enough of that!

Now the Young'un picked up his basket and marched into the teashop, shouting: "Look here, yer old bitch, why did yer beat me yesterday?"

True to form, the old woman leapt to her feet and replied: "You little guttersnipe! I've nothing to say to you. What do you mean by coming in here and using bad language to me?"

"An' if I call yer a filthy bawd, a dirty old bitch, who gives a fart for what you think?"

The old woman saw red. She grabbed the boy and started beating him.

The Young'un squealed. Screaming, "'Ow dare yer beat me!" he threw his basket out into the street. The old woman sought to tighten her grip on him, but shouting: "Just you dare!" he took hold of her waist and butted her in the stomach with his head. He would have knocked her over, but for the wall which prevented

Chapter 25

her from falling. While the Young'un was employing all his strength to pin the old woman to the wall, the Midget bounded into the teahouse, his robe tucked into his belt for action. When the old woman saw who it was, she made a desperate attempt to stop him. However the boy pinned her down with might and main and she couldn't move. All she could do was shout: "The Midget's coming!" Within the room the terrified Jinlian rushed to secure the door, while his Nibs tried to hide under the bed. The Midget charged the door and tried to push it open. But it wouldn't budge. All he could do was shout: "You oughter be ashamed of yourself!"

Jinlian continued to hold the door, but she was getting desperate. "You're always boasting about your fighting skills," she hissed at her lover. "But in an emergency like this you're useless. Even a paper tiger is enough to scare you." She obviously wanted him to come out and fight the Midget and then make good his escape. The lover, in his hiding place under the bed, finally caught on. He crawled out and said: "My dear, it's not that I can't, I just wasn't sure what was best." He flung open the door and shouted: "No violence!" The Midget tried to grab him, but his Nibs caught him with his left foot. Now the Midget being very short, the kick took him in the solar plexus and sent him flying backwards. He collapsed on the ground. His Nibs, having floored his adversary, fled amid the confusion. The Young'un, seeing things weren't looking good, released the old woman and vanished. As for the neighbours, well, they knew Xi-men Qing's power and influence, they weren't minded to interfere.

When Mrs. Wang went to help the Midget up, she found he was bleeding from the mouth and his face was as yellow as wax. She called to Jinlian, telling her to bring a bowl of water to revive him. The two of them supporting him under the shoulders got him out the back way and back to his house, where they put him into his bed and he went to sleep.

Well, this is the way it was going:

Poor three-inch midget, what can you do?
That bugger Xi-men's too much for you!

When the wife has the lover bash her true lord,
Adultery's taking a worse crime on board.

Nothing more happened that night. Next day, his Nibs, hearing there had been no repercussions, went back as usual for his assignation with Jinlian. Their great hope now was that the Midget would die.

For five days the Midget lay sick, unable to move. What is more, when he wanted a bowl of soup it didn't come, when he wanted water, it didn't come. It was in vain that he called to his wife. In fact he was obliged to watch her go out each day all powdered and adorned. And when she came back, her face was flushed. More than once he fainted from the violence of his rage. But no one paid him the least attention. Finally he called to his wife and said to her: "I know perfectly well what you're up to, I caught you in the act. You even egged on your lover to kick me in the chest, and now here I am hanging between life and death, while you two live it up together. Well, whether I live or die makes little difference, there's nothing I can do to stop you. But my brother's a different matter, you ought to know what he's like. When he returns, which he will do sooner or later, do you suppose he'll stand by idle? If you have any feelings at all, help me now to get better and I won't tell him anything when he comes back. But if you refuse to look after me, just wait till he comes, he'll have a few things to say to the pair of you."

Jinlian left without saying a word in reply, but she told Mrs. Wang and his Nibs exactly what the Midget had said. When her lover heard this, it was as if someone had thrown a bucket of cold water over him. "Oh my God! Captain Wu, the killer of the tiger of Jingyang Pass?" he said. "Of course I know him, he's the toughest customer in the whole of Qinghe! Listen, we've been indulging ourselves all this time, okay, we're happy as can be, but we must be crazy! All this you've just told us, whatever are we going to do about it? It's terrible."

Mrs. Wang responded with a scornful laugh. "Well, really!" she said. "You're the helmsman and I'm only crew, yet I'm not afraid. Just look at you, trembling with fear!"

Chapter 25

"Just because I'm a man," his Nibs replied, "it doesn't mean I can resolve a situation like this. Have you anything to suggest that will help us to cover up?"

"What do you want from this, a long-term affair or just a quickie?"

"What do you mean, long-term or a quickie?"

"If it's to be a quickie, you'd best say goodbye to each other right now. When the Midget recovers, you can pay him something in compensation and when Wu Song gets back there won't be any trouble. Later, if Wu Song's sent off somewhere again, perhaps you can see each other. That's how it would be for just a quickie. But if you want it long-term, if you want to meet each other without all these alarms and disturbances, then I've got a plan, only it's not so easy to tell you about it."

"Mother Wang, please tell us. We do want it to be long-term."

"In order to carry out this plan we need something which most people don't possess, but which you, as heaven will have it, do happen to keep in your house."

"If you said you wanted my eyes, I'd cut them out and give them to you. What is it?"

"At the moment, that poor fool is seriously ill. We must strike while the iron's hot. Go and get some arsenic and we'll get the young lady to buy some medicine for the heart and mix the arsenic with it. That'll settle the dwarf. Then all it needs is a good thorough cremation and there won't be any trace. So when Wu Song comes back, what can he do? You know the saying, 'Brother and sister-in-law should leave each other alone'; and then that other saying, 'The first marriage is to please your family, the second is to please yourself.' What can a brother-in-law say? You just have to be discreet for a few months, until the mourning period is over, and then you can marry the girl. Well, that's what you'll get if you have it long-term, a lifetime's joy, as they say. How does that strike you?"

"Mother Wang, what a proposition!" cried his Nibs. "But they do say, 'If you want to have an easy life, you'll have to work for it.' All right then, in for a penny in for a pound!"

"Of course, it's like they say, 'if you're weeding, get the roots out, kill the growth, else in spring they'll start to sprout.' Now, off you go and get the arsenic, and I'll tell her what to do. Only don't forget, you're going to owe me a lot!"

"Of course," he said. "You don't need to tell me that!" There's a poem about this.

From love's delights they can't abstain;
They'd like to have them spread more thick,
Little aware that there's more pain
In Wu Song's blade than arsenic.

It was not long before his Nibs returned, bearing a small package containing arsenic, which he handed to the old woman. The latter went to Jinlian and said: "I'm going to tell you how you can give him the medicine, dear. Didn't you say he'd been asking you to help him get better? Well then, what you must do is pay him some special little attentions. Then when he asks you to get him medicine, you can mix the arsenic with some heart medicine. If he resists at all, just pour it down his throat and get out of the way. When the poison gets into his stomach it's going to tear it to shreds and he'll start screaming, so you must cover him with the bedclothes because you don't want anyone to hear. Get a basin of hot water ready and a hot towel. When the poison begins to work he'll bleed from all the seven orifices, and he'll bite his lips, which will leave marks. So when he's dead you must take the bedclothes off him and clean him with the hot towel to remove all traces of blood. Then you only have to stick him in the coffin and have him taken out for cremation. You see, it's dead simple."

"It sounds all right," said Jinlian, "only I'm afraid I'm not strong enough and I won't be able to arrange the body when I have to."

"That's no problem. Just knock on the wall and I'll come over and help you."

"Make a thorough job of it, the two of you," said his Nibs. "I'll be over first thing in the morning to find out how you got on." With that he left. The old woman took the arsenic and rolled it in her fingers to turn it into powder and then gave it to the girl to keep.

When Jinlian got home and went upstairs to see the Midget, he

Chapter 25

was hardly breathing and looked as if he was at death's door. She sat down beside him and pretended to cry.

"Why are you crying?" the Midget asked.

Wiping away the tears, she said: "I was wrong, I know, but that blighter led me astray. How could I know he was going to kick you like that? I've been told of some good medicine and I wanted to go out and buy it for you, but I was afraid you might think badly of me if I left you again."

"Don't worry," the Midget said. "If you help me get better, we'll say no more of this business, we'll wipe the slate clean. When my brother comes back I won't mention it. Go and get that medicine for me, quickly!"

Jinlian took some change in coppers and went over to Mrs. Wang's. She sat and waited while Mrs. Wang went to buy the medicine. Then she took the medicine home and went upstairs to show it to the Midget. "This medicine is for the heart. The doctor said you were to take it at midnight and then cover yourself with two quilts so that you will sweat. In the morning you'll be able to get up."

"That's wonderful," the Midget said. "You're very good to me my dear. I shall try to sleep for a while now. Wake me up at midnight for the medicine."

"You sleep now," she said. "I shall watch over you."

Gradually it grew dark and the girl lit the lamps in the bedroom. She went downstairs and heated a basin of water, and also warmed a damp towel. She listened for the watch, and when the third watch was sounded at eleven she took the poison and poured it into a cup and poured out a bowl of hot water. She took all this upstairs. "Where's the medicine, dear?" she called.

"Under the mat, beside the pillow," the Midget answered. "Prepare it and give it to me, quickly!"

She turned back the mat and took the medicine and poured it into the cup. She mixed the two powders and poured hot water into the cup. She took a silver hairpin from her hair and stirred it till it was evenly mixed. Then, supporting the Midget with her left hand she gave him the medicine with her right. After the first sip, the Midget said: "This medicine is horrible, dear!"

"What does that matter, so long as it cures you?" she said.

When he'd taken the second mouthful, she tipped the cup and poured it down his throat. Then she quickly released him and jumped off the bed. He groaned and said: "That medicine's given me a dreadful stomach ache. Oh, the pain's terrible, I can't bear it!"

She got the two quilts at the foot of the bed and pulled them over him, covering his face completely.

"I can't breathe," he cried out.

"The doctor said I had to make you sweat so you'd get better sooner."

When he tried to cry out again, she was afraid he might put up a fight, so she jumped on the bed and sat on him, pressing down the covers tightly with both arms. He hadn't a hope of freeing himself:

> *His insides are frying, a fire is eating his liver, a blade of ice has pierced his heart, his stomach's being churned by a steel knife. Cold grips his body, blood seeps from the orifices. His teeth are tightly clenched, as the three souls prepare to depart for the realm of the unjustly dead; his throat is burning, as the seven spirits head for the place of judgement. The world of the dead's about to receive another poison victim while the world of the living loses an accuser of adultery.*

He groaned twice and struggled for breath a little longer, and then finally the stomach burst and the Midget — ill-fated wretch! — was still.

When she pulled back the covers, she saw that he had bitten his lips and was bleeding from all seven orifices. Suddenly terrified, she jumped off the bed and went to knock on the wall. Mrs. Wang heard the signal and came to the back door and coughed. Jinlian ran downstairs to open the door. "Is it done?" Mrs. Wang asked.

"It's done," she answered. "But I've no strength left in my arms and legs. I can't clear up."

"Don't worry about that, I'll help you," said the old woman. She rolled up her sleeves and poured out some hot water. She threw the warm towel into it and took it upstairs. After turning back the

Chapter 25

covers she started wiping the Midget's mouth and lips. Then she cleaned away all traces of blood from the other points where it had seeped out. She placed the clothes on top of the body and then the two of them manoeuvred it down the stairs and laid it out on an old door. They combed the hair, put on a cloth cap, and dressed him, putting on new socks and shoes. They covered the face with a piece of fine white silk. Finally they covered the body with a clean quilt. Then they went back upstairs to tidy up there. When they had finished, Mrs. Wang went home.

Next the girl set up a tremendous hullabaloo, falsely mourning the death of her lord and master. As the reader well knows, there are generally three ways in which a woman weeps: with tears and noise, the kind of thing we call weeping; with tears, but silently, which we call crying; noisily but with no tears, what we call keening or wailing. Well, on this occasion the woman wailed all night. In the early hours of the morning, before it was light, his Nibs came, in great excitement to hear the news. Mrs. Wang gave him a detailed account. He took out some silver and gave it to her to buy a coffin and the necessary for the funeral. Then he conferred with Jinlian.

"Now my husband is dead, I have to depend on you for everything," she said.

"There's no need to tell me that," he said.

"There's one thing that's urgent," Mrs. Wang said. "Mr. Ho, the coroner, is a very careful person. I'm afraid he may smell a rat and refuse to allow the funeral to go ahead."

"Don't worry about that. I'll have a word with him myself. He won't want to oppose me."

"Then you'd better go and do it at once, Your Honour, don't waste any time."

His Nibs left.

When it was fully light, Mrs. Wang went to buy the coffin. She also bought candles and incense, paper money and suchlike. On her return she helped Jinlian prepare the food for the offering and lit the special lamp which accompanies the spirit of the dead person. Now the neighbours all began to arrive to inquire what had happened. The girl covered her pretty face and falsely wept.

"But what did your husband die of?" they all wanted to know.

"He had heart disease," she replied. "It got worse and worse. I could see it was hopeless. He went last night around midnight." She began to snivel and sob again. The neighbours all knew perfectly well that the death was suspicious, but they didn't like to go on questioning her, so they merely tried to console her by saying: "Well, his spirit is fled now, and the soul has departed for other regions. Try not to upset yourself too much." She made a show of thanking them and they went away.

Mrs. Wang had the coffin delivered and went to fetch the coroner, whom most people knew as Uncle Ho. She had already bought everything necessary for the funeral, including a number of kitchen utensils. She now sent for two monks, who would be needed later on to watch over the body. Meanwhile, Uncle Ho had sent along some assistants to get everything ready.

It was almost noon when Uncle Ho set out himself. He was in no particular hurry. When he got to the beginning of Redstone Road, he met Xi-men Qing, who called out: "Where are you going, Uncle?"

"I'm going over to inspect the body of Wu Da, the bread-seller," he replied.

"Do you mind accompanying me a moment? I'd like a word with you."

Uncle Ho went with Xi-men Qing to a little wineshop on the corner of the street, where they found a quiet room to sit. "Please take the place of honour, Mr. Ho," said his Nibs.

"I'm just a simple man, how should I presume to sit down with Your Honour?"

"Please don't stand on ceremony. Do sit down."

When they were seated a bottle of the best wine was ordered. The waiter brought dishes of vegetables and fruit, together with the wine, which he poured for them. Uncle Ho was becoming quite suspicious. Privately he was thinking, "This man has never invited me before, there must be some special reason for this." They had been drinking there about an hour when his Nibs suddenly took from his sleeve ten taels of silver and placed them on the table. "Please don't despise this, Uncle," he said. "Later on I'll find a way to express my gratitude more suitably."

"But I've done nothing for you," Uncle Ho said, "nothing at all. How can I take your money? Even if there is something you'd like me to do, I can't accept the money now."

"Please, for my sake, Uncle, take it and then we can talk."

"Say whatever you wish, Your Honour, I am listening."

"It's not something special, and in any case, the family will presently be rewarding you for your pains. It's just that you are going along to lay out the body of Mr. Wu and I want you to make sure everything is done nicely; it would be a good idea to cover the body with an embroidered quilt, that's all."

"If that's all it is, there's no problem at all. How can I accept your money for this?"

"If you don't take it, I shall be offended."

Now Uncle Ho knew very well that this man was a crook and had many government officials in his pocket, so he thought it best to accept the gift. After they'd had a few more cups, his Nibs called the waiter and told him to make out the bill and come round to his shop to collect the money next day.

They went downstairs together. As they were going out of the door, his Nibs said: "Don't forget, Uncle. Keep it to yourself and I'll reward you later on."

Uncle Ho was now highly suspicious. "There's something very odd about this business," he said to himself. "I haven't seen the body of the Midget and here he is giving me all this money. There must be something going on." When he arrived at Wu Da's, his assistants were waiting around outside.

"What did Wu Da die of?" he asked them.

"They say in there he died of heart disease," they said.

When Uncle Ho drew back the curtain and went in, Mrs. Wang received him. "We've been waiting a long time for you, Mr. Ho," she said.

"There was some business that held me up," he said, "that's why I'm a little late."

At this point Jinlian, who was dressed in plain white funeral clothing, started crying loudly inside.

Chapter 25

"You must control yourself, madam," Uncle Ho said. "However sad, he's departed now."

The girl covered her eyes and said: "It's so awful sir! I never thought that my husband's heart disease would carry him off so suddenly, leaving me here like this!"

Uncle Ho examined her closely. He was thinking: "I'd only heard about the Midget's wife, I never actually saw her till now. So this is what the Midget managed to get himself by way of a wife! I'm beginning to understand why his Nibs offered me that money!"

He now proceeded to the examination of the body. He pulled back the shroud and lifted the piece of silk. However, when his sharp and perceptive eyes took in the body, Uncle Ho gave a startled cry and fell to the floor. He was seen to be bleeding from the mouth, his fingernails were blue and his lips purple. His face had a yellowish tinge and his eyes were glazed. His whole body resembled the moon setting behind the mountain in the hour before dawn, and anyone would have said his life was like a lamp at midnight when the oil's exhausted.

But if you want to know how it went with Mr. Ho after this, you must read the next chapter.

Chapter 26

Uncle Ho attends the funeral and steals some bones; Wu Song makes an offering of some human heads!

Now when Mr. Ho fell to the ground, his assistants rushed to help him, and Mrs. Wang said: "He's having a fit. Quickly, get some water!" After two mouthfuls had been administered, Mr. Ho began to stir and gradually regained consciousness. Mrs. Wang said: "Take Mr. Ho home, we can arrange this matter later." Two of the assistants carried him home, using a door as stretcher. All his family, young and old, came out to meet them and he was put to bed and went to sleep. His wife wept. "He was in the best of humours when he went out," she sobbed. "And now look what sort of a state he comes back in. I've never known him to have one of these fits before."

But as she sat there crying at the bedside, Uncle Ho, having made sure that the assistants were out of earshot, nudged her with his foot and said: "You don't need to worry; there's nothing wrong with me. On the way to Wu Da's to lay out the body, just at the entrance to his street, I met Xi-men Qing — you know, his Nibs, the one that has the medicine shop in front of the government offices. He treated me to a cup of wine and then gave me ten taels of silver and said, 'When you lay out the body, just make sure everything's properly covered, will you?' Well when I got to the house, I could see the wife was not a good sort of person, so I was already practically certain something was wrong. And when I took off the shroud and looked at the body, I found the face was dark purple, blood had seeped out of all the apertures, and the lips bore the marks of his own teeth. I was convinced he'd died of poisoning. I would have announced this, but then I thought, no one's going to stick up for the Midget, and I would only be making an enemy of his Nibs. Obviously I didn't want to stir up a hornet's nest. So the best thing to do was turn a blind eye and let them get on with the funeral. But then, the Midget has a younger brother, the one who killed the tiger on Jingyang Pass the other day and was made a captain. He's the sort that could kill a man without batting an eyelid. Sooner or later he's going to come back, and that could mean big trouble."

His wife said: "I also heard that the other day the Young'un — old Qiao's son, you know, who lives in one of those back alleys — went to Redstone Road to help Wu Da set a trap for his wife's lover and caused a commotion in the teahouse. That must have something to do with it. You'd better question the Young'un, discreetly of course. Actually, this business shouldn't be too difficult to manage. Just get your assistants to go and deal with the body and find out when they're going to hold the funeral. If they're going to keep the coffin in the house till Wu Song comes back, then it's all perfectly above board. Even if they want to take it out for burial immediately, let them. But suppose they plan to cremate it, then there's something fishy. When the time for the ceremony comes, you'd better find a time when no one's looking and pinch two pieces of bone. Put them together with the ten taels of silver and you'll have evidence. If Wu Song doesn't ask any questions when he comes back, then forget about it. We won't have upset his Nibs and we'll have made a little profit for ourselves into the bargain."

"I've a wonderful wife," Uncle Ho said, "how clever she is!" He called his assistants and said to them: "I can't go myself because I have these fainting fits. So you must go and see about the body. Ask them when the funeral is going to be, and then come back and tell me. If they give you any silver or silk, you can share it amongst you. But make sure everything's done properly. If they give you money or silk for me, don't accept it."

The assistants went to Wu Da's, as instructed, to oversee the business of putting the body in the coffin and positioning it correctly, and then returned to inform Mr. Ho: "The mistress of the house says the funeral will be in three days' time and the body will

Chapter 26

be taken and cremated outside the town." They left after dividing up the money.

Uncle Ho said to his wife: "It's just as you predicted. I'll have to find the right moment to go along and take those bones."

Meanwhile Mrs. Wang had been busying herself: she told Jinlian to watch over the body all night and invited four monks on the second day to recite Buddhist scriptures. Early on the third day the coroner's assistants arrived to carry out the coffin. There were also a number of neighbours and local people to see the dead man off. Jinlian followed, dressed in mourning and shedding false tears for her late husband. When they arrived at the cremation ground outside the town, the fire was lit. At this moment Uncle Ho appeared, carrying some paper money. Mrs. Wang and Jinlian welcomed him, saying: "Mr. Ho, we're so glad to see you're better."

"I bought a basket of bread off Mr. Wu the other day," Ho said, "and I hadn't paid him. So now I've brought this paper money to burn with him."

"What a conscientious person you are, Mr. Ho!" Mrs. Wang said.

Ho lit the money and burnt it. Then he set about the business of the cremation. Mrs. Wang and Jinlian thanked him. "It's really kind of you to help like this, Mr. Ho. When we go back, we must find a way to show our gratitude."

"It's always a pleasure to be of use," he replied. "Now, why don't you two leave all this to me and go and look after your friends and neighbours in the funeral hall? I'll keep an eye on things for you here."

As soon as they had departed, he took a pair of tongs and picked two pieces of bone out of the fire. He dipped them quickly in the tank reserved for this purpose. They had turned completely black. He hid the bones away and then went and mingled with the crowd in the funeral hall for a while. When the coffin had been consumed by the flames, the fire was put out and all the bones were collected and immersed in the tank, after which the neighbours all went home. Mr. Ho took his two pieces of bone home and wrote out a label recording the exact date and the names of those present at the ceremony and wrapped them together with the money in a canvas bag which he stored in his house.

When Jinlian returned home, she set up a memorial tablet in front of the niche for the ancestors' spirits, bearing the words: "In memory of Wu Da, my late husband." She placed a glass lamp before the altar and decorated it with Buddhist invocations, paper gold, pieces of gold and silver, coloured paintings and suchlike. From now on, she and her lover could disport themselves freely in the bedroom every day; it was no longer as formerly when they were obliged to steal their pleasure furtively in Mrs. Wang's parlour, for now there was absolutely no one in the house to hinder them. They could stay together the whole night if they wished. Often his Nibs would not return home for four or five nights on end. Of course no one in his household liked this state of affairs. And in the end such womanizing can only ruin a man. Catastrophe inexorably approaches. As the poem says:

> *Who love's delights can view with enlightened eyes*
> *Knows luck in love is actually a curse.*
> *To marry a woman plain as daily rice*
> *Will shield your heart from shocks and spare your purse.*

So now all day long his Nibs and Jinlian played undisturbed, leading a life of total debauchery, quite unconcerned about what people might think. For by now, not one of the neighbours, far or near, but knew everything. Since they were all scared of his Nibs, however, and knew what a crook he was, no one dared to meddle.

Nevertheless, as the proverb says: "Pleasure contains the seeds of sadness, in misfortune relief is born." Time passed quickly and soon over a month had gone by. Wu Song, in accordance with the governor's instructions, had escorted the convoy to the residence of the governor's relative in the Eastern Capital, delivering the letter and handing over the baskets and boxes. He had spent a few days looking round the city, while he waited for the reply, and then with his party set out for Yanggu again. The whole journey, there and back, had lasted about two months: it was early spring when he started, and here he was returning at the beginning of summer. Even during the journey something already made him feel uneasy. He felt somehow both a physical and a mental disquiet. On arrival he would have liked to go and see his brother at once, but first he had to report to the government office and deliver the reply.

The governor expressed great satisfaction. When he had read the letter, and learnt that the delivery of the valuables had all gone without a hitch, he rewarded Wu Song with a large silver ingot and entertained him with a banquet. Of this no more.

Finally Wu Song went back to his room, and changed his clothes, shoes and socks. He put on a new headdress and, locking the door behind him, headed for Redstone Road. When the neighbours on both sides saw Wu Song was back they had such a shock the palms of their hands became sticky with sweat. "Look out for domestic storms now!" they whispered to each other. "If he's back, don't expect him to stay quiet, a firebrand like that! He's bound to raise hell!"

Meanwhile, Wu Song had arrived at the door. When he drew back the curtain and walked in, the first thing he saw was the altar with the plaque bearing the scant inscription "In memory of my husband, Wu Da." He was dumbfounded. At first he stared in horror, wondering if there was something wrong with his eyes. Finally he called out: "Sister-in-law, it's me, Wu Song."

At this moment his Nibs and Jinlian were upstairs making love. His Nibs shit himself when he heard Wu Song's shout. He fled at once, by the back way and out through Mrs. Wang's.

"Please have a seat, brother-in-law, I'll be with you in a minute," Jinlian shouted. Now, since the time she poisoned her husband, not once had she worn mourning for him. Instead she had dolled herself up in the most garish fashion for the benefit of his Nibs and in aid of their mutual pleasures. When she heard Wu Song downstairs, she rushed to wash and clean off all the powder and paint, tore off all her jewellery, her pins and her earrings, discomposed her artfully arranged tresses and removed her red skirt and embroidered robe, replacing them with the rough shirt and skirt of mourning. This done, she descended, snivelling and moaning, to the room below.

"Sister-in-law, enough, stop crying!" said Wu Song. "Tell me when my brother died. What did he die of? And whose medicine did he take?"

Between sobs she replied: "Just ten days or so after you were gone he began to have terrible heart pains. It went on for about eight or nine days. He consulted fortune-tellers but he wouldn't take any medicine. The doctors couldn't do anything for him. He just went and died. He has left me heartbroken!"

Next door, Mrs. Wang heard the noise and her heart misgave her. She hurried round to assist her neighbour in dealing with this crisis. Wu Song was just saying: "But my brother never had an illness of this kind before. How could he suddenly get sick and die just like that?"

"How can you say that?" interrupted Mrs. Wang. "Like the storms of the sky, which arise without warning, human misfortune strikes at any time. Who can count on tranquillity for long?"

"I was so thankful for this lady's help," Jinlian added. "I was so helpless. She was the only one, none of the other neighbours offered me any help."

"Where is he buried?" Wu Song asked.

"I was all alone," the girl said. "I didn't know how to find a burial plot. What could I do? After three days we cremated him."

"How long is it since he died?"

"In two days it will be time for the seventh week ceremony."

Wu Song remained plunged in thought for a long time. Finally he left and went to the government offices, where he unlocked his door, entered and changed into mourning clothes. Then he asked a soldier to prepare him a piece of rope which he tied about his waist. He also concealed on his person a knife with a long blade and short handle, sharp-edged but thick, together with a quantity of silver. He told the soldier to lock the door, and they went off to purchase rice, flour, seasoning and so on, opposite the government offices, and also some incense, candles and paper money. With these supplies they headed back to Wu Da's house. It was evening when Wu Song knocked on the door.

Chapter 26

When Jinlian opened, Wu Song told the soldier to go and prepare the food for the offering. He lit a lamp and placed it before the altar with his own hands, and arranged the wine and the dishes. At nine o'clock, when everything was ready, he prostrated himself before the altar and spoke: "Brother, your soul is still near. In life you were weak and helpless, and now your death is unclear. If you were the victim of ill-treatment or injustice, if anyone harmed you in any way, appear to me in a dream and I will avenge you." So saying he poured the wine and burnt the paper money, and then began loudly to lament. He wailed so loudly that the neighbours trembled, every one of them. Jinlian in her room accompanied him with feigned weeping.

When the display of grief was done, Wu Song gave the food and wine of the offering to the soldier. He asked for two mats and told the soldier to sleep in front of the door, while he spread his mat out and slept before the altar. Jinlian retired upstairs to sleep, closing the upstairs door.

Shortly before midnight Wu Song, who had been tossing and turning, unable to sleep, looked at the soldier and saw that he lay there as motionless as if he were dead, snoring loudly. He got up and looked at the glass lamp before the altar. The flame was vacillating and weak. He heard the watch: three beats and three taps, signifying midnight. He sighed and sat down on the mat again. He began muttering to himself: "My brother was always weak and unresisting and I still can't be sure about his death." Hardly had he formulated this thought when from beneath the altar there arose a current of cold air, which seemed veritably to curl itself about his bones and fill him with ice. The lamp went out. The paper money on the wall began to flutter and fly in all directions. This glacial emanation made Wu Song's hair stand on end. As he gazed fixedly at the altar, a vague figure crept out from beneath it and cried: "Brother, I had a terrible death!" Wu Song had no time to see clearly. When he approached to question the apparition, the cold air ceased and the figure vanished. Wu Song fell back onto the mat. He sat there asking himself if he was dreaming or not. He turned to look at the soldier. The soldier was still sleeping soundly. "There must be something wrong with my brother's death," Wu Song decided. "He wanted to tell me about it, but my vital force frightened the spirit away."

He decided to keep this experience to himself and wait till daylight before making up his mind what to do. The poem says:

> *In life an idiot, ridiculed by most,*
> *The Three-Inch Midget's now a clever ghost.*
> *The power that in a brother's feeling lies*
> *Can make the injured spirit materialize.*

Slowly day dawned. The soldier got up and heated some water. Wu Song washed and rinsed his mouth. The woman came downstairs and said to Wu Song: "You seem to have had a bad night, brother-in-law."

"Tell me," Wu Song said, "what did my brother really die of?"

"How is it you've forgotten?" she said. "I told you last night, he died of heart disease."

"What medicine did he take?"

"I can show you, it's here."

"Who ordered the coffin?"

"I asked the neighbour, Mrs. Wang, to buy it for me."

"And how was it carried out?"

"Mr. Ho, the coroner, supervised everything."

"Well, now I know everything I must go and report to the office. I'll be back later." He left, followed by the soldier, but at the entrance to Redstone Road he asked the soldier: "Do you know this Mr. Ho, the coroner?"

"How come you don't remember, Your Honour?" the soldier said. "He came to congratulate you only a little while back. He lives in an alley off Lion Avenue."

"Take me there."

When they reached Uncle Ho's front door, Wu Song said: "You can go now" and the soldier departed. Wu Song raised the curtain and shouted: "Is Mr. Ho there?"

Uncle Ho had just got up. When he heard Wu Song was looking for him, he was so scared he felt his hands and feet begin to shake. He didn't even wait to put on a headdress but went and got the silver and the bones, which he concealed on his person

Chapter 26

before going to greet Wu Song. "When did you get back, Captain?" he asked.

"I got here yesterday. I'd like to have a word with you. Would you be so good as to spare me a few minutes?"

"Of course, Captain. But let me offer you some tea."

"Please don't trouble."

The two men went to a little wineshop on the corner of the street and seated themselves. When Wu Song ordered two measures of wine, Uncle Ho rose to his feet protesting: "You refused my offer just now, Your Honour, how can I accept hospitality from you?"

"Please be seated," Wu Song said.

Now Uncle Ho already pretty well guessed what was coming. However, when the landlord poured the wine, Wu Song simply drank his without saying a word. This made Uncle Ho even more apprehensive. His hands were sweating. He tried making conversation but Wu Song still said nothing, he simply didn't open his mouth. Eventually, after a number of cups, Wu Song suddenly reached inside his clothing, took out the knife and slammed it into the table!

The landlord looked on in horror, but certainly he was not going to intervene! Uncle Ho went green. He scarcely dared to breathe. Wu Song rolled up his sleeves, pulled the knife out of the table, pointed it at Uncle Ho and said: "I don't know much about fine manners, but I do know that every crime has its author and every debt has to be paid. Don't be afraid. Just tell the truth. Tell me in detail everything you know about my brother's death. If you do this I won't touch you. On my honour I promise you that. But if you're anything less than completely honest with me, I swear this dagger will put five hundred holes in you and turn you into a sieve. So watch out and just tell me straight, what did my brother's body look like?" When he finished speaking, he gripped his knees with his hands and fixed Uncle Ho with a ferocious gaze.

Uncle Ho responded by producing the bag that was concealed in his sleeve and which he now placed on the table, saying: "Don't be angry, Captain. This bag is capital evidence."

Wu Song took the bag and opened it up. Inside he saw the two pieces of blackened bone and the ten taels of silver. "How is this evidence?" he asked.

"I am afraid I do not know all the circumstances of this case," Uncle Ho began. "What I do know is that on the twenty-second of the first month I was sitting at home when Mrs. Wang, the teashop proprietress, came to fetch me to examine the body of Mr. Wu. As I was approaching Redstone Road on the same day, I met Mr. Ximen, the owner of the medicine shop. He stopped me and asked me to go with him to a wineshop to drink a bottle of wine. Once there he took out a quantity of silver which he gave to me and said, 'When the body is prepared for burial, make sure everything is done properly.' Well, I knew him for a crafty devil and didn't see how I could refuse. After drinking and taking the silver, I went to Mr. Wu's house. When I lifted the shroud I could see traces of blood around the orifices and teeth-marks on the lips, which are all signs of death by poisoning. I would have denounced the crime, but there was no plaintiff. The wife of the deceased had already said that he died of heart disease. Knowing it would be dangerous to speak out, I bit the end of my tongue and pretended to have a fit. They carried me home and it was my assistants who went to perform the routine preparations for burial. I received no payment for it myself, not a penny. Three days later I heard that they were taking the body off for cremation, so I bought some paper money and went there to the mountain pretending to pay my respects. I managed to shake off Mrs. Wang and the wife of the deceased and secretly collected these two pieces of bone, which I took home with me. The fact that they have turned black is proof of death by poisoning. On this piece of paper I have written the exact date and the names of those present. That is my statement, Captain. You may check it for yourself."

"And the lover's name?" Wu Song asked.

"I know nothing about that," Uncle Ho said. "But I heard a rumour about a certain Yunge, known as the Young'un, who sells pears. This young lad, it seems, went with Mr. Wu, your brother, to the teahouse with the intention of catching the lovers at it. The whole street knew about it. If you want the exact details, Captain, you'd better question this Yunge."

"Very well!" said Wu Song. "In that case we'll go and look for him together." He put away his knife, packed up the bones and the silver again, and paid for the wine. Then he set off with Uncle Ho for the Young'un's house.

They reached the Young'un's door just as the young monkey appeared, toting a wicker basket, on his way back from buying rice. "Hey there, Young'un!" Uncle Ho called out. "The Captain here is looking for you. Do you know who he is?"

"I seen him the day they brought in the big tiger," the Young'un said. "Wotcha want with me?"

Actually the young rascal had more or less guessed, so he quickly added: "There's just one thing. Me old dad's over sixty and there' ain't no one else to look after 'im, so I wouldn't want to have to go and sit in gaol on account of you!"

"Don't worry young man," said Wu Song, taking out five taels of silver. "Take this for your father's living expenses and then come with me because I want to talk to you."

The Young'un thought to himself: "This will cover a good three or four months expenses. So even if I do have to go to the tribunal with him, it don't signify." He went in to give his father the silver and the rice and then accompanied the other two to a winehouse on the corner of the street. Wu Song ordered food for three and then addressed the Young'un. "Young man, you're very young but you carry all the responsibility of supporting your old father, that's why I wanted you to have the funds I've just given you. You can be useful to me, and if matters are satisfactorily concluded, I shall give you another fifteen taels or so, to provide you with a little capital. Now please tell me in detail how it came about that you went with my brother to the teahouse to surprise the lovers."

"If I tells yer," the Young'un said, "please, yer mustn't get angry. It were on the thirteenth of the first month. I 'ad a basket of pears and I were looking for Mr. Xi-men, 'oping to make a sale, but I couldn't find him nowhere. Then while I were making inquiries someone said: ''Is Nibs's at Mrs. Wang's teashop in Redstone Road. He's with the wife of Wu Da, what sells the bread. He's having it off with her, an' he goes there every day now.' Well I goes straight round there to find 'im. But that old bitch Mrs.

Wang stops me and won't let me go inside. I told her what I thought of her and she started beating me and chucked me out — threw my pears all over the street, too. I were so angry I went and found your brother and told 'im everything. So 'e got this idea of going there to catch them in the act. 'Don't be in such a hurry,' I told him. 'That Xi-men Qing's a crafty bugger and 'e knows how to fight; if yer don't get 'im the first time 'e'll accuse you and you'll be the one what's in the shit. Look, I'll meet you here tomorrow at the end of the street. You go and finish yer sales quickly and I'll watch to see if 'is Nibs goes into the teahouse. If he does, I'll go in first. You get rid of yer carrying-pole and wait. When I throw out the basket, you rush in and catch them at it.' So I goes back to the teahouse with another basket of pears. I give the old bitch a taste of my tongue and she came and 'it me and I threw me basket out into the street and butted the old cow and pushed 'er up against the wall. When Mr. Wu barged in I held her back so she couldn't stop 'im, but she got to shout 'Wu Da's coming!' So of course them two inside blocked the door. So there's Mr. Wu 'ollering away outside the door, which was all 'e could do. And then suddenly that bastard Xi-men Qing opens the door and charges out. He floored Mr. Wu with one kick. I see the woman come out and she went to help Mr. Wu up but 'e weren't moving. So I got out quick. About a week later I 'eard that Mr. Wu was dead. But I don't know 'ow 'e died."

"Is all this true?" Wu Song asked. "You'd better not lie to me!"

"If it were in front of the judge I'd say exactly the same," the Young'un said.

"I believe you young man," said Wu Song. He told the landlord to bring the food and paid the bill when they'd finished eating, and then the three of them left. As they went downstairs Uncle Ho said: "I have to be going now."

"Oh no, please come with me," Wu Song said. "I need the two of you as witnesses." He took them both with him to the magistracy.

"Well, what is it Captain?" the magistrate said when he saw them.

Chapter 26

鄆哥大鬧授官廳

"My brother, Wu Da, has been cruelly murdered, poisoned by my adulterous sister-in-law and her lover, Xi-men Qing. I request justice, Your Honour!"

The magistrate questioned Uncle Ho and the Young'un. Then he called a meeting of his staff. Now all of these officials, not to mention the magistrate himself, received money from Xi-men Qing, so the unanimous verdict was: "This matter is too hot to handle." The magistrate went back to Wu Song and said: "Wu Song, you're a member of my administration, you really ought to know the law better. What it says is, 'For a charge of adultery produce the two lovers; for a charge of theft show the stolen goods; for a charge of assault demonstrate the wounds.' Now you haven't even got your brother's body. Nor did you catch the lovers in the act. All you've got to go on is the word of these two. And you want to base criminal charges on that? It would just look like a personal vendetta. You can't rush into it like that. You'd better go away and think it over. We've got to observe the proper procedure."

Wu Song took out the two blackened bones, the silver and the paper and said: "Here is my reply, Your Honour. No one can say I invented this!"

After examining the objects, the magistrate said. "Very well, you had better go now and leave the matter in my hands. If there is a case to answer I will have the culprits arrested and questioned."

While the magistrate continued his deliberations, Wu Song detained Uncle Ho and the Young'un in his quarters. Meanwhile, his Nibs had heard about it and sent a trusted friend to the government offices to offer money to everyone. Consequently when Wu Song returned to the court next morning to urge the magistrate to make the arrests, what did he find? The magistrate had been bought. He simply returned the bones and the silver saying: "Wu Song, people want to make trouble between you and Xi-men Qing and you shouldn't listen to everything they say. This affair is most unclear, your case would never succeed. Remember the words of the philosopher, 'If that which is before your eyes can prove illusory, what trust should be put in words spoken behind your back?' You must temper your impetuousness." The superintendent of prisons also put his oar in: "In a criminal offence of this nature, Captain, it is necessary to be able to show a body, wounds, physical effects, circumstantial evidence and the culprit's traces. In the absence of any one of these five elements, one cannot instigate an inquiry."

"If Your Honour will not accept the case," Wu Song said to the magistrate, "I shall have to change my tactics." He collected the bones and the money and returned them to Uncle Ho's safekeeping. Then he went back to his quarters and told the orderly to serve Uncle Ho and the Young'un with food and drink. Telling them to wait, because he would be back soon, he left, taking a number of soldiers with him. He provided himself with an inkstone, brush and ink. He bought four or five pieces of paper, which he carried himself, and told two of the soldiers to buy a pig's head, a goose, a chicken, a bucket of wine and an assortment of dried fruit, all of which was to be prepared in the house. It was late afternoon when he and the soldiers reached Wu Da's. Jinlian had already heard that the magistrate had rejected his case and was full of confidence. Feeling she had nothing to fear, she received them quite insolently.

"Please come down, sister-in-law, I'd like a word with you," Wu Song said.

She took her time. When she finally came down, she said: "Well, what is it?"

"Tomorrow is the end of the seven week period. Since you must have caused the neighbours a lot of distress lately, I've brought some wine in order to thank them on your behalf."

"There's no reason to thank them!" she said scornfully.

"One should always be polite," Wu Song said. He told the soldiers to place two candles in front of the altar, brightly illuminating it, and to burn a stick of incense and arrange some paper money. Next the offerings were laid out, the plates piled high with food, together with the wine and assorted fruit. One of the soldiers was sent to warm the wine at the back, while others arranged tables and chairs by the door, and still others guarded the entrance. When he was satisfied with these arrangements, Wu

Song called his sister-in-law: "Get ready now to receive your guests. I'm going over to invite them."

He went first to Mrs. Wang's. "There's no reason to trouble yourself, Captain, there's nothing to thank me for," she said.

"I know you've had a lot of trouble, Mrs. Wang," he said. "Of course there's a reason. You must come and take a cup of wine and something to eat, you can't refuse!"

In the end she accepted the invitation. She locked up and went round to Wu Da's by the back way.

"You take the host's place, sister-in-law," Wu Song said, "and let Mrs. Wang sit in front of you."

The old woman had already heard from his Nibs that Wu Song's attempt to bring a case had failed, so she sat down and drank with an easy mind. Both of them were thinking: "There's not much he can do now."

Wu Song also invited another neighbour, Yao Wenqing, proprietor of a silver shop. "I'm overwhelmed with work, you must excuse me," Yao said. "Besides, I don't want to bother you."

But Wu Song wasn't having it. "A cup of weak wine won't take long," he said. "Please come." Wu Song went round to another neighbour's. This was Mr. Zhao, Zhao Zhongming, that is, who had a shop selling the paper objects that are burnt at funerals. "I'm afraid I can't leave the shop," Zhao said. "You'll have to excuse me."

"Impossible," said Wu Song, "the other neighbours are already there." Mr. Zhao found he couldn't get out of it and Wu Song dragged him back to the house. "Old people must be honoured like relatives," he said. "Please sit beside my sister-in-law."

Next, Wu Song went to invite Hu Zhengqing, who had a shop across the road selling cold wine. Mr. Hu had formerly worked for the government and he found the invitation somewhat suspicious. But although he did not at all want to go, Wu Song dragged him off willy-nilly and seated him next to Mr. Zhao.

Then Wu Song asked Mrs. Wang who lived next door to her. "Old Mr. Zhang who sells stuffed dumplings," she replied. Mr. Zhang was at home and had quite a shock when he saw Wu Song coming. "Captain, what can I do for you?" he said.

Chapter 26

"Our house has disturbed everyone in the neighbourhood," said Wu Song. This old man was also prevailed upon by Wu Song to come to the house, where he was made to sit next to Mr. Zhao. And why, you may ask, had the earliest guests not gone away by now? Because the soldiers were guarding the doors of course, front and back, they were all being watched like prisoners.

So now Wu Song had invited these four neighbours, together with Mrs. Wang and Jinlian making six people in all. He moved a chair for himself and sat down a little to one side. The soldiers were told to lock the front and back doors and the one at the back was called on to pour the wine. At this point Wu Song bowed to the company and announced: "Esteemed neighbours, please pardon my lack of courtesy and the informality of this invitation."

They all replied: "But we did nothing to celebrate your return. We oughtn't to let you go to all this trouble."

Wu Song only smiled. "It's so little. Please, I shall think you are laughing at me."

The soldier went on pouring the wine. The neighbours were secretly fearful, because they just didn't know what was going on. After three more rounds had been drunk, Mr. Hu got up to leave, saying: "I'm a busy man, you know."

Wu Song cried out: "You can't leave. Now that you're here you must stay a little longer, I don't care how busy you are."

This left Mr. Hu in a quandary, like the well with fifteen buckets, seven going up and eight going down. He said to himself: "If he really wanted to invite us out of politeness, why should he treat us like this, refusing to let us go?" Nevertheless he was obliged to sit down again.

"More wine," Wu Song said, and the soldier poured a fourth round. In the end they had seven rounds, and everyone felt as if they'd been at a thousand of Empress Lü's banquets, where those who refused a cup were beheaded. Then at last Wu Song called the soldier to clear away the cups, saying they'd drink again later. He wiped the table clean, but when everyone got up to leave he stopped them with a gesture: "I've something to say first. Is there any one of you good people who can write?"

Mr. Yao said: "Mr. Hu here writes beautifully."

"Then may I trouble you, Mr. Hu?" Wu Song said, rolling up his sleeves and suddenly producing the sharp knife. He gripped the handle in his right hand, resting his thumb against the guard, and glared round at the company ferociously.

"Worthy neighbours," he began, "seeing that every crime has an author and every debt has to be paid, I need your help as witnesses." At this point he seized his sister-in-law with his left hand and pointed at Mrs. Wang with his right. The four neighbours were so shocked they could only stare, dumbfounded. Though they looked at each other in horror, no one dared utter a sound. Wu Song continued: "Please forgive me, friends, but you have nothing to fear. Although I'm a rough and ready sort of fellow and I fear nothing, not even death, and it's my principle that crimes must be paid for, injustice avenged, I certainly intend you no harm. I merely need you as witnesses. However, if any of you should try to leave before the end, I'm afraid you will have to allow me to change my mind. I should be obliged to give him six or seven cuts with my knife, and it would make no difference if I had to answer for it with my life." Everyone continued to stare open-mouthed and no one dared raise a finger.

Wu Song now looked at Mrs. Wang and began to shout: "Now you old bitch hear this! My brother's death is all on your head and I shall be dealing with you in my own time!" Then he turned to Jinlian: "As for you, you trollop, listen to me! If you have any hope of being spared, you'd better tell me the whole truth about how you plotted against my brother's life!"

"Brother-in-law, you're talking nonsense!" Jinlian said. "Your brother died of a weak heart, what fault is it of mine?"

Before she could even finish, wham! Wu Song's knife stuck quivering in the table! Wu Song seized her by the hair with his left hand and punched her in the chest with his right. He kicked over the table and swung the girl over it, forcing her down in front of the altar, where he stood on her to keep her from moving. He pulled the knife from the table with his other hand and pointing it at Mrs. Wang said: "Confess, you bawd!" Seeing there was no way for her to escape, the old woman said: "Don't be angry, Captain, I will tell you everything."

Chapter 26

On Wu Song's orders one of the soldiers brought paper, ink, brush and inkstone and laid them out neatly on the table. Wu Song pointed his knife at Mr. Hu and said: "May I trouble you to write everything down, exactly as you hear it."

"I will, I will," Mr. Hu stammered. He ground some ink, took up the brush, spread out the paper and said: "Now then Mrs. Wang, your confession!"

"It's really nothing to do with me," she said, "I don't know what you want me to say."

"I know everything, damn you! You've no way out! If you don't start talking I shall cut this one's head off and then I shall kill you!" He drew the blade of his knife softly across the girls face, twice. She began to scream: "Brother-in-law, forgive me! If you'll let me go I'll tell everything!"

Wu Song flung her on her knees before the altar and bellowed: "Talk then, slut!"

Half fainting with terror, she began to confess. She told everything, from the moment she was lowering the curtain and dropped the pole on Xi-men Qing to the making of the clothes which led to the affair. Finally she came to the part where the Midget was kicked and the plan to poison him was devised, and how Mrs. Wang incited her. She told it all, from start to finish, and Wu Song had Mr. Hu write everything down.

"You ungrateful wretch!" Mrs. Wang cried, "You've told them everything, what am I supposed to say now? You've left me no chance!" And so she too was obliged to make a clean breast of it and Mr. Hu also wrote down her declaration. When the record was complete, from beginning to end, the two accused were made to sign it and then the four witnesses added their full names. Wu Song told the soldiers to take off their belts and used them to tie the old woman's hands behind her back. He rolled up the declaration and put it in his breast pocket. He told the soldiers to bring a bowl of wine and placed it as an offering before the altar. Then he dragged Jinlian to the altar and forced her to her knees. He told the old woman to kneel beside her. Then he said: "Brother, whose spirit is not far from here, your little brother will wash away the injury which was done to you!" He told a soldier to burn some paper money. The girl now understood that her situation was desperate and set up a terrified shrieking. But Wu Song pulled her over backwards and planted both feet on her shoulders. He tore the clothing from her breast and — it's slow in the telling but happens in a flash — with one slash of the knife he opened her up. Placing the knife between his teeth he plunged both hands inside and tore out the heart and liver and placed them on the altar. Then, wham! one more blow cut off the head. There was blood everywhere. The four horrified neighbours covered their faces. They were so shocked by this savagery that no one dared to stir. No, they would do whatever he said. Wu Song sent one of the soldiers upstairs to fetch a bed cover, which he used to wrap the head in. He wiped the knife and returned it to its sheath, washed his hands and then announced: "Worthy neighbours, I apologize to you. But I must still ask you to go upstairs and wait for me till my return." The neighbours looked at each other, but no one thought of disobeying, so upstairs they went. Wu Song told a soldier to take the old woman up too and lock the door. Two soldiers were left on guard downstairs.

Taking the head with him, Wu Song now hastened to Xi-men Qing's medicine shop. When the manager appeared, Wu Song greeted him and said: "Is your boss there?"

"He's just gone out," the manager said.

"Please step this way with me," Wu Song said. "I want a word with you."

The manager was not unacquainted with Wu Song's ways and he dared not refuse. Wu Song led him apart into a quiet alley and then turned to him and said: "Do you want to die or do you want to live?"

"Please, Captain!" the man protested. "I am sure I have never done anything to offend you!"

"If you want to die, you can refuse to tell me where your boss has gone. But if you want to live you'd better tell me truthfully where he is."

"He ... he ... he went with a friend," the man stammered, "to have a drink ... in the wineshop, the wineshop under Lion Bridge."

Chapter 26

Wu Song was off like a shot. The manager however stood there as if paralysed and it was quite some time before he returned to the shop.

When he reached the wineshop under Lion Bridge, Wu Song barged straight in and asked the landlord. "Who is Mr. Xi-men drinking with?"

"Some kind of merchant, I think. They're upstairs, in the room overlooking the street."

Wu Song tore up the stairs. He paused outside the room. His Nibs was in the window seat playing host. Opposite him was his guest and there were two hostesses sitting one on either side. Wu Song shook the head loose from its wrapping. It rolled out, still dripping with blood. Taking the head in his left hand and the dagger in his right, he lifted the curtain and as he entered tossed the head right in his Nibs' face!

His Nibs recognized Wu Song at once. With a cry of horror he leapt onto the chair and started to climb onto the window sill, thinking to escape that way. But when he saw the street below he knew it was too high to jump. Panic seized him. Then Wu Song — it's slow in the telling but happens in a flash — placed a hand on the table and vaulted onto it. With his foot he swept off all the plates and dishes, the two hostesses watching paralysed with fear. The other guest, the merchant, had fallen over backwards in his eagerness to get out of the way. His Nibs in desperation feinted with his hand and launched a flying kick. Wu Song was too intent on getting to grips with him; though he had seen the kick coming, it caught his right hand and sent the knife flying out of the window, to land in the middle of the street below. Seeing his attacker disarmed, his Nibs' confidence revived. He feinted with his right and hit out with his left, aiming at Wu Song's chest. Wu Song ducked and came in under his opponent's guard; with his left hand he grabbed the back of his adversary's neck while with his right he seized his left leg and gave a heave, crying "Down you go!"

Now, one, Xi-men Qing was hampered by the spirit of the man he had wronged; two, heaven's tolerance was ended; and three, he was no match in strength for Wu Song. So he went hurtling

The Marshes of Mount Liang

Chapter 26

through the window, head over heels, to smash in the street below, where he lay, as they say, *in extremis*. Imagine the shock of those who were passing on either side of the street! Next thing, Wu Song bent to pick up the head of the adulteress beside the chair, rushed with it to the window and leapt down into the street. First he picked up his dagger. Then he went to inspect Xi-men Qing, where, half dead already, he lay stiffening on the ground with only his eyes moving. Steadying him with one hand, Wu Song cut off his head with a single blow. He tied the two heads together, and with the heads and his knife sped back to Redstone Road. When the soldiers opened up for him he went to offer the two heads on his brother's altar. He poured the libation of cold wine and proclaimed: "Brother, whose spirit is not far off, may you soon enjoy the peace of heaven! Your brother has avenged you. I have killed the betrayer and his paramour! Soon I will burn a memorial tablet."

Wu Song now told the soldiers to bring the neighbours downstairs. Mrs. Wang was placed in front, closely guarded. Still holding the knife, Wu Song raised the two heads and addressed the group as follows: "I have just one more thing to say to you all and then I am done."

The four of them crossed their hands deferentially and said: "Please speak Captain, we are listening."

What Wu Song had to say is of some importance, because of some later consequences:

The hero of Jingyang Pass into prison hurled;
Yanggu's captain turned monk, wandering the world.

But if you want to know what Wu Song said, you must read the next chapter.

Chapter 27

On the Mengzhou road the Ogress sells meat pies; Wu Song meets the Gardener at Crossways Rise!

Wu Song was addressing the four neighbours. He went on immediately: "In order to avenge the crime committed against my brother I have meted out appropriate justice and should I pay for it with my life I still can have no regrets. But I am afraid it has been disturbing for all of you. I know not what fate awaits me now, not even whether I shall live or die, but first I am going to burn an offering to my brother's spirit. Whatever goods there are in this house, may I presume on the kindness of you four good people to sell them on my behalf, in order that the proceeds may serve to cover my expenses during and after trial? For I intend to go to the magistracy next and give myself up. All I ask of you is not to extenuate my crime but simply to bear witness to the truth." So saying he took the votive tablet and the paper money and burnt them. There were two trunks upstairs. He brought them down and opened them and handed the contents over to the neighbours to sell. Then with the old woman still in his custody and carrying the two heads, he set off for the magistracy.

The news had spread throughout Yanggu by now, and there were countless onlookers in the street. When the magistrate heard he was at first horrified but he initiated a hearing at once. Pushing the old woman into the court before him, Wu Song knelt and placed the murder weapon and the two heads on the ground before the bench. The scene was like this: Wu Song knelt on the left, the old woman was kneeling in the middle and the witnesses on the right. Wu Song took out the statement taken down by Mr. Hu and rehearsed what had taken place, from start to finish. The magistrate called the clerk of the court to question Mrs. Wang, who confirmed everything. The evidence of the four witnesses provided further corroboration. Mr. Ho and the Young'un were also called, and their evidence tallied as well. An assistant of the coroner and a clerk were ordered to accompany all those involved to Redstone Road to examine the corpse of the woman and then to the wineshop under Lion Bridge to examine Xi-men Qing's corpse. Having prepared a full report on the deaths, the officials returned to the magistracy to have it placed on the court's record. The magistrate ordered cangues to be brought and fitted on Wu Song and the old woman who were forthwith committed to prison. The witnesses were ordered to be detained at the magistracy.

Now the magistrate knew Wu Song was an honest and brave man and remembered how he had carried out his mission to the capital, so he wanted to protect him. After contemplating Wu Song's good points, he called the registrar and said: "Seeing that Wu Song is such a worthy fellow, I think we ought to revise that statement. We must change it to read, 'Owing to the fact that when Wu Song went to perform a sacrifice to the spirit of his dead brother his sister-in-law tried to prevent him, a quarrel arose. The said sister-in-law tried to throw down the altar to his brother's spirit and Wu Song, trying to defend it, accidentally killed her in the struggle. Subsequently a fight took place with Xi-men Qing, who was the woman's lover and had tried to intervene on her behalf. The fight continued till the evenly matched contestants were close to Lion Bridge where Xi-men Qing was fatally wounded and died.'" This new version was read out to Wu Song and then a full report was prepared to be sent along with all the witnesses to the provincial governor at Dongping, thus transferring the case to a higher court.

Although Yanggu was only a small place, it was not without its public spirited citizens and some of its richest men offered Wu Song financial assistance, so he was provided with wine, food, money and rice. First he went back to his room and gave all his things into the keeping of the orderly, setting aside some twelve or thirteen taels of silver for the Young'un's old father. The men under his command for the most part were prompt in delivering wine and meat to him.

The clerk of the court, armed with an official order collected the statement, Uncle Ho's silver and bones, the women's confessions, the murder weapon and all the witnesses, and set off for Dongping.

When they arrived at the court-house, a huge crowd of onlookers was milling about the entrance. When the Governor, Chen Wenzhao, heard of their arrival, he initiated a hearing at once.

Governor Chen was an intelligent official. He already had some knowledge of the case. He called in all the witnesses and the accused and having read the Yanggu magistrate's report and the various confessions, and depositions, questioned each person in turn. He placed the evidence, including the murder weapon, under seal and had it all taken to the archives. He committed Wu Song to prison, but not before his cangue had been exchanged for a lighter one. The old woman on the other hand was given a heavier cangue and confined in a death cell. The clerk of the magistrate's court was sent back to Yanggu with an official reply. The Governor also gave orders for Uncle Ho, the Young'un and the four neighbours. "Let the six of them return to Yanggu and remain quietly at home in case this court should need to summon them again. And let Xi-men Qing's wife remain here in custody of this court. A detailed verdict will be handed down on receipt of the imperial instructions."

Uncle Ho, the Young'un and the rest together with the official from the magistrate's court, went back to Yanggu, while Wu Song remained in gaol where the soldiers took him food.

Governor Chen was highly sympathetic to Wu Song, knowing him to be a brave and upright man, and he regularly sent people to inquire after his well-being. Consequently all the prison staff made sure he was provided with food and drink, exacting not the least payment in return. Moreover, Governor Chen again altered the original report in Wu Song's favour. He lodged a full report on the case with the provincial court and at the same time entrusted a secret document to someone totally reliable and instructed him to ride day and night to the capital on a certain confidential mission. The Governor had friends there in the Ministry of Justice and they exerted their influence on the provincial court. As a result the following judgement was delivered:

> *Insomuch as Mrs. Wang acted as an instigator of adultery and incited a wife to murder her husband by poisoning; and insomuch as she encouraged the said wife to obstruct Wu Song and prevent him from carrying out the rituals in commemoration of his brother thus indirectly provoking a murder; and insomuch as she encouraged illicit sexual relations in defiance of all morality; for all these crimes this court sentences her to death by dismemberment.*
>
> *And insomuch as Wu Song notwithstanding the fact that he was acting in response to his brother's murder has taken the lives of Xi-men Qing and his paramour and given the impossibility of overlooking this crime despite the fact that he voluntarily gave himself up to justice this court sentences him to forty strokes of the cane followed by banishment to a distance of not less than five hundred miles. The adulterous couple also merit the severest of penalties but being dead none needs to be imposed. This sentence shall have immediate effect.*

On receipt of the verdict Governor Chen acted immediately. Those who had been detained, that is to say, Uncle Ho, the Young'un, and the four neighbours together with Xi-men Qing's wife, were all summoned to hear the sentence.

Wu Song was fetched from prison. After his sentence had been read to him, his cangue was removed and the forty strokes administered. However, as all the prison officers respected him, only a few of the strokes actually touched him. A seven and a half catty cangue with iron spikes was then locked round his neck and, unavoidably, he was branded on the cheeks with the two rows of "golden seals." After this he was informed that the prison fortress at Mengzhou was to be his place of exile. The others, on the provincial court's instructions, were released and allowed to proceed quietly home. Mrs. Wang was now brought out to hear her sentence. The imperial judgement was read out, her crimes were written out on a placard, she was made to sign her confession. She was then thrown on the "wooden donkey" and nailed down with four nails and three cords. The Governor of Dongping having pronounced the dread words, "Dismember her!", she was brought out and paraded through the streets amid the rolling of drums and booming of gongs, preceded by the placard and followed by official staff-bearers, with two knives held on high and paper flowers waving in the wind, to the market-place, where she was hacked to pieces.

While Wu Song, who was already wearing a lighter cangue for the journey, was watching the execution of Mrs. Wang, one of the former neighbours, Mr. Yao, came with the money that had been obtained from selling the things in the house. He left after handing it over to Wu Song. The court now issued an official order and two guards were detailed to escort Wu Song and deliver him safely to Mengzhou in accordance with the Governor's instructions. Before they left, the orderly gave Wu Song back his things and returned home. Then Wu Song and his escort set out on the road to Mengzhou.

The two guards knew very well what a good reputation Wu Song had and they looked after him most attentively, taking good care not to insult him in any way. Since they treated him so well and made no difficulties, Wu Song used the funds he was carrying liberally. At each wayside inn where they stopped he bought food and drink and shared it with them. But enough of this.

The murders had been committed around the beginning of the third month and Wu Song had been in gaol for two months, so it was nearly the sixth month as they travelled towards Mengzhou and the sun was blazing down, weather to roast a stone and melt metal. The only way to travel was in the cool of the early morning. One day when they had been going a little more than three weeks they came to a highway, and at about noon they were on top of a ridge. "Let's not stop here," Wu Song said. "It's better to go down the other side and look for somewhere to buy food and drink."

"Agreed," said the two guards.

They hurried down the hill. Away in the distance they saw a group of thatched cottages under a cliff; and the sign of an inn showed among some willows beside a stream. "Look!" exclaimed Wu Song. "Isn't that an inn?" As they hastened on down they came upon a woodcutter carrying a load of firewood. "Can you tell us what place this is?" Wu Song asked him. "This here be the Mengzhou road," he answered. "And over there, by that wood, see, at the bottom of the hill, that be the famous Crossways Rise."

So Wu Song and his guards pressed on till they reached Crossways Rise, where they found a huge tree, so immense that four or five men together could not have encompassed its girth, all twined about with a mass of withered creepers. A little way beyond this tree was an inn. A woman was sitting outside, beside the window. She wore a green bodice and she had a great many gold pins and rings on her head and wild flowers stuck in her hair. When she saw Wu Song and the guards approaching, she rose to greet them. Her skirt was of bright red silk and her face was thickly rouged and powdered. The bodice was cut low, revealing a peach-coloured gauze undershirt, and it had a row of gold buttons. Here is her picture:

> *Her lowering brow betrays a fearsome spirit, her eyes gleam with murderous light; her waist is coarse as a pulley block, her arms and legs clumsy as a workman's mallet; her rough skin is thickly daubed with make-up and a double layer of grease-paint reaches to the edge of her matted hair; gold bracelets bind the she-devil's arms, a red skirt reflects her hellish nature.*

Leaning against the door, she greeted them: "Come in and rest your feet, gentlemen. We've good wine and good meat here, and good pies too if you've a fancy for them."

Wu Song and the guards entered. The tables and stools were made of cypress wood. The guards put down their batons and took off their packs, and everyone sat down. Wu Song removed his pack and put it on the table. He divested himself of his belt and his cotton shirt. Then the guards said: "There's no one here to see. We'll take it upon ourselves to relieve you of that cangue, so you can enjoy a cup or two of wine more freely." They opened the seals, removed the cangue and put it under the table. Then they too took off their shirts and hung them on the window-sill. The woman now approached and said, with a friendly smile: "How much wine is it to be, gentlemen?"

"No need to ask how much," said Wu Song, "just warm it and bring it, and cut us four or five catties of meat as well. We'll pay for it all together."

"We've also got some lovely pies," the woman said.

"You can bring us twenty or thirty, then, as a snack," said Wu Song.

With a gleeful chuckle the woman disappeared inside and came out holding a big pitcher of wine. She laid three bowls and three sets of chopsticks on the table and then brought two plates of meat. After three or four rounds of wine had been served and drunk without a pause, she returned to the kitchen and brought out a basket of pies which she placed on the table. The two guards began to help themselves. Wu Song took one and opened it up to see what was inside. "What's in them, hostess?" he said. "Human flesh or dog meat or what?"

The woman giggled and said: "You are a caution sir! Where in the wide world would you find pies like that, made with human flesh or dog meat? Our pies have always been made with good buffalo meat."

"Well, I've had many dealings with the rivers and lakes fraternity," said Wu Song, "and I've often heard the saying, 'To the great tree at Crossways Rise what traveller dares to venture? There the fat ones are chopped up for pies, the thin ones go to the bottom of the river.'"

"Wherever did you get that story from, sir? You must be making it up!"

"There are some hairs in this pie meat, and they look to me remarkably like pubic hairs. That's what makes me suspicious."

Wu Song continued his questioning. "How come your husband's not around?" he asked.

"My husband's gone out on business and he isn't back yet."

"So you're all on your own here then," he said.

She smiled to herself. "The bastard's really asking for it, he thinks he can make a pass at me! It's like the moth seeking the flame in which it will perish! No one can say as I'm the one that started it, but I'll settle his hash, never fear." Aloud she said: "You oughtn't to pull my leg, sir. Come on, have another bowl or two and then you can go and rest in the shade of the tree. If it's peace and quiet you want, you'll find it in this house and no mistake!"

When Wu Song heard this he thought to himself: "The woman's up to something. I'll play along with her for a bit." Out loud he said: "This wine of yours is a bit thin. If you've got something better, let us try a few cups."

"We've got a really first-rate brew," she said, "but it's a bit cloudy."

"Excellent. The cloudier it comes the better I like it!"

Secretly exulting, she went in and fetched a pitcher of the cloudy wine. Wu Song examined it and said: "Now that's what I call good wine, only it would be better warm."

"You're a real connoisseur, aren't you sir? I'll warm it up and we'll see how you like it then." To herself she was thinking: "It's the poor devil's fate. He even wants it warmed! That'll just make the drug work faster. Played right into my hands, he has!"

When she'd warmed it she brought it back and poured three bowls, saying: "Try this then gentlemen!"

The two guards had no thought of holding back, they attacked the wine with gusto. But Wu Song said: "It's not my custom to drink without food, hostess. Cut us some more of that meat to go with it." He waited till she had gone back inside and then emptied his bowl in a dark corner. Then he smacked his lips and exclaimed: "Ah, now that's good wine! That's a wine that really warms the cockles of the heart!"

Needless to say, the woman had not gone to cut any meat. All she did was take a turn round the house. When she returned, she clapped her hands and cried: "They're going, they're going!" And sure enough, the two guards found the sky was spinning and the earth swaying under their feet, and in a moment, paf! they fell flat on their backs with their mouths open. Wu Song also shut his eyes tight and collapsed beside the bench. He heard the woman say, with a chuckle: "Got you, now, you cheeky twit, you've drunk the water that washed my feet!" Then she shouted: "Number two,

Chapter 27

number three, in here, double quick!" At this two yokels shambled in and carted the two guards off inside, while the woman went to the table and picked up Wu Song's backpack and the packs belonging to the two guards and felt them carefully. Reckoning that there was some quantity of gold and silver inside, she said delightedly: "That's three good pieces of merchandise I've got us today, that'll easily do for two days' supply of pies. And on top of it there's this!" She took the bags inside and then came back to watch while her two minions tried to move Wu Song. But try as they might they couldn't shift him. Stretched out inert upon the floor, he seemed to weigh a ton. Watching the two of them straining away and unable to move him, she began to curse them: "You feeble buggers, all you know how to do is eat and drink, you're useless! I suppose I shall have to come and lend a hand myself. Well, this ugly great so-and-so thought he was going to make a pass at me. He'll sell as good buffalo meat, the great fat lump! The other two bastards are stringier, they'll only do for water-buffalo. Let's get this one inside, we'll cut him up first." As she was speaking she took off her green bodice and removed the red skirt. Thus stripped for action, she approached Wu Song and lightly heaved him upright. Thereupon Wu Song grasped her firmly, pinning her arms to her sides and pressing her to his chest, while he caught her legs in a scissors grip, using the whole weight of his body to subdue her. She squealed like a pig having its throat cut. Her two assistants were about to come to her aid, but Wu Song let out such a roar that they hung back in terror. The woman was forced to the ground. All she could do was gasp: "Please sir, have mercy!" All the fight had gone out of her. It was a case of:

> She thought to drug the tiger beater,
> She looked to bake a load of pies;
> Only she couldn't take the banter,
> Or the true hero recognize.
> Now instead of selling the meat,
> She squeals like a pig whose throat is slit.

At this moment a man carrying a load of firewood appeared. He put his load down by the door and seeing Wu Song pinning the woman to the ground bounded into the room, shouting: "Easy now! Let her off, sir, please! I'd like a word with you."

Wu Song spun round and put up his fists, keeping his left foot on the woman to hold her down. He looked at the newcomer who was wearing a black silk cap, pinched in at the sides, a white cotton tunic, breeches with knee-guards, hemp shoes and a belt with pouches. His face was craggy, with prominent cheekbones and covered with a ragged stubble. He looked to be about thirty-five.

The man returned Wu Song's stare and with his arms tightly crossed said: "Can I ask your name?"

"I make no secret of it," Wu Song said, "neither on the road nor at home. I am Captain Wu Song."

"You're not the one who killed a tiger on Jingyang Pass, are you?" said the other.

"You've got it!" said Wu Song.

The man bowed and prostrated himself, saying: "I've heard so much about you, what an honour to be able to meet you!"

"Would you happen to be this woman's husband?"

"That I am, and I regret that she couldn't see what was staring her in the face. Please tell me how she has offended you, Captain. I beg you to pardon her, for my honour's sake." It was a case of:

Violence surrenders to a smile;
And manners get the better of ill will;
The good man's truth and manliness, no less
Subdues the jealous spirit of the Ogress.

Seeing the husband's manner was so correct, Wu Song quickly released the woman and asked: "You two are evidently something out of the ordinary. Would you tell me your names?"

The man ordered his wife to get dressed quickly and come and prostrate herself before the Captain.

"I was a little rough just now," Wu Song said, "please forgive me, dear lady."

"No, I've eyes but I couldn't recognize a good man," she said. "I was very wrong, Uncle, please pardon me. And please come inside and sit down."

Chapter 27

武都頭十字坡過張青

Wu Song asked again: "What are your names, you two?"

"I am Zhang Qing," the man said, "and I used to be gardener at the Guangming Temple. But I lost my temper in a stupid argument and did in the monks and burnt the temple down. Seeing as there were no witnesses the police let me alone, so I was able to come here and set up as a highwayman under the big tree. Then one day this old fellow with a carrying-pole comes by, and I thought because of his age I could easily get the better of him. We fought, and after more than twenty passes a blow from his pole knocked me right off my feet. It turned out that in his youth he'd been a famous footpad. Anyway, he saw I was pretty nifty on my feet and he took me back with him to the city, where he taught me all his tricks and even made me a present of this lady, his daughter, so I became his son-in-law. But how can anyone make a living in the city? There was nothing for it, I had to return to my old haunts. I came back here, built a thatched house and started this wineshop. Actually what we do is, we keep an eye out for travellers and merchants. Any likely looking customers, we poison their drink and when they're dead we chop 'em up to sell as buffalo meat. We turn the skinny ones into mince meat for pie fillings. Every day I take a load round the villages to sell, that's what I do in the daytime. I've a good many connections among the rivers and lakes fraternity and they call me Zhang Qing, the Gardener. And as for this woman of mine, her family name is Sun. She learnt all her father's old tricks and people call her Sister Sun, the Ogress.

"Well, anyway, I heard the missis screaming when I came home just now, but I'd never have guessed it meant I was about to meet you here, Captain! I've told her about this you know many a time. 'Sister Sun,' I said, 'there's three kinds of people you should never touch. The first are those monks, what they call the wandering monks. In the first place they're not much good to us anyway, and secondly, they're people who've renounced the world.' And you know, we nearly did do one of the buggers in the other day, an incredibly powerful fellow, used to be commandant under the orders of old Marshal Zhang of Yanan district. Lu Da his name used to be, he had some trouble over killing a certain Master of

Guanxi with three blows of his fist and had to flee to Mount Wu Tai, shave his head and become a monk. Because he's got tattoos all over his back the rivers and lakes folk know him as the Flowery Monk, Lu Zhishen. He's got a solid steel staff, you know, that weighs a good sixty catties. Well, when he came through here, my old lady, she thought he looked good and fat so she chucked the drug in his drink and carted him off to the workshop. She was just about to start carving him up when I came home, thank God! The moment I clapped eyes on that incredible staff of his, I gave him the antidote, pronto. After that I paid him my respects and we became brothers like. They do say he's recently seized the Temple of the Precious Pearl on Twin Dragon Peak and fortified himself there, together with some fellow they call Yang Zhi, the Blue-Faced Beast. I've had letters from him inviting me to join him, but I haven't been able to make it yet."

"Yes, I've often heard about those two among the rivers and lakes," Wu Song said.

"Now the thing I really do regret is, there was one of those shaven-pates, giant of a man he was, that really did come to grief here. I came back just a bit too late, she'd already got the arms and legs off. All that's left to show for him now's one of those iron circlets monks have, a black cassock and his monk's certificate. Nothing much in any of that, you'd say. But there was these two remarkable objects he had with him. One was this rosary made of little skulls, a hundred and eight of them all told. The other was a pair of monk's swords, made of the purest white steel. I reckon that old monk had accounted for quite a few men in his time, because, do you know, even now you'll hear a strange moaning out of those swords in the middle of the night! I'm really sorry I didn't get back in time to save that man! I often think of him.

"Well, as I was saying, I told the missis, 'The second kind you mustn't touch is those young performing women who wander the rivers and lakes. They're on the go all the time, moving from one province to the next, giving performances, and it's really tough for them to make a living. If you meddle with one of them, the word'll get round, and they'll proclaim it from the stage that us daredevils of the rivers and lakes aren't gentlemen at all.' That's what I told the wife, see. And I said to her, 'There's a third kind you must leave alone, that's the convicts and escorted prisoners, there's plenty of good fellows among them, you don't want to harm them.' I never dreamed she would disobey my instructions like this and give offence to you, Captain. Lucky I came back a bit early. Sister Sun, whatever gave you such an idea?"

"I didn't mean to do anything," the Ogress replied. "But I could see the gentleman's bag was well stuffed, and besides, I was annoyed because he made an improper suggestion, that's what made me do it."

"Cutting off heads and wading in blood is more in my line, I don't go around insulting ladies," said Wu Song. "But I just happened to notice you were showing a lot of interest in our bags. I got suspicious, so I said something a bit suggestive on purpose to encourage you to show your hand. I poured that bowl of wine away and pretended to be drugged until you tried to move me. Then I grabbed you, and even thumped you, I'm afraid my dear lady, I do beg you to forgive me."

The Gardener became very jovial. He invited Wu Song to step inside and be their guest. Wu Song said: "Won't you first rescue the guards, Brother?" The Gardener led him into the workshop, where a number of human skins were stretched on the walls and from the beams hung five or six human legs. The two guards had been flung down on the carving block. "Please release them now, Brother," Wu Song said.

"Can I ask what your crime was? And where you were being sent to?"

Wu Song recounted how he had killed his sister-in-law and her lover, omitting no detail, while the Gardener and his wife made no secret of their admiration. At the end of it, Zhang said: "I'd like to make a suggestion, if you'll let me?"

"Please, speak frankly," Wu Song said.

The Gardener then slowly unfolded his idea. There were to be important consequences for Wu Song:

He'll kick up a row in the town of Mengzhou,
And create quite stir in the Fortress of Peace.

Chapter 27

Truly he was the kind that can ...

*Throw down an elephant, vanquish a buffalo,
Lay hands on a dragon or capture a tiger.*

But if you want to know what it was the Gardener said to Wu Song, you must read the next chapter.

Chapter 28

Wu Song cuts a dash in the Fortress of Peace; The Young Master's ousted from Happy Woods!

Well, what the Gardener said to Wu Song was this: "Don't think I'm nasty-minded, Captain, but rather than you go and suffer in prison, wouldn't it be better if we finish off those guards of yours right now? You could stay here with us for a while. Afterwards, if you agree to become an outlaw, I'd personally send word to the Temple of the Precious Pearl on Twin Dragon Peak and arrange for you to join Lu Zhishen's band. What do you say?"

"It is very good of you, Brother, to show such concern for my welfare," said Wu Song, "but there's just one thing. All my life I've fought only with bullies. These two guards have been kind to me and looked after me well, they've done everything they could for me on the journey. If I let any harm come to them, heaven will not pardon me. If you really want to please me, for my sake let them off, don't do them any harm."

"Since you're so magnanimous, Captain, I'll give them the antidote at once."

The Gardener told the two assistants to get the guards down off the carving block. His wife prepared a bowl of the antidote and then he pulled them by the ears and made them swallow it. In less than an hour they awoke as if from a dream and sat up. When they saw Wu Song, they said: "However did we get so drunk in this place? That wine must be really something! We hardly touched a drop and it knocked us out cold. We must remember this place. We'll come and try their wine again on the way back."

Wu Song couldn't help laughing, and the Gardener and the Ogress joined in. The guards couldn't make out what was going on. Meanwhile the two assistants went and slaughtered chickens and geese and cooked them and set out dishes and cups. The Gardener ordered a table and chairs to be placed under a vine-covered trellis at the back and invited Wu Song and his guards out into the garden.

Wu Song made the guards take the place of honour, while he and Zhang the Gardener sat with the Ogress on one side. The two assistants poured the wine and came and went with plates of food. The Gardener plied Wu Song with wine. When evening came he got out the two monk's swords to show Wu Song. They were indeed of the very finest steel and more than one day's work had surely gone into their making. The two men reminisced about the heroes of rivers and lakes and told many a tale of killing and burning. At one point Wu Song said: "That noble and generous fellow, Song Jiang of Shandong province, known as the Opportune Rain, has had to take refuge with Mr. Chai in his country residence, because of some affair he got involved in." On hearing this talk the two guards suddenly became terrified and threw themselves down on their knees. Wu Song said: "Surely you can't suppose I intend you any harm, after you've looked after me for such a space? All this talk of the heroes of rivers and lakes is nothing to be frightened of, there's no way we would want to harm good people. Just drink up and tomorrow when we reach Mengzhou I'll give proof of my gratitude."

They spent the night at the Gardener's. Wu Song wanted to leave in the morning but the Gardener wouldn't let him go and insisted on their staying another three days. Wu Song was moved by the attentions of the Gardener and his wife and since Zhang was his elder by five years formally pronounced him his elder brother.

Now Wu Song announced his intention of leaving again, but not before the Gardener had organized a send-off party. The Gardener returned all their things to them, the duffle bag and the packs, and gave ten taels or so of silver to Wu Song and two or three taels in loose change to the guards. Wu Song divided his among the guards. Then the cangue was fitted again and the seals replaced. The Gardener and his wife saw them to the gate and they set off for Mengzhou. As the poem says:

Chapter 28

*His new brother's counsel
Is to join the robber rout.
But he's no mind to cancel
The justice meted out
For his killing of the woman
Who acted like a whore:
For he's no common felon
Without regard for law.*

It was not yet noon when they reached the city. They went straight to the government offices and presented the documents from Dongping district court. When the governor had examined these, Wu Song was taken into custody and a receipt was sent back with the two guards. We say no more of them.

Wu Song was immediately consigned to the prison fortress. When he arrived there, he found a big plaque bearing three characters which read: "Fortress of Peace." The guards took him to his cell and then went to hand in the documents and get a receipt. No more of this.

Once Wu Song was ensconced in his own cell, a dozen or so of his fellow inmates came to see him. "You're new here," they said, "so if you happen to have anything in your pack there, a letter of recommendation or some spare cash, you'd better have it ready. The chief warder will be here in a minute and you'll need to give him something. Then if they do give you the disciplinary beating, that's meant to soften you up, they'll go easy on you. But if you haven't got anything for him you'll really cop it! We're all in the same boat here, that's why we're warning you. You know the saying, 'When the rabbit dies the fox mourns; creatures feel for their own kind.' We were afraid since you've just come you might not know about these things, that's why we thought we'd better tell you."

"Thank you all for your good advice," Wu Song said. "I do happen to have something here, and if he speaks to me nicely I shall reward him. But if he's rude, I shan't give him a cent!"

"Oh no!" the others exclaimed, "That's not the way at all. You know what the ancients said, 'Fear not the law but him who wields the law.' And there's that proverb too, 'When you walk under the eaves, better keep your head down.' You want to watch out you know!"

They'd hardly finished speaking when someone shouted: "The chief warder's coming!" At this they all dispersed.

Wu Song took off his pack and sat down in his cell. Next thing, in comes the gaoler shouting "Where's the new prisoner?"

"That's me," said Wu Song.

"What's the matter with you? Are you blind or something? Why wait for me to ask? Aren't you the fellow who killed the tiger on Jingyang Pass and was made captain in Yanggu? You oughter be smart, how come you don't know what's what? Think you can face me out, do you? Why, you couldn't even beat up a cat!"

"And you're just making a big noise because you think I ought to bribe you! Well you won't get a cent!" Wu Song said. "All you'll get is a taste of my fists! I have got some money, but I shall keep it to buy myself wine. What are you going to do about that? Why, you haven't even got the power to send me back to Yanggu!"

After the head warder had departed in high dudgeon, the other convicts crowded round Wu Song. "Now you've done it!" they said. "In a minute you're really going to be sorry! He'll have gone off to report to the Warden, you can count on it. It's not likely you'll get off with your life!"

"I'm not scared of him. I'll treat him the same way he treats me. If he's reasonable, I'll be reasonable too; if he wants a fight, that's what he'll get!"

Hardly had he finished speaking when three or four prison guards marched in demanding to know where the prisoner, Wu Song, was. "Here I am, you fools, did you think I'd run away?" Wu Song answered sarcastically. "I don't see the need for all this shouting!" Ignoring this they marched him off to the administration office to see the prison Warden. Several guards brought him in and the Warden barked out orders for the cangue to be removed. "Prisoner, in accordance with the original decree of Emperor Wude, our forefather, every newly arrived prisoner receives one hundred disciplinary lashes. Guards, secure the prisoner and administer the punishment!"

Chapter 28

"Keep your hands off!" Wu Song warned. "If you want to beat me, go ahead, but you don't have to hold me. If I dodge a single blow, you can call me a coward and start again. If I so much as make a sound, you can say I'm not the hero of Yanggu!"

All the onlookers laughed. "The fellow's crazy," they said, "he's committing suicide! Well, let's see how he can take it."

"Come on then, if you're going to beat me try to do it properly," said Wu Song. "Don't hold anything back or I shall feel insulted."

This provoked further mirth. But as the guards took up their sticks in readiness, a cry rang out. Standing by the Warden's side was a man of about twenty-five, of average height and pale complexion, bearded and bewhiskered, his head bound about with a white scarf and sporting a black silk tunic. One hand was wrapped in a white bandage. He now spoke a few words in the Warden's ear. Thereupon the latter said: "Newly arrived prisoner Wu Song, tell us about the illness you contracted on the journey."

"I contracted no illness on the journey," Wu Song said. "I drank, I ate everything available, and I marched."

"The fellow was sick on the way here," the Warden said. "I can see from the look of him he's only just recovered. The beating will be postponed."

The guards on either side whispered to Wu Song: "Quick, say you've been ill. He's doing you a favour. All you've got to do is say you're feeling bad."

"But I'm not, I'm perfectly fit," Wu Song protested. "Beat me and be done with it. I don't want to put this beating in store and have it hanging over me. Let's get it over with as soon as possible."

Again there was laughter all round. Even the Warden was grinning. "The man's obviously still delirious with fever. He's sweating and spouting nonsense, I shall pay no attention to him. Take him back to the lock-up."

Several guards escorted Wu Song back to his cell. The other convicts gathered round and said: "Are you really going to tell us you didn't have some special letter of recommendation for the Warden?"

"Definitely not."

"In that case this postponement doesn't look good at all. They'll come and finish you off in the night."

"And how do you think they'll do it?"

"This evening they'll feed you two bowls of dry brown rice and some salted fish. As soon as you're full, they'll take you down to the dungeons, tie you up and roll you in straw mats, stop up the seven apertures and put you upside down on the wall. In less than an hour you'll be gone. It's what they call 'hanging the pot'."

"Is that the only method they've got?"

"There's another where they tie you up and get a sack and fill it full of sand and squash you under it. Same as before, in less than half an hour you're a goner. That's called 'sandbagging'."

"What else can they do?"

"Isn't that horrible enough? What would they need more for?"

Hardly had the convicts finished speaking when a guard entered, carrying a hamper, and asked: "Which of you is the new prisoner, Captain Wu?"

"I am," said Wu Song, "what do you want with me?"

"The Warden sends this snack for you."

Inside the hamper were a big pot of wine, a plate of meat, a bowl of noodles and a big bowl of broth.

"I suppose they're giving me this snack because they're coming to kill me later," Wu Song thought to himself. "Well anyway, I may as well eat now, let's take things one at a time."

When he had drained the wine and polished off the meat and noodles, the man returned and cleared away the things.

Alone in his cell, Wu Song considered his situation. "Now we shall see what they're going to do with me," he thought fatalistically. But as night fell, the same man entered again with another hamper. "What have you come for?" Wu Song asked him.

"I've been sent to give you your dinner."

He had brought several plates of vegetables, another big pot of wine, a plate of roast meat, a bowl of fish soup and a big bowl of rice. "After all this," Wu Song said to himself, "they'll definitely be coming to kill me. Well, let them. At least I won't be a hungry ghost when I die. So let's eat first and think about things after."

As soon as he had finished, the man collected the dishes and left. But in a little while he returned with another man. One was carrying a bath-tub, the other a big bucket of hot water. "Your bath, Captain," they said.

"I suppose they'll start on me when I've had my bath," he thought. "Well, I'm not afraid of them. I may as well spruce myself up a bit."

The two men filled the bath and he got in. When he'd washed, they handed him a bathrobe and a towel. He dried himself and dressed and then one of the men poured away the bath water and removed the bath, while the other brought a rattan mat and a mosquito-net. After hanging the mosquito-net, spreading the mat and placing a cool pillow on it, he bade Wu Song good night and departed.

Wu Song closed the door and bolted it. "What does all this mean?" he was thinking to himself. "Well let them do what they like. I'll know sooner or later." He laid his head on the pillow and slept soundly all night.

At daybreak Wu Song unbolted the door of the cell and the man who had served him the day before reappeared carrying hot water for washing. He invited Wu Song to wash his face and rinse his mouth with the water he provided for the purpose. He also brought a barber who combed Wu Song's hair, tied it in a knot on top of his head and covered it with a cap. Following this another man entered with a hamper from which he produced plates of vegetables, a big bowl of broth and a big bowl of rice. "I've no idea what you're up to," Wu Song thought, "but I'm going to eat anyway." When he'd eaten, a pot of tea was produced, and when he'd drunk the tea, the man who'd brought the food came back and said: "You're not very comfortable here, Captain, you'll be better off if we move you into the next room. It's a more suitable place for us to serve your tea and food."

"This is it!" Wu Song thought. "But I'll just go with him and see what happens."

While one man collected Wu Song's pack and bedding, another led him from his cell to somewhere on the opposite side of the corridor. They opened the door and inside was a spotlessly clean bed, with table and benches recently placed along either side. When he saw this, Wu Song thought to himself: "Here was I thinking they were about to take me down to the dungeons, how come they bring me somewhere like this! It's much better than the cell."

Wu Song sat there till midday, when the man came again with a hamper and a bottle of wine. Opening up the hamper he laid out fruit of four kinds, a cooked chicken and a quantity of steamed rolls. He carved the chicken, poured out the wine and invited Wu Song to eat. "What is going on?" Wu Song wondered. In the evening, there was more food and Wu Song was invited to bathe and lie down in the cool. "I believed it would be exactly as the other convicts said," he thought. "Then how is it they keep treating me so nicely?"

On the third day they brought him food and wine, same as before, and when he had breakfasted he went out for a stroll in the prison grounds. There he came upon a gang of convicts carrying water, chopping firewood and doing a variety of jobs, all under the baking noonday sun. It was high summer and nowhere was there any relief from the heat. Standing with his hands behind his back, Wu Song asked these convicts: "Why are you working in the sun like this?"

The convicts laughed. "Listen, friend, simply to be allowed to work this way is heaven on earth for us. How on earth could we expect to sit on our arses keeping cool? Them as don't have the means to bribe the gaolers are locked up in the great dungeon, live or die, it's all one to them, they'll pass the rest of their days like that, loaded down with chains."

After this Wu Song went to take a turn around the Temple of the Heavenly Prince. Next to the paper-burner was a block of granite with a hole in it, a massive stone, which served as occasional support for a flag-staff. He went and sat on this stone for a while, and then went back to his room and sat on the floor, turning things over in his mind, till the man came again with wine and food. To cut a long story short, Wu Song spent several more days in that room, and each day good food and wine was brought him and no attempt whatsoever was made to harm him. He simply did not know what to make of it.

Chapter 28

Finally one day when the man came at noon with food and drink, Wu Song could hold back no longer. Placing his hand on the hamper, he asked: "Who is your master? Why do you keep bringing me all this?"

"I told you, didn't I? I'm a servant of the Warden's household."

"But you still haven't answered my question. This food and wine you bring me each day, who is it told you to bring it? And what does he want of me?"

"Actually it's the Warden's son who's sending it."

"But I'm only a convict, I haven't even halfway done anything for the Warden, so why send me all this?"

"Who am I to say? I'm just obeying the Young Master's orders. He says to go on bringing you the stuff for five or six months and then he'll explain."

"Stranger and stranger! Are they trying to fatten me up before they do me in? It's a bloody conundrum and I just don't see how I'm ever going to solve it. But there's something fishy about all the food, so how can I be comfortable eating it? Tell me, this Young Master of yours, what's he like? How does he know me? I won't eat any more unless you answer."

"Remember when you'd just arrived, sir, in the administration office, the one who had a white dressing and a bandaged hand? That's the Warden's son."

"Do you mean the one in the black tunic standing right next to the Warden?"

"That's the one."

"Wasn't he the one who told them to stop when they were about to give me the beating?"

"Right sir. It was the Young Master that spoke up for you, that's why they didn't beat you."

"This is really odd! I'm from Qinghe, he's from Mengzhou, we've never met before, so why's he so concerned about me? There's got to be a reason. Listen, this Young Master of yours, what's his name?"

"His name's Shi En, and he's a martial arts expert, so people call him the Golden-Eyed Tiger."

"He's obviously a good man. Ask him to come here and see

me. If you do that I can accept his food and wine. If you don't get him to come, I refuse to touch anything."

The servant began to object. "The Young Master told me not to say anything about it. He said I was to serve you five or six months before he'd meet you."

"Shut up. Just tell your Young Master to come here and meet me."

At first the man was too scared, but when Wu Song began to lose patience he was obliged to go back and report what Wu Song had said.

After a long wait the Young Master rushed in and prostrated himself before Wu Song, who hurriedly returned the compliment, saying: "I am a convicted criminal under your jurisdiction, I cannot claim the honour or your acquaintance, yet recently you saved me from a severe beating and now every day you provide me with excellent food and wine, all of which I have done nothing to deserve. I have done you no service. To be thus rewarded without reason renders one unable either to eat or sleep in peace."

"I have long been familiar with your name, my friend, it has sounded like thunder in my ears," said the Young Master, "but an unfriendly fate kept us apart and I could not contact you. Now it is my good fortune that you are here and I would have come to greet you at once, only I was ashamed because I had nothing suitable to give you."

"I believe I heard your servant say that I was supposed to wait several months and then you would speak to me about something. What exactly was it you wanted to speak to me about?"

"The idiot doesn't know how to behave. He had to blurt it all out when he ought to have been keeping his mouth shut!"

"Really sir!" Wu Song protested, "all this shilly-shallying about, you'll drive me crazy. For heaven's sake, can't you tell me right out what it is you want of me?"

"Well, since the clod has let the cat out of the bag, I suppose I'd better explain. Because you're such a strong man, there is something I'd like to ask you to do, no one but you is capable of it. But because you must be tired from the journey here and haven't had time to recuperate, I want you to rest for a few months first. Then,

Chapter 28

施恩義奪快活林

when you've fully recovered your strength, I'll tell you all about it."

"Your Honour," Wu Song said scornfully, "last year on Jingyang Pass after I'd been sick with malaria for three months, and was drunk into the bargain, I was able to throw down a great tiger and kill it with just three blows of the fist and a couple of kicks. What do you suppose I'm capable of now?"

"But I'm not going to tell you today. Not till you've had a bit more rest and got your strength back fully."

"You still think I'm not strong enough? All right. There's a big block of stone I saw yesterday outside the Temple of the Heavenly Prince, what do you suppose it weighs?"

"I should think about four or five hundred catties."

"Let's go and see if I can lift it."

"Finish this wine first."

"Time enough for that when we come back."

The two men went to the Temple of the Heavenly Prince. When the convicts saw Wu Song with the Warden's son, they all bent low and saluted. Wu Song began to rock the stone a little. He grinned and said: "I'm really getting out of shape, I can't shift it."

"A stone that weighs four or five hundred catties, that's not to be taken lightly," said the Young Master.

"Do you really believe I can't lift it?" Wu Song said scornfully. "All right, everyone, stand back and watch this!" He removed the upper part of his robe and tied it about his waist, and then with single jerk lifted the stone clear off the ground. Then he threw it with both hands. It plunged to the ground, sinking in to a depth of a foot. The onlookers marvelled at what they saw. Wu Song went to the stone and lifted it again and tossed it into the air. It rose to a height of ten feet. Wu Song caught it in both hands as it descended and replaced it gently in the original spot. He turned to the Young Master and the crowd. His face was unflushed, his heartbeat regular and his breathing easy. The Young Master stepped forward and embraced him and then prostrated himself, saying: "You're not just an ordinary human! You're a god!" The convicts all echoed his words: "A god, truly a god!"

Chapter 28

His strength is a miracle, wondrous to see.
He's filled with true power in the highest degree.
The hand of this hero the universe appals
He tosses the stone like a juggler his balls.

The Young Master now took Wu Song into his private residence and made him sit down.

"Now you must tell me what it is you want me to do for you," Wu Song said.

"Let us just sit a little, till my father comes, then I'll be ready to explain it to you."

Wu Song did not conceal his disgust: "Now look here, Your Honour, if you want someone to do something for you, it's no good messing around like a young girl, never coming out with anything clearly, that's not a man's way of going about it. Even if it's something terrible I'll do it for you. But don't imagine I'm going to flatter you, you'll not catch Wu Song doing that!"

So the Young Master, standing quite still with his hands clasped together, expounded the business to Wu Song. And it was as a result of this that Wu Song was to display his fearsome aptitude for killing, to bring to bear once more the full force of his tiger-killing might. Truly,

When his two fists strike, a thunderbolt falls,
A flying kick from him raises a storm.

But to know what it was the Young Master told Wu Song you must turn to the next chapter.

Chapter 29

The Young Master reigns again on the Mengzhou road; Wu Song drinks his fill and beats the Door-God!

Now when the Young Master stepped forward and said: "Brother, please be seated and I will recount to you in full a matter of the utmost importance to me," Wu Song replied: "Hold nothing back, if you please. But stick to the point and tell it straight."

"I had the fortune to acquire in my youth," the Young Master began, "some degree of competence in the martial arts, from masters who belonged to the rivers and lakes fraternity. That is why in Mengzhou they have bestowed on me the name of Golden-Eyed Tiger. I run a little trading centre here, outside the East Gate, at a place called Happy Woods. We get a crowd of merchants from the north, and there are over a hundred lodging houses, together with twenty or thirty money changers and gaming houses. Partly relying on my own powers and partly by conscripting some eighty or ninety hardened convicts from the prison camp, I have been able to set up an establishment of my own and also to receive contributions from all of the money changers and gaming houses.

"At least, that's how it is normally. Even the travelling singers and other ladies of easy virtue are obliged to speak to me first on arrival before they are allowed to ply their trade. These affairs provide a regular income, bringing in something like two or three hundred taels of silver a month. It's what I live on.

"Recently, however, one Colonel Zhang was posted to the prison garrison here from Dongluzhou, and he brought with him a certain individual named Jiang Zhong, an enormous fellow, immensely strong, known therefore throughout the rivers and lakes as Jiang the Door-God. And in addition to his size and strength he's an expert fencer with sword or staff, equally good with his fists and feet, and a formidable wrestler! He boasts of remaining unbeaten three years running in the contest on Mount Taishan and insists he hasn't a rival in the world! So now this villain marches in and appropriates my territory. I didn't want to let him get away with it, but he beat me up so badly I was in bed for two months! The other day when you came my head and hand were still bandaged and even now the scars haven't healed completely.

"Well, I had thought of getting together a group of my people and going to pay him back, but the trouble is he can call on the support of Colonel Zhang and his guard, so if I attack him I'm going to have problems right here in the prison fortress. I'm eaten up with rage and there's nothing I can do to get even. But I've heard so much about your reputation for valour, so what would you say to helping me get my own back? If you did I'd be able to die in peace. I was only afraid that after such a hard journey you'd not have the necessary energy and strength, that's why I said I'd wait a few months before putting this proposition to you. My fool of a servant couldn't keep his mouth shut and blurted it out. Anyway, that's the truth of it."

Wu Song laughed when he heard all this, and said: "This Door-God, how many heads has he got and how many arms?"

"Just one head and two arms, what do you expect?"

"Well, supposing he had three heads and six arms now, and all the strength of Nazha the Ogre, then perhaps I might be afraid of him. But you say he's only got one head and two arms and he's nothing like Nazha. So what's there to be afraid of?"

"I just don't have the strength or the skill to defeat him."

"I don't want to brag but all my life I've used what powers I have to combat bullying and injustice. If it's like you say, then why are we sitting here? If you've got some wine, bring it along, we'll drink it on the way. I'm going there with you right away. You'll see, I shall give that scoundrel the same treatment I gave the tiger. And if I should punch him a bit hard and he dies, well, I'm quite prepared to forfeit my life."

"Sit down, brother, please. Wait till my father comes. We'll go

Chapter 29

when the time's right, there's no point in rushing things. Tomorrow I'll send someone to reconnoitre and find out if our man is at home. If he is, we'll go the next day. If he's away we'll reconsider. It would be a pity to go all the way there for nothing. Besides, we might just alert our quarry and give him a chance to play some trick on us."

"Small wonder he defeated you!" Wu Song replied impatiently. "That's not the way a man does things. If we're going to do it, come on! Forget all this talk about today and tomorrow, let's go! What difference does it make if he's expecting us or not?"

Just at this moment, as the son was attempting in vain to restrain Wu Song, the father came out from behind the screen and said: "Bravo! I've been listening to you all this time. I'm delighted to see you. Your presence here is like a ray of sunshine, so far as this son of mine is concerned. Please come with me into the back room for a moment."

Wu Song followed him inside. The Warden requested him to be seated.

"I am a convict, Your Honour, how can I sit in your presence?" Wu Song said.

"Nonsense! My son is most fortunate to have found a champion of your stature. There's no call for false modesty."

So Wu Song, with a deprecatory bow, sat down. But the Young Master remained standing. "Why don't you sit down too?" Wu Song said to him.

"In the presence of my father?" he replied. "Please brother, just make yourself comfortable."

"How can I, with you standing like that?"

"If that's how you feel, since there's no one else present ..." said the Warden, motioning his son to sit down.

Servants brought wine, fruit and nuts and a variety of other snacks. The Warden with his own two hands offered Wu Song a cup, saying: "Everyone pays tribute to your great courage, my friend. Now, this business venture of my son's at Happy Woods, it's not just a question of personal gain, you know, it actually helps Mengzhou to grow, improves the tone of our district, you might say. But that so-called Door-God has seized control by force, in full public view. Without the benefit of your help there's no way we can satisfy our need for revenge. Don't refuse my son. Empty this cup of wine, accept his sincere homage and allow him, as a mark of the respect in which he holds you, to call you elder brother."

"I have no talent or learning, who am I that your son should honour me like this?" Wu Song said. "It's tempting fate to accept unmerited praise." But he drank the wine and the Young Master prostrated himself four times. Wu Song immediately returned the compliment and henceforth they called each other brother. Wu Song went on drinking enthusiastically that day till he was very drunk and had to be helped to his room. We say no more of this.

Next day father and son had a talk. "Wu Song was dead drunk last night," they agreed, "he must be still affected. How can we expect him to go today? We'd better pretend the man we sent to reconnoitre has told us the enemy is not at home and we have to postpone the mission." So the Young Master went to Wu Song and said: "It can't be today. The scout has learnt that the fellow is away. Let us go tomorrow after lunch."

"No matter," said Wu Song. "If it has to be tomorrow, it gives me another day to stoke up my anger."

When they had breakfasted and drunk tea, the Young Master and Wu Song went for a stroll outside the camp. On their return they discussed spear technique and compared some moves with the fist or staff. Since it was midday, the Young Master invited Wu Song to the residence and ordered wine for him and some dishes to go with it. Impossible to say how many cups were drunk. But Wu Song began to notice that when he wanted to drink the Young Master only pressed more food on him, and he started to feel rather annoyed. After lunch they parted and Wu Song went back to the guest-room. When the two servants came to prepare his bath, Wu Song asked: "Your Young Master today kept urging me to eat more but he wouldn't offer me any more wine. Why was that?"

"I can tell you about that, sir, because actually this morning the two of them was talking about it. They wanted you to go today, see, only they thought you was pissed last night. They was afraid you couldn't bring it off 'cos you'd have a hangover. That's why they didn't want to give you wine. They're going to ask you to go and finish the business tomorrow."

"You mean they think that if I'm drunk I'll make a mess of it?"

"That's about the size of it."

That night Wu Song couldn't wait for dawn to come. He rose early and washed and rinsed his mouth. He put on a swastika scarf and an earth-coloured tunic, tied at the waist with a red satin belt. He bound his legs with gaiters reaching to the knee and wore eight-buckled canvas shoes. He stuck plasters over the convict's tattoos on his cheeks. Soon the Young Master came to take him to breakfast in the residence. When Wu Song had eaten and drunk tea, the Young Master said: "A horse is ready for you in the stables."

"There's nothing wrong with my legs, what do I need a horse for," Wu Song said. "There's just one thing I need you to do for me."

"Tell me what it is without fear. I couldn't possibly refuse."

"When we leave the camp, I want to observe the rule of 'For every sign take three'."

"Tell me please, what is this rule? I've never heard of it."

"I'll explain. If you want me to defeat the Door-God, every time on our journey we lay eyes on an inn sign, you must invite me to have three bowls of wine. Without those three bowls you won't get me past an inn. That's the rule of 'For every sign take three'."

This gave the Young Master pause. "From the East Gate to Happy Woods, it's a good five miles," he said. "Establishments where they sell wine, well, at a guess there must be twelve or thirteen of them. Three bowls in each, that'll come to something like thirty-six bowls before we get there. You'll be drunk, won't you? Then how can you deliver the goods?"

Wu Song found this exceedingly funny. "You think if I'm drunk I don't have strength," he said. "But it's the opposite, if I'm not drunk I don't have strength. With a little drop of wine in me I've got a little bit of strength, if I'm half drunk I've got half my full strength. But when I'm completely drunk something seems to inspire me! If I hadn't had all the force of being drunk, how do you think I'd have killed the tiger on Jingyang Pass? I was totally pissed that day and I did the job easily, I was brim-full of strength and energy."

"I didn't realize you were like that," said the Young Master. "Our wine is very good, too, I was just afraid that if you got too drunk you wouldn't be able to do the job, that's why I didn't offer you more and let you drink your fill. Since the wine only increases your strength, we'd better send two of the servants on ahead with some of our good wine, some fruit and nuts and other dishes, to wait for us along the road. Then we can enjoy the journey."

"Now that's very much to my liking," said Wu Song. "That'll put me in exactly the right mood for tackling the Door-God. Without wine, I might not know how to go about it. I'm going to knock him into kingdom come for you, people will laugh to see him in such a state."

The Young Master made the arrangements at once, sending two servants off with the wine and food on a carrying-pole, providing them also with a small sum of cash in coppers. Meanwhile the Warden, unbeknownst to the others, selected a dozen stalwart men whom he ordered to follow at a distance in case there was need of assistance.

So the Young Master and Wu Song set off from the Fortress of Peace, leaving Mengzhou by the East Gate. They had not gone more than a few hundred yards when beside the highroad they saw an inn, its sign sticking out from under the eaves. The servants were there already, waiting for them. The Young Master invited Wu Song inside and made him sit down. The servants had the wine ready and were about to serve it, when Wu Song said: "None of your tiny cups, please. Serve it in big bowls and make sure there are three of them." The servants accordingly produced big bowls and poured the wine. Wu Song did not hang back. He drank off three bowls at once and rose to go. The servants hurriedly cleared up the things and rushed on ahead. Wu Song gave a satisfied smile. "That's beginning to work now. Let's go!" he said. So off they went.

It was late summer, fiercely hot, though a little autumn breeze had started up, and the two men loosened their clothing. They

Chapter 29

had not gone half a mile when they came to a place not quite big enough for a village, where they could see another inn sign emerging from a clump of trees. Penetrating this grove, they found themselves before a little country inn:

Along the old road in the village stands an inn beside a stream. Willows cast deep shade before the door, lotus are aflutter in a pool; the inn flag dances in the autumn breeze, a short screen of rushes excludes the sun's harsh rays. On the dresser pitchers of rough wine glimmer, by the stove a heady young brew steams. Even before a bottle is unstoppered the scent carries five miles, making three neighbouring households drunk.

The Young Master paused at the door and said: "This is just a country tavern, selling cheap rough wine, do you have to drink here?"

"Sour or salt, sharp or rough — just as long as it's wine, I've got to have my three bowls. That's the rule, 'For every sign take three'."

So in they went and sat down, while the servants produced fruit and nuts to go with the wine. Wu Song drank off his three bowls and got up to go. The servants hurriedly cleared up and rushed off again. The two friends left the inn and in less than a mile they found another inn beside the road. Wu Song entered, drank his three bowls and left. But enough of this. Wu Song and the Young Master continued their journey thus: at each inn Wu Song entered and drank his three bowls. Yet although he must have drunk something like ten bottles, he was not, so far as the Young Master could see, drunk.

"How much further is it to Happy Woods?" Wu Song asked his companion.

"Not far. Do you see that wood over there, on the horizon? That's it."

"Since we're nearly there, you'd better go and wait for me somewhere. I'll go and find him on my own."

"That's fine by me. I know where to go. But do be careful. Don't underestimate him."

"Don't worry about that. Just tell the servants to stay with me.

If there are any more inns on the way I shall want to drink more."

The Young Master told the servants to follow the same procedure as before and then went his own way, while Wu Song continued on. In a little more than a mile he downed another nine cups or so. It was around noon and the sun was exceedingly hot, in spite of the light breeze, and the wine began to mount to his head. He opened the front of his tunic. Although less than three quarters drunk, he pretended to be totally intoxicated, deliberately lurching and stumbling, tilting one way, then swaying back. When he reached the wood, the servants pointed and said: "That's Jiang, the Door-God's inn, over there where the road forks."

"We've arrived then," said Wu Song. "You lot had better go and hide and keep well clear till I've knocked him out." Skirting the wood in order to approach from behind, he saw a man in a white linen tunic, built like the wooden guardian at a temple door. This character had set up a folding chair under a locust tree and was sitting there with a fly whisk in his hand, enjoying the cool. Here's the description of him:

> *The face devilish, the countenance coarse; the body a mass of purple flesh, with bulging blue veins; the face adorned with brown curling whiskers and a few wild strands beside the lips. Crazy staring eyes, glinting beneath the brows like stars. This is truly one of the two ugly door-gods, not the god-like semblance of a hero!*

Still feigning drunkenness, Wu Song staggered along, casting sideways glances at the man and saying to himself: "That big fellow must be the Door-God." He gave him a wide berth. Thirty or forty paces further on at the fork in the road he came upon an impressive inn. A flag-pole sticking out from under the eaves carried a sign on which was written in four large characters: "Bellavista Wines and Beverages." A closer look revealed a green railing in front of the entrance on which were displayed two banners respectively bearing the following messages, in gold characters: 'In drunkenness the world grows bigger' and 'In the wine pot the days grow longer.' An outhouse on one side of the

Chapter 29

inn yard contained a butcher's table, with chopping-block, chopper and other tools of the trade, while on the other side was a stove and firewood for making steamed bread; inside the main building was a row of huge wine vats, half buried in the ground and more than half full. In the middle was a counter behind which sat a very young girl: this was in fact the Door-God's concubine, recently acquired in Mengzhou, where she had been a hostess in one of the houses of pleasure in the entertainment district and known for her renderings of operatic songs.

Leering drunkenly at the girl, Wu Song erupted into the room and sat down at a place opposite the bar. Pressing both hands on the table, he ogled the girl, who responded by turning her head away.

There were five or six waiters on duty. Wu Song pounded the table and shouted: "Who's in charge here?" A waiter approached and asked: "'Ow much wine was you wantin', sir?"

"I'll have two measures first, just to try."

The waiter went to the bar and asked the girl to serve out two measures of wine. From the bucket she ladled out a bowl and warmed it, then presented it to Wu Song, saying: "'Ope you enjoys it, sir."

Wu Song picked it up and smelt it. He shook his head. "This is dreadful stuff, dreadful! Change it!"

The waiter saw he was drunk. He went back to the bar and said: "Better just give him something else, miss."

The girl took the wine and poured it away, then drew off some wine of a better quality. The waiter warmed a bowl and took it to Wu Song, who sipped and exclaimed: "This isn't any good either! Change it, double quick, or you'll be sorry."

Swallowing his annoyance, the waiter took the wine back to the bar and said: "Reckon as 'ow you'll 'ave to change it again, miss. Best not to argue — 'e's drunk an' 'e's looking to pick a quarrel. Just give 'im some of the best."

The girl ladled out some of the best wine and gave it to the waiter, who set the pitcher down and warmed a bowl. Wu Song drank it and said: "Now, this is more like it!" After a while he asked: "Tell me, waiter, what's the owner's name?"

"'Is name's Jiang," the man replied.

"Are you sure it's not Pimp?" Wu Song said, smirking.

The girl heard this and said to herself: "The swine's pissed, he's come here looking for trouble."

The waiter said to her: "'E's from the back of beyond, you can see that, 'e don't know nothink, don't you listen to 'is bleedin' nonsense!"

"What was that you said?" Wu Song asked.

"It's a private conversation," the waiter said. "Just shut up and drink your wine!"

"Waiter, tell the young lady behind the bar to come over here and have a drink with me," Wu Song said.

"Are you crazy or somethink? She's the boss's woman."

"So what? That doesn't prevent her having a cup of wine with me does it?"

"You lousy beggar!" the girl shouted in a fury. "You oughter be dead!" She flung open the bar flap and was about to rush out.

But Wu Song had already slipped his arms out of that earth-coloured tunic of his and knotted the sleeves around his waist. Pouring the pitcher of wine over the floor, he dashed behind the bar, colliding with the girl. With Wu Song's strength what hope did she have against him? One arm grasped her by the waist, while the other demolished her elaborate coiffure. Lifting her bodily over the bar, he hurled her towards where the wine was stored. With a resounding splash, the unfortunate girl landed right in the middle of a big vat of wine. As Wu Song bounded out from behind the bar, some of the more athletic waiters tried to rush him. Wu Song was ready for them. He caught one and lifted him easily, flinging him away so that he landed head first in a wine vat. Another charged and he grabbed him by the head and hurled him into another wine vat. Two more charged and he knocked them both down, one with a punch and the other with a kick. The first three were now in the wine vats and struggle as they might they could not get out. The next two lay motionless on the floor. Most of the establishment's forces had now been reduced to a pile of shit. There was just one who got away. "That bastard's gone off

Chapter 29

to get the Jiang the Door-God," Wu Song said to himself. "I'd better go and meet him. If I beat him up out on the road, it'll give the people something to laugh at." So saying he strode out of the inn.

The other waiter had indeed rushed off to tell Jiang the Door-God. The latter received quite a shock. He struggled to his feet, knocking over the folding chair and flinging away the fly whisk. Wu Song was waiting for him. They met in the middle of the road. Now although Jiang the Door-God was big, his strength had been sapped by recent bouts of drinking and sex, together with the unexpectedness of the event. He was in such a hurry he had no time to stop and think. Wu Song was built like a tiger and equally determined to beat him. Deceived by Wu Song's appearance of drunkenness, the Door-God rushed in without thinking. It's slow in the telling but happens in a flash. Wu Song started by feinting with a right and left to the head, then turned suddenly and danced away. Enraged, the Door-God lunged after him and was caught with a flying kick to the groin. As he doubled up, clutching himself with both hands, Wu Song whirled around and caught him again with his right foot, fair and square on the temple, toppling him over backwards. Stepping forward and planting a foot on his chest, Wu Song raised that fist the size of a barrel and began pounding him in the face.

Now this routine we have just described — that's to say, feinting with both hands, turning, kicking with the left foot, landing, turning again and kicking with the right foot — has a name. It's called 'jade bracelet steps and mandarin duck footwork.' It was something Wu Song had practised all his life, he had no equal for it.

Jiang the Door-God now lay beaten on the ground and crying for mercy. "I'll spare you, but only on three conditions," Wu Song told him.

"Spare me sir, I beg you. Even three hundred conditions, I accept them all," cried the Door-God, prostrate at Wu Song's feet.

Pointing a finger at Jiang, Wu Song proceeded to tell him the three conditions. And as a result, certain changes occurred:

Chapter 29

Changes are made to head and face, a new master is sought;
The hair is cut, the eyebrows plucked, a man goes forth to kill.

But if you want to know what the three conditions were, you must read the next chapter.

Chapter 30

❦

**The Young Master makes three visits to Death Row;
Wu Song reaps havoc at Flying Clouds Quay!**

Now when Wu Song was treading down Jiang the Door-God and said: "If you want me to spare your life you must agree to three conditions," and the latter replied: "Just tell me what they are, I'll agree to them!", here is what Wu Song told him: "Condition number one is that you give up Happy Woods and restore it entire, with all its goods and chattels, to its rightful owner, the Young Master Shi En — incidentally, who told you to steal it from him in the first place?"

"Yes, yes, I accept," said the Door-God in a hurry.

"And number two is that you get all the bosses and leading lights of Happy Woods to come and beg forgiveness of the Young Master."

"Yes, I accept!"

"And number three, as soon as you've made restitution in full, you quit this place and take yourself back where you came from, double-quick. I don't want to see you in Mengzhou again. If you stay I shall beat you up every time I see you. As many times as I catch you, you'll get a beating, and you'll be lucky if I only half kill you, I might finish you off completely. Understood?"

"Yes, yes, yes, I accept everything!" the Door-God babbled, desperate to save his life.

Wu Song hauled him to his feet. His face was black and blue and his lips swollen; his neck was twisted sideways and blood was streaming from his temples. Pointing a finger at him, Wu Song said: "Look at you, you blackguard, you're nothing compared to the great tiger of Jingyang Pass which, with just three blows of my fist and two kicks I actually killed. You'll get exactly the treatment you deserve. So look sharp and make restitution. If I think you're dragging your feet, just the least little bit, I'll have your life!"

Now that he knew it was Wu Song he had to do with, Jiang couldn't have enough of ducking and bowing and pleading for mercy. At this very moment, the Young Master appeared at the head of the twenty or thirty stalwart troops who had been sent to lend a hand. When they saw Wu Song had already defeated the Door-God, they made no secret of their approval. Everyone crowded around him.

Wu Song made a sign to the Door-God and said: "The rightful owner is back, you can clear off now, but first tell everyone to come and apologize."

"Please come inside and sit down," the Door-God said.

When Wu Song and the others entered the inn, they found the floor was swimming in wine, while the two waiters and the woman still scrabbled at the sides of the wine vats. When the woman managed to drag herself out her face was bruised and her skirt was sopping, wet through with wine. The other waiters had vanished.

Wu Song and his friends sat down and the Door-God shouted: "You lot, look sharp, get the place cleaned up!" Next he ordered a cart. The woman's belongings were loaded onto it and she was dispatched. Then several unharmed waiters were found and sent off to the village to summon some of the bosses. When they arrived at the inn the Door-God had them apologize to the Young Master on his behalf.

Wine was brought, of the best, with some dishes; a table was laid and everyone was invited to sit. Wu Song gave the Young Master the place of honour, above the Door-God, and ordered big bowls for everybody. The wine was poured.

After several bowls, Wu Song rose to speak. "Gentlemen, when I was banished here, after killing someone in Yanggu, I heard that this establishment in Happy Woods, which had been set up as a trading centre by Mr. Shi the younger, had been misappropriated by Jiang the Door-God and a bunch of his thugs, who were thus depriving the rightful owner of his livelihood. Maybe you all think I'm working for the Young Master, but you're wrong, there's nothing between us. It is simply that I have always made it my habit to combat injustice. When I come upon something unfair I gird my loins and rush to help, without fear or favour. Today I intended to beat the life out of this Jiang and rid the world of a pest. But out of consideration for you I decided to spare him. However, I've told him he's got to clear out tonight. If he doesn't leave, next time he meets me he's going to end up like the tiger on Jingyang Pass."

When they understood that this was the Wu Song who killed the tiger of Jingyang Pass, they all expressed their regrets at Jiang's behaviour and said: "We beg you not to get excited. Just let him move out and restore everything to the owner."

Jiang was too scared to even open his mouth. The Young Master, after checking the inventory, repossessed the inn. The shamefaced Jiang thanked all present, obtained a cart, loaded his things onto it and took himself off. Of him we need say no more.

Wu Song now invited the neighbours and the celebrations went on till they were quite drunk. It was already late when they dispersed and Wu Song slept soundly till morning.

When the Warden heard that his son had regained control of the inn at Happy Woods, he mounted and rode over to thank Wu Song personally. The celebrations in Wu Song's honour continued for days. By now the people of Happy Woods all knew Wu Song's reputation and no one omitted to pay his respects. The inn was tidied up and repaired, and opened for business again. The Warden went back to the business of administering the Fortress of Peace.

The Young Master sent out spies to discover, if they could, where Jiang and his family had taken themselves off to, but their whereabouts remained a mystery. So he settled down to his work and paid Jiang no further heed. He invited Wu Song to stay on at the inn. The Young Master's business flourished, profits more than doubling. Every betting shop and stall in the place handed over money with interest. The Young Master had gained tremendous status from Wu Song, and he honoured Wu Song as he might his own mother and father. Of the Young Master and his continued management of Happy Woods we shall say no more. It was a case of:

> *What was obtained by force, to force again is lost;*
> *Mostly the way of virtue's the way to gain the most.*
> *Happy Woods once more o'erflows with happiness.*
> *Evil requites the wicked, the innocent gain redress.*

The days slipped by and soon a month had passed. The fierce heat of summer soon gave way before the autumn equinox. Fresh breezes dissipated the sultry heat. Autumn had arrived.

But to cut a long story short, one day when the Young Master was sitting in the inn chatting with Wu Song about martial arts, a couple of soldiers appeared at the inn door leading a horse. Entering, they asked the owner: "Which is Captain Wu Song, killer of the tiger?"

The Young Master recognized the speaker as one of the aides of the Mengzhou garrison commander, General Zhang Mengfang. He stepped forward and asked: "What do you want with Captain Wu?"

The officer replied: "His Excellency has heard that Captain Wu is a brave soldier. He has sent us with a horse to fetch him. Here is the order."

The Young Master examined it. Privately he was thinking: "General Zhang is my father's superior — my father is under his command and so also, as a convicted prisoner, is Wu Song. I'd better advise him to go."

So he spoke to Wu Song: "These officers have been sent from General Zhang's headquarters to fetch you. They've even brought a horse for you. What do you think you should do?"

Wu Song, always straightforward, didn't prevaricate. "Since he's calling for me, I'd better go and see what he wants." He changed his clothes and cap and accompanied by with one of the retainers mounted and rode with the officers to Mengzhou.

Arriving at the General's residence, he dismounted and followed the officers in, till they stood at the entrance to the hall where General Zhang awaited them. The General smiled to himself when Wu Song arrived. "Let him come in," he said, "I want to see him." Wu Song entered and saluted, then stood to one side respectfully with his arms crossed.

"I have heard you are a strong and valiant soldier," the General said, "the sort who fears no enemy, one who'd be loyal through thick and thin. I need such a man on my staff. Would you be prepared to serve as my personal aide?"

Wu Song knelt and thanked the General. "I am a convict from the prison camp," he said. "If you show me this enormous favour, of course I shall be your faithful servant, yours to command in any service."

General Zhang expressed his satisfaction. He ordered food and drink and plied Wu Song with wine till he was quite drunk. He had a room off the main gallery furnished for Wu Song to sleep in. Next day servants were sent to the Young Master's to fetch Wu Song's luggage. From now on Wu Song lived at General Zhang's and the General required his company at all hours, constantly inviting him into his own quarters to eat and drink. Wu Song had the run of the residence and was treated like one of the family. The General commanded a tailor to equip Wu Song with a complete set of autumn clothes.

Wu Song found all this very flattering. But he said to himself: "Apparently the General is determined to advance me. He hasn't once let me out of his sight since I came, and I've no time even to go and see the Young Master at Happy Woods, who's most likely been sending people to see me but they're not allowed in."

The fact is that since his arrival the General seemed to have taken a great fancy to Wu Song. If anyone with some official business requested Wu Song's help and Wu Song spoke to the General, the latter always agreed to everything. So people gave Wu Song gifts of gold and silver and silk and suchlike. Wu Song bought a wicker trunk and locked these gifts up in it. Of this no more.

Time sped by and soon it was the Mid-Autumn Festival. What a fine mid-autumn scene it was:

The jade disk shines coldly in the sky; the autumn breeze blows softly. On the path by the well the Wutong leaves are fallen; the pond is choked with weeds. Mournful is the cry of the first geese, anxious the music of the winter cricket. Tossing in the wind the willows are half stripped; glistening with raindrops the hibiscus flaunts its beauty. Autumn's breath even-handedly urges on the season's changes; moonlight envelopes river and hill.

To celebrate the festival, General Zhang arranged the feast in an interior court, beneath the Ducks and Drakes Tower, and he invited Wu Song. But when Wu Song saw that there were ladies present, he just drank one cup and was about to turn round and leave. The General stopped him with a shout: "Where do you think you're going?"

"Sir!" Wu Song replied. "You are feasting with the female members of your family, it is not correct for me to be here."

The General treated this as absurd. "Nonsense!" he said. "I respect you as a man of integrity and invited you on purpose to come and feast with us, like one of the family, why should you withdraw?" He told Wu Song to sit down.

"But I am a convict," Wu Song protested. "How can I sit with Your Excellency?"

"My dear fellow," the General said, "why be so difficult? There are no outsiders present, there's nothing to stop you sitting down."

Wu Song went on protesting his unworthiness and trying to leave, but the General would have none of it, and insisted that he sit down with them. In the end Wu Song saluted respectfully and seated himself as far away as possible, maintaining a respectful posture. The General told the maids to offer Wu Song wine. After half a dozen cups the General ordered more snacks and then a complete dinner was served — and repeated. All this time they chatted about martial arts.

"When real men drink, it shouldn't be from small cups," the General said. "Bring a big mug and pour for our friend here."

Wu Song was immediately served with several mugs of wine. Moonlight was now flooding through a window on the east. Wu Song was quite drunk. He had lost all his inhibitions and just kept on drinking.

Chapter 30

The General called for one of his favourites, a girl called Yulan, to sing for them. Here's what Yulan was like:

Fair as a lotus, with cherry lips and eyebrows drawn in a curve like the blue line of distant mountains and, lying beneath, a pair of eyes bright as autumn waters. A graceful slender waist girt with a green skirt that allows but a precious glimpse of the feet. The white body delicately perfumed, the arms lightly encased in sleeves of scarlet silk. A peacock brooch to restrain luxuriant locks. Holding the ivory clappers high above her head she struts the stage.

So motioning to Yulan, the General said: "There are no outsiders here, no one but my good friend Captain Wu. Why don't you sing us some Moon Festival songs? Let us hear your voice."

Yulan picked up the clappers, curtsied and launched into a Mid-Autumn song by Su Dongpo:

When will the moon be bright again?
Cup in hand, ask the clear sky.
Who knows in the palaces of heaven what year
It is tonight? I would ride the wind there but fear
The cold of those remote and beauteous regions
Would be more than I could bear.
I shall get up and dance with shadows,
There is nothing like it among men.
The blind is pulled right up
And moonlight floods the room, banishing sleep.

Hate should not be. And why
Is the moon so often full at parting?
Men have their joy and grief, their partings and reunions,
The moon has its light and dark, waxing and waning,
It has ever been thus, that there is nothing perfect.

Let us just hope for life, and that miles apart
The sight of beauty may join our hearts.

When she had finished, Yulan put down the clappers, curtsied and stood to one side.

"Yulan, bring us a round of wine," said the General.

She took up a tray at once, while a maid filled the bowls. Then she took the wine round, offering it first to the General, then to his wife and finally to Wu Song. The General ordered the bowls to be filled to the brim. During all this, Wu Song would not raise his eyes. He received the wine where he sat apart, emptied the bowl in one go to the health of the General and his lady, and quickly put it back.

Pointing to Yulan, the General said: "This girl is clever and quick-witted, she's an excellent musician and a good hand at needlework. If you don't have any objection, I propose that within the next few days, whenever it's most auspicious, you can get married."

Wu Song jumped to his feet, bowed and said: "I am nobody, how could I possibly presume to marry somebody from Your Excellency's household? I should really be making a fool of myself."

"If I suggest it," said the general, "I mean it. There's no point in arguing. I never go back on my word."

By this time Wu Song had drunk a dozen bowls in quick succession and the wine was beginning to rush to his head. It is to be feared that he was no longer in complete control of himself. He rose to his feet and bowing to the General and his wife returned to his room off the main gallery. But when he went inside, he found the wine and food lay heavy on his stomach and he couldn't sleep. So he changed and took off his cap, picked up a club, and went to practise in the centre of the hall, under the light of the moon. After executing several movements, completing several routines, he glanced up and saw from the sky that it was well past midnight. He returned to his room and was about to undress and go to bed when he heard a cry of "Thief! Thief!" from the inner chambers of the residence. "The General has been so kind to me," he said to himself, "if there's a thief in his quarters it's my duty to go and help."

Seizing his club, he hastened to the inner chambers. Here he met the singer, Yulan, rushing out in a panic. "A thief has got in," she shouted, "he's gone into the garden!"

Chapter 30

Club in hand, Wu Song dashed into the garden to investigate. He looked around but saw nothing. He turned and hurried back inside. But he failed to observe a wooden stool which was suddenly thrust out from the shadows, so that he tripped and fell. Immediately half a dozen soldiers appeared and shouted: "We've got him!" They fell on Wu Song and trussed him up with hemp rope.

"It's me!" Wu Song shouted. But they had no intention of letting him explain. At this moment a blaze of lamps and candles flooded the building. From the hall where he was sitting, General Zhang bellowed: "Bring him here!" The soldiers dragged Wu Song stumbling into his presence.

"I'm not the thief, I'm Wu Song," the captive shouted.

When he saw who it was the General exploded. His whole face changed. "You bloody convict!" he shouted. "So you're the thief, are you, a villain with the heart and soul of a dog! And I was fool enough to give you a leg up, to try to help you. I would have denied you nothing, why, I even asked you to drink with us, to sit and eat with us! I had plans for you, I would have given you an official post. Is this the way you repay me?"

Wu Song cried: "But sir, I've done nothing wrong! I came to catch the thief, how can you take me for the thief? I'm a man of honour, I don't do things like that!"

"Don't deny it, you shameless villain! Take him back to his room and search it for stolen goods."

The soldiers escorted Wu Song back to his room, where the wicker trunk was opened. On top there were a whole lot of clothes. Underneath they found silver wine cups and platters, a treasure trove of several hundred taels. Wu Song stood gasping in amazement, he couldn't believe his eyes. The soldiers carried the trunk back to the hall. On seeing it, the General burst out again: "You bloody convict, have you no conscience? The stolen goods have been found in your trunk, you can't deny it! It's right, what they say, 'You can't judge a man by his appearance.' On the outside you look like an ordinary human being, but inside you've the heart and soul of a thief! Now that there's proof you haven't a leg to stand on." He gave orders for the stolen goods to be put under seal and taken to the strong room for safekeeping and said he would deal with the thief in the morning. Wu Song loudly protested his innocence, but no one would listen to him. The soldiers, having disposed of the loot, placed him in a cell under guard. The General meanwhile had quickly sent someone to inform the magistrate and bribe the court officials.

Next day at dawn, when the court was already in session, with the magistrate, his assistants, bailiffs and guards all present, Wu Song was brought in. The stolen goods were produced and a confidant of the General's presented an affidavit giving details of the robbery. Having perused this document, the magistrate ordered his officers to tie Wu Song up. The gaolers then brought out the instruments of persuasion and placed them in full view. When Wu Song tried to explain, the magistrate interrupted: "This fellow is a banished convict, of course he's going to steal, no doubt the mere sight of riches was too much for him. In view of the fact that we have the stolen goods, clear evidence of the crime, there's no need to listen to his rubbish, just take him away and beat him soundly."

Each of the gaoler's assistants took a split bamboo and started raining down blows. Wu Song understood clearly that there was absolutely nothing he could do but submit and produce a confession: "On the fifteenth of this month I saw in the quarters of the General a quantity of silver wine cups and platters. My greed was aroused and I found an opportunity to purloin it under cover of night for my own personal advantage."

After this confession the magistrate said: "There you are! With this scoundrel it's simply a case of the mere sight of riches being too much for him, that's all there is to it. Take him and fit him with a cangue." The gaolers took Wu Song away, fitted the cangue and locked him away in a cell for condemned men.

When they took him down into the dungeons, Wu Song thought: "The awful thing is, it was all a trap that bastard General Zhang set for me, and I fell for it. If ever I come out of this alive he's going to be sorry!"

The gaolers committed Wu Song to the dungeons where he wore chains on his feet at all times and his hands were secured by wooden manacles, allowing him not the slightest relief.

Meanwhile, what of the Young Master? The matter had already been reported to him and he had gone hurriedly to the prison fortress to consult his father. "Obviously Captain Zhang is behind this, carrying out Jiang the Door-God's revenge on his behalf. He has bribed General Zhang and they concocted this scheme to destroy Wu Song," said the Warden. "No doubt he sent someone to pay off everyone concerned. After receiving money and gifts they wouldn't give Wu Song a chance to explain. Evidently they want him dead. But I've been thinking: Wu Song's crime does not merit the death penalty. All we've got to do is buy over a couple of gaolers and we can easily protect him whilst he's there. When he gets out we'll have to think of something else."

"The head gaoler at present is a fellow called Kang, who's a very great friend of mine," said the Young Master. "Suppose I go and ask him to help?"

"Well, it's on your account that Wu Song is suffering persecution, what better time to help him than now?"

The Young Master collected up a few hundred taels of silver and went off to see Kang the gaoler at his home. But Kang was out. The Young Master told one of his family to go to the gaol and inform him. In a little while Kang returned and spoke with the Young Master.

The Young Master told him the whole story. "I'll tell you the truth," said Kang. "All this is the doing of Captain Zhang and General Zhang. They've not only the same name, they're sworn blood brothers as well. At present Jiang the Door-God is hiding in Captain Zhang's house. He got the captain to bribe General Zhang and they cooked up this scheme between them. Jiang has bribed absolutely everybody, we've all had money from him. In the court the magistrate is quite ready to let him call the tune. They'd like to finish Wu Song off, but there's one person involved in the case, the clerk of the court, a fellow called Ye, who won't consent. That's the only reason they can't touch him. You see, this law official is an upright and honest man, he won't agree to the death of an innocent party, that's why Wu Song is still untouched. After what you've just told me, sir, I shall look after him myself, so far as the gaol is concerned. I'll go over there and make things a bit easier for him right away. In future he shan't suffer a moment's unease. What you'd better do is quickly send someone to talk to Mr. Ye and ask him to speed up the sentencing, then your man will be safe."

The Young Master took out a hundred taels of silver for Kang, but the latter refused. He refused three times before finally accepting it.

The Young Master left and returned to the fortress. He sought out someone who knew Ye well and sent him a hundred taels of silver, asking him to treat the case as urgent and get a sentence as quickly as possible. In fact Ye knew all about Wu Song's good qualities and was inclined anyway to help him. He had already classified the case as doubtful but knew the magistrate had received General Zhang's bribes and would not countenance a light sentence. However, the charge against Wu Song was one of theft, which was not a capital offence, so what they were aiming to do was to let the case drag on, while they planned a way of ending Wu Song's life in the gaol.

Now after receiving the hundred taels of silver from the Young Master and learning that Wu Song had been framed, the clerk of the court willingly reduced the charges in the indictment and agreed to help save Wu Song by procuring a sentence as soon as the preliminary detention was completed.

Next day the Young Master prepared great quantities of wine and food and got Kang to take him to the gaol and admit him to see Wu Song and give him the provisions. By this time Kang had already checked up on Wu Song and his conditions had been improved. The Young Master also took along twenty or thirty taels of silver which he distributed among the prison staff. As he took out the food and drink and encouraged Wu Song to eat, the Young Master whispered in his ear: "It's absolutely clear that the trouble you are in was all contrived to get Jiang his revenge and to destroy you. But take heart, do not despair. I've already sent a message to Clerk Ye. He knows all about you. As soon as you've served out your term here you'll be sentenced and allowed to leave and then you can take what action you like."

As soon as Wu Song's conditions were relaxed he had formed

Chapter 30

the intention of trying to escape. But when he heard what the Young Master had to say, he changed his mind.

After thus reassuring Wu Song, the Young Master returned to the fortress. Two days later he again prepared food and drink and some money, and got Kang to admit him to the prison to see Wu Song. They talked and he regaled Wu Song with food and wine. He also administered some small change in tips for the prison staff.

A few days later the Young Master once more prepared food and drink and had some clothes made, and through the good services of Kang again got himself admitted to the prison, where he invited everyone to drink and gave them money so they would take good care of Wu Song. He made the latter change his clothes and take some wine and food.

Now that he knew the way, the Young Master visited the prison three times in just a few days. He had become over-confident and his visits were observed by one of Captain Zhang's men who reported the fact. Captain Zhang passed the information on to General Zhang. General Zhang in turn sent someone carrying presents for the magistrate to report the matter to him. The magistrate, since he was corrupt and in their pay, ordered that the prison be constantly inspected and any strangers detained and questioned. The Young Master was told of this and thereafter did not dare go back again, so it was left to Kang and the other gaolers to take care of Wu Song. But the Young Master went regularly to Kang's house, where he received the news and was able to keep up with all the developments. Of this no more.

For the next two months or so, Ye did all he could to talk the magistrate round. He often explained the ins and outs of the case to him. Thus the magistrate learnt that General Zhang had received considerable sums of money from Jiang the Door-God, and that they were in cahoots with Captain Zhang to trap and destroy Wu Song, and he said to himself: "You lot have been receiving money for all this, but you want me to do the dirty work." He began to lose his enthusiasm for the job and neglected it.

When he had done nearly sixty days, Wu Song was brought forth from the prison and the court ordered the cangue to be removed. The clerk of the court read out the charges and the sentence was announced: twenty strokes of the cane and banishment to the prison camp at Enzhou, the stolen goods to be restored to the owner. General Zhang had to send one of his people to collect the stolen goods. Wu Song received the twenty strokes, had his cheeks tattooed with the golden seals and was fitted with a seven and a half catty iron-spiked cangue. A certificate was made out and two officers detailed to escort him. A deadline was fixed for his departure.

The two officers, bearing the certificate, led Wu Song from the court. The flogging he received, since the old Warden had spent his money so freely and since the friendly clerk of the court was overseeing it, and since the magistrate knew that Wu Song had been the victim of a plot, was not at all severe; in fact he got off lightly.

Wearing the cangue and closely guarded by the two officers, Wu Song left the town, inwardly seething with anger. They had gone about half a mile when they came to an inn by the highway, from which the Young Master emerged to greet Wu Song. "I've been waiting for you," he said. His head was bandaged and his arm was in a sling.

"I haven't seen you for so long," Wu Song said. "How did you come to be in this state?"

"I'll tell you," said the Young Master. "After that time when I came to visit you three times in a row, the magistrate got to hear about it and started sending people to make random checks at the gaol and General Zhang also sent men to watch the gates on every side. I couldn't come to see you again, but I got news of you at Mr. Kang's. Then a fortnight ago when I was at the Happy Woods inn, Jiang the Door-God reappeared, with a gang of thugs. They beat me up really badly and Jiang insisted that I get all the locals to come and apologize. He seized the inn again, like before, and took over all the fixtures and stock. I had to stay home, I wasn't even able to get up from my bed. But today when I heard you were banished to Enzhou I got two padded coats for you for the journey. And there's two cooked geese here as well that I want you to have."

The Young Master invited the two guards. He suggested they should all go to an inn. But the guards refused, making a great fuss about it: "Wu Song is a vicious thief, if we accepted your offer, we'd really be in hot water at the government offices. You'd better clear off, unless you want to be beaten up."

The Young Master saw it was no good. So he took out a dozen taels of silver and offered them to the guards. They would not accept. Instead they indignantly urged Wu Song to get a move on.

The Young Master ordered two bowls of wine which he made Wu Song drink, and tied a bundle round his waist and attached the two geese to his cangue for him. Then he whispered in Wu Song's ear: "Inside the bundle are the two padded coats and some loose change wrapped up in a scarf. I want you to eat well on the journey. There's also a pair of hemp sandals with eight eyelets. You must watch out during the journey. Those two bastards don't seem to harbour good intentions."

Wu Song nodded. "No need to tell me, I'd already noticed. But even if they were twice as many I wouldn't fear them. You go home and rest and please don't worry. I can handle it."

The Young Master bade Wu Song goodbye with tears in his eyes. Of this no more.

Wu Song and his two guards set out. When they had gone a mile or two, the guards began to talk quietly among themselves. "Where's them two got to then?" Wu Song heard them say. He silently considered this. "You fools, you've given it away," he thought contemptuously, "I suppose someone was going to come along and knock me on the head!"

Wu Song's right hand was secured by the cangue but his left hand was free. So he grasped the geese which were attached to his cangue and applied himself to eating, without looking at the two guards. After a mile or so he was attacking the second of the cooked geese. He held it down with his right hand and tore pieces off it with his left. Eating occupied all his attention. A mile or so more and he had accounted for both the geese. They were now about three miles from their starting-point, when two men appeared ahead of them, standing by the roadside. These two carried halberds and had swords stuck through their belts. They

Chapter 30

waited, and then, when Wu Song and his guards were passing, fell into step beside them. Wu Song was able to observe certain signs expressive of a hidden meaning passing between the guards and the two who carried halberds. He also noticed that they were embarrassed when he caught their eye, but he said nothing and pretended he hadn't seen.

Before they had gone much further they came to the edge of a vast area of rivers and fish-ponds. On all sides were desolate creeks and broad channels. The five men reached a place where the water was crossed by a bridge of broad wooden planks. There was a tall structure beside it bearing a sign which read: "Flying Clouds Quay." At this point Wu Song innocently asked: "What do you call this place?"

"Are you blind or what?" the two guards replied. "Can't you see that sign next to the bridge there, what says 'Flying Clouds Quay'?"

Wu Song came to a halt and said: "I want to wash my hands, then."

As the two with halberds approached him he gave a shout of "In you go!" and with a flying kick sent one of them sailing head over heels into the water. The other hurriedly tried to turn round, but Wu Song's right foot was already poised and it propelled him into the water with an enormous splash. The two guards were terrified and wanted to get off the bridge and run for it, but Wu Song shouted: "Where do you think you're going?" With one wrench he broke the cangue in two and hurled it from the bridge. One of the guards collapsed from shock, the other made a run for it, but Wu Song charged after him and felled him with one blow of the fist. He picked up a halberd which was floating on the water and fell on the guard, striking several blows. The guard expired on the spot. Wu Song then turned back and dealt with the one who had fainted, cutting him to pieces. The two in the water had struggled to the shore and were hoping to escape. Wu Song gave chase and cut one of them down. He shouted to the other: "If you tell me everything, I'll spare you!"

The second halberdier said: "We work for Mr. Jiang. Our master made the plan together with Captain Zhang. They sent us to help the guards, the idea was to take care of you."

武松大鬧飛雲浦

"Where is your master right now?"

"When we left he was with the Captain and the General — they were all at General Zhang's house, drinking wine in the Ducks and Drakes Tower, waiting for us to go back and report."

"Well, in view of all this I find I can't let you off after all," Wu Song said. He raised his blade and brought it down again. The man was dead.

He detached the swords and took the best one. He tipped the two corpses into the water. Then he wasn't sure if they were both dead, so he picked up the halberd again and thrust it into each of the bodies several times.

Now he stood there on the bridge, looking around him and thinking: "I've killed these four stooges, but the big shots, the two Zhangs and Jiang, are still getting off scot-free. Where's the satisfaction in that?"

Halberd in hand he stood there, for a moment undecided. Then he knew what to do. He turned back and headed at full speed for Mengzhou.

If he hadn't, things would have been different. He would never have killed so many corrupt men, or released so much pent-up anger.

In the painted hall, the bodies point this way and that,
In the red light of the candles, the room is swimming in blood.

Well, exactly what happened when Wu Song returned to Mengzhou you can read about in the next chapter.

Chapter 31

In Ducks and Drakes Tower the General's blood will spill;
The false pilgrim Wu Song comes to Centipede Hill!

General Zhang was listening to his namesake Captain Zhang boasting about how he had accomplished Jiang the Door-God's revenge by having Wu Song done to death, and none of them had the slightest idea that the four would-be assassins had all been killed by Wu Song at Flying Clouds Quay. And Wu Song meanwhile stood on the bridge for a long while, pondering what to do. As he hesitated, his anger mounted till it seemed to fill the sky. "Until I have killed General Zhang," he said to himself, "how will I ever settle this spleen of mine?" So he went over to the corpses and took the swords from them, choosing the best and sticking it through his belt, and selected a good halberd and shouldered it, and then turned back in the direction of Mengzhou.

Night was just falling as he entered the town. The houses were already shut up, every door was locked:

> At the Nine Luminaries incense fills the air and bells are being struck. A big round moon hangs in the sky, a few stars prick heaven's vault. In brigade headquarters a bugle insistently calls; in Five Drums tower the water clock drips steadily. One after another ladies steal back to their bedchambers, gentlemen close the curtains.

When Wu Song entered the town he went straight to General Zhang's and prowled along the boundary wall of the compound till he came to a place where there was a stable. He crouched down and listened. It sounded as if the groom had gone inside the residence and was still in there. As he waited, the side-door creaked open and the groom emerged, carrying a lantern, while someone shut the door from the inside. Wu Song remained hidden in the shadows. Just at that moment, listen! ... the drum beat the hour. It was half-past eight. He watched the groom climb onto the hay to hang up the lantern, then spread out his blanket, undress and lie down to sleep. Wu Song approached the stable door and started to make a noise.

"I've only just gone to bed!" the groom yelled. "If you're counting on stealing my clothes you've cocked up, mate!"

Wu Song propped his halberd against the wall, drew his sword and began to rattle the door.

This was too much for the groom. He leapt out of bed, just as he was, stark naked, grabbed a pitchfork, and then removed the beam which secured the door. Before he even had time to open it, Wu Song had given it a mighty shove and crashed through. He knocked the groom on the head and subdued him in a trice. Before the groom could cry out, in fact, he had seen the sword glinting in the moonlight, and his legs turned to jelly. He was far too terrified to do more than produce a strangled cry of "Mercy!"

"Do you know me?" Wu Song asked.

Only when he heard the voice did the groom realize it was Wu Song. "Please sir, I 'ad nothing to do with it, be merciful!" he cried.

"Just tell me the truth. General Zhang, where is he right now?"

"'E's with Captain Zhang and Mr. Jiang, they been drinking all day. They're still at it, over there in the Ducks and Drakes Tower."

"Are you telling the truth?"

"Cross me heart an' hope to die!"

"It's no good, I can't let you go!" Raising his arm, Wu Song killed him with a single cut. He kicked the body aside and returned the sword to its scabbard. Then by the light of the lantern he undid the clothes from the Young Master that he had fastened round his waist and exchanged what he was wearing for the two new items of clothing. He fastened them securely, girded on sword and scabbard and wrapped some loose silver in the groom's quilt and stuffed it in his bag which he hung up on the door. Then he propped the two leaves of the gate against the wall and after blowing out the lantern slipped out to retrieve his halberd before mounting the gate and climbing onto the wall.

Chapter 31

There was just a little moonlight now, as Wu Song sprang from the wall down into the garden. He first opened the side-door and went to replace the leaves of the stable gate. Then he turned and went back inside again, closing the side-door so that it looked as if it was bolted, although he did not replace the beam. Following this he headed towards a light, which turned out to be coming from the kitchen. Two maids were standing beside the soup cauldron, grumbling: "All day they've 'ad us running after them and still they don't go to bed. It's nothink but 'Bring us more tea.' And them two guests oughter be ashamed, gettin' theirselves pissed as newts like that! They don't never think of goin' off to bed, just jabber, jabber, jabber!"

While these two maids were nattering on about their grievances, Wu Song put down his halberd, drew the bloodstained sword at his waist, gave the door a mighty shove so that it opened with a groan, and charged in. He grabbed the first of the maids by the hair and killed her with one cut. The other would have run off, but her feet were as if nailed to the floor. She wanted to scream but she seemed to have lost her tongue. She was literally struck dumb.

Now, forget about two simple servant girls, had it been yours truly, I too would have been speechless, I can tell you!

Wu Song raised his arm and killed this one with one blow. He dragged the two corpses in front of the stove. He extinguished the lamp and with the aid of the moonlight streaming through the window advanced into the house.

Of course Wu Song had been a member of the household, he knew the geography. Stealthily he reached the stairway leading up into the Ducks and Drakes Tower. Feeling his way carefully he crept up the stairs. By this time all the attendants had taken themselves off, fed up with waiting. So just the three of them were there, General Zhang, Captain Zhang and Jiang the Door-God, still talking. Jiang's fawning tones reached the ears of Wu Song where he stood listening on the landing: "It's all thanks to you, sir, that I can have my vengeance. I shall never be able to repay your great kindness!"

"I only did it for the sake of my friend Captain Zhang here," the General replied. "Otherwise I wouldn't have touched the business. Well, it's cost you a penny or two, but you've the satisfaction of knowing you've settled the blighter's hash. Any time now they'll be making their move, so I think we can say he's as good as dead. Finish it off at Flying Clouds Quay, that's what I told 'em. They'll be here in the morning to make their report."

Captain Zhang chipped in: "Four of them against one, it can't possibly go wrong. Even supposing he had several lives, he'd still be a goner!"

Jiang added: "I told my people to go along too. I said to lend a hand and come back and report when it's over."

Indeed it was a case of:

Behind closed doors the truth is heard;
Revenge is waiting in the wings.
Before the cold the cricket sings,
The Reaper's call can't be deferred.

When Wu Song heard all this, the flaming pillar of rage in his heart grew ten thousand feet tall, splitting the sky's vault. With the sword brandished in his right hand, the fingers of his left hand tense, he charged into the room.

Three or four decorated candles were blazing and in several places moonlight filtered in, so the room was clearly illumined. The drinking vessels had still not been cleared away. Jiang the Door-God was sitting in a folding chair. When he saw Wu Song he had such a shock his heart, liver and lungs leapt into his mouth.

It's slow in the telling but happens in a flash. Before Jiang could offer any resistance, Wu Song brought his blade down, just the once, slashing down across the man's face and chopping right through the chair. Only as Wu Song turned and raised the sword again did General Zhang start to move his feet. But as he did so Wu Song's sword caught him, slashing from the ear to the neck and he crashed to the floor.

So these two lay there, nearer to death than life. But Captain Zhang was after all a military man of no mean ability, so although drunk he still had some fight left in him. Having seen the other two cut down, and not rating his own chances of getting away,

Chapter 31 169

he picked up a folding chair and moved in. But Wu Song was ready and checked the attack. Then he brought all his strength to bear. It matters little that Captain Zhang was drunk, even if he'd been stone-cold sober he'd never have matched Wu Song's phenomenal strength. He lost his balance and toppled backwards. Wu Song was onto him and cut off his head with one blow.

Now Jiang the Door-God was a pretty tough customer. He had just managed to struggle to his feet again. But Wu Song lifted his left foot and felled him again with a flying kick. He held him down and cut off his head. Turning, he cut off General Zhang's head as well. Seeing that there was meat and wine on the table, he now picked up a wine jar and drained it at a single draught. After three or four more he went to one of the bodies and cut off a piece of cloth. He dipped this in the blood and went and wrote in big characters on the whitewashed wall these words: "The tiger-killer, Wu Song, did this." He then took the drinking vessels and stamped them flat, stuffing several inside his shirt front. Before he could leave he heard the general's lady shouting: "The gentlemen upstairs are all drunk. You two, run up and assist them!"

She had hardly finished speaking when two men could be heard coming upstairs. Wu Song slipped to the side of the landing. When they appeared he saw it was two of the household servants who had previously been involved in his capture. Standing in the shadows he let them go by and then barred the door. Inside the room they immediately saw the three corpses lying in a pool of blood. They stared at each other in horror, unable to utter a sound — you know the feeling, when your scalp seems to split into eight pieces, or some one pours a bucket of iced water over you! They were about to retreat, but Wu Song had crept up behind them. His sword arm rose and fell, and one was cut down. The other knelt on the floor and begged for mercy. "It's no good, I can't let you off," Wu Song said. He held him and chopped off his head. From all this killing the pavilion was swimming in blood, bodies could be seen lying everywhere in the flickering light of the candles. Wu Song said to himself: "It had to be all or nothing; kill a hundred, you can only die for it once." Sword at the ready, he went downstairs.

"What's all the hullabaloo upstairs?" the General's wife was inquiring as Wu Song rushed in. At this monstrous sight she shrieked: "Who are you?"

But Wu Song's sword was already flying. It caught her square in the forehead and she fell with a shriek right there in front of the pavilion. Wu Song held her down but when he tried to cut off her head the sword wouldn't cut. Baffled, he saw by the light of the moon that the blade was completely blunted. "So that's why I couldn't get her head off," he thought.

He slipped out of the back door to get his halberd again and threw away the blunt sword. Then he turned and went back to the tower. A lamp could be seen approaching. It turned out to be the singing girl, Yulan, the one he'd had the trouble with before. She was accompanied by two children. When the light of her lamp fell on the General's wife where she lay dead on the floor, Yulan screamed: "Merciful heaven!" Wu Song raised his halberd and ran her through the heart. He also killed the children, a single thrust to each. He went to the central hall, bolted the main door and returned. He found two or three more young girls and stabbed them to death too. "Now at last," he said, "my heart is eased. Now it's time to stop." He threw away the scabbard, picked up his halberd, went out of the side-door, took from his shirt front the drinking vessels he had squashed and put them in the sack he had left in the stable, tying it on at his waist. And off he strode, halberd in hand. Reaching the city wall, he thought: "If I wait for the gates to open I'll be caught. Surely the best thing to do is to climb the wall now, while it's still dark, and clear off." So he leapt up onto the wall.

This Mengzhou was only a small place and the wall was of packed earth and not too high. Peering down from the parapet, he felt around with his halberd, holding it with the point reversed. Then he vaulted down, leaning his weight on the halberd. Steadying himself with the shaft, he landed beside the moat. The water gleamed in the moonlight, but it was not more than one or two feet deep. It was real October weather and everywhere the springs were dry. Standing by the moat he took off his shoes, leggings and knee guards, hitched up his clothing and waded across to the other bank. Then he remembered that in the package the Young Master had given him there was a pair of hemp sandals with eight eyelets. He took them out and put them on. As he heard the drum beat for half-past one in the morning, he told himself that finally his rage had been fully appeased. "Well," he said to himself now: " 'Tis fine to stay in Liang hall, but in the end its comforts pall'. I'd better beat it!" Halberd in hand, he took an eastward path.

As the poem says:

To wield the sword was his only intention,
But he also finds some drink on the way.
One against many, he kills his opponents;
A murderous heart makes the murderers pay.
So many angry ghosts to detain him,
What hope can he have of getting away?

That night he went on walking till after five. The sky was still dark, day had not yet dawned. It had been a hard night and Wu Song was exhausted. Besides, the wounds from his beating were hurting again and he simply couldn't take any more. When he saw a little old temple, surrounded by trees, he entered it at once, dropped his halberd, took off the pack to use as a pillow and flung himself down to sleep.

He had only just closed his eyes when two hooks were thrust into the temple from outside, pinning him to the ground, while two men charged inside and quickly subdued him, tying him up with a rope. The four villains now began to discuss him: "This bugger's good and fat. The boss'll be real pleased with 'im!"

Struggle as he might, Wu Song could not escape. They picked up his pack and his halberd and hauled him off to the village, like a sheep to market, harrying him along so fast that his feet barely touched the ground. All the way they were discussing him among themselves. "Did you see? The bugger's all covered in blood, what's 'e been up to? D' you suppose we've caught a thief?"

Wu Song kept quiet and listened. They'd not gone more than a mile or so when they came to a thatched hut. They pushed Wu

Song inside. Through a doorway on one side a lamp was burning. They stripped off his clothes and tied him to a pillar.

When he looked around, Wu Song saw hanging from a beam beside the stove two human legs. "I've fallen into the hands of a bunch of real cutthroats," he thought to himself. "Now I'm going to die uselessly. If I'd known this was going to happen, I might just as well have gone to Mengzhou and turned myself in. I'd have died at the hands of the executioner, of course, but at least I'd have left a reputation behind me."

Holding the pack the four who had brought him in cried: "Boss! Mistress! Come and look! We got a lovely piece of goods here!"

There was an answering cry from inside: "Coming! Don't begin yet! I'll come and do the carving myself!" And in less time than it takes to drink a cup of tea, a couple appeared from the back, first a woman, and behind her a big man. They both took a good long look at Wu Song. "Why, if it isn't Uncle!" the woman exclaimed. "'Course it is, it's our old friend," the man said.

And now at last Wu Song realized that these two were none other than the Gardener and the Ogress. The four who had brought him in, much chastened, hurried to undo the rope and return his clothes so that he could get dressed. His head cloth was torn so they gave him a felt hat to put on.

In fact, Zhang the Gardener had quite a number of establishments like the inn at Crossways Rise, that's why Wu Song hadn't recognized his surroundings.

The Gardener now invited Wu Song inside, and after the exchange of courtesies said with a great show of concern: "How did you get like this, my old friend?"

"It's a long story," said Wu Song. "After I left you and went to the Fortress of Peace, I received great favours from the Warden's son, the Young Master, nicknamed the Golden-Eyed Tiger. We hit it off at once and he kept me supplied every day with wonderful food and drink. He had an inn, you know, to the east of the town at Happy Woods, a most profitable place, that was pinched from him in broad daylight by a certain villain known as Jiang the Door-God, a protégé of one Captain Zhang. The Young Master told me all this. Well, I could see it wasn't right. I beat that Jiang the Door-God up one day when I was drunk and got Happy Woods back for the Young Master, who valued me highly after this. Afterwards, this Captain Zhang bribed General Zhang and they hatched a plot. The General invited me to join his staff, but it was all a trap, the purpose being to accomplish Jiang the Door-God's vengeance. The evening of Mid-Autumn Festival, the cry went up that a thief had got in. They decoyed me into the house and meanwhile hid some silver cups in a chest of mine. Then they arrested me and handed me over to the Mengzhou court, accused of theft. I was beaten till I confessed and locked up. The Young Master managed to get in to see me by bribing everyone and I was not ill-treated after that. And then thanks to the rectitude and generosity of the clerk of the court, their plot to destroy me failed. It turned out also that the gaoler, Kang, was a friend of the Young Master's — they did all they could to let me off lightly. I was sentenced to a flogging and banishment to the prison camp at Enzhou.

"Yesterday evening when I was being taken out of town, would you believe it? — that General Zhang produced another plot. He got Jiang the Door-God to send two of his people to collaborate with the police guards in killing me. They made their move when we got to Flying Clouds Quay, a lonely spot. But I got in two kicks first and dumped the two henchmen in the water. Then I got those bloody guards, each with a halberd thrust, killing them and chucking them in the water. I reckoned I had to work off my anger, so I returned to Mengzhou. At half-past eight, after entering the stables and killing a groom, I scaled the wall and killed two maids in the kitchen. In the Ducks and Drakes Tower I killed General Zhang, Captain Zhang and Jiang the Door-God, and afterwards two attendants. I went downstairs again and dealt with the General's wife and daughters and the singer. I left at once, by jumping down from the city wall. After a mile or two I was exhausted and my wounds were hurting, I could go no further. So I went into a little temple intending to rest a while. That's when I was tied up by these four."

Wu Song's four assailants now flung themselves on the floor

Chapter 31

and said: "We works for Mr. Zhang, we does. We bin losin' a lot at the tables, see, so we went to try an' make a bit in the woods. We seed you a-comin' down the path, all drippin' with blood, like. An' then you lays down on the ground inside the temple. We 'adn't got no idea 'oo you was. But Mr. Zhang tell us only to take 'em alive, see, so we just used the 'ooks to pin you down. If 'e 'adn't give us that order, like as not we'd've done you in. Honest, we couldn't see what was starin' us in the face. We treated you 'orrible, sir. 'Ow can you ever pardon us?"

The Gardener and his wife explained happily: "We were worried, see. That's why I've been telling them to bring the goods back alive. 'Course they didn't know what was in my mind." The Gardener turned to the gang: "Listen, you lot: if our friend here hadn't been tired, forget about the four of you; if you'd been forty you still wouldn't have got near him."

In reply to this they knocked their heads on the ground.

"If it's money for gambling you want," Wu Song cried, "I can help you out." He opened his pack and took out a dozen taels of silver for them to divide. When they expressed their gratitude, the Gardener also produced two or three taels and distributed them.

"Well" said the Gardener, "You can't imagine how worried I've been. After you left I was sure you were going to get into some kind of scrape or other. Anyway, I knew you'd be back sooner or later. So I says to this ere lot, 'Every time you get hold of some goods, see that you bring 'em back alive.' You see these idiots, sometimes they can take the slower ones alive, but if someone puts up a fight they just kill him. So now I don't let them take any knives along, only the hooks and some rope. When I heard them calling just now I had some misgivings, I can tell you. I told 'em straight off not to do anything till I'd been and had a look. And who should it be then but our old mate!"

"We heard all about your beating up Jiang the Door-God," the Ogress added, "how you took him apart, even when you were drunk. Everyone said it was amazing! Some of the traders from Happy Woods told us about that, but we didn't hear what happened afterwards. You must be tired though, why not go and have a little sleep? We can talk later."

The Gardener showed Wu Song to his room so he could rest, and then they both went to the kitchen to prepare some very special dishes and wine of the best for entertaining Wu Song. Soon this was ready and nothing lacked but for Wu Song to wake up and join them. There's a poem here:

When authority sleeps the long knives awaken,
All's out of kilter when justice is far.
But forget how in palaces evil is rampant
From the rivers and lakes, deliverance is near.

Meanwhile, back in Mengzhou at General Zhang's, it was early morning before all those who had hidden dared come out. Their cries aroused the household servants and the guards on duty outside, who immediately raised the alarm when they viewed the scene. Yet no one emerged from the neighbouring houses. Not until almost full daylight did anyone go to the government office to report the incident. The governor was horrified by what he heard. He hurriedly sent to determine the number of dead and the assassin's point of entry and escape. After making sketches and diagrams the investigators returned and reported: "The murderer entered by way of the stables where he killed the stable boy and discarded two items of old clothing. He then proceeded to the kitchen where he killed two maids beside the stove and abandoned one of the murder weapons by the back door, a blunted knife. In an upper room he killed General Zhang and two of his retinue. Two visitors, Captain Zhang and Jiang, alias the Door-God, were also killed. On the whitewashed wall the murderer wrote in big characters using a rag dipped in blood, "The tiger-killer, Wu Song, did this." The body of the mistress of the house was found downstairs and outside were those of Yulan, her two attendants and three little girls — in all a total of fifteen dead. Six items of silverware were missing."

The governor immediately ordered the gates of Mengzhou closed and commanded officers of the militia and police, together with local authorities in the city and districts, to carry out a thorough search in order to apprehend the criminal Wu Song. The next day police authorities from Flying Clouds Quay arrived to report that four people had been murdered: there were bloodstains under the bridge and four corpses floating in the water. In response to this report the governor sent the sheriff to have the four bodies retrieved and examined. Two were local policemen whose next of kin prepared the bodies for burial and lodged a formal complaint, demanding that the culprit be arrested and sentenced to death. The city gates remained closed for three days while a door-to-door search was carried out; every household, every family, no one escaped questioning. The governor put out an order underlining the responsibility of all local authorities at every level — district and ward, urban and rural — to assist in the search and bring the murderer to justice. A full description of Wu Song was circulated, giving his birthplace, age, physical appearance and bearing, with sketches, and announcing a reward of three thousand in cash. Anyone with knowledge of his whereabouts was to report it immediately and would receive the due reward. Anyone found to be harbouring the criminal or giving him food would be charged as an accomplice and sent up for trial with him.

When Wu Song had been staying at the Gardener's for a few days, it became clear that the situation was far from good. Police were pouring out of the city to search the villages and countryside. In view of this, the Gardener felt obliged to say: "Listen, it's not that I don't want you to stay because I'm worried about my own skin, but this thing's really hotting up. They're knocking on every door. What I'm afraid is that if something was to go wrong, you'd blame us. But I do know of a really safe refuge for you, and I'd tell you about it right away if I thought you were prepared to go there."

"I've been thinking too," said Wu Song. "I can see they aren't going to let the matter rest, so I'll never be really safe here. As for family, I had just the one brother and he was cruelly murdered by my sister-in-law. I came here only recently and fell into a trap. I've no home or family left, so if you do know of a good place for me, I shall go there, why not? You'd better tell me where it is."

"It's in Qingzhou," the Gardener said. "There's this temple there called Temple of the Precious Pearl, on Twin Dragon Peak.

Lu Zhishen, the Flowery Monk and a pal of his called Yang Zhi, the Blue-Faced Beast, have made themselves a stronghold there, a base for pillaging and plundering. The local militia and the anti-bandit brigade daren't so much as look them in the face, you'll be perfectly safe if you go there. Anywhere else they'd catch up with you sooner or later. Those two have often written to me and asked me to join their company and it's only because I'm attached to my own home that I didn't go. I'll write a letter for you to take, telling all about your situation, and I'm sure they'll have you, for my sake."

"You're quite right," said Wu Song. "I've been thinking that too. Only I wasn't sure the time was ripe. But I'm a murderer now, it's an established fact and I've nowhere to hide. It's the best possible plan. Please write the letter and I'll be off today."

So the Gardener penned a full account and gave the letter to Wu Song. They were in the middle of a farewell dinner when the Ogress pointed a finger at her husband and said: "You can't let him go like this, he's going to get himself caught."

"What do you mean? Why should I be caught?" said Wu Song.

"There's police notices everywhere and a reward of three thousand on your head. They've got pictures of you and all your personal details posted up everywhere. And there's the two golden seals on your face, plain for all to see. If you go ahead, it's just a foregone conclusion."

"We can always stick a couple of medicinal plasters on his cheeks," said the Gardener.

"Trust you to come up with something cock-eyed like that," said the Ogress. "How's that supposed to fool the police? I've got a better idea, only I don't know if you'll like it."

"I'm in a tight spot, I can't afford to be fussy," said Wu Song.

"Well, but promise not to get angry if I tell you," said the Ogress.

"Don't worry, I won't," said Wu Song.

"A couple of years back we had one of them travelling monks come through here. We put him down, and he did us for several days' pies. We've still got his metal circlet, a set of clothing, a black cassock, a short coloured silk sash, a certificate, a set of one hundred and eight beads in the shape of human skulls, a shark-skin scabbard with two monk's swords of snow-white patterned steel — you saw those two swords yourself, brother, often at night there's a kind of keening comes from them. Now you're in such trouble your best chance is to cut your hair and become a monk. When we've put the patches on your cheeks to hide the golden seals, this monk's certificate will be all the passport you need. He had just about your age and looks, it's like it was preordained. If you use his name and don't stop, who's going to ask questions? What do you say?"

The Gardener clapped his hands. "She's right! I'd forgotten all about that!"

It was a case of:

The pursuit is hot, he's in a spot,
He's in the tightest corner;
Now it's the best escape he's got,
To become a holy brother!

"Well brother, what do you say?" the Gardener asked.

"It's not a bad idea," said Wu Song, "only I'm afraid I don't look much like a monk."

"Let's try dressing you up," the Gardener said.

The Ogress went and fetched a bundle, from which she took a variety of clothing. They made Wu Song change everything. "It's as if they'd been made for me," said Wu Song, when he saw the things. He put on the black robe, fastened the sash, took off his hat to loosen his hair, then doubled it back and secured it with the circlet, and hung the beads round his neck. The Gardener and the Ogress both applauded the effect. "It must have been ordained in a previous life," they said. When he saw himself in a mirror, Wu Song roared with laughter. "Why are you laughing?" the Gardener asked. "I look so funny, I'm really like a monk," Wu Song replied. "Now cut my hair please."

The Gardener took the scissors and cut Wu Song's hair in front and behind.

Filled now with a sense of urgency, Wu Song packed his bag and was eager to be off at once. But the Gardener said: "Listen brother, I don't want you to think me greedy, but you'd better leave General Zhang's silver drinking vessels here. I'll give you some loose silver for them to use on the journey. It's by far the best way."

"Just as you say brother." Wu Song fetched them out and gave them to the Gardener, who gave him the equivalent in loose silver. He put this away in his purse, tied it and hung it on his belt.

When Wu Song had eaten and drunk his fill, he thanked the Gardener and his wife, hung the two swords on his belt and prepared to leave that evening. The Ogress took out the monk's certificate and stitched a special cover for it, which she made Wu Song wear round his neck, next to the skin. Wu Song thanked them both. Just before he left, the Gardener said: "Be very careful on the journey. You must be moderate in everything. Eat and drink little, don't get into quarrels, and do all the things a monk does. Keep calm always and don't cause scandal. Write and let us know, if you can, when you get to Twin Dragon Peak. We don't expect to remain here long. I wouldn't mind betting we'll soon be packing up too and moving to the mountain to join the band. Look after yourself, brother, and please give my regards to Lu Zhishen and Yang Zhi."

As he marched off, Wu Song put his hands in his sleeves and adopted the mincing gait of a monk. The Gardener and his wife exclaimed in admiration: "He's a perfect monk!" Here's the picture:

> *The hair in front falls in a fringe to the brows, it straggles to his shoulders at the back. The black robe envelopes him like an ominous cloud, the coloured sash binds him about like the mottled python's coils. The metal circlet glitters on his forehead like a fiery eye; the vest reveals the contours of an iron frame. The two swords give off a deadly autumn chill, the rosary of skulls wafts unease about him as he goes. Before him, the man-devouring yakshas bow down perforce, even the fierce door-gods who guard the scriptures needs must lower their gaze.*

After bidding the Gardener and his wife farewell that afternoon and leaving the crossroads of the tree behind him, Pilgrim Wu chose a lonely road. It was November, when the days are short and night falls in the blink of an eyelid. He had barely gone fifteen miles when he came to a steep hill. By the light of the moon he began to climb, step by step. He calculated it must be somewhat after seven o'clock. When he reached the top he looked about him and saw that the moon rising in the east was flooding the landscape with light. At that moment he heard laughter, coming from a clump of trees ahead. "That's odd!" he thought. "Who can be laughing on a lonely moor like this?" He headed for the trees to investigate, and there among a group of pines he found a small family shrine, composed of a dozen or so thatched rooms. In one of these a double-leafed window was flung open and revealed a man holding a woman and gazing at the moon while engaged in lustful dalliance. When Pilgrim Wu saw this, his gorge rose. "This is supposed to be a holy man, living here in the wilderness as a hermit, and look what he gets up to!" he exclaimed, unsheathing the two swords at his waist, which glittered like polished silver.

Gazing on his swords in the moonlight, he said to himself: "The blades are good, but I have yet to set them to work. Let's try them out now." He hung one of the swords on his wrist and returned the other to its scabbard. He drew back the long sleeves of his robe and tied them behind his back. Then he approached the shrine and knocked on the door. The window at the back closed at once. Pilgrim Wu picked up a stone and began hammering on the door with it. Thereupon a side-door burst open and out popped an acolyte. "Who do you think you are?" he scolded. "What do you mean by kicking up such a row in the middle of the night, banging on people's doors like this?"

Pilgrim Wu fixed the lad with a glare and shouted: "This bloody acolyte is meat for my sword!" Almost before he'd finished speaking, the acolyte's head fell, splat! on the ground. Then there was a great roar from within: "Who has the temerity to kill my acolyte?" and out leapt the gentleman who had been seen in the window. Brandishing two double-edged swords, he set upon Wu Song.

Wu Song greeted this with a great shout of laughter: "Only too happy to oblige," he bellowed. "Just what the doctor ordered!"

The Marshes of Mount Liang

With that he drew the second sword from its scabbard and engaged the stranger with both weapons. The battle waged to and fro, back and forth, in the light of the moon, the stranger's double-edged blades glinting frostily, Wu Song's swords filling the air with chilly light.

Long they fought, locked together as if in a lover's embrace. On they went, until the hawk had taken the hare, so to speak. It was after a dozen bouts that a piercing scream rang out over the hillside, and one of the two contestants fell. Then:

A man's head rolls among the cold shadows,
Amid baneful thickets the blood wells out.

Now who was it died, which of the two was it that fell? To learn this you must read the next chapter.

Chapter 32

❦

Wu Song gets drunk and beats Red Star;
The Dandy treats Song Jiang with honour!

When those two had fought a dozen bouts, Wu Song, the false pilgrim, sold the stranger a dummy. He deliberately allowed him to come in with both weapons at once, then dodged aside and, taking careful aim, struck a blow — just one. The stranger's head fell one way and his body slumped on the stone path.

"You there, inside! Young woman! Come out!" Wu Song shouted. "I won't harm you, I only want you to tell me what's going on."

The woman emerged from the hut and prostrated herself.

"No need for ceremony," Wu Song said. "Just tell me, what place is this? What's the relationship between you and that priest?"

Weeping, she replied: "I am the daughter of Squire Zhang who lived at the bottom of the hill. This is our family shrine. I don't know where the priest is from. He came to spend a night with us and said he was an expert in magic and *fengshui*. My parents made the mistake of letting him stay at the manor and asked him to come here and inspect the siting of our shrine. He took them in completely and they allowed him to stay on. Then one day he saw me and after that he refused to leave. Within a few months he brought about the death of both my parents, and my family, and forced me to live here with him. The acolyte was kidnapped also. This place is called Centipede Hill. The priest decided the *fengshui* was good here, so he started calling himself 'Taoist Wang, the Flying Centipede'."

"Don't you have any other relatives?" Wu Song asked.

"A few, but they're just farmers. They wouldn't dare argue with him."

"Does he have any valuables?"

"He collected two or three hundred taels of silver."

"Then you'd better go and get it, because I'm going to set fire to the shrine."

"Do you want something to eat and drink, Father?" she asked.

"I wouldn't say no, if there is anything."

"Then please come inside."

"You haven't got someone lying in wait for me in there, have you?"

"I wouldn't dare! I've only got one life!"

Wu Song followed the woman into the building and saw a table beside the window loaded with food and drink. He took a big bowl of wine and polished it off. Then, when the woman had collected up all the valuables, he started a fire inside. The woman offered the bundle of gold and silver to him, in return for sparing her life.

"I don't want your stuff," he said. "You'll need that to live on. Go on now, take yourself off!"

She thanked him humbly and set off down the hill. Wu Song dragged the bodies into the fire to cremate them, stuck his swords back in their scabbards and left that same evening, following a winding path across the hills towards Qingzhou.

He travelled for ten days or so, and everywhere he came to, every village, wayside inn, market town or local centre, there were posters advertising Wu Song as "wanted." Despite this, because of his disguise no one questioned him on the road.

It was December and the weather bitterly cold. One day he had bought wine and food for the journey, but fighting the cold was still a problem. He climbed a small hill and saw a high mountain ahead which looked exceedingly steep and dangerous. Descending from his vantage point, he marched on another mile or two till he saw an inn. There was a stream running past the gate and behind the house a wilderness of scattered rocks and broken ground. It was this kind of remote country inn:

> *The door faces a stream, at the back are beds of reeds and water chestnuts; beside the rough perimeter fence plum trees display*

their ivory blossoms; in front of the window pines sway their gnarled green limbs; on the dark tops of tables and chairs, china cups and bowls are ranged. The yellow clay walls are decorated with pictures of tipsy gods and poets; a blue pennant dances in the winter wind; two lines of verse welcome the customers. The mere smell of a place like this makes the horseman yearn to call a halt, the sailor to head for harbour.

So Pilgrim Wu descended from his vantage point and hastening to the inn entered and sat down. "Landlord, bring two measures of wine!" he called. "I'll order food later."

"I'll tell you the honest truth, Reverend. The only wine we've got is some plain country brew, and as for meat, we're right out of it."

"Bring me the wine, then. It'll do to keep the cold out."

The landlord went and got the two measures of wine, which he poured into a large bowl for Wu Song, and gave him also a dish of cooked vegetables as a stopgap. Wu Song finished the wine in a trice and called for more, which the landlord supplied, again in a large bowl. Wu Song concentrated on drinking. He had been half drunk on the way, even before he climbed the hill. Now, with these additional four measures and the effect of the north wind, the wine rose to his head. He began to kick up a row: "Landlord, are you quite sure you haven't got anything else? If not, then please give me something from your own table. Of course I'll pay you for it."

The landlord grinned. "I've never seen a monk like you," he said. "You think of nothing but eating and drinking. But where do you suppose I'd get anything? Not a hope, Father!"

"I wouldn't take your food without paying, why won't you sell it to me?"

"I told you already, I've only got this ordinary wine, what else can I sell you?"

While this discussion was in progress, a tall man walked into the inn, followed by two or three others. Here's how this gent struck Wu Song:

His headdress is the red of a fish's tail, his gown the green of a mallard's head. On his feet he wears a pair of strong boots, about his waist is knotted a length of red cloth. He has a round face and big ears, broad lips and a determined set to his chin. He is well-built and his age is about twenty-five. This young gentleman is proud and heroic in his bearing and not at all given to venery.

When the tall gent and his pals walked into the inn, the landlord greeted them effusively: "Please, sir, please, take a seat."

"Have you done what I ordered?" the newcomer asked.

"The chicken and the meat are all ready," the landlord replied. "We were just waiting for your arrival, sir."

"How about my special bottle of Qinghua wine?"

"It's right here, sir!"

The tall gent took his party to the table opposite and sat down at the head, while his companions seated themselves lower down. The landlord fetched a bottle of special wine, removed the stopper and poured it into a big white jug.

Wu Song was watching all this out of the corner of his eye. He could tell it was fine vintage wine from the bouquet wafted towards him on the breeze. When he smelt it, Wu Song's throat really began to feel dry and he found it hard to resist slipping closer to grab some. At this point the landlord went off to the kitchen and returned with a pair of roast chickens and a plate of selected meats which he placed before the newcomer. He added some dishes of vegetables and began to ladle out the wine into cups. When Wu Song compared this with what was in front of him, a miserable plate of boiled vegetables, there was nothing he could do to control his anger. For indeed, the eyes were fed but the stomach stayed empty. The wine he had drunk, too, was having its effect. He crashed his fist down, shattering the table, and shouted: "Landlord, come here! What a cheating bastard you are!"

The landlord remonstrated: "Please calm yourself, Father. If you want more wine, you've only to ask."

Wu Song glared at him and shouted: "You've got no principles, you bastard. All that vintage wine and chicken and meat and stuff, why wouldn't you sell it to me? I offered you good money."

Chapter 32

The landlord said: "The wine, the chicken and the meat are all what the gentleman brought himself, he's only paying for the table."

But Wu Song was still hungry, he wasn't interested in explanations. "Bollocks! Bollocks!" he bellowed.

"I've never seen a monk as wild as you!" the landlord protested.

"What do you bloody well mean by calling me wild?"

"And I never heard a monk using such language!"

This was too much for Wu Song, who leapt to his feet and thrust his five fingers in the landlord's face, dealing him a blow which sent him reeling. The tall man sitting opposite was furious when he saw this. One half of the landlord's face was completely swollen and for a long time he was unable to rise. The stranger jumped up and pointing to Wu Song said: "You bastard, you're certainly not obeying the religious rule, you're far too ready with your fists and feet. I thought a monk was supposed never to give way to his emotions!"

"Okay, so I hit him, what's it to do with you?" Wu Song said.

The man said angrily: "For your own good, I'm warning you, priest. Keep a civil tongue in your head!"

This so enraged Wu Song that he overturned the table. "Who the hell do you think you're talking to!" he bellowed.

"You lousy beggar," the other answered, undismayed. "Are you looking for a fight? That's really tempting fate, you know!" Then, pointing his finger at Wu Song, he went on: "Come outside then, priest, and let me teach you a lesson!"

"Do you think I'm scared? Do you really think I won't hit you?" Wu Song shouted, and took up a position near the door. The other man slipped through the door and Wu Song followed him. But when the man saw how big and strong Wu Song was, he opted for discretion and took up a defensive stance. Wu Song charged straight in, blocking his opponent's defensive blow. The other was thinking to repel him by main force, but he reckoned without Wu Song's massive strength. With a jerk Wu Song grappled him to his chest, then with a twist he had him over, as easily as someone up-ending a little child. The man did not get in a single blow or kick. When his companions saw this, their hands shook and their legs went limp, no one dared to intervene. With one foot on the man's chest, Wu Song raised his fist and let it fall. After twenty or thirty blows he dragged the man to his feet, and threw him into the stream in front of the door. There was now a great uproar from the man's companions; chaos reigned. Finally they went down to the stream and fished their friend out. Supporting him, they disappeared in a southerly direction. The landlord, meanwhile, who had been knocked senseless and half paralysed by the blow, escaped into the back of the house and hid.

"All right," said Wu Song, "since you've all gone, I may as well take some sustenance!" He took a bowl and started ladling out the wine into a cup and set about some serious drinking. The chickens and the meat on the table were still untouched. He didn't bother with chopsticks, but tore off chunks with both hands and wolfed them down. In less than an hour he had eaten most of it. Now full, and not a little drunk, with the sleeves of his robe knotted behind his back, he left the inn and marched off along the bank of the stream. But the north wind tired him and his legs could scarcely carry him, so he veered this way and that along the path. He was scarcely more than a mile from the inn, skirting the side of an earthen wall, when a yellow dog appeared and started barking at him.

So there was Wu Song, with this big yellow dog yapping at his heels. He was very drunk and needed no excuse for a quarrel. This dog that went on barking and barking infuriated him, so he drew the sword from his left-hand scabbard and bounded after it. The dog fled along the bank of the stream, still barking. Wu Song struck out at it, but he struck empty air. He used such wild force that he went head over heels into the stream and couldn't get out.

The winter moon was in the heavens and it was the dry season, but although there were only a few inches of water, it was unbearably cold. When he managed to crawl out, drenched to the skin, he saw his sword lying in the water. He bent down to fish it out and splash! in he fell again! He was still floundering about in the water when on the other bank, beside the perimeter wall, a

Chapter 32

bunch of people appeared. The foremost of them was a tall man with a felt hat, a goose yellow surcoat, carrying a staff, and behind him came a dozen or so fellows with pitchforks and peeled staves. One of these pointed and said: "That there bugger in the stream's the one as hit little brother. Little brother were looking for you just now, but 'e couldn't find you. So 'e went and got up a party of twenty, and they buggered off to the inn to nab 'im. But 'e's turned up here!" He had scarcely finished speaking when the man who had been beaten appeared in the distance. He had changed his clothes and now carried a halberd. There were twenty or thirty retainers with him, complemented by a bunch of lads from the village. Wielding clubs and spears they advanced behind their leader with much shouting and whistling as they searched for Wu Song. When they reached the earthen wall, they saw him. The leader pointed and shouted to the man with the goose yellow robe: "That's him, that's the damned priest who beat me up!"

"Tie him up and take him up to the manor for a good thrashing," said the man in goose yellow.

"Move!" shouted the leader of the other party. His followers obeyed. The wretched Wu Song was too drunk to escape. As he still struggled to climb out he was seized and dragged onto the bank. They took him to a big manor house on the other side of the stream, surrounded by a whitewashed wall, shaded by hanging willows and stately pines and set in a walled compound. They dragged him inside, stripped him naked, took his swords and his bundle, tied him to a big willow tree and sent for a rattan cane to flog him.

They had just applied the first few blows when someone emerged from the manor and asked: "Who's that you're beating there?"

The two gentlemen joined their hands in greeting and said: "Let us tell you what happened, master. We went with two or three friends and neighbours to have a drink at the inn down the road and this damned monk came and picked a fight with us. He beat younger brother up badly and chucked him in the stream. His face was all cut and he could have died of the cold if his friends hadn't rescued him and brought him back. After he'd changed his clothes

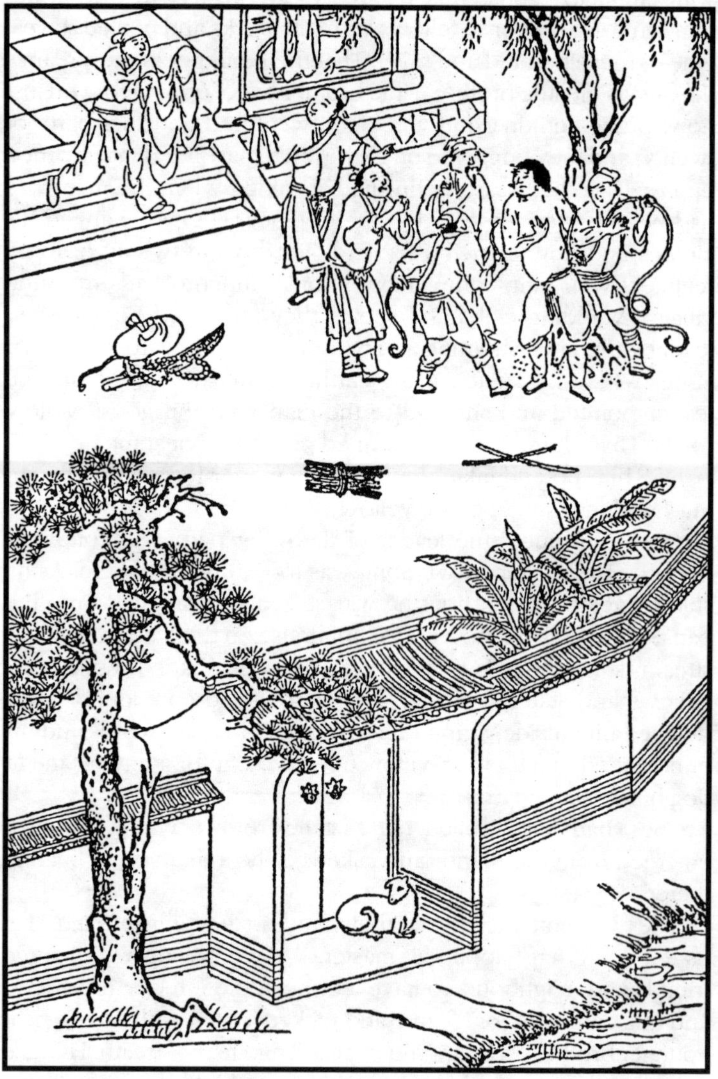

Chapter 32

and got together a party he went to look for the monk. The bastard had finished off our food and wine and got himself drunk and fallen in the stream. So we brought him here to give him a good thrashing. Now you can see he isn't a monk at all; he's got a couple of golden seals on his face, only the crafty bugger had combed his hair down to hide them. He must be an escaped criminal on the run. We're going to get to the bottom of this first and then we'll send him off to the police for them to deal with."

The one who had been beaten interjected: "What's the point of questioning him? The blighter really hurt me. I won't get over it for months. Surely the best thing is to kill him. We can burn the body and then I'll be properly revenged." So saying, he raised the cane and was about to resume the beating. But the other man stopped him: "Don't beat him, brother. Let me have a look at him first. It sounds as if he might be a good fellow."

By this time Wu Song was beginning to sober up. He could hear all right, but he kept his eyes tight closed, and when they beat him he didn't utter a sound. Walking around him, the other man saw the wounds on his back. "Hallo!" he said, "this looks like an official flogging, and the scars are still fresh." He came round to the front of Wu Song, stretched out his hand and lifted the hair to take a good look. Suddenly he exclaimed: "Why, isn't it my old friend, second brother Wu?"

Now Wu Song opened his eyes wide and saw the other. "Well, if it isn't my friend!"

"Quickly, untie him!" the other man shouted. "He's my brother!"

The man in the yellow robe, and the other who'd been beaten, got quite a shock. "How can this monk be your brother, master?" they stammered.

"He's the one I've so often told you about, the one who killed the tiger of Jingyang Pass. He's Wu Song. I didn't know he'd become a pilgrim."

The two brothers hurriedly untied Wu Song and sent for some dry clothes for him. Then they escorted him into the thatched hall. When Wu Song wanted to prostrate himself, the other man, who was obviously overjoyed, raised him up and said: "You still haven't quite got over your hangover, brother. You'd better sit down for a bit and talk."

The pleasure of this meeting did much to sober Wu Song up. Hot water was called for, so he could wash and he was given a pick-me-up. Then he ceremoniously expressed his thanks and they began to chat of old times.

Now this person was none other than that famous native of Yuncheng, Song Jiang the Just.

"I thought you were at Mr. Chai's," Wu Song said. "What are you doing here? Or am I dreaming?"

"After you left Mr. Chai's I stayed there six months. But I didn't know how things were at home, I was afraid my father might be in trouble. First I sent my younger brother, Song Qing, back to see. Later I received a letter from home which said, 'Thanks to the good offices of Sergeants Zhu and Lei, there has been no more trouble with the law. Only you are still "wanted" and there's a general warrant out for your arrest.' The business had in fact calmed down.

"Meanwhile a certain Squire Kong from these parts had been sending for news of me. After my brother returned home and told them I was at Mr. Chai's, Squire Kong sent someone to Mr. Chai's to take me back to his place. This place where we are is called White Tiger Mountain, and this is Squire Kong's estate. That young fellow you had a fight with is the squire's younger son. He's Kong Liang, and because his nature is impetuous and he is always getting into fights, they call him Red Star. The fellow in yellow is the elder son; he goes by the name of Kong Ming, nicknamed Blazing Comet. They're both very keen on fencing, so I've been giving them a few lessons, that's why they call me master. I've been here six months and I'm planning to move on to Windy Fort. I was thinking of setting off in the next few days. I heard all about your exploits when I was at Mr. Chai's, how you killed the tiger on Jingyang Pass and became a captain in Yanggu, and I heard that you'd fought and killed Xi-men Qing. But I don't know where you were banished to or how you became a monk."

"Yes, after I left Mr. Chai's and said goodbye to you," Wu Song explained, "I came to the Jingyang Pass and killed the tiger and had it taken to Yanggu where the governor made me captain. And then my sister-in-law behaved disgracefully — she had an affair with this Xi-men Qing and poisoned my brother. I killed them both and gave myself up to the authorities. At first my case was dealt with in the district, but then it was transferred to Dongping, where Governor Chen came to my rescue and had me banished to Mengzhou." He went on to tell how he ran into the Gardener and his wife, the Ogress, at the crossroads, how in Mengzhou he made the acquaintance of the Young Master and beat up Jiang the Door-God, and later killed General Zhang and fourteen others and escaped to the Gardener's again. He explained why the Ogress advised him to dress as a monk, how he tried out his swords on Centipede Hill, killing Wang, the Taoist and how he got drunk at the village inn and beat up the younger Kong. All his affairs, from beginning to end, he recounted to Song Jiang. The two Kong brothers listened spellbound. When he finished, they humbly prostrated themselves. Wu Song hurriedly returned the compliment, saying: "My behaviour was disgraceful, forgive me, please forgive me!"

The two brothers said: "We couldn't see what was staring us in the face! It's all our fault."

"Since you're so kind," said Wu Song, "might I ask you to have my certificate dried and the letter and my luggage and clothes. And I wouldn't want to lose those two swords or the beads."

"Don't worry about all that," the brothers said. "We've already sent someone to fetch your things and it will all be restored to you."

Wu Song thanked them. Then Song Jiang invited Squire Kong to come and meet Wu Song. Squire Kong ordered wine and arranged a banquet. Of this no more.

That evening Song Jiang invited Wu Song to share his room and they talked far into the night about the things which had happened during the past year or more, and Song Jiang received much pleasure from it. Wu Song was up at dawn next day. After washing and rinsing his mouth he went and breakfasted in the main hall. Kong Ming kept him company. Kong Liang, or Red Star, though still sore from the beating, also helped entertain him. Their father, Squire Kong, ordered goats and horses killed and arranged a banquet. During the day some neighbours and relatives from the village came and visited. There were also some retainers who came to pay their respects, to Wu Song's great satisfaction. After the banquet, Song Jiang asked Wu Song: "Where are you planning to go after this?"

"As I told you last night," Wu Song said, "the Gardener has written me a letter so I can go to the Temple of the Precious Pearl on Twin Dragon Peak, where Lu Zhishen, the Flowery Monk has joined a band. The Gardener intends to go to the mountain himself later on."

"That's good," said Song Jiang. "To tell you the truth, I had a letter from home recently in which they said that the commander of Windy Fort, Colonel Hua Rong, 'the Archer,' keeps writing and asking me to go and stay with him, ever since he heard about my killing Yan Poxi. We're not far from Windy Fort here, and for several days I've been thinking of going. The only reason I haven't started yet is the weather looked uncertain. Sooner or later I'll go, so why don't we go together?"

"I'm afraid it might not bring you luck if you took me along." Wu Song said. "You see, my crime is very serious, it won't easily be forgiven. That's why I think that to go to Twin Dragon Peak and become an outlaw is my only way out. Besides, dressed as a monk I couldn't very well travel with you, it would make people suspicious. And if there was some kind of fracas, you'd be implicated. Anyway, we're friends till death. I just don't think it's a good idea to compromise Colonel Hua's fort, that's all. You'd better let me go to Twin Dragon Peak. If fate favours us and death does not intervene, there may be an amnesty and it will be time enough then for me to come and see you."

"Since you're so faithful to the emperor, heaven will protect you. And as you've obviously made up your mind, I won't try to dissuade you. But do stay and keep me company a few days longer before you go."

So they both stayed another ten days at Squire Kong's on White Tiger Mountain. And when they did finally make up their minds to leave, the squire was most reluctant to let them go. He managed

Chapter 32

to detain them a few more days, but after that Wu Song was determined to get going and Squire Kong had to content himself with organizing a farewell banquet. He entertained them for a whole day, and the following morning a new set of monk's clothing was presented to Wu Song, together with the black robe, the monk's certificate he was supposed to carry, the letter, the circlet for his hair, the set of beads, the swords and some other valuables. And everyone contributed fifty taels of silver for his travelling expenses. He put on the circlet, attached the beads to his belt, strapped on the two swords, packed his bag and tied it to his belt. Likewise Song Jiang took up his halberd, stuck the sword through his belt, and donned his felt hat. They both bade farewell to Squire Kong. The two sons ordered some retainers to carry the luggage and accompanied them for the first five miles or more of the way before saying farewell. Then Song Jiang slung his pack on his back, saying: "There's no need for the servants to come any further. We'll go on now by ourselves." The two Kong brothers said goodbye and returned to the manor. Of them no more.

We now follow Song Jiang and Wu Song as they continue their journey, chatting along the way, marching on till evening and then stopping for the night. Next day they rose early, ate and departed. They travelled ten miles or more after breakfast and came to a place called Dragonsborough, situated at a crossroads. Song Jiang asked the people there: "We want to get to Twin Dragon Peak and Windy Fort, which road should we take?"

"They're both in different directions," was the answer. "If you want to go to Twin Dragon Peak you take this road leading westwards. If you want Windy City, you take the road which heads east, past Windy Mountain."

Song Jiang listened carefully and then said: "Dear brother, we have to part now, so let's drink three farewell cups together first."

Parting is the theme of a poem attributed to *Huan Xisha*:

Parting's hard, when the time comes to shake hands and go. All those shared scenes of mountain and forest draw to a close. Your heart is lonely, your resources are exhausted. When you break your journey grief weighs your spirit down, in the rest house there's nothing to do but sit and twiddle your thumbs. *The long evening passes in solitary contemplation, slowly, oh so slowly.*

Pilgrim Wu said: "I'll go with you a little way and then turn back."

"There's no need," said Song Jiang. "As the saying is, 'You can go with your friend a hundred miles, but in the end you still must part.' Remember you've got a long way to go yourself. Try to get there as soon as possible. Once you've joined the company, be moderate in your drinking. If there's an amnesty, you can try to persuade Lu Zhishen and Yang Zhi to give themselves up. Maybe you'll be sent to serve on the frontier, win yourself a good name with your sword and be able to establish a family. That way you'll know you haven't lived in vain. I myself have but little talent and although people can trust me, I shall never be successful. But you are such a great hero, you will certainly perform great and memorable deeds. Please do not despise my words. We shall meet again one day, I hope."

After these words they drank a few more cups, then paid the bill. When they left they walked together till the edge of the town, and at the crossroads Wu Song prostrated himself four times. Song Jiang was sentimental from the wine and was most loath to say goodbye. Again he said to Wu Song: "Dear brother, do not forget what I said. Be moderate in your drinking. And look after yourself! Do look after yourself!"

Pilgrim Wu Song now took the road to the west. For the reader's information, he went straight to Twin Dragon Peak and joined up with Lu Zhishen and Yang Zhi. We shall leave him there.

Song Jiang meanwhile after saying goodbye to his friend turned east and set his course for Windy Mountain. He missed Wu Song. After a few days' travel he saw Windy Mountain, looming in the distance. Here's what it was like:

On all sides jagged ridges; dangerous peaks all around. Gnarled and ancient pines harbour eagle's nests; from forked branches of old trees dangle twisted vines. Waterfalls that hang in the air produce a cold blast that gives you goose pimples; amid the play of

Chapter 32

green shadows light dazzles the eye producing fearful visions. The sound of water carries from deep channels, the woodcutter's axe rings out; crowded peaks rear up, mountain birds call; herds of tailed deer leap through the thorns; packs of foxes howl as they roam in search of prey. This has to be either a monk's place of retreat, or a robber's lair.

Song Jiang saw that mountain looming before him. It was a wonderful sight, all covered in thick forest, a delight to the eye. Feeling he could never have enough of looking at this scenery, he continued on for several stages without thought of finding somewhere to stay the night. When he realized that it was getting late he began to be worried. "If it was summer, I could spend the night anywhere in the woods," he thought. "But unfortunately it's the middle of winter. It's wild weather and the nights are bitterly cold, I'd never survive. Besides, suppose I should meet some dangerous wild animal, how could I defend myself? Most probably I would lose my life." So he took a little path to the east. After walking about two hours, he was so preoccupied that he failed to notice a rope stretched across the path close to the ground and it tripped him. A bell rang out through the forest and four or five men who were waiting in ambush leapt out shouting and overpowered him. They took his halberd and pack and after lighting torches they dragged him off up the mountain. All Song Jiang could do was lament his fate. Soon he was a captive in the mountain fortress.

When he looked around him by the light of the torches, he found he was surrounded by a wooden palisade. In the middle was a thatched hall. Three chairs with tiger-skin covers were placed on a dais and beyond there were over a hundred thatched huts. His captors took Song Jiang, trussed up like a festival dumpling, and tied him to one of the main pillars. Some soldiers who were in the hall said: "The chief is still sleeping, don't go and tell him now. Wait till he's slept off his wine, then you can invite him. We'll cut out this big idiot's heart and liver to make the chief a pick-me-up soup, and we can all have some fresh meat."

Bound to his pillar, Song Jiang was thinking to himself: "My God, what a fate! and all because I killed a strumpet! How my whole life is changed into bitterness! Who would have thought my mortal span was destined to finish here!" He saw the soldiers lighting many lanterns and candles. His whole body was numb with cold, he hadn't the least freedom to move; all he could do was gaze helplessly around him, lower his head and sigh.

About eleven to twelve o'clock some soldiers appeared from behind the hall and shouted: "The chief's getting up!" They turned the lights up higher in the hall. Watching out of the corner of his eye, Song Jiang saw this chief enter. His hair was bound in an oval bun and covered with a red silk turban, he wore a robe of burgundy cloth. He seated himself on the middle one of the three chairs with tiger-skin covers. Here's what he looked like:

Round-eyed, with brown hair and whiskers quite sandy;
His stature's heroic, his spirit the same.
In rivers and lakes they call him the Dandy.
Although in reality Yan's his true name.

This stalwart was a native of Laizhou in Shandong and his name was Yan Shun. He was nicknamed the Dandy. He had once been a dealer in livestock, until he lost his capital and was obliged to take to the greenwood and turn robber. So having awoken from his drunken sleep, the Dandy took the middle one of the three chairs and said: "Where did you get this great ox from, boys?"

"We were just setting up an ambush behind the mountain when we heard the bell go off among the trees," they replied. "It was this poor idiot, marching all alone with a pack on his back. He'd blundered into the trip-rope. So we thought we'd bring him here, chief, to make you a pick-me-up."

"Excellent," said the Dandy. "Quickly then, go and tell the other chiefs to join me."

A moment later two men were seen approaching the hall one from each side. The one on the left was little more than five feet tall, but he had piercing eyes. If you'd like to know more about his appearance, here you are:

Chapter 32

> *Dressed in a robe of blue patterned silk,*
> *Haughty of mien but in nature most coarse.*
> *Covetous, lustful, strong as an oak,*
> *Wang is his name but he's known as Short-Arse.*

This gentleman was from the Huai Valley and his name was Wang Ying. Because he was so small the rivers and lakes fraternity had dubbed him "Short-Arse." He had once been a carter, but seeing so many riches on the road gave him ideas and he robbed a merchant, got sentenced for it, escaped from prison and took refuge on Windy Mountain. He and the Dandy had taken over the mountain as a base for robbery.

The man on the right was exceptionally pale and clear complexioned. He had a moustache and a little pointed beard. He was a fine figure of a man, tall and slender, with broad shoulders. He wore a red turban. Want to know what he was like? Here you are then:

> *A robe of pure gold and dark glossy green,*
> *A supple wolf's waist, girded so tightly.*
> *Though as fearsome a robber as ever was seen,*
> *He's known to the others as Gentleman Whitey.*

He was from Suzhou and his name was Zheng Tianshou. Because of his pale complexion people called him "Whitey." He had been a silversmith, but from childhood was addicted to fencing with spear and staff, and drifted into the rivers and lakes way of life. Happening to pass Windy Mountain, he ran into Short-Arse, and the two of them fought half a dozen evenly poised bouts. The Dandy, seeing the newcomer was talented, invited him to join them on the mountain, so Whitey took the third chair.

When the three chiefs were seated, Short-Arse said: "Come on now, lads, give us a real good pick-me-up! Let's have this great Ox's heart and liver out double-quick! We'll have 'em in a sweet and sour soup."

One of the soldiers brought a big brass basin full of water and placed it in front of Song Jiang, while another soldier rolled up his sleeves and brandished a sharp knife, of the kind specially adapted to scooping out hearts. The man with the water plunged both hands in and splashed water on the area around Song Jiang's heart — a person's heart, you understand, is a region where the blood is hot; cold water disperses the hot blood, so that when you take the heart and liver out it's particularly crisp and delicious. When the soldier also sprinkled water on Song Jiang's face, the latter heaved a sigh and said: "O wretched Song Jiang, your life must end here!"

The moment the Dandy, with his own ears, heard those two words, he shouted to the soldier to stop splashing the water: "What's that he said about 'Song Jiang'?" he asked.

"He said 'O wretched Song Jiang, your life must end here'," replied the soldier.

The Dandy rose to his feet and said: "You there, do you know Song Jiang?"

"I *am* Song Jiang," came the reply.

"Which Song Jiang are you?" said the Dandy, approaching closer.

"I am Registrar Song Jiang of Yuncheng in Jizhou."

"You don't mean to say you are Song Jiang of Shandong, the Opportune Rain, the one who killed Yan Poxi and fled to the rivers and lakes?"

"You know all about that then? Yes, I am he."

Appalled, the Dandy seized the soldier's knife and cut the bonds. Then he tore off his own burgundy robe and wrapped it around Song Jiang. He placed him on the middle one of the tiger-skin chairs and ordered Short-Arse and Whitey at once to get down on their knees. All three knocked their heads on the ground. Song Jiang slipped off the chair to return the compliment. "Why are you honouring me like this, instead of killing me? What does it mean?" he asked, bowing to the ground.

The three chiefs remained kneeling there together. "I would like to take that knife and gouge my own eyes out, for failing to recognize a great man," the Dandy said. "If I hadn't been and looked for myself, and made these inquiries, we could easily have finished off a righteous man. I thank my stars that you were impelled to speak out your own name, for how else would I have

Chapter 32

learnt the truth? I have frequented the rivers and lakes and roamed the greenwood for many a year now, and I know well your reputation for bravery and generosity, for helping the needy and supporting the oppressed; but it had never been my fortune to meet you face to face. Today heaven has ordained our meeting and my dearest wish is fulfilled."

Song Jiang replied: "What poor talent can I lay claim to, that you should so overestimate my worth?"

"It is well known how you respect men of honour and receive heroes, you are renowned throughout the known world. Who does not honour you? How the stronghold in the Marshes of Mount Liang has prospered in recent times everybody knows, and people say it is all due to your efforts. What I would like to know, however, is why are you alone and what brings you here?"

One after another, Song Jiang told them about the rescue of Chao Gai, the killing of Yan Poxi, the sojourn with Mr. Chai and Squire Kong and how he was now heading for Windy Fort to find Colonel Hua, the Archer — to the manifest delight of the three chiefs. Afterwards they had clothes brought for him and then goats and horses were slaughtered and they feasted until dawn. At the end of the evening soldiers were called to help Song Jiang to bed.

They were up betimes and Song Jiang recounted more of his adventures on the road, and when he told of the prowess of Wu Song, they stamped their feet and lamented: "Just our luck! If only he'd come to us, how splendid that would be! Why did he have to go there?"

But enough of all this. Suffice it to say that Song Jiang stayed about a week on Windy Mountain and every day he was entertained with drinking and feasting.

It was now well into the last lunar month and in Shandong it's the custom to visit graves on the twenty-fifth. Some of the robbers came up from the foot of the mountain and reported: "There's a sedan chair coming along the main road, with an escort of half a dozen soldiers, and they're carrying two boxes, looks like they're heading for a grave site to burn paper money."

Now Short-Arse was a great lady's man. When he heard this

report, he assumed the sedan chair must be carrying a lady, so he mobilized thirty or forty troops and prepared to set off down the mountain. There was nothing Song Jiang or the Dandy could do to dissuade him. Off they went, brandishing pikes and beating a gong. Song Jiang, the Dandy and Whitey went on with their drinking.

When Short-Arse had been gone four or five hours, one of the scouts returned and reported: "The soldiers ran off before Chief Wang got to them. The sedan chair was taken, with a lady inside. There was only a silver incense burner, nothing else of value."

"Where have they taken the lady?" the Dandy asked.

"Chief Wang has taken her to the hut on the mountain," the man replied.

The Dandy laughed. But Song Jiang said: "I suppose our friend Wang Ying has designs on her, but that's not the behaviour of a gentleman."

"Our friend has difficulty in controlling himself, it's his one big failing," said the Dandy.

"Then let's all three of us go and reason with him," said Song Jiang.

So the others took Song Jiang to Short-Arse's place on the mountain. They pushed open the door and found Short-Arse trying to make love to a woman. When he saw them he thrust the woman away immediately and asked them to sit down.

"Whose wife are you, madam?" Song Jiang asked. "What business causes you to be abroad in such a season?"

Blushing, she took a step forward and offered her humble respects before replying: "I am the wife of the governor of Windy Fort. My mother passed away and this is her anniversary, so I was on my way to burn offerings on her grave. Obviously I would not be travelling if it were not needful. I implore you to spare my life!"

Song Jiang received a shock. "Here I am, on my way to stay with Colonel Hua, and this must be his wife," he said to himself. "Obviously I'm obliged to help her!"

He asked her: "Why didn't your husband, Colonel Hua, accompany you to the grave?"

"I am not Colonel Hua's wife," she replied.

"But you just said you were the wife of the governor of Windy Fort!"

"But you see, recently Windy Fort has been given two governors, a civil one and a military one. Colonel Hua is the military governor. My husband is the civil governor, Governor Liu Gao."

Well, Song Jiang was thinking to himself, if her husband is a colleague of Colonel Hua's and if I don't rescue her, it certainly won't look very good when I arrive there tomorrow. So he turned to Short-Arse and said: "There's something I'd like to say to you, my friend, but I don't know if you're prepared to listen."

"Say whatever you like," said Short-Arse.

"In general, a hero indulging in fornication provokes ridicule. And from what this lady says, she is the wife of an important official. Don't you think, for my sake, and for the sake of chivalry, you might let her go, so she can be reunited with her husband?"

Short-Arse replied: "Listen here, I've never had a woman of my own to be my consort here; besides, it's these high and mighty officials who grab all the women nowadays, why are you so concerned about her husband? Can't you just indulge me in this little thing?"

Song Jiang went down on his knees and said: "If it's a wife you want, I can find you a much better one later. Only this woman is the wife of an official who is my friend's colleague, so please, just let her go!"

The Dandy and Whitey helped Song Jiang up, saying: "Get up, please, this is a simple concession to make!" Song Jiang thanked them profusely.

Seeing Song Jiang was so serious about wanting to rescue the woman, the Dandy didn't wait to hear Short-Arse's wishes, he simply gave the order for the sedan chair bearers to take her away. The woman herself, when she heard this, bowed down before Song Jiang as reverently as someone laying out candles before a shrine, intoning: "Thank you, Great Sir!"

"It's not me you must thank," said Song Jiang. "I'm not the chief here, I'm just a visitor from Yuncheng."

She left at once after expressing her thanks. The two chair bearers, glad to get away with their lives, bore her off down the mountain, flying along as if they were only sorry their parents had endowed them with no more than one pair of legs.

Short-Arse was much out of countenance, but he said nothing. Song Jiang drew him aside into the main hall and tried to console him: "Dear friend, do not be upset. Come what may, I shall find you a wife who will completely satisfy you. I always keep my word."

The other two started laughing. Short-Arse was still angry, but Song Jiang treated him with such ceremony that he could not show his feelings and he joined in the laughter. The feasting now continued on the mountain. Of this no more.

Now when their mistress was snatched, the soldiers from Windy Fort had to return to the fort and report to Governor Liu that the bandits from Windy Mountain had taken their mistress. Governor Liu was furious when he heard this, and swore at them for their incompetence and for abandoning their mistress. He beat them ferociously. "But there's only a few of us," they protested, "how could we stand up against thirty or forty of them?"

"Shut up!" he shouted. "If you don't go and get her back I'll have you thrown into dungeons and tortured!"

Well, there was no escape for them, nothing for it but to enlist seventy or eighty troops from the fort and set off with spears and staves to do their best to rescue her. To their surprise, when they were half way there they met the two bearers racing down the mountain with their mistress. "How did you escape?" they asked.

"The blighters carried me off to their mountain stronghold," she replied. "But when they heard I was Governor Liu's wife, they were so scared they quickly paid their respects and told the bearers to take me back."

The soldiers said: "Please have pity on us and tell the Governor we rescued you, to save us from punishment."

"That story suits me all right," she said.

The soldiers prostrated themselves in gratitude and then closely surrounding the chair they set off. When they saw how fast the bearers went, the soldiers said: "In the city you two generally carry the chair at a snail's pace. How come you can go so fast now?"

"Actually we're exhausted," the bearers said, "but these blows on the back keep driving us on."

"Are you seeing ghosts or something? There isn't anyone behind you!"

Only then did they dare turn round and look. "Aiyo!" they exclaimed. "We were running so fast we must have been kicking ourselves on the back of the head!" This provoked general laughter.

Pressing round the chair they all arrived at the fort. Governor Liu was delighted. "Who rescued you?" he asked his wife.

"When those blighters kidnapped me I resisted their advances so they were going to kill me. But when I said I was the governor's wife they didn't dare, in fact they couldn't wait to pay their respects. Then these fellows came and delivered me by force."

When Governor Liu heard this he ordered a dozen bottles of wine and a pig to be brought as a reward for the soldiers. Of this no more.

As for Song Jiang, after saving the lady he stayed another week at the mountain stronghold, but then he wanted to go and find Colonel Hua and began to say his farewells. Since they could not persuade him to stay, the three chiefs laid on a little farewell celebration, and each gave him some money, which he wrapped in his bundle. The day he was leaving he rose early and washed and rinsed his mouth, breakfasted, packed his things, said goodbye and set off down the mountain. The three chiefs, bringing wine, nuts and food, accompanied him more than five miles in the direction of the main road. They all drank before the final parting. Still reluctant to see him go, they said: "Brother, on your return from Windy Fort, you have to come and see us again at the stronghold."

Song Jiang, luggage on his back and halberd in hand, simply said: "We're sure to meet again." Then he saluted and left them.

Now, had yours truly been present at that time, I'd have taken him by the shoulder or grasped him round the waist, forcibly to restrain him. For just because he insisted on going to stay with Colonel Hua, Song Jiang all but met with an untimely death and no decent burial! But indeed,

*Troubles are sent by Heaven to try us,
Who can predict life's ups and downs?*

Whom Song Jiang met when he went to find Colonel Hua, you must read the next chapter to find out.

Chapter 33

Song Jiang goes to see the lights;
Hua Rong with his colleague fights!

Now Windy Mountain was no great distance from Qingzhou, a mere thirty miles or so in fact. And Windy Fort was situated at a main crossroads in Qingzhou district, at the place called Windy City. Windy Fort had been established here at Windy City for the very reason that this crossroads connected three dangerous mountain regions. It contained a garrison of three or four thousand, and was just one stage away by road from Windy Mountain.

On the day in question the three chiefs returned to their stronghold on the mountain, while Song Jiang went on alone. With the pack on his back, he made his way to Windy City. On arrival there he asked one of the inhabitants where he could find Colonel Hua.

"The garrison headquarters is right here in the town," the man answered. "There's a compound on the south which is the residence of the civil chief, Mr. Liu. Colonel Hua's residence is in the compound to the north."

Song Jiang thanked his informant and directed his steps northward. The guards at the main gate asked his name and went inside to report. Immediately a young officer rushed out, pulled Song Jiang to one side and prostrated himself. Here's what he looked like:

White teeth, red lips, bold eyes, strongly drawn eyebrows, the waist narrow but the shoulders broad as an ape's. He knows how to manage a mettlesome steed or skilfully launch a hawk. He can split the willow twig at a hundred paces and the strength of his arm is wondrous to behold; he bends the bow round as the autumn moon and his feathered shaft scatters the winter stars. The Archer they call him; this scion of great leaders is actually Hua Rong.

The young officer who appeared was indeed none other than Colonel Hua, the military commander of Windy Fort. After his most respectful greeting, Colonel Hua ordered his men to take Song Jiang's luggage, halberd and sword and escort him into the main hall. Here, after inviting Song Jiang to take a comfortable seat, he prostrated himself again four times, before rising and saying: "It's, let me see, nearly six years now since we parted and I've thought of you many a time. I heard that you killed a harlot, there are notices up everywhere demanding your arrest. When I learnt you were in such trouble I felt as if I was sitting on a mat full of pins. I wrote many times to your home to ask about you, I don't know if you got the letters. But now at last heaven has rewarded me, it is my great good fortune to have you come here. This meeting makes me happy for life." He prostrated himself yet again.

Song Jiang raised him up, saying: "Please brother, this courtesy is excessive. Be seated, I beg of you, and let me tell you my story."

Colonel Hua sat down opposite, and Song Jiang recounted the killing of Yan Poxi, the sojourn with Mr. Chai, the meeting with Wu Song at Squire Kong's, his capture by the Windy Mountain band and meeting with the Dandy ... and so on. He left nothing out. Afterwards Colonel Hua said: "To think that you've been through so much! I'm so glad you've come here now. You can stay with me a year or two, we'll have plenty of time to decide what to do later."

"If my younger brother had not written urging me to go to Squire Kong's, it was always my intention to come and spend a little time with you," said Song Jiang.

Next Colonel Hua invited Song Jiang to sit in the inner hall while his wife came and paid her respects, followed by his younger sister. Then he sent him off to change his clothes, including his shoes and stockings, and bathe in scented water, while a feast was being prepared in the inner hall.

At the banquet that day, Song Jiang gave Colonel Hua a full account of how he had rescued Governor Liu's wife. Colonel Hua scowled when he heard this and said: "That was a mistake. What did you go and rescue the woman for? What an opportunity to shut her mouth!"

"How strange!" Song Jiang said. "I heard she was the wife of the governor of Windy Fort. It was for the sake of your colleague I insisted on her release, that's why I refused to listen to the protests of Wang Ying. So what's all this?"

Colonel Hua said: "You don't understand. Don't think I'm boasting, but this Windy Fort is strategically vital for Qingzhou and if I was in sole command you'd never have all these bandits from far and near creating mayhem here. But now I've got this miserable louse over me as civil governor! He's not only a civilian, he's also totally incompetent. Since he took office all the local property owners have been swindled and the law's been turned upside down, he'll stop at nothing. I'm a soldier and deputy governor, and every day that fool does something to drive me crazy. I could kill him, the dirty bastard! Why the hell did you rescue his wife? That woman is evil, I tell you, she drives her husband on to every kind of shamelessness, ruining good men, indulging in bribery and corruption ... the cow deserves to be humiliated! Yes, you should never have rescued the bitch!"

Song Jiang rebuked him for this tirade: "Brother, you're wrong there. Remember the old saying, 'Resentment should be purged, not fed.' You and he are colleagues, even if he has some faults, you should ignore the failings and see the good side. You really shouldn't be so prejudiced!"

Colonel Hua relented: "I'm sure you know best, brother. Next time I see Mr. Liu at the office I'll tell him how you rescued his lady."

"I expected no less of your generosity, brother."

Colonel Hua and his family continued to ply Song Jiang with food and drink from dawn to dusk. In the evening a bed was set up for him in a room off the inner hall. Next day the feasting went on. But we will not bore you with any more of this.

For the next week or so Song Jiang continued to enjoy Colonel

Hua's hospitality in the fort. Colonel Hua had in his employ a number of personal aides. One of these gentlemen, in turn, was given each day an amount of money for incidental expenses and charged with taking Song Jiang around to witness the activity on the streets of Windy City, to see the beauty spots, the palaces, monasteries and temples, and to visit places of entertainment. From now on one of these aides always accompanied Song Jiang, keeping him entertained with visits to the town.

It goes without saying that in Windy City there were quite a few brothels, teahouses and wineshops. One day, after Song Jiang and his companion had spent a little time in one of the pleasure houses and been to see some temples and monasteries on the outskirts, Taoist and Buddhist, the aide suggested a drink at one of the wineshops in town. When they were leaving, the aide took out money to pay. But Song Jiang refused to let him and paid with his own money, and when he returned he did not tell Colonel Hua about this. Song Jiang's drinking companion of course was delighted: he'd saved his money and he'd also had a very good time. A different companion was allotted to take Song Jiang out each day and every time it was Song Jiang who paid. Soon there was no one in the fort who did not love and honour him.

It was almost a month after Song Jiang came to Colonel Hua's. Winter was ending and spring just beginning and the lantern festival was almost upon them. The townsfolk busied themselves discussing the placing of lanterns and making preparations for the festival. A collection was taken up, and in front of the temple of the Lord of Earth a small turtle mountain was constructed — the top was festooned with coloured streamers and hundreds of decorated lanterns. Inside the temple itself all kinds of events were organized. Everyone erected stands in front of their door, all vying to exhibit the most splendid display of lanterns. Every imaginable activity was on offer in the city and although it obviously could not equal the capital it still seemed a very heaven on earth.

Song Jiang was drinking with Colonel Hua in the compound on the day of the lantern festival. The weather was splendid, clear and sunny. In the morning Colonel Hua rode over to the barracks to give instructions for a hundred or so troops to keep order in the town in the evening, assigning a body of men to each of the four gates. Before noon he returned to the fort and invited Song Jiang to have a snack.

"I've heard there are to be illuminations in the town tonight," said Song Jiang. "I'd like to see them."

"I would take you myself," said Colonel Hua, "but unfortunately I'm on duty, so I'm not free to go with you. You'd better go to see the illuminations with some of my people and come back early. When I get home I'll drink a few cups with you to celebrate the festival."

"Splendid!" said Song Jiang.

Soon it was evening and a bright moon was rising in the east. Song Jiang with two or three of Colonel Hua's personal aides strolled along the bank of a stream. When they reached the centre of town they saw the illuminations: on the stands before each house coloured lanterns were hung, painted with many a famous tale. There were lanterns too decorated with paper cut-outs in the likeness of peonies, hibiscus and lotus flowers and in all manner of wondrous shapes. Walking hand in hand our friends came to the turtle mountain. Then they saw:

> *Amid the stones of the mountain two dragons play in water; sunset clouds illume a solitary crane gliding through the sky. Lotus lamps and plum blossom lamps cast pools of coloured light; lamps in the shape of water-lily and hibiscus create a host of dancing colours. Silvery moths vying in brilliance flutter in pairs around perfumed spheres, silvery trees try to outshine each other like patterned banners or jade curtains. Local airs and country rhythms are shouted out under the coloured lanterns; girls of the silk trade stroll and laugh together in the flickering light of the candles. Though it may lack the elegance of fine music, this celebration of nature's bounty has many years of tradition behind it.*

After admiring the turtle mountain, they wandered off towards the south. Another five or six hundred paces brought them to a particularly brilliant display of lights where a small group of people were gathered at the gate of a high walled compound, whence a lot of noise was proceeding. Amid the sound of gongs and fifes, the spectators were applauding. It was a group of masked dancers. Song Jiang was rather short and he couldn't see through the crowd, so his companions, who knew some of the performers, cleared a path through the crowd for him. At this moment some piece of rustic clowning by the dancers made Song Jiang guffaw.

Now it so happened that Governor Liu and his wife with several other ladies were watching within this compound. When the governor's wife heard Song Jiang laughing, she recognized him by the light of the lamps and pointed him out to her husband, saying: "That short dark fellow there, he's one of the blighters who kidnapped me the other day on Windy Mountain."

Governor Liu reacted immediately. He called half a dozen of his attendants and told them to apprehend the dark fellow who was laughing. Song Jiang heard the order and made to leave. But he had hardly passed more than ten houses when they caught up with him, pouncing and carrying him off, as the black hawk seizes a red swallow, or the merciless tiger devours a little lamb. They took him inside the compound, bound him with four ropes, and dumped him in front of the courtroom. His four companions, seeing him arrested, rushed back to inform Colonel Hua.

Governor Liu was waiting in the courtroom and ordered the prisoner to be brought in. They shoved him forward in front of the bench and forced him to his knees. Governor Liu shouted: "You, a brigand from Windy Mountain, how dare you come here brazenly to see the lights? Now you're caught, have you anything to say for yourself?"

Song Jiang replied: "I am a merchant from Yuncheng. My name is Zhang, Third Brother Zhang. I am an old friend of Colonel Hua's. I only arrived a few days ago. I was never a robber on Windy Mountain."

At this point the wife slipped out from behind the screen and shouted: "Who are you expecting to fool, you cheeky devil! Have you forgotten how you wanted me to call you big chief?"

"With respect, madam, you must be mistaken," Song Jiang

Chapter 33

宋江夜看小鰲山

replied. "Don't you remember that I told you then I was a merchant from Yuncheng and was a captive there, not at liberty to leave the mountain?"

Governor Liu said: "If you were a captive, held there by force, how were you able to come and see the lights?"

The woman added: "You liar! When you were up there on the mountain you sat among the leaders as bold as brass and I had to call you chief! What sort of a captive is that?"

"Madam," said Song Jiang, "have you forgotten that it was I who secured your release? Why are you so determined to make me out a bandit?"

The woman was furious. She pointed at Song Jiang and scolded: "The lousy beggar, beating's the only thing he'll understand!"

"Quite so!" said the Governor, and called for split canes to be brought.

After two successive floggings, Song Jiang's wounds all opened, his skin split and fresh blood poured out. Then manacles were called for to secure him, and a prison cart, which was to take Third Brother Zhang from Yuncheng next day to the provincial court.

Now his companions had rushed back to inform Colonel Hua, who was devastated when he heard and immediately wrote a letter which he sent with two able members of his staff to Governor Liu's. The guards at the gate went inside and reported that there was a letter from Colonel Hua. Liu Gao ordered the bearers to be admitted and they presented the letter. The Governor broke the seal and opened it:

> Hua Rong respectfully greets his colleague and begs to inform the Governor that his cousin Liu Zhang recently arrived from Jizhou, on going to witness the illuminations, had the misfortune to offend in some way. If the Governor will pardon him, Hua Rong will be eternally grateful. Hua Rong begs the Governor to overlook the inadequacy of his style.

That put the lid on it. Liu Gao tore the letter into little pieces and yelled: "That bastard Colonel Hua doesn't know what's what! He's supposed to be a government official. Yet he's in league with the bandits, and what's more, he's lying to me. The prisoner has already confessed to being Third Brother Zhang, the Yuncheng bandit, how can he be called Liu? Really, it's too much! Does he imagine I'll let him off just because he says his name is Liu, the same as mine?"

He told the guards to throw the bearers of the letter out. Unceremoniously ejected, they returned to the fort in great haste and told Colonel Hua what had happened. "My poor friend!" Colonel Hua exclaimed. "Bring my horse!" He donned his best uniform, slung his bow over his shoulder, grasped his spear and galloped off to Governor Liu's residence, accompanied by thirty or forty men all fully armed. When the guards saw him they dared not stand in his way. His expression was terrible and it struck so much fear into them that they fled in all directions. Colonel Hua charged in and dismounted in front of the courtroom, spear in hand, while his troops deployed. "I wish to speak to Governor Liu!" he bellowed.

Liu Gao heard and was so terrified his spirit fled, his senses scattered. He had a healthy respect for Colonel Hua's martial prowess and had no intention of coming out to meet him. Seeing the Governor would not come out, Colonel Hua waited there a little while, then ordered his men to search the buildings on either side. The search soon revealed Song Jiang in a side-room off the main hall, where he had been hung from a rafter, all trussed up and loaded with padlocks, his legs flayed and bleeding. Some of them freed him, cutting the ropes and smashing the padlocks. Colonel Hua ordered him to be taken home at once. Colonel Hua mounted again and brandishing his spear shouted out as follows: "Governor Liu, you are supposed to be an official, what call have you to insult Hua Rong? Doesn't everyone have relatives? What do you think you're playing at, dragging my cousin into your house and calling him a bandit? What a nerve! You haven't heard the last of this!" At the head of his troop he galloped back to the fort, to take care of Song Jiang.

Now when Governor Liu realized that Colonel Hua had freed the prisoner, he immediately detailed several hundred men to go to Colonel Hua's and seize him again. Amongst these men were

花榮大鬧清風寨

Chapter 33

two new instructors. Although they were relatively skilled with arms, they could not match Colonel Hua's military art, but they did not dare disobey Liu Gao. At the head of their troops, they rushed to Colonel Hua's fort. The guards went in to report this arrival. It was not yet light, and the two hundred or so soldiers remained milling about at the gate. No one wanted to be first to enter since they feared Colonel Hua's prowess.

When it got lighter, it was seen that the gates were wide open, and Colonel Hua was revealed sitting in the courtroom. In his left hand he held a bow, in his right a drawn arrow. As the crowd pressed about the gate, Colonel Hua raised the bow and shouted: "You there, you men, haven't you heard that there's a cause of every wrong, a collector of every debt? Liu Gao sent you here, but do you really want to die for him? You two instructors are not yet familiar with my skill. I'm going to give you a little demonstration with the bow. After that, if you really want to die for Liu Gao, then feel free to just step inside. I am now going to put an arrow through the knob on the end of the weapon of the door-god on the left." He fitted an arrow, bent the bow to its limit and wham! the arrow struck the very middle of the knob on the end of the door-god's weapon. Everyone seeing this trembled. Colonel Hua took a second arrow and cried: "Now everyone watch while I shoot the red tassel on top of the head of the door-god on the right." Another arrow whizzed off and flew straight to its target. The two arrows now stuck quivering in the two leaves of the door. Colonel Hua took a third arrow and shouted: "Now watch my third arrow. This one is destined for the head of the instructor dressed in white!"

With a cry of "Aiya!" this individual turned and fled. The rest followed, amid a tumult of shouts. Colonel Hua ordered the gates closed and retired to the inner hall to see Song Jiang. "I failed you, brother," he said, "allowing you to suffer this injury."

"It's nothing," replied Song Jiang. "But I am afraid that scoundrel Liu Gao won't leave you alone now. We ought to devise a plan of some sort."

"I'd give up this post for the sake of having it out with that louse!"

"Who would have thought that the woman would return hatred for kindness, inciting her husband to give me such a beating! I should have given my true name in the first place. Only I was afraid that the Poxi affair was known, that's why I said I was Third Brother Zhang, a merchant from Yuncheng. Still, it was a bit much of Liu Gao, trying to turn me into Third Brother Zhang the bandit from Yuncheng and send me up to the district court in a prison cart! He got it into his head I was the chief of the Windy Mountain bandits and from then on all the talk was of beating and execution. If you hadn't come to my rescue, nothing I said could have shifted him, I'd never have convinced him, not in a month of Sundays!"

"And my idea, you see, was that since he's a scholar he ought to respect somebody with the same name, that's why I wrote 'Liu Zhang.' It didn't occur to me he could be so lacking in human feelings. But now you're safely here and we'll have plenty of time to decide what to do later."

"I think that's a mistake," said Song Jiang. "Since you rescued me by force the whole affair needs careful thought. Remember the old saying, 'When you eat beware of choking, when you walk watch out for tripping up.' You've openly robbed him of his prize, he immediately sent troops to get me back and you scared them off, I don't see how he can let the matter rest. He'll certainly report you. I'd better leave tonight, then you can repudiate me and it'll just look like the usual difference of opinion between the military and the civil arm. Even supposing he does capture me again, he'll have nothing on you."

Colonel Hua said: "I'm just a soldier, I'm afraid ... I don't have your logic and foresight. Only I'm afraid with your wounds you won't be able to travel."

"That won't stop me," said Song Jiang. "One shouldn't delay in an emergency. I can hold out till I reach the mountain."

That afternoon ointment was applied to Song Jiang's wounds and he ate some food. His luggage he left at Colonel Hua's. At dusk two soldiers escorted him out of the camp. He started his journey that same night. Of this no more.

Meanwhile Liu Gao's men had struggled back to the barracks

Chapter 33

one by one. "Colonel Hua is such a tough nut, no one wants to get within reach of his arrows," they said. "Give him an arrow and he'll shoot you as full of holes as a sieve," the two instructors added. "That's why no one can get near him."

But not for nothing was Liu Gao a scholar. His mind was deep and devious, and he was full of schemes. Here is what he had worked out: "After this incident, I think we can count on Colonel Hua's sending the bandit straight off to Windy Mountain tonight. And tomorrow he'll come to me with excuses. So even if it went to court, it would look like a difference of opinion between the civil arm and the military. That way I'd never be able to get even with him. But tonight I'll send a score of men to set an ambush at the second milestone. If heaven favours me and we catch him, I'll have him quietly locked up here and send someone in secret to the provincial court to request a military escort to come and get him. They can take Colonel Hua in at the same time, and they'll both be finished off together. That way I'll be left in sole command of Windy Fort. I won't have to put up with that fellow's insolence any longer."

That very evening he dispatched a troop of around twenty well-armed men. At approximately nine o'clock they returned with Song Jiang, tightly bound. "Just as I hoped," Liu Gao gloated. "Now take him and lock him up in the inmost court and don't breathe a word to anyone." He made out an official report at once, carefully sealed and marked urgent, and entrusted it to two of his most reliable men to deliver by night to the Qingzhou district court.

Next day, Colonel Hua, assuming Song Jiang had got away to Windy Mountain, sat at home and considered things. "I don't see that there's anything he can do," he said to himself. So he gave the matter no further thought. Liu Gao also kept quiet. Nothing was said on either side.

Now the court was actually in session in Qingzhou. The governor had the double surname of Mu-Rong, and the given name Yanda, and he was an elder brother of one of the concubines of the current emperor, Huizong. Relying on the influence of his sister, he made his own rules in Qingzhou, riding roughshod over the people, intriguing against friends and colleagues and in general doing exactly as he liked. He was just on the point of going home for breakfast when his assistants came in with the urgent letter from Liu Gao. It concerned a case of banditry. What he read shocked him: "Colonel Hua is the son of a high-ranking official," he said. "What's he doing consorting with the bandits of Windy Mountain? It's a most serious crime, certainly not something to be condoned." He summoned the commander of the district militia and ordered him to Windy Fort.

This commander was General Huang Xin. On account of his notable military ability, the people of Qingzhou went in awe of him and referred to him as the Tamer of Three Mountains. For there were in the district of Qingzhou three dangerous mountains: Windy Mountain, Twin Dragon Peak and Mount Peachblossom. These were all areas to which bandits and outlaws resorted, and Huang Xin was always boasting that he would put down the gangs on all three. Hence his nickname, the Tamer. After reporting to the court and receiving the Governor's order, the Tamer chose fifty seasoned troops and equipped himself for battle. That same evening, brandishing his double-edged sword, he set off for Windy Fort. He dismounted in front of Liu Gao's office. Liu Gao received him and took him into the inner hall. After the exchange of courtesies a banquet was organized and the troops were suitably regaled. Afterwards Song Jiang was brought out for the Tamer to see. "No need for questions," said the latter. "Get a prison cart at once and shove the scoundrel inside." A piece of red silk was bound round Song Jiang's head and a paper pennant stuck in it bearing the words, "Third Brother Zhang, the Yuncheng bandit, leader of the Windy Mountain rabble." Song Jiang dared not protest, he was obliged to submit to their will.

"Does Colonel Hua know that you've got Zhang?" the Tamer asked Liu Gao.

"I took him at night, at nine o'clock," Liu Gao replied. "I locked him up secretly here in the residence. Colonel Hua must think he's got away because he's just sitting at home doing nothing."

"In that case it's easy. Tomorrow lay in plentiful supplies for a feast in the main hall of the fort and set an ambush of fifty or so

Chapter 33

men all around it in advance. I will go myself to Colonel Hua's residence and personally invite him to attend. The reason I'll give as follows: 'His Excellency, Governor Mu-Rong has heard that the military and civil authorities are not in accord and has sent me with express orders to arrange a meeting.' Once we've lured him into the hall I shall give the signal by dashing my cup to the floor. Then we go into action and capture him."

The plan was agreed on that night, and early next morning the ambush was set in the rooms on either side of the main hall, while the semblance of a feast was created in the hall itself. The Tamer then mounted and rode to Colonel Hua's residence, taking only a few men with him. When the guard reported, Colonel Hua asked: "Why has he come?"

"The word is that General Huang Xin has some special business with you," the man replied.

This was enough to bring Colonel Hua out to receive him. The Tamer dismounted and Colonel Hua asked him in. After the exchange of formalities, Colonel Hua asked: "May I inquire, General Huang sir, what business brings you here?"

"I have the honour to bear the Governor's commission. He told me that for some unknown reason the civil and military authorities here are not in accord. He fears that your personal animosity may cause you to neglect your public duties. He has sent me to organize a feast so that the two of you may be reconciled. This has already been arranged in the great hall, so I request you to mount and accompany me thither."

"Of course I would not think of intriguing against Liu Gao," said Colonel Hua easily. "He also has an official appointment here. It's just that he is always finding fault with me. But it was far from my intention to upset the Governor. And now I have given you all the trouble of coming here. How can I make amends?"

The Tamer, bending his ear and speaking very softly, said: "The Governor puts his trust in you alone. If there are any military emergencies, Liu Gao is only a civilian, he would be no use for dealing with them. All you need to do is follow my advice."

"I am deeply grateful to you, sir," Colonel Hua said.

The Tamer suggested they leave at once, but Colonel Hua said:

"Please honour me, sir, by accepting some wine before we go."

"Before a conference a cup or two of wine is not a bad idea," the Tamer said.

Finally Colonel Hua called for the horses and they rode together to the main compound where they dismounted and taking Colonel Hua by the hand the Tamer led him into the main hall. Here they found Liu Gao already waiting for them. Now the three were assembled, Liu Gao ordered wine and the servants took Colonel Hua's horse away and closed the main doors. Colonel Hua was completely unsuspecting. Confident in the fact that the Tamer was a soldier, he assumed he could not possibly harbour any ill intentions.

The Tamer, holding a cup of wine, now spoke to Liu Gao as follows: "The Governor has heard that the civil and military authorities do not see eye to eye and he is most concerned. He has sent me here to bring the two of you together. Whatever happens he hopes that the two of you will always put your duty to the Emperor first and act in accord if the need should arise."

Liu Gao said: "Call me a fool if you like. No doubt it's due to my lack of experience as an administrator that I have caused the Governor this distress. In fact there's no real quarrel between us, it's just gossip."

The Tamer smiled approvingly and said: "That's splendid."

Liu Gao drank the wine and the Tamer poured another cup and said to Colonel Hua: "In view of what Mr. Liu has just said, that it is mere idle gossip, nothing more, I would like you to drink this cup."

Colonel Hua took the cup and drank it. Then Liu Gao took another cup and filled it and said to the Tamer: "Please do us the signal honour of drinking." The Tamer took the cup and raised it in his hand and looked very deliberately around him. At this moment a small group of soldiers effected an entry and the Tamer dashed the cup to the floor. Immediately there was a sound of cheering outside and on both sides of the hall forty or fifty hardened troops were revealed. In a moment they had overpowered Colonel Hua. "Tie him up!" the Tamer shouted.

Chapter 33

"But what have I done?" Colonel Hua cried.

"You'd best keep quiet!" said the Tamer with a sneer. "You're a villain and you're in league with the Windy Mountain bandits, traitors to the Emperor one and all, that's what! Because of your former reputation, I've tried to keep it quiet. Lucky for you I haven't brought in all your family."

"Where is your evidence?" Colonel Hua cried.

"I'll give you evidence all right! I'll show to you a true and indubitable villain, you shall know all. Guards, bring him out!"

A moment later a prison cart, complete with paper banner and red inscription, was rolled into the room. In it was Song Jiang! The two men stared at each other, dumbstruck.

"Anyway, it's out of my hands," the Tamer roared, "because the accuser is Liu Gao!"

"But that's nothing, it's nothing," Colonel Hua protested. "This is my relative. He's from Yuncheng. You can't make him out to be a bandit. Take the matter to court and let the court give judgement."

"All right, I shall do just that. I'm sending you up to the district capital for trial. You'll get your judgement there." He told Liu Gao to assemble an escort of a hundred men.

Colonel Hua said: "General Huang, you tricked me into coming here. All right then, you've got me, so send me to the court and let them decide. Only since I'm a soldier like yourself, please allow me to keep my uniform and just send me in a prison cart."

"No problem," said the Tamer. "It shall be as you say. And Liu Gao shall go too to give evidence. He shall not be allowed to harm the prisoners in any way."

The Tamer and Liu Gao mounted their horses and with the two prison carts, surrounded by a thirty or forty man military escort and a hundred guards from the fort, travelled with all dispatch to Qingzhou district court. And this was to have an important result:

In the conflagration a hundred households will burn;
Amid the swords and axes two thousand lives are lost.

And truly it is as they say,

*Trouble's cause is trouble's target, so hold your horses,
Malice seeks who malice uses, so watch your step.*

Of how Song Jiang was taken to Qingzhou and how he finally managed to escape, you can read in the next chapter.

Chapter 34

On the Qingzhou road, the Tamer fights a battle; Thunderclap comes to the field of desolation!

So there was General Huang Xin, the Tamer, on horseback, sword in hand, and Governor Liu riding beside him, dressed in armour and bearing a trident, together with an escort of one hundred and fifty or so seasoned troops armed with tasselled spears or staves, and short swords stuck in their belts. A double roll of the drums, a clash of cymbals, and they were off on their mission to deliver Song Jiang and Colonel Hua to Qingzhou.

They had not travelled much over ten miles from Windy Fort when they were confronted by a forest. They had reached a defile through the mountains, and the guards pointing ahead said: "There are lookouts among the trees," and refused to go on.

"Why have you stopped?" the Tamer asked, looking down from his horse.

"There's men concealed in the forest there, watching," he was told.

"Pay no attention to them, just keep going," the Tamer ordered.

But as they were about to enter the forest, dong! dong! — twenty or thirty big gongs sounded all together. The troops began to panic, they were on the point of fleeing.

"Stop!" the Tamer ordered. "I want you to spread out!" To Governor Liu he shouted: "Guard the prison carts!"

Liu was too terrified to make an answer. "Heaven help us, heaven preserve us!" was all he could get out, together with mumbled promises to pay for a thousand copies of the classics and endow three hundred temples, if only heaven would spare him. Terror had turned him part green and part yellow, like a ripe melon. The Tamer, however, was a real soldier, by no means devoid of courage. He spurred his horse forward to investigate: hundreds of enemy troops were pouring out of the forest on all sides, each one tall and strong, all with fierce expressions and blazing eyes, their heads bound with red cloths, all wearing padded robes, with swords in their belts and long spears in their hands. In no time at all they had surrounded the convoy. Three heroes now leapt out of the forest. One wore black, one green and one red. Each had a head scarf emblazoned with a gold swastika and carried sword and halberd. There they stood, blocking the way. The one in the middle was Yan Shun, the Dandy; Short-Arse Wang was in the lead; and bringing up the rear was Whitey Zheng Tianshou.

They now cried in unison: "Travellers must halt here and pay the toll of three thousand ounces of gold, before they are allowed to proceed."

"You villains!" the Tamer shouted down at them. "This is intolerable! Can't you see the Tamer of Three Mountains is here?"

All three glared at him. "Oh that's who you are, is it?" they said. "But you still have to pay the toll, otherwise you're not allowed to pass."

"I bear the Emperor's commission and I am travelling with a prisoner, what's this nonsense about a toll?"

"Who cares about your Emperor's commission? If you were the Emperor himself riding in state you'd still need the gold. If you haven't got it, you can leave your prisoners here as a gage while you go and fetch it."

"You scum! How dare you!" shouted the enraged Tamer, and ordered the drums to be beaten and the gongs sounded. Then he slapped his horse and brandishing his sword charged the Dandy. Acting as one, the three heroes levelled their halberds and attacked the Tamer. Since all three of them came at him at once, the Tamer needed all his strength and energy just to fight ten bouts. What chance had he of prevailing against the three of them? As for Liu Gao, he was a civilian and he had no thought of joining in. Given the strength of the opposition, his one idea was to flee. The Tamer now began to fear he would be taken, to his eternal dishonour. He was obliged to turn his horse and gallop back the

Chapter 34

way he had come, while the three chiefs pursued him, halberds levelled.

Mindless now of his troops, the Tamer galloped right back into Windy City. When the troops saw the Tamer turn his horse, they let out a great cry, abandoned the prison carts and fled in all directions. Only Liu Gao remained. Seeing the situation had turned so ugly, he frantically pulled his horse's head round and gave it three blows with his whip. The horse broke into a gallop but immediately ran into a trip-wire and came crashing down. The enemy rushed forward and seized Liu Gao. They also captured the prison carts.

Colonel Hua had quickly broken out of his prison cart and snapped his bonds. He then smashed the other cart and rescued Song Jiang. Some of the troops held Liu Gao while others caught his horse and three other horses that had been pulling the carts. They stripped Liu Gao and gave his clothes to Song Jiang, and sent the horses on ahead to the mountain. The three heroes, together with Colonel Hua and the troops, carried the bound and naked Liu Gao back to the mountain retreat.

The way all this came about was like this: the three heroes, in the absence of any news from Song Jiang, had sent some of their men down the mountain to reconnoitre in Windy City, where they heard people saying: "The Tamer threw his cup on the floor as a signal and Colonel Hua and Song Jiang were seized, flung into a prison cart and bundled off to Qingzhou." It was this news that caused the three to muster their troops and march in a flanking movement to block the main road ahead of the party, whilst posting scouts along all secondary routes. By these means they came to rescue our two friends, capture Liu Gao and return with them all to the mountain.

It was evening when they reached the mountain retreat, after nine o'clock. They all went to the assembly hall. Colonel Hua and Song Jiang were asked to join the company and the three hosts feasted them, pressing food and wine upon them most liberally. The Dandy ordered wine for all the troops. Colonel Hua expressed his gratitude to his rescuers: "You have saved our lives and repaired the injustice done to us. Song Jiang and I will never

Chapter 34

be able to repay you for this. One problem remains: I still have my wife and younger sister in Windy City, and the Tamer is sure to seize them. How can we rescue them?"

The Dandy said: "Don't worry, Colonel, I don't imagine the Tamer will dare to touch your wife; if he does, she will probably be brought along this road. Tomorrow we'll go down and get your wife and sister back for you." He sent men down at once to reconnoitre.

"I am deeply obliged to you," said Colonel Hua.

Song Jiang now said: "Bring me that scoundrel, Liu Gao."

"Tie him to the pillar," the Dandy said. "We'll cut out his heart and liver for your gratification."

"I'll do it with my own hands," Colonel Hua said.

"You bastard!" Song Jiang said to Liu Gao. "I never did you any harm or gave you cause to hate me, why did you listen to that bitch's slanders? Now we've got you, what have you to say for yourself?"

"No point in asking," Colonel Hua said, and plunging his knife into Liu Gao's breast ripped out his heart and presented it to Song Jiang. The soldiers cleared away the corpse.

"Well, this piece of filth is dead now," said Song Jiang, "but that bloody wife of his lives on, that's one score still unsettled."

"Don't you worry about that," said Short-Arse. "I'll go and get her myself tomorrow. This time she has to be mine." Everyone laughed.

They went on drinking, and in the end all retired to rest. When they rose next day, they discussed how to attack Windy Fort. The Dandy said: "The men had a tough time yesterday. Today they'd better rest. It'll be time enough if we go tomorrow."

"That's reasonable," said Song Jiang. "Men and horses need rest to regain their strength, there's no point in rushing things."

We shall now leave them to their preparations in the mountain retreat, and join the Tamer. After he galloped back to the barracks in Windy City, he immediately reinforced the guards at the four gates. Then he composed a report and told the two instructors to ride post haste and deliver it to Governor Mu-Rong.

Hearing that urgent news of a military crisis had come, the

Governor went into session at once. This is what he read in the Tamer's report: "Colonel Hua is a traitor, he has joined the Qingzhou bandits. At this moment Windy City is indefensible, the situation is desperate, please send a competent general at once to secure the place." Horrified, the Governor sent for General Qin, divisional commander of Qingzhou, to come at once to discuss the military situation.

This General Qin was a native of Kaizhou beyond the mountains. His given name was Ming, but because of his volatile temper and his raucous voice people called him Thunderclap. He was from a long line of famous warriors, and his weapon was a wolf-tooth mace, which he wielded with irresistible ferocity. On receiving the Governor's summons, he hurried to the government office. Respectful greetings completed, the Governor handed him the Tamer's report and bade him read it.

"Those bandits are getting too confident by far," the General said, "but don't you worry, I'll raise a force immediately and I promise I'll capture the buggers, or else never see you again!"

"If you delay, General," the Governor said, "I'm afraid Windy Fort will fall."

"Who'd think of delaying in a situation like this?" the General said. "I shall raise an army at once and in a few days' time we'll be off."

The grateful Governor ordered wine and food and dry provisions to be taken to the city boundary for the troops.

The news that Hua Rong was a turncoat had enraged General Qin Ming. He mounted his horse and galloped round to his headquarters where he mustered a force of a hundred cavalry and four hundred foot and ordered them to parade outside the city, prior to embarking on the campaign. Meanwhile Governor Mu-Rong had some bread made in a temple garden outside the city; big bowls were also laid out and a quantity of wine warmed. Each man got three bowls of wine, two rolls and a slice of meat. It was all just ready when the troops began marching out of the city. Here they came in their neat ranks:

The banners and pennants dance like flames, the pikes and lances are thick as a field of hemp. Divided into ranks of eight, the column advances like a great snake, sufficient indeed to instil fear in the heart of god or demon. Dark green or fiery red are the tassels on their weapons, embroidered in rich hues the standards that they bear. A tumult of horses' hooves approaching and receding — the whole world seems threatened; to which side will victory belong?

It was still early in the day when General Qin Ming paraded his troops and led them forth from the city in orderly ranks, under a red banner which bore the words "General Qin Ming, commander in chief." Governor Mu-Rong watched Thunderclap riding out in full battle array and indeed it was a glorious sight:

A fluttering flame is the plume on his helm,
His surcoat's the reddest you'll find in the realm;
His linked armour glitters like stars in the sky,
His boots are dark green, like the mountains so high.
An avenging Fury, he straddles his mount,
The flash of his breastplate's like cash beyond count.
His cudgel is cruel but prettily made,
When angry his eyes seem to start from his head;
His character's sudden as thunder in spring,
This is the picture of General Qin Ming.

Well, as Thunderclap rode out from the city, he found Governor Mu-Rong waiting beyond the city wall to reward the troops. He quickly handed his arms to a soldier and dismounted to speak with the Governor. After an exchange of courtesies, the Governor took a cup and spoke some words of encouragement to the General: "Make sure you turn the situation to good advantage and come back quickly, singing a song of victory!"

When the troops had been treated, a signal gun was fired and Thunderclap bade the Governor farewell. He sprang into the saddle, the ranks formed up and at his command, shouldering their weapons, they marched on Windy Fort.

Now Windy Fort lay south-east of Qingzhou, but to go due south, skirting round the side of Windy Mountain, was deemed quicker. Before long they were travelling along a small road just north of the mountain.

Meanwhile in the mountain retreat on Windy Mountain the scouts had made a thorough reconnaissance and returned to make their report. Everyone was ready for their attack on Windy Fort, when the news came in: "Thunderclap is on his way with a big army!" They all stared at each other in horror. But Colonel Hua said: "There's no need for anyone to be afraid. They always say that in an emergency, when the enemy's almost upon you, the best thing is to put up a good fight. Let the troops have as much food and drink as they can take. Now, here's what we must do. First we must fight hard, and secondly we must use our heads. We shall do so ... and so .... What do you say to that?"

"It's a great plan," said Song Jiang. "That's just what I would have recommended." Having laid their plans, Song Jiang and Colonel Hua dismissed the troops so that each could make his own preparations. For himself, Colonel Hua selected a reliable mount, a good set of armour, bow and arrows and an iron spear. All were then ready and waiting.

Meanwhile Thunderclap had been leading his troops towards Windy Mountain and had arrived within two or three miles of it. Here they encamped. They were up at dawn. When they had breakfasted a signal gun was fired and they set off in the direction of Windy Mountain. They chose their route across a wide empty space so that the troops could spread out. When their drums began to beat, immediately in response a shattering crash of gongs sounded on the mountain and enemy troops began to pour forth. Thunderclap reined in his horse, rested his wolf-tooth mace and stared. Colonel Hua was advancing down the mountain, his troops pressing about him. When they reached the bottom, gongs were sounded again and the men formed ranks. Colonel Hua on horseback raised his iron spear and shouted a salute to Thunderclap. The latter merely replied: "Colonel Hua, you come from a family of military men, serving the Emperor. You have been appointed commander of a fort, with a wide jurisdiction. You draw a salary from the government. What cause have you ever had for complaint? Yet now you consort with brigands! You're

Chapter 34

a traitor to the Emperor and I've been sent to arrest you. You'd better dismount and submit to being bound, it will save us all a lot of unpleasantness."

Colonel Hua brushed this aside: "General, be so good as to hear what I have to say. Do you really think I would betray the Emperor? The fault lies entirely with Liu Gao, who with absolutely no justification turned a private vendetta into a public cause, and so persecuted me that I now have no home to go to, no country I can call my own. If I take refuge here, temporarily, it is because I am obliged to. I beseech you to look into the affair and lend me your help."

"Get off your horse and surrender, what are you waiting for?" Thunderclap responded. "Cut the talk, you're just trying to confuse us." With that he called for the drums to be beaten again, whirled his mace about his head, and charged Colonel Hua.

"Thunderclap, you're a fool," Colonel Hua sneered. "Can't you see I was just giving you a chance? I spoke respectfully because you're my commanding officer, don't imagine it was because I'm afraid of you." So saying he levelled his spear and charged Thunderclap.

There under Windy Mountain the two of them fought a desperate battle. Truly it was an irresistible force meeting an immovable object. They really tested each other, those two warriors:

> *A pair of raging tigers from the southern mountains, two green dragons of the northern sea. When a dragon is angry its horns bristle with menace, when the tiger is enraged its teeth and claws are terrible to behold; terrible the teeth and claws, like silver hooks embedded in a fuzzy velvet ball, menacing the horns, like a blur of yellow leaves shaking on a gold tree. The weapons whirl and clash, the steel spear tip never far from its target; the combat surges to and fro, the wolf-tooth mace displaying a thousand tricks. When the wolf-tooth mace strikes down it misses the head by only a hair's breadth. When the steel spear darts towards the heart it stops but half a finger's breadth away. The wielder of the spear affrights the firmament; the owner of the dancing wolf-tooth mace*

rages like lightning rending the clouds. One is the awesome general, upholder of the state, the other is the black star, protector of the nation's boundaries.

Well, they went on fighting and after forty or fifty bouts there was nothing to choose between them. Eventually Colonel Hua dodged aside and turning his horse back towards the mountain vanished along a narrow trail. Thunderclap rode furiously in pursuit. Colonel Hua laid his spear in the rest and reined in his horse. He took the bow in his left hand, selected an arrow and bent the bow into an arc, twisted round and let fly. The arrow, as if to deliver a warning, struck the red tassel off Thunderclap's helmet. This stopped him in his tracks. He recovered quickly and set spurs to his horse, eager to close for the kill. But the enemy troops had all disappeared up the mountain, while Colonel Hua had taken a different path back to the mountain retreat.

When he saw they had all disappeared, Thunderclap was more furious than ever. "These bloody bandits, the nerve of them!" he roared. He ordered drums and gongs to be sounded for an attack up the mountain. The troops advanced cheering, the infantry leading the way. They had negotiated several ridges, when suddenly wood and stone missiles, bottles of lime and molten metal began to rain down on them from the slopes above. The troops in front were unable to pull up in time and fifty or more were killed. The remainder had to beat a retreat.

Thunderclap was a hot-headed man, and a fire had now been lit in his brain that nothing would do to extinguish. After reaching the bottom with his troops, he began looking for another way up. This search continued till midday, when gongs rang out on the western flank of the mountain and a bandit column emerged from the trees and undergrowth. But when Thunderclap charged to encounter them, the gongs ceased and the bandits disappeared. And when Thunderclap looked for the way they had come, there was no proper road there at all, only some woodcutters' paths, and even these were blocked with a tangle of tree trunks and branches and offered no practicable route.

He was just about to order his men to open up a path when

some soldiers arrived and announced: "There's gongs being struck over to the east and an enemy column is advancing there."

Thunderclap marshalled his forces and raced over to the eastern end of the mountain. But when he arrived the gongs were silent and the enemy had disappeared. Thunderclap galloped about in all directions searching for a route, but all he found was a tangled mess of felled trees and branches blocking the paths.

At this point scouts returned and reported: "There's gongs and enemy troops over to the west." Thunderclap slapped his horse and galloped back to the western end of the mountain, but when he got there, no drums, no enemy. Well, as you know, Thunderclap was not a patient man; by now he was grinding his teeth together as if he intended to grind them to powder.

Just then, from where they were on the western side of the mountain, infuriatingly, they heard the gongs sounding with redoubled vigour over on the east. They raced back to the east, but there was not a bandit to be seen. The bandits had all vanished into thin air.

Fuming with anger, Thunderclap was just about to order his men to force a route up the mountain, when shouting was heard over to the west.

Thunderclap's fury knew no bounds. Frantically goading on his troops he raced westwards. They searched high and low, but not a soul did they see! "Look for a way up the mountain!" Thunderclap commanded.

"There's no proper route on this side," one of his men said. "The only real way up's over there on the south-east. If we try and get up this way, we'll get ourselves into serious trouble."

"We'll take the proper road then, and we'll do it right away," said Thunderclap. He chased his men to the south-east.

It was getting dark by now. The troops were worn out with marching. When they reached the bottom of the mountain all they wanted was to make camp and eat. At this point torches were seen moving about high up on the mountainside, and a cacophony of drums and gongs began to sound. All Thunderclap's anger was renewed, and he ordered a detachment of fifty horse into the attack. They were met with a hail of arrows from the tree line above and many of them were hit. Thunderclap had to withdraw. He told the troops now just to concentrate on preparing food. But the fires had hardly been lit when eighty or ninety torches were seen moving down the mountain, amid a shrill sound of whistling. Thunderclap was just about to go after them when suddenly the torches all went out at the same time. Although there was a moon that night, it was masked by clouds and only a glimmer of light filtered through. But Thunderclap was now too angry to sit still, so he ordered his men to light torches and burn the trees down. Just then drums and fifes were heard somewhere up the mountain. Thunderclap galloped towards the sound. Then he saw that on the summit a dozen or more torches had been lit. Up there Colonel Hua and Song Jiang were revealed, drinking together. This vision caused Thunderclap almost to suffocate with rage. He reined in his horse and began to hurl insults at them from below. Colonel Hua shouted back: "General Qin, you shouldn't get so worked up. Go away and rest now; tomorrow we'll engage in a little fight to the death — your death."

"You traitor! Come down here! I'll have three hundred bouts with you right now, and then we'll see!"

Colonel Hua merely laughed. "General Qin, you're too tired. If I beat you now there's no honour in it. Go back and rest and come again tomorrow!"

Still more enraged, Thunderclap continued to shout insults up the mountain, while looking for a way up. But he feared Colonel Hua's arrows so he had to be satisfied with the insults.

At this point a cry went up among his own ranks. Thunderclap hurried down to see what was going on and found that fire arrows and blazing missiles were being hurled down in that quarter. And behind the missiles a company of crossbowmen were causing havoc. Thunderclap's troops, yelling blue murder, rushed to take cover in another part of the mountain where there was a deep ravine.

It was now past midnight. The troops were sheltering from the crossbow bolts, all complaining bitterly, when a great flood came rushing down from the head of the stream, engulfing the men and horses that were gathered there in the river bed. Each man was obliged to fight for his life. Those who managed to climb out onto the bank were immobilized by the enemy with hooked poles and carried as prisoners up the mountain. Those who couldn't crawl out drowned in the flood. Thunderclap's rage was now beyond description, it was as if his brain was melting. But just then he saw a small path leading off on one side. He urged his horse forward up this path. Before he had gone fifty paces, man and horse crashed head over heels into a concealed pit. Fifty men with hooks who were lying in ambush on either side dragged Thunderclap out, stripped him of his armour, uniform, helmet and weapons, and tied him up. Then, having rescued his horse, they transferred him and it to the Windy Mountain retreat.

Now all these tricks, of course, had been thought up by Colonel Hua and Song Jiang. First they had their men draw Thunderclap's forces this way and that, now to the east, now to the west, in order to tire them out, taking care themselves never to remain fixed in one spot. They had dammed up the waters of two streams with sandbags in advance, waiting until nightfall, then forcing the troops into the bed of the stream and releasing the pent-up waters. The resulting flood finished off Thunderclap's army. Thunderclap had brought more than five hundred troops, remember. More than half of these were overwhelmed by the flood and paid with their lives. Those who were captured alive numbered around a hundred and seventy while eighty good horses were seized, not a single one having got away. And on top of all this, Thunderclap himself was caught in the trap.

When the group who had captured Thunderclap returned to the camp it was almost dawn. The five leaders were sitting in the assembly hall. Thunderclap was brought bound before the dais. Colonel Hua immediately leapt to his feet and went to meet him, personally loosening his bonds and helping him up onto the dais, then prostrating himself before him. Thunderclap hurriedly returned the compliment. Then he said: "I am your prisoner. You could beat me to death if you wished. Why do you honour me like this?"

Colonel Hua knelt and said: "Our men didn't respect you, really they were unmannerly. Please forgive us." So saying he took clothes and gave them to Thunderclap to put on.

"That leader of yours, who is he?" Thunderclap asked.

Colonel Hua replied: "That is my friend and brother, the Yuncheng registrar, Song Jiang. And the other three are the chiefs of this stronghold, Yan Shun, Wang Ying and Zheng Tianshou."

Thunderclap said: "I know those three. But this registrar Song, would it by any chance be the person they call the Opportune Rain, Song Jiang the Just from Shandong?"

"That is correct, I am he," said Song Jiang.

Thunderclap hurriedly prostrated himself and said: "I have heard so much about you, I never expected to have the honour of meeting you here today!"

Song Jiang did not fail to return the courtesy at once.

Noticing that Song Jiang had a problem with his leg, Thunderclap asked: "Excuse me for asking, but is there something the matter with your leg?"

Song Jiang accordingly told him his story, from the time he left Yuncheng to the occasion when Governor Liu flogged him to get a confession.

Thunderclap simply nodded and said: "We only heard one side of the story and we got things all wrong. When I get back to headquarters I will put Governor Mu-Rong in the picture."

The Dandy insisted that Thunderclap stay a few days, and to this end slaughtered buffaloes and horses for a big feast. The captured enemy soldiers were all housed at the back of the mountain retreat, and were well supplied with wine and food.

After several cups, Thunderclap rose to his feet and said: "Gentlemen, since you have been so generous as to spare my life, please return to me my helmet and armour, my horse and my weapons, and let me go back to the capital."

The Dandy replied: "General, with respect: you came from Qingzhou with five hundred men and now you've none left. How can you go back? Governor Mu-Rong is bound to hold you responsible. Wouldn't it be better to stay here a while, even if this is a God-forsaken outlaws' retreat? No doubt this place of ours is

Chapter 34

beneath your dignity, but surely it's only sensible to shelter here for a time? Everything we get here is shared between us, clothing comes in whole suits, isn't that better than going back to suffer the insults of the bigwigs?"

Thunderclap stepped down from the dais before giving his reply: "All my life I've served the Emperor, in death I shall serve him too. The court made me a general and appointed me divisional commander. I've never been given any cause for dissatisfaction. How can I become a bandit and betray the Emperor's trust? If you want to kill me, go ahead. But don't expect me ever to join you."

Colonel Hua stepped down from the dais and took him by the arm. "My respected friend, do not be angry. Let me tell you this: I too come from a line of military commanders, but like it or not I've been obliged to take refuge here. Still, if you are unwilling to become an outlaw how could we possibly force you? All we ask is that you sit down for a while till we finish eating, then we'll return your armour, helmet, horse and weapons."

Thunderclap still refused to sit down, so Colonel Hua went on: "General, you've been exhausting your strength and energy for a day and a night, you yourself are almost too tired to stand, how can your horse continue unless he's fully fed?"

When he thought about it, Thunderclap could not but agree. So he went back to the dais and sat down again to eat and drink with them. The five leaders took the cup in turn and toasted him. Thunderclap, being thoroughly tired out and unable to resist the entreaties of all of them, drank himself into a stupor and had to be helped to his bed. After that the others went about their business. Of this no more.

It was already after ten when Thunderclap awoke next morning. He leapt from his bed, performed his ablutions, and was eager to leave. The others tried to persuade him not to go: "Have some breakfast first, General. Afterwards we'll all come and see you off."

But Thunderclap was an impatient man. He couldn't wait to be off down the mountain. So they quickly organized some food and drink, then fetched him his helmet and armour and helped him dress. His horse was brought out and his wolf-tooth mace. Men were sent on with these to wait at the bottom. Then the five of them accompanied him down. When they said goodbye, his horse was brought and his weapons. Thunderclap mounted, took his mace, and taking advantage of the daylight left Windy Mountain. He travelled with all speed and reached the crossroads around noon. Far off in the distance he seemed to see a cloud of smoke and dust, but there was not a single passer-by. Thunderclap had a premonition that something was wrong. When he reached the city walls, where there used to be a hundred dwellings, he found that all had been burnt to the ground and everywhere lay broken tiles and debris, and countless bodies of men and women. Horrified, Thunderclap spurred his horse and cantered across this scene of desolation till he reached the city wall. When he shouted for them to open the gates, the drawbridge remained up. Troops were on the alert, with banners and flags waving and ballista missiles piled up ready. Reining in his horse, Thunderclap again shouted for them to lower the drawbridge and let him in. They had already seen it was Thunderclap. A drum started to beat and a confused hubbub arose.

"I am General Qin," Thunderclap shouted again, "why don't you let me in?"

Governor Mu-Rong now appeared on the battlements and shouted back angrily: "You traitor, do you know no shame? Many ordinary citizens lost their lives and many houses were burnt down when you attacked us yesterday. And now you have the nerve to come here and try to tempt us into opening the gates! What a mistake the Emperor made in giving you responsibility! See how you perform your duty! But I've already sent a report to the Emperor and sooner or later you'll get your desserts, you'll be captured and cut into a thousand pieces!"

Thunderclap was outraged: "Your Honour, yesterday I lost my troops and was taken prisoner by the bandits on the mountain. I've only just managed to get free, how could I possibly have attacked the town?"

"Do you suppose I don't know that horse of yours?" the Governor replied. "And your armour, your weapons, your helmet?

Chapter 34

Everyone in the town clearly saw you inciting the bandits to kill and burn, what's the point in denying it? If you expect me to believe you were defeated and captured, how come not one of the five hundred troops came back to report? Now you've come to persuade us to open the gates so you can fetch your family. Well, we've already executed your wife. If you don't believe me, take a look at her head!"

Some soldiers held up a spear with the head of Thunderclap's wife on the end. Thunderclap was a hot-tempered man, but when he saw the head of his wife, his breath seemed to stop and his heart to shrivel up. Words failed him utterly. All he could do was curse his fate. But now ballista missiles began to rain down on him from the town walls and he was forced to withdraw.

Much of the ground was still covered in flames from fires which had not been put out. He turned his horse and cantered back over the field of debris. At first in his despair he wanted to find a place to die. He considered this for a long time, but then he gave his horse its head and galloped back the way he had come. He had not gone more than three miles when he saw a body of horsemen emerging from the forest, five leaders out in front. They were of course Song Jiang, Colonel Hua and the other three, with a couple of hundred men. Song Jiang inclined and said: "Why aren't you back in Qingzhou, General? Where are you going now, all on your own?"

Thunderclap replied angrily: "Some swine, unfit to inhabit the earth, some accursed villain who deserves to roast in hell, pretended to be me and attacked the city, destroyed people and houses, killed innocent folk and brought about the death of all my family. There'll be no escape for him now, be he in heaven or under the earth. When I find him I shall beat him till I smash this mace into smithereens."

Song Jiang said: "Calm yourself, General. You've no wife now, but don't worry. Allow me to act as a matchmaker for you. I've got something in mind already. Please come with us, it's not easy to tell you about it here. If we go back to the mountain retreat it will be easier to explain. Let us go together now."

There was little alternative but to comply, so Thunderclap

returned with them to the mountain. The journey was uneventful. When they reached the gatehouse they dismounted and entered the camp. Some of the men prepared wine and food in the assembly hall and the five leaders invited Thunderclap in and gave him a place in their midst. Next all five threw themselves on their knees while Thunderclap hastily returned the compliment by kneeling also. Then Song Jiang began: "Please don't be angry with us, General. Yesterday, you remember, we were trying to persuade you to stay, and you were absolutely fixed against it. So I devised a plan. I got one of the men to make himself up like you, wearing your armour and helmet, riding your horse and carrying your mace, and attack Qingzhou, inciting the bandits to kill people. The Dandy and Short-Arse Wang reinforced them with another fifty men, and made it look as if it was you trying to get your family out. This killing and arson was intended to put paid to your idea of going back. But now we must apologize for this."

This account increased Thunderclap's anger, and he sorely wished to challenge Song Jiang and the others. At the same time, he couldn't help thinking: "In the first place, it's probably the fault of my stars, and secondly, they've let me off quite lightly, and then again, I don't know if I could actually handle them. I'd better swallow my anger." So he said: "You may have meant well when you asked me to stay, but you've done me irreparable harm in causing the death of my wife and all my family."

Song Jiang said: "But without this, how would you ever have submitted? Now that you've no wife, I know that Colonel Hua has a younger sister who is very virtuous. I will sponsor the match and provide a dowry and give you a house. What do you say?"

Thunderclap, seeing they all showed him such respect and kindness, resigned himself to going along with them. The company placed Song Jiang in the middle, Thunderclap at the head and Colonel Hua next to him and the other three in the places that befitted them. They drank to the accompaniment of loud music, and all the while discussed how to attack Windy Fort.

Thunderclap said: "Should be easy, no need for you to spend a lot of thought on it. The Tamer is my subordinate. What's more, he was my pupil in martial arts. Anyway, we've always got along fine. I'll go tomorrow and get him to open up for me. Once I'm inside, I'll tell him to surrender and join us. I can marry Hua Rong's sister and we can also take Liu Gao's wife, so you can all have your revenge and wipe the slate clean. I'll make it my joining gift, how about that?"

"That is indeed handsome of you!" said Song Jiang delightedly. "It pleases us immensely!"

When the feast broke up that day they all went to rest. They rose early next day, breakfasted and put on their uniforms. Thunderclap mounted and preceded them down the mountain. Mace in hand, he galloped towards Windy City.

Now when the Tamer had returned to Windy City, he first alerted the military authorities and posted soldiers from the camp to keep a strict watch night and day, reinforcing the guard on all the gates. He decided against making any sortie, but regularly sent out scouts, who reported no sign of reinforcements from Qingzhou. When they came to him and said that Thunderclap was outside the gates, alone, on horseback, asking for the gates to be opened, he mounted and galloped off to see for himself. Having ascertained that the rider was indeed alone, with no escort, he gave orders for the gates to be opened and the drawbridge lowered. He personally met Thunderclap and escorted him in. The latter dismounted in front of the main hall and the Tamer invited him to enter. After the exchange of courtesies, the Tamer asked: "Why have you ridden here all alone, General?"

Thunderclap first told him all about how he had lost his army, and then said: "Song Jiang the Just of Shandong, he whom they call the Opportune Rain, is truly a noble and generous man. All brave men under the sun honour and respect him. When I was on Windy Mountain recently I joined the band. You too are without family attachments, why not listen to my advice and join them too? You won't have to put up with the insolence of civil administrators."

"Since the advice comes from you, how can I not follow it?" the Tamer said. "I had not heard that Song Jiang was on the mountain. When did he arrive?"

Thunderclap laughed. "Remember that prisoner you were escorting the other day, Third Brother Zhang, the Yuncheng bandit? That was he. He was afraid to give his real name, because it might remind people of the sentence against him. That's why he called himself Zhang."

The Tamer stamped his foot. "If I'd known it was Song Jiang I'd have let him escape on the way. I knew nothing about it, I only heard Liu Gao's version. To think I nearly caused his death!"

While Thunderclap and the Tamer were talking in the hall, thinking of setting out shortly, one of the guards entered and announced: "Two columns of troops, with drums and fifes, are marching on the town."

They both leapt on their horses and rode to encounter the enemy. When they reached the town gates, they saw a great cloud of dust, a deathly cloud which obscured the sky:

Two army columns are heading for the town;
Four heroes on the mountain are coming down.

How Thunderclap and the Tamer "encountered the enemy" you will hear in the next chapter.

Chapter 35

Shi Yong delivers a letter at the inn; The Tamer shoots a goose on the wing!

When Thunderclap Qin Ming and Huang Xin, the Tamer of Three Mountains stood at the gates looking out, they saw the two approaching columns were almost upon them. In fact, one column was led by Song Jiang and Colonel Hua, the other by Yan Shun, the Dandy, and Short-Arse Wang. In each there were more than a hundred and fifty men.

The Tamer at once ordered the guards to lower the drawbridge and open the gates, and both columns entered the town. Song Jiang had already issued an order: no citizen was to be touched, no soldier harmed. But the southern barracks was to be reduced and Liu Gao's family all executed.

Short-Arse first seized Liu Gao's wife for himself. The troops then loaded all the property — money, valuables and other goods — onto carts. Buffaloes and sheep were also appropriated in large numbers. Colonel Hua went to his own residence and loaded his valuables and other items onto carts and picked up his wife and younger sister. There were some local servants who were all sent home. When all the leaders had packed their things, a column of men and horses moved out of Windy City and headed for the mountain.

Carts, people and horses having arrived in the camp, Whitey Zheng Tianshou invited everyone to meet in the hall. The Tamer, after he and the others had paid their respects, seated himself one place down from Colonel Hua. Song Jiang gave orders for a residence to be prepared for Colonel Hua's family and Liu Gao's possessions to be divided up equally among the troops.

By now Short-Arse had secreted the woman in his own house. "Where is Liu Gao's wife?" the Dandy asked him.

"This time you've got to let me have her as my slave," replied Short-Arse.

"Have her if you want her," the Dandy said, "but bring her here now because I've got something to say."

"And I want to question her too," said Song Jiang.

When Short-Arse brought her in, the woman wept and pleaded.

"You shameless hussy," Song Jiang shouted. "I rescued you because you were the wife of an official, why did you repay me with lying accusations? You're our prisoner now, what have you got to say for yourself?"

The Dandy sprang forward and said: "What's the good of asking her, the filthy bitch?" With that he drew his sword and with one cut severed her head from her body.

Short-Arse, seeing his woman decapitated, was furious. He snatched up a halberd and was about to attack the Dandy, but Song Jiang and the others intervened.

"Yan Shun was right to kill the woman," Song Jiang said. "Look what happened before, when I told you to free her and let her be reunited with her husband. It didn't stop her turning round and asking her husband to do me in. My friend, if you had kept her by you, sooner or later you'd have come to regret it. Anyway, I'm going to find you a better one, someone who will prove entirely satisfactory."

"That's exactly what was in my mind," said the Dandy. "If I hadn't killed her, it wouldn't have been any good, sooner or later she would have done us serious injury."

They were all trying to talk him round but Short-Arse remained silent. The Dandy told some men to remove the corpse and clear up the blood, and a celebration feast was prepared.

Next day with Song Jiang and the Tamer as sponsors and the Dandy, Short-Arse and Whitey as witnesses, a marriage was arranged between Thunderclap and Colonel Hua's younger sister. The dowry was provided by Song Jiang and the Dandy. There was feasting for four or five days.

About a week after the wedding, a scout got wind of something and came up the mountain to report: "There's a rumour that Governor Mu-Rong of Qingzhou has sent a report up to the Emperor saying that Colonel Hua, Thunderclap and the Tamer are in rebellion. They say a big force is being raised to destroy them and sweep Windy Mountain clean."

The leaders, when they discussed the news, were all agreed: "This place is too small. We can't afford to become too attached to it. If a big force is sent, they've only got to surround us and then what can we do?"

"I've a proposal," said Song Jiang. "But I don't know if it will meet with your approval."

"Let's hear what it is," they all said.

"There's a place to the south of here," Song Jiang said, "called the Marshes of Mount Liang. It's a hundred leagues in circumference. There, in the Place of Many Meanderings and in Duckweed Marsh, Leader Chao Gai has assembled a company of almost five thousand, foot and horse. In their home in the marshes the government troops and anti-banditry forces dare not meet them face to face. Why don't we marshal our men and go to join them?"

"If this place exists it sounds ideal," said Thunderclap. "The only thing is, without an introduction are they likely to receive us?"

Song Jiang responded happily by telling them the story of the birthday convoy and its treasure. He told also of the letter Liu Tang delivered and the gift of gold, and how this led to the death of Yan Poxi and his taking refuge with the outlaws.

Thunderclap was quite excited. "In that case those people owe you a favour," he said. "We should waste no time. Let's pack up and leave at once."

So it was decided. A dozen carts were procured. Onto them were loaded families, valuables, clothing, baggage and other items. The horses, around three hundred of them, were to be taken along. Some of the men did not want to go: they were given silver and told they were free to leave. Those who did want to go were incorporated with Thunderclap's soldiers into an army four or five hundred strong. Before they left, Song Jiang divided them into three columns. They were to pose as government troops sent to subdue Mount Liang.

When these preparations were completed and all the carts loaded, the barracks was razed to the ground. The three columns then set off. Song Jiang and Colonel Hua led off with fifty foot soldiers and fifty cavalrymen, closely guarding six or seven carts and the families. Thunderclap and the Tamer followed with ninety horses and the provision carts. The Dandy, Short-Arse and Whitey brought up the rear with fifty horses and two hundred men. Thus they all left Windy Mountain and took the road for Mount Liang. Anyone who met them on the road could see clearly displayed the banners proclaiming that they were government troops sent to suppress bandits, for which reason no one dared interfere with them. After travelling nearly a week they had put a considerable distance between themselves and Windy Mountain.

Now between Song Jiang and Colonel Hua, riding at the head of the first column, which also incorporated the carts bearing the families, and the last group of men and horses there was a distance of six or seven miles. The leaders had now arrived at the place called Twinhills. Here there are two hills, identical in shape, with a broad stretch of the highroad running between them. As the two leaders proceeded, they heard gongs and drums from the hillside up ahead.

"There must be bandits ahead," said Colonel Hua, stopping suddenly and taking out his bow, which he tested and then put back in its case. Ordering the cavalrymen behind to stop the carts, Song Jiang and Colonel Hua rode forward with a score of horsemen to reconnoitre.

Less than a quarter of a mile further on they came upon a group of horsemen, perhaps a hundred of them, surrounding a young warrior. Here's how this young fellow was dressed:

> On his head a three-cornered cap, with gold badge and jade pin; for dress, an embroidered coat, richly decorated with a bold pattern of flowers; armour like the scales of a fire dragon, a belt fastened with an agate clasp. He rides a charger like a dragon

smeared with red grease and wields a halberd with carved red shaft and squarish blade. Behind him every single one of his followers is clad in red, both coat and armour.

This young stalwart rode with his halberd held athwart. He was shouting in the direction of the mountain: "I want to fight! Today we'll find out who's best, today we'll find the winner!"

Immediately on the other slope a group of horsemen appeared from behind a ridge, over a hundred of them headed by a young man dressed in white. This is what he looked like:

On his head a three-cornered cap with a white jade emblem. For his dress, a suit of fine steel chain mail, covered with a thousand spots of cold frost. His white silk coat outshines the sun and his silver patterned belt rivals the moon. The horse he sits on is a pure white Arab, in his hand he twirls a steel halberd with a silver bound shaft. Behind him every single one of his followers is clad in white, both coat and armour.

This young stalwart also carried a halberd with a square blade and a carved shaft. So on one side it was all plain white banners and on the other all flaming red. Then on each side a flag dipped, one red, the other white, and amid rolling drums and musical flourishes the two riders without a word levelled their lances, spurred their horses and joined battle, each striving for victory. Colonel Hua and Song Jiang reined in their horses to watch. What a ferocious contest it was!

The pennants flutter, garments float in the wind. Like whisps of flying cloud brushing the earth reflecting red shadows, like fires sweeping through the grass in the light reflected from snow. Like in the winter garden the red tea flower vying with the white plum, like in lush spring gardens the pear's powder contending with the peach's rouge. The one turned toward the south and the heat of the sun, like a red stove whose flames lick at the sky. The other oriented to the west and Venus, like Mount Tai dipping its head into the jade well.

The two of them wielding their square halberds fought more

than thirty bouts and victory inclined neither way. Colonel Hua and Song Jiang began to applaud. As Colonel Hua gradually edged his horse forward to see better, he realized that the two contestants were on the brink of a deep ravine.

Now each of the halberds was adorned near the tip with a decorative tassel, one in the form of a leopard's tail, the other a multi-coloured streamer, and in one of their encounters these threads became entangled. Try as they might they could not separate their weapons.

When Colonel Hua saw this he steadied his horse and with his left hand took his bow from its case, whilst with the right he took an arrow from the quiver and fitted it to the string. Stretching the bow to its fullest extent, he aimed carefully at the leopard's tail and the point where the strings were entangled, and loosed the arrow. With just the one shot he cut the entangled strings and immediately the two weapons flew apart. Two hundred men watching exclaimed in admiration.

The two warriors stopped fighting and galloped towards Song Jiang and Colonel Hua. Bowing deeply in salute, they asked: "May we please inquire the archer's name?"

Colonel Hua replied: "This famous fellow is the Yuncheng registrar Song Jiang the Just of Shandong, otherwise known as the Opportune Rain. I am Hua Rong, commander of Windy Fort." When they heard this the two young men stuck their halberds in the ground, dismounted and threw themselves down before Song Jiang and Colonel Hua saying: "These names are known far and wide!" Song Jiang and Colonel Hua also dismounted and raised them up, saying: "Please tell us your names." The one in red said: "My name is Lü Fang. I am from Tanzhou. Because Lü Bu was always my hero I studied the use of the square halberd and everyone calls me the Little Duke. I was selling medicines in Shandong, but I lost my capital and was unable to return home. So for the time being I set up as a robber here at Twinhills. Recently this fellow came along and wanted to seize my hideout. He could have had just one of the hills, but no, that wasn't good enough for him, so every day we come here and fight it out. But what I never dreamt was that I was destined to meet you here today!"

Song Jiang then asked the one in white his name. "I am Guo Sheng," he said, "from Jialing in Xichuan. I was a trader in mercury, but I lost everything in a storm on the Yellow River and couldn't return home. I had learnt the use of the square halberd from Major Zhang in Jialing and because I was pretty handy with it people called me the Halberdier. I heard from the rivers and lakes fraternity that someone who could use the square halberd had occupied this site at Twinhills so I came here to measure my skill against his. We've been fighting for ten days now, but neither of us has had the advantage. But what a surprise to meet you here today! I count it a blessing from heaven!"

Song Jiang now recounted the previous events and then said: "Since we have met, will you allow me to make peace between you" The two consented willingly. As the poem says:

A mere brass chain, to beat apart hard steel,
That's quite a feat.
An arrow tip, to separate two blades,
It's also pretty neat.
But let me tell you this, and don't you doubt it:
The firmness of a hero's mind can split
The toughest metal — there's no two ways about it.

The others had now come up with them and were duly introduced. Lü Fang invited them all to his mountain retreat, where oxen and horses were slaughtered for a feast. The next day it was Guo Sheng's turn to provide the entertainment. Song Jiang suggested they should both enlist and go with the company to Mount Liang to join Chao Gai's band of robbers. The young men were over the moon at this suggestion and agreed at once. When their two forces had been mustered and their possessions collected they were ready to leave at once. But Song Jiang said: "Wait a minute, we shouldn't travel like this. If we all go together to Mount Liang, there's five hundred or so of us and they'll have scouts outwatching on all sides. Suppose they think we really are an anti-bandit force? That wouldn't do at all! Let Yan Shun and me go first and tell them. The rest of you can follow later, still in your three columns."

"You think of everything," Colonel Hua and Thunderclap said admiringly. "That's the best plan. We can start at intervals. You start half a day earlier. We'll marshal our forces and follow."

We shall leave the others at Twinhills, preparing to set out at intervals and we shall go along with Song Jiang and the Dandy, riding off with a dozen men as an advance party to Mount Liang. They rode for two days. Then, having travelled till noon, they found a large winehouse beside the road. Song Jiang said: "The men are all tired, let's stop for some wine before going on." So the two leaders dismounted and went into the shop, telling the men to loosen their saddle girths and follow.

Inside they found that there were only three large tables and a few small ones. One of the large tables was already occupied by one man. He was very tall, and had a sallow complexion and angular cheekbones, lively eyes and a sparse growth of hair on his chin. Song Jiang called the landlord over and said: "We're a large group. The two of us will go and sit inside there, if that's all right. Please ask that customer to move to another table and leave the big one free for our men to have a few drinks."

"I'll arrange it," the landlord said.

Song Jiang and the Dandy went and sat inside and ordered the wine. The men were to have large bowls, three bowls each, and if there was meat they would buy some for everyone, but first pour the wine. The landlord, seeing the group had filled all the seats around the stove, went over to the customer, who looked pretty much like a policeman, and said: "Sorry to trouble you, constable, but would you mind moving to leave this big table for the men belonging to those two officers inside?"

The man took exception to the form of address and protested angrily: "I thought it was supposed to be first come first serve! Who cares about some bloody officers' men? Want to change places, do they? Well, I bloody well won't!"

The Dandy reacted angrily: "Do you hear how rude he is?" he said to Song Jiang. Song Jiang restrained him, saying: "Let him be! Don't stoop to his level."

The man turned his head and gave Song Jiang and the Dandy a very dirty look.

The landlord said anxiously, "Sir, please have a regard for my business. I don't see anything wrong with changing places."

The man began to swear. He struck the table and said: "You bloody so-and-so, you don't know anything, you think because I'm on my own you can browbeat me into changing places. Well I wouldn't bloody move it was for the Emperor himself. If you don't buzz off, you'll get acquainted with my fists!"

The landlord said: "What have I said to upset you?"

"You wouldn't dare say anything to upset me," the man said.

This was all too much for the Dandy, who said: "You're really too big for your boots. If you don't want to change, all right. But just stop throwing your weight around."

The man leapt to his feet, grabbed his staff and answered: "If I choose to tell him off, what's it to do with you? There's only two people in the world I'd listen to, the rest I rate no higher than the mud under my feet."

The Dandy was furious. He picked up a stool and was about to hit the other with it, but Song Jiang, finding something remarkable in the fellow's manner of speech, stepped between them and said soothingly: "There's no need to fight. I'd like to ask you, those two people you'd listen to, who are they?"

"You'll get a shock if I tell you," the other said.

"Tell me their names."

"One is a descendant of Emperor Chai, that's Chai Jin, the Little Whirlwind."

Song Jiang nodded to himself and said: "And who's the other?"

"The other's also a great gentleman. He's the Yuncheng registrar, Song Jiang of Shandong, known as the Opportune Rain."

Song Jiang gave the Dandy a surreptitious smile. But the Dandy had already put the stool down.

"Those two aside," the man went on, "I'm not afraid of anyone, not even the Emperor himself."

"Hold on," said Song Jiang. "Let me ask you another question. Both the gentlemen you mentioned are known to me. Where did you meet them?"

"You know them, do you? Well, I'll tell you no lies. Three years back I stayed more than four months at Mr. Chai's. Only I never met Song Jiang."

"Would you be interested to meet Blackie, then?" Song Jiang asked.

"I'm on my way to find him right now," said the other.

"Who told you to look for him?"

"His younger brother, Song Qing, alias Iron Fan. He gave me a letter for him."

This delighted Song Jiang. He took the other by the arm and said: "'If fate decrees a meeting a thousand miles are nought, if it's not destined you'll miss what's right next door.' I am Song Jiang, whom men call Blackie!"

The man took a good long look and then threw himself down, saying: "Heaven be praised for this meeting. It could all so easily have gone wrong. I'd have gone all the way to Squire Kong's for nothing!"

Song Jiang now took him inside and asked: "Is anything wrong at home?"

"Let me tell you," he said. "My name is Shi Yong and I'm from Daming. I used to run a gaming house and locally I was known as the Guv. But I hit a man at the tables and killed him so I had to run. I took refuge at Mr. Chai's. I was always hearing about you from the rivers and lakes people who came by and I went to Yuncheng to find you, but they told me you'd had to leave. I met your younger brother and when he heard I'd come from Mr. Chai's he told me you were at Squire Kong's estate on White Tiger Mountain. Seeing I was so keen to meet you he gave me a letter to deliver to you at Squire Kong's. He said if I saw you to tell you to go home at once."

This worried Song Jiang. "How long did you stay at my house?" he asked. "Did you see my father?"

"I was only there the one night. I didn't have time to see the Squire before I left."

Song Jiang now told Shi Yong about the plan to go to Mount Liang.

Shi Yong said: "I've been hearing about you all the time from the rivers and lakes fraternity ever since I left Mr. Chai's, about your valour and generosity, how you help the needy and succour the poor. If you're going there to join the outlaws please take me along, you must!" "Certainly I will, one more is nothing. Come now and meet the Dandy." Song Jiang told the landlord to pour three cups. After they'd drunk, Shi Yong pulled the letter out of his pack and gave it to Song Jiang, who noticed at once that the envelope had been sealed upside down and without the customary message "in peace." He became even more worried. He hurriedly tore it open and read. Half-way through he came to these words: *Father became ill at the beginning of February and has now passed away. He is still lying in his coffin at home; we are waiting for you to return home for the funeral. Please, please do not delay! Your grief-stricken brother, Song Qing.*

Song Jiang gave a stricken cry and almost passed out when he read this. His heart was pounding and he began to revile himself in this fashion: "Unfilial, contrary son, how ill you have acted! Your old father is dead and you couldn't act like a human son, you're no better than an animal!" He began to knock his head against the wall and weep loudly. The Dandy and Shi Yong did their best to restrain him. But he went on weeping wildly and it was a long time before he came to his senses. "Don't be so hard on yourself, brother," the other two kept urging.

"Don't think I'm unfeeling or wish to let you down," Song Jiang said to the Dandy. "It's just that I can't help thinking of my father; now he's gone I must hurry back this very night, so you'll just have to go on to Mount Liang by yourselves."

"Brother, since your father is no more, even if you do return home you won't be able to see him," said the Dandy. "Everyone's parents must die, you must try to accept it. Take us there first and afterwards I'll accompany you home to the funeral. That'll be time enough. You know the old saying, 'A headless snake can't walk.' If we go without you it's most unlikely they'll let us stay."

"But I'll lose too much time if I take you there first, I can't accept that. I'll write a detailed letter for you explaining everything. You can take Shi Yong along too, when the rest catch up you can all join them on the mountain together. I didn't know about my father's death until now. But now that heaven has chosen to inform me, a day seems like a year and I'm on fire with impatience. I don't need my horse or any attendants, but I must hasten home this very night." There was nothing the Dandy and Shi Yong could do to persuade him not to leave.

Song Jiang asked the waiter for brush, inkstone and paper, and wrote a letter, in which he repeatedly urged their case, weeping while he wrote. He put the letter in an envelope without sealing it, and handed it to the Dandy. He borrowed Shi Yong's sandals with eight eyelets, stored some silver on his person, buckled on a sword and took Shi Yong's short staff. Refusing to touch food and drink, he wanted to leave at once. The Dandy said: "Why not wait until General Qin and Colonel Hua get here? You can have a word with them first, there'll still be time."

"No, I'm not waiting," said Song Jiang. "You can take my letter, there'll be no problem. Friend Shi, please explain to everyone for me — tell them how unfortunately I have to go home for the funeral and ask them to forgive me." And then wishing he could accomplish the journey in a single stride, he raced off all alone, heading for home.

The Dandy and Shi Yong, having paid for all they had had, including the snacks, set off with the rest of the men, Shi Yong riding Song Jiang's horse. A mile or two further on they found a large hostelry where they decided to spend the night and wait for the others. Next morning about eight, the rest of the company caught up with them. The Dandy and Shi Yong greeted them and explained about Song Jiang's going off to the funeral. The others were critical: "Why on earth didn't you persuade him to stay?"

Shi Yong explained: "When he heard his father had died he even wanted to kill himself, nothing would have made him wait, he simply had to rush home. He wrote this letter for us, explaining everything, and told us to go on without him. He said when they saw this letter there would be no problem."

Colonel Hua and Thunderclap, having read the letter, put the following proposal to everyone: "We're already embarked on this business, to go back is as difficult as to go on. We can't return where we came from, and it would be difficult to disperse. The only thing is to go ahead. Let us seal the letter and go on to Mount Liang and see. If they won't have us, we'll have to think of something else."

The nine leaders, riding together now, with an army of five hundred, gradually drew nearer to the Marshes of Mount Liang and began to look for the way to the mountain stronghold. As they were traversing an area of reedbeds, they heard the sound of gongs and drums wafted towards them over the water. And then suddenly the mountain and the whole countryside were filled with coloured banners, and two fast boats were shooting out from the marshes. The first of these was manned by forty or so troops with the leader seated in the bow: this was Leopard's Head Lin Chong. The second boat carried a slightly smaller number of troops and the leader seated in the bow was Liu Tang, the Red-Haired Devil. Lin Chong in the first boat now shouted out: "You lot, identify yourselves! Under whose orders are you? How can you have the audacity to come here and try to arrest us? Don't you realize you'll be killed, every man jack of you? Don't you know the reputation of our Marshes of Mount Liang?"

Colonel Hua, Thunderclap and the others quickly dismounted. Standing there on the bank they shouted: "We are not government troops. We have a letter from our friend, Song Jiang, and we've come to join your band."

"If you've got a letter from Song Jiang," Lin Chong shouted, "please proceed to the inn of Zhu Gui. We'll need to see the letter first, and then we'll invite you to a meeting."

A green flag was run up on the boat and immediately a smaller boat shot out from the reeds. Aboard it were three fishermen. One of them looked after the boat while the other two stepped ashore and said: "Come with us, all the commanders." One of the two patrol boats now displayed a white flag, some gongs sounded and the two boats sped off.

The group were amazed by all they saw. "What organization!" they exclaimed. "How can government troops take this lot on? Compared with this our little outfit is nothing at all!"

They followed the two fishermen. Making a big circuit they came to the inn of Zhu Gui, the Dry Land Crocodile. When he heard what they had to say, the Crocodile invited them in and introductions were carried out. Then he had two oxen killed and wine and food were distributed. Having examined the letter, he went to the pavilion over the water and fired off the whistling arrow in the direction of the reeds on the opposite bank. A fast boat appeared at once. The Crocodile gave orders to the troops in it to take the letter to the mountain stronghold. At the inn pigs and sheep were slaughtered to feast the nine leaders, and their troops were temporarily quartered round about.

Next day at eight o'clock the military leader of Mount Liang, "Professor" Wu Yong, appeared at the inn to welcome them. They were introduced to him one by one. After the exchange of courtesies and a good many questions, thirty or so empty boats arrived to pick them up. Wu Yong and the Crocodile invited the nine leaders to embark, followed by the families, carts, troops and baggage. All were carried over in the various boats to Golden Sands Landing on the other side. They disembarked and there on the path among the pine trees the leaders of Mount Liang with Chao Gai at their head came ceremonially to receive them amid a thunderous roll of drums. All nine having been presented to Chao Gai, he invited them up the mountain. Riding on horses or in sedan chairs everyone arrived at the assembly hall, where they saluted each other in pairs.

The left-hand row of chairs was now taken by Chao Gai, the Professor, the Taoist Gongsun Sheng, Leopard's Head Lin Chong, Liu Tang the Red-Haired Devil, the Ruans, Du Qian, Song Wan, the Crocodile and Bai Sheng (the Daytime Rat, who had escaped from Jizhou gaol a month or two earlier and joined the others on Mount Liang — the Professor had sent someone to bribe the gaolers so he could escape). Occupying the right hand row were Colonel Hua, Thunderclap, The Tamer, the Dandy, Short-Arse Wang, Whitey, the Little Duke, the Halberdier and Shi Yong. Burning joss-sticks were set between the two rows of chairs and an oath of loyalty was sworn by both sides. There was much blowing of flutes and tapping of drums, and oxen and horses were slaughtered for a grand feast. Meanwhile the new troops were entertained outside the hall by the lesser chiefs. Quarters

Chapter 35

were prepared at the rear of the stronghold for the families. Thunderclap and Colonel Hua spoke at the feast in praise of Song Jiang's many good qualities and told of the revenge killings on Windy Mountain. The leaders of Mount Liang were most impressed. They told also of the halberd contest between the Little Duke and the Halberdier, and of how Colonel Hua's arrow severed the threads and parted the halberds. Chao Gai didn't quite believe this part and was heard muttering to himself: "Hm, can he really be so accurate as he claims? One day we'll set up an archery contest and see."

The drinking went on that day till they were all half drunk and many dishes were consumed. Then the leaders said: "Let us go and walk on the mountain for a while; we'll come back afterwards and continue the feasting."

Everyone assented and they went to stroll on the mountain and enjoy the fine views. They had gone down as far as the third entrance gate when they heard in the sky the honking of some migrating geese. Colonel Hua was thinking to himself: "Chao Gai didn't believe it just now about my shooting the threads. I'd better try and give them a little demonstration of my skill right away. I must show them what I can do so they'll respect me later." His eyes searched the company till he saw someone who was carrying a bow and arrows. He asked for the bow and took it in his hand and examined it. It was a finely crafted weapon with rich decorations and was well suited to his purpose. He took a good arrow and said to Chao Gai: "Perhaps you remember hearing just now how I broke the threads on the halberds — I think you were all a little sceptical. Do you see that flock of geese there, away in the distance? I'm not trying to boast, but with this arrow I will shoot the third in the flock through the head. Only please don't laugh at me if I miss." Fitting the arrow to the string, he stretched the bow to its fullest extent, aimed carefully and loosed the arrow. What they then saw was this:

> *The painted bow is bent into a full moon; the feathered shaft zooms like a shooting star. The hand that draws the bow is strong, the arrow speeds towards its goal. The winging geese prove no*

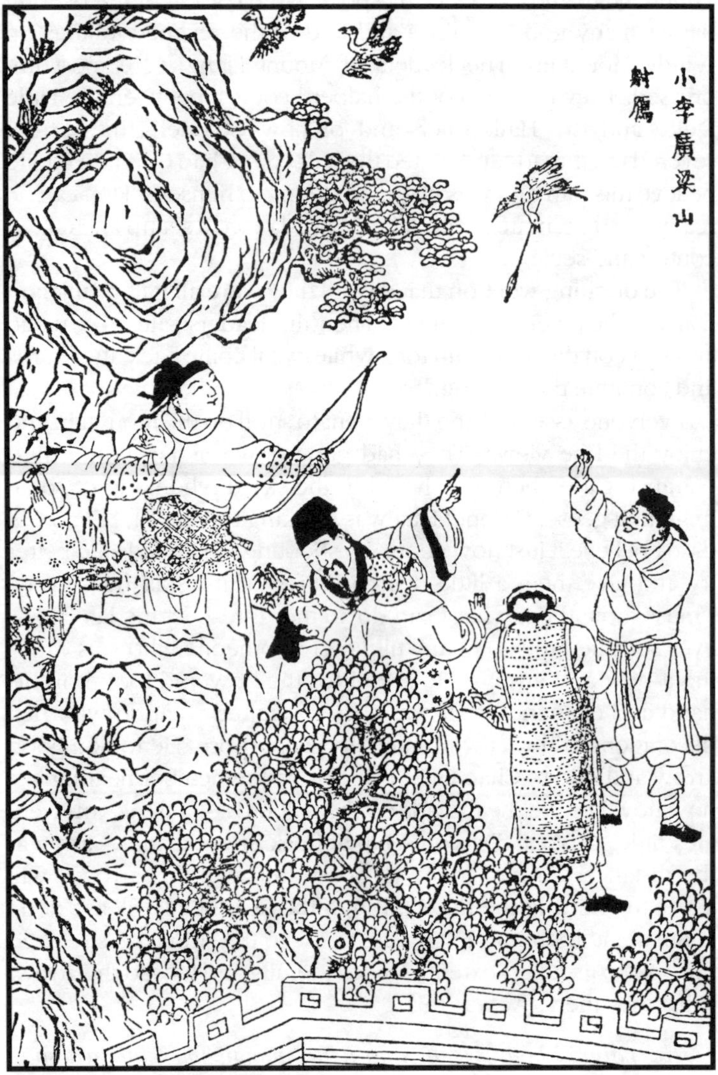
小李廣梁山
射雁

more elusive than a target stretched in the air; the arrow homes in like metal drawn to a magnet. A falling shadow among the clouds, a startled cry amid the grass. The line of geese is sundered in the sky; the company of heroes continues to assemble.

When Colonel Hua shot his arrow, it was of course the third bird in the flock that tumbled from the sky and fell on the hillside. A soldier was sent at once to fetch it. The arrow had transfixed its head! Chao Gai and the others were astounded. They were lavish in their praises of Colonel Hua's archery. The Professor said: "Never mind about Li Guang, the great Yang Youji himself could not have bettered that! Our stronghold is really lucky to get this man!" From then on Colonel Hua was honoured by all and sundry on Mount Liang.

They now returned to feasting in the hall and continued till evening, when everyone went to rest. Next day a further banquet was arranged and each of them was allotted his proper place in the hierarchy. Thunderclap was now seated below Colonel Hua because the latter was his brother-in-law. Colonel Hua was given the place next to Leopard's Head Lin Chong in fifth position, so Thunderclap was sixth, Liu Tang the Red-Haired Devil seventh, the Tamer eighth. Then after the three Ruans came the Dandy, Short-Arse, the Little Duke, the Halberdier, Whitey, Shi Yong, Du Qian, Song Wan, the Crocodile and Bai Sheng: twenty-one leaders in all. When the places had been decided and the welcoming feast concluded, they set about building more big boats, extra accommodation and new carts, laying in provisions, making new weapons, armour and helmets, preparing flags and banners, clothing, crossbows, arrows and so on, so that all was in readiness for repelling the government troops. Of this no more.

Meanwhile Song Jiang, after leaving the wineshop, had been travelling day and night to reach home. At four in the afternoon he was on the outskirts of his village and stopped for a little rest at headman Zhang's inn. This Zhang was an old friend of Song Jiang's family. When he saw Song Jiang's unhappy expression and the tears in his eyes, he said: "You haven't been home for a year and a half, Registrar. Today you ought to be happy! How come you look so sad, is something troubling you? You ought to be pleased about the amnesty, your sentence must at least be reduced."

"That's as may be," said Song Jiang. "But a sentence is not all there is in life. How do you expect me not to be miserable when my old father, my one and only father, is dead?"

Zhang burst out laughing. "You are a one," he said. "Making jokes like that! Why, His Worship the Squire was right here drinking in this place of mine not an hour past. What do you go and say something like that for?"

"Please don't make fun of me," said Song Jiang, taking out the letter and showing it to Zhang. "My younger brother, Song Qing, says quite clearly that our father passed away at the beginning of February this year and he wants me to go home for the funeral."

"What an extraordinary thing!" Zhang exclaimed. "I tell you, he was here drinking in the company of Squire Wang from Eastside, just about noon today. Why would I tell you a lie?"

Song Jiang was beginning to feel very puzzled. He could not make this out at all. He remained plunged in thought for a long time. But as soon as evening came, he bade the innkeeper farewell and hurried towards his home.

When he entered the house, there were no signs of activity. When they saw Song Jiang, the servants all came to pay their respects. "Are my father and brother at home?" he asked them.

"Every day he's had such a craving for the sight of you, sir," they said. "He'll be overjoyed you're here. He just got back from drinking with Squire Wang of Eastside, over at old Zhang's, and he went to his room to sleep."

Song Jiang was greatly moved. He threw down his short staff and entered the thatched hall. Immediately Song Qing rushed up to receive him and prostrated himself. When he saw his brother, who was not dressed in mourning, Song Jiang exploded. Pointing an accusing finger at him, he shouted: "You heartless little monster, what do you mean by it? Father's inside, apparently, why ever did you write that letter to torment me? Two or three times I thought of killing myself. I cried till I was almost out of my mind. How could you be so unnatural!"

Chapter 35

Before his brother could begin to explain, the Squire himself rushed out from behind the screen and said: "Don't be angry, my son. It's nothing to do with your brother. It was because I kept thinking every day how badly I missed you, so I told your brother to write and say I was dead and you must come home quickly. I had heard, too, that there were many robbers on the White Tiger Mountain, and I was afraid they might catch you and persuade you to become an outlaw, a man without honour or respect for his family. That's why I was so anxious to say something that would make you come home. Then Shi Yong turned up from Mr. Chai's and agreed to deliver a letter to you. The whole thing was my idea, it was nothing to do with your brother, so don't blame him. I had just returned from old Zhang's when I heard you'd come home."

After hearing this, Song Jiang pressed his fist to his brow and bowed low before his father, grief and joy mingling in his breast. "Do you happen to know how the case against me stands nowadays?" he asked. "There's been an amnesty so the sentence ought to be reduced. That's what old Zhang was telling me just now."

Squire Song said: "Before Song Qing returned, Sergeants Lei and Zhu were most helpful. There was a general warrant out against you, but no one came to bother me again. Perhaps you wonder why I summoned you home. Well, I heard recently that the Emperor has named his heir and an amnesty has been proclaimed to celebrate it. All criminals throughout the land are to have their sentences reduced by one degree. So even if you were discovered and brought to trial, the most you could get is banishment, it couldn't be the death penalty."

"Do Sergeants Zhu and Lei still come to the house?" Song Jiang asked.

"I heard just the other day," said his brother, "that they've both been transferred. Zhu Tong has been posted to the Eastern Capital, and Lei Heng has gone I don't know where. Recently two new officers, both called Zhao, joined the police department in the provincial capital."

"But you've been travelling my son, you must be tired," said the Squire. "Go to your room now and get some rest."

There was great happiness in the house that night. But of this no more.

Now the sky has darkened, the hour is late. The jade hare is rising in the east. It must be about eight o'clock and all in the manor are sleeping. Suddenly at the front and back doors a great hubbub arises. What is it? On every side there are torches, all around the manor house, and confused shouts of "Don't let Song Jiang get away!" The old Squire ceaselessly curses his fate.

Well, but for this things might have been different. We would not have seen:

On the river bank the heroes all assembled;
In busy streets displays of courage and resolve.

If you want to know how Song Jiang escaped after being arrested at the manor house, you must read the next chapter.

Chapter 36

The Professor speaks of the Magic Messenger; Song Jiang meets the White Water Dragon!

What happened next was that Squire Song set a ladder against the wall and climbed up to see what was going on. A forest of torches revealed a hundred men or more, led by the two new police sergeants from district headquarters. These sergeants were two brothers called Zhao Neng and Zhao De.

The two of them now said: "Squire Song, if you've any sense you'll hand over your son, Song Jiang. We'll take care of him. If you try to prevent his coming to trial, we'll take the lot of you in, yourself included."

"And when is he supposed to have come back?" the Squire asked.

"Quit fooling around!" said Zhao Neng. "There's witnesses saw him come here from old Zhang's, where he'd been drinking. He was followed here. You can't possibly deny it."

Song Jiang, standing beside the ladder, said: "There's no point in arguing with him, father. I'll give myself up, there's no reason not to. I've got friends in the district court, and the provincial court as well. Besides, if there's been an amnesty the sentence will have to be reduced. There's nothing to be gained by talking to these blighters. The Zhaos were always a bad lot. Now these two have managed to wangle themselves a promotion. They've never had any kind feelings towards me. It's a waste of time trying to talk them round."

"But it's all my fault," the Squire wailed.

"Don't worry, father," said Song Jiang. "Maybe it's not such a bad thing if my case comes to trial. Suppose I had gone off to seek refuge among the rivers and lakes, I'd certainly have met up with a bunch of cutthroats and arsonists. Then if I'd been captured, how would I have been able to look you in the eye? As it is, if I'm banished to another province I don't suppose it's forever, one day I shall return. Eventually I shall be there to look after you, father, when you die."

"All right then," the Squire said. "And I shall give a little something to everyone to make sure you get a good place of exile."

So Song Jiang now climbed the ladder and called out: "Stop making such a racket. There's been an amnesty and my crime no longer calls for the death penalty, so wouldn't you two sergeants like to step inside and take a cup of wine or two first? We'll go to the court afterwards."

"Don't try anything on," growled Zhao Neng. "You're not trying to trick us, are you?"

"Do you think I'd want to get my father and brother into trouble?" said Song Jiang. "You're perfectly safe to come in."

Song Jiang descended the ladder and opened the manor gates. He invited the sergeants to sit in the main hall and that night chickens and geese were killed and the wine flowed. The troops and hangers-on were all entertained as well and some silver and other gifts were found for them. The sergeants each received silver ingots amounting to twenty ounces, "for their pains." Indeed this was a case of:

A policeman smells money: he gives you a smile.
No money? Then count on a look full of bile.
That's why they speak of money's good looks,
And say money can laugh at the statute books.

The two sergeants stayed the night at Song Jiang's. Next morning shortly after dawn, they were all ready and waiting outside the courtroom. It had just become light when the magistrate opened the session. The two sergeants brought in the prisoner, Song Jiang. The magistrate, Shi Wenbin, expressed his satisfaction and invited Song Jiang to make a statement. Song Jiang took the brush and wrote as follows:

Unfortunately last year in the autumn having secured the services of Yan Poxi as concubine and finding her to be unsuitable an altercation arose and I accidentally killed her, in a moment of drunkenness. Having previously fled from justice, I now submit myself to the judgment of this court and declare myself willing to accept any punishment without question.

Having read this deposition, the magistrate ordered Song Jiang to be remanded in custody.

Now when they heard Song Jiang had been captured, everyone in the town was sorry for him and went to the government offices to plead for leniency, urging his normal good qualities. The magistrate himself, in his heart, was very much inclined to pardon him. He accepted Song Jiang's deposition and ordered him to be detained but without cangue or fetters, Squire Song bought the goodwill of all and sundry with money and gifts. By this time Mrs. Yan had been dead for six months, so there was no plaintiff. And Third Brother Zhang, the loss of his mistress being already past history, did not see any point in making himself an enemy. The findings were drawn up and after the due sixty days handed over to the court in Jizhou. The governor having reviewed the case and seeing that it fell within the amnesty's terms for clemency ordered twenty strokes of the cane and banishment to Jiangzhou prison camp. The provincial officials all knew Song Jiang and also had received gifts. He was supposed to be beaten before being exiled, but as there was no plaintiff or witness against him everyone was able to help him out and make sure he was not hurt. The court imposed the cangue and an iron seal and two guards were assigned to escort him. No doubt they were called Zhang Something-or-Other and Li Somebody-Else.

When the two policemen bearing the order brought Song Jiang out in front of the courtroom, his father and brother were there waiting for him with wine for the two guards, and some silver which they presented to them. They made Song Jiang change his clothes. When he had tied his pack and put on hemp sandals, Squire Song took his son aside and said by way of encouragement: "Jiangzhou is a good place, rich in fish and rice. I spent good money to get you sent there. You'll be able to manage there very well. I'll send your brother to see you from time to time. And I hope there'll be other people passing that way who can take letters. But in order to get there you'll have to pass the Marshes of Mount Liang. If they come down from the mountain and try to seize you and get you to join them, please don't listen or you'll give people reason to call you disloyal and unfaithful. Try to bear this in mind always. Travel slowly. If heaven is kind, you'll soon come back and be reunited with your father and brother."

Song Jiang was in tears as he said goodbye to his father. His younger brother accompanied him on the first stage of his journey. Before they parted, Song Jiang said to his brother: "Don't grieve for me. The only thing that bothers me about this sentence is that I have to turn my back on hearth and home when father is getting on in years. Brother, please keep a constant watch on things at home, don't on my account come to Jiangzhou and leave father all alone with no one to look after him. I have many friends among the rivers and lakes fraternity who'd all be willing to help me, I'll always have somewhere to go for money if I need it. If heaven smiles on me I shall most certainly be back one day!"

His brother wept as he said goodbye and then returned home to look after their old father. We shall leave him there.

Song Jiang and the two guards proceeded on their way. Since they'd had money from him, and since he was generally accounted a good fellow, they were very helpful to him on the journey.

After one day's travelling they stopped at an inn, where they cooked themselves some food and Song Jiang bought wine for the others. Song Jiang said to them: "I'll be frank with you. The way we are taking at the moment lies quite close to the Marshes of Mount Liang. There are some brave men up there on the mountain who, if they hear my name, are liable to come down and seize me. I'm afraid they might rough you up a bit. Tomorrow let's get up a bit earlier and choose a smaller road — even if we have to walk a bit further it will be worth it."

"If you hadn't said anything we wouldn't have known," they said gratefully. "We know some roundabout ways, you can be sure we won't run into them."

This is what they agreed in the evening, and next morning they rose and breakfasted at dawn. When they left the inn they chose an obscure route. But when they'd gone about ten miles, a group of men appeared on the hillside in front of them. Song Jiang cursed his luck. Who should it be but Liu Tang, the Red-Haired Devil, with fifty men, bent on killing his guards? Zhang and Li were terrified. They knelt cowering on the path, trying to make themselves as inconspicuous as possible.

Song Jiang called out: "Hold, brother, who do you want to kill?"

"Those two cowards, of course. What do you expect?" Liu Tang replied.

"Don't dirty your hands, give the sword to me and let me do it!" The two unfortunates bewailed their fate. "This time we're really in for it!" they exclaimed.

"But why do you want to kill these two guards?" Song Jiang asked as he took the sword.

"Our friends on the mountain sent out spies who heard about your arrest. We wanted to go and get you out of Yuncheng gaol, but then we heard you weren't there any longer and weren't too badly off. Later we heard you'd been banished to Jiangzhou, but we were afraid we might get the wrong road, so everyone was told to go in different directions to lie in wait for you and invite you up the mountain. Surely the best thing to do with these two is to kill them?"

"This is not something which will help me, you know. On the contrary, you are trying to ruin my reputation. If you're so determined to destroy me, you'd better take my life. I'd rather die." So saying, Song Jiang held the sword to his own throat.

The Red-Haired Devil hurriedly stopped him, saying: "Please, don't be so hasty!" and took the sword from him.

Song Jiang said: "If you have any feeling for me, let me go to Jiangzhou prison camp and wait till I have served out my sentence. Then when I return I will come and see you."

The Red-Haired Devil said: "But I dare not listen to that. The military commander, 'Professor' Wu Yong, and Colonel Hua are waiting to greet you up on the main road. Please allow me to invite you to discuss matters with them."

Song Jiang said: "But that's exactly what I intended. I want to discuss it all with you."

Soldiers were sent on to report and in no time at all the Professor and Colonel Hua were seen galloping towards them, followed by a dozen riders. They dismounted, courtesies were exchanged, and then Colonel Hua said: "Why have they not removed the cangue?"

"Dear brother," Song Jiang said, "what are you saying? This is a penalty imposed by our national law, how can you dare to touch it?"

"I understand your meaning," said the Professor pleasantly. "It's quite all right, we won't make any attempt to keep you on the mountain. But Leader Chao Gai has not seen you for such a long time, he really would like to have a heart-to-heart talk with you. He invites you to spend just a little time on the mountain. After that we'll send you on your way."

"Professor, you're the only one who understands me," said Song Jiang. After helping up the two guards, he said: "I don't want them to have any cause for fear. Even if I were to die, please do not harm them."

The two guards said: "We owe you our lives, Registrar."

The whole body of men now left the road and went to an area of reedbeds beside the water. Already there was a boat there waiting. When they arrived at the main route up to the stronghold, mountain sedans were summoned to carry them. They paused for a rest at the Golden Pavilion. Men were sent to every part of the mountain to summon the leaders to a meeting and they all gathered in the assembly hall. Chao Gai spoke: "Ever since that time you saved our lives in Yuncheng, dear brother, and we found sanctuary here, not a day has passed without my recalling our indebtedness to you. If you will allow me now to invite you to honour our little place with your presence, my gratitude will know no bounds."

Song Jiang replied: "Since we parted and I killed that trollop and fled to the rivers and lakes a year and a half has passed. It was my intention to pay you a visit here on the mountain, only I happened to run into Shi Yong at a country inn and he gave me a letter from home which said my father had passed away. Actually it was all because my father feared I might join you and enter the band — that's why he sent me the letter to get me to go home. Although I have been sentenced, I have received great kindness from all the authorities and have got off very lightly. Now I'm banished to Jiangzhou, which is a pretty good place. I come here in obedience to your summons, which I would not dream of refusing. But now that I have seen you I cannot stay long, so let us part immediately."

"Why such a hurry?" Chao Gai said. "Please stay a little longer."

They both sat down together. Song Jiang told his guards to sit behind him and not leave his sight.

Chao Gai had the various leaders come and pay their respects to Song Jiang. They sat in two rows, while the lesser chiefs poured for them. Chao Gai took the cup first and then passed it to all in turn, from the military commanders, "Professor" Wu and Taoist Gongsun Sheng down to the Daytime Rat. After only a few rounds Song Jiang rose to his feet and said: "Dear friends, much as I appreciate your kindness to me, I am a sentenced criminal and I must not tarry here. It is time for me to say goodbye."

"Your attitude is really very strange," said Chao Gai. "I know you don't want any harm to come to the two guards, but why not just give them some money and send them away? They can say they were attacked by us here on Mount Liang, no one can reasonably punish them for that."

"Don't talk like that!" Song Jiang said. "That's not the way to help me out. Indeed it's the way to ruin me. I've an old father at home, I must always remember that. I have never afforded him all the honour he deserves. How can I violate his commands, how can I consent to sully his name? Previously I got carried away and I really was on the point of joining you. But heaven ordained that I should run into Shi Yong at that country inn and thus I was led to go home. My father explained why he thought it better for me to receive my sentence and suffer exile, he was most insistent on it. Just before I left he again urged me not to sacrifice the family honour to my own convenience, never to disgrace the family name, to spare my father such shame and horror. For this reason he told me and my brother that if we had no regard for his wishes we would be going against heaven's will; if we broke his commands we would show ourselves to be unfilial and dishonourable men, and in that case for what purpose had we lived? So if you are not willing now to let me leave, I would prefer to receive death at your hands." When he finished speaking, the tears flooded down and he flung himself on the ground.

Chao Gai, the Professor and Taoist Gongsun Sheng together raised him up and said: "If you are so determined to go to Jiangzhou, then be at ease for this one day and tomorrow morning we will escort you down the mountain."

Over and over again they begged him to stay and drink with them just for one day. They wanted the cangue to be removed but he would have none of it. He insisted also on remaining with his two guards.

Song Jiang did stay that night, but he was up early next morning, impatient to be off. The Professor said: "I want to tell you something. I have a dear friend who works as a warder at the Jiangzhou prison camp. He is Dai Zong, generally known as Superintendent Dai. He has a certain magic power: he can travel three hundred miles in a day, which is why people call him the Magic Messenger. He's entirely honourable and generous. Last night I wrote this letter for you to take. When you're there you can get to know him. Then if you have any problem he can let us know."

Since they could not hold onto Song Jiang, the leaders gave him a farewell feast. A tray of gold and silver was presented to him and the guards also got twenty taels. Then, carrying Song Jiang's luggage for him, they escorted him down the mountain before one by one taking their leave of him. The Professor and Colonel Hua accompanied him further, another six or seven miles down the road. Then they too went back to the mountain.

So Song Jiang with his escort took the road to Jiangzhou. The two guards, having seen that enormous army on the mountain and observed how they all bowed down before Song Jiang, and having just been given all that money, took the greatest possible care of him during the journey. They had been travelling

Chapter 36

something more than a fortnight when they came to a spot where a steep hill faced them. The guards said: "Good! Once we're past this hill it'll be the river, and after that the route to Jiangzhou is all by water. Not far to go at all."

Song Jiang said: "The weather is oppressive. Let's get this hill over with first and then look for somewhere to stay."

"Right you are," they said. They pressed on up the hill. It took them half a day's march but when they reached the top they were in sight of an inn on the other side, nestling against the hillside, with a gnarled old tree beside the door and surrounded by thatched huts. When they reached that tree's shade the inn sign was plain to see. It was a sight that brought great relief to Song Jiang's heart and he said to the guards: "We're truly hungry and thirsty. It turns out there's an inn here, so let's get some wine before we go on."

They went in. The two policemen put down their baggage and leant their staves against the wall. Song Jiang left them the place of honour and sat down at the bottom of the table. They waited a long time and no one came out, so Song Jiang shouted: "Can't you see there are customers?"

"Coming! Coming!" came a shout from inside and a big fellow emerged from a side-room. Here's how he looked:

Red curly beard in a horrible tangle,
Staring red eyes like a terrifying tiger,
With exactly the look of a fiend from the underworld,
It's no wonder they dubbed him Hell's Executioner.

This man who came out was wearing a torn head-cloth, a cotton vest which left his arms bare and a piece of linen wrapped about his waist. He looked at Song Jiang's party and barked out a salute. "How much wine would you like, gentlemen?" he asked.

"We've been travelling and we're hungry," Song Jiang said. "Have you any meat in the house?"

"All we've got is boiled beef and rough country wine," the man replied.

"That'll do fine. Bring us two catties of beef and a measure of wine, to begin with."

Chapter 36

"Don't take it amiss, sirs, but here in the mountains what we say is 'pay first before you drink'."

"Pay first before you drink," Song Jiang repeated. "That's all right by me. Just wait while I find you the money." He opened his bundle and took out some change. The man standing on one side watched surreptitiously. Seeing the pack so deep and heavy, so full of substance, he secretly exulted. He took Song Jiang's money and went inside to fill a jug of wine and cut the meat. He brought out the meat and put down three bowls and three pairs of chopsticks. He then poured the wine.

The three men talked as they ate. "Recently among the rivers and lakes there are said to be some nasty customers around. Many a good man has fallen foul of them. Maybe the wine or food is drugged and knocks them out. Then they're cut up and the flesh is used for pie fillings. But it's hard to believe. How could such things be true?"

The innkeeper laughed sardonically. "If that's what you think, you'd better not eat or drink. Of course my stuff is all laced with drugs!"

Song Jiang laughed. "Our friend here heard what we were saying, so he's having a joke with us!"

"Let's have some warm wine," the guards said.

"I'll go and warm it then, if that's what you want," the innkeeper said.

When he returned he poured three bowls of warm wine. Hungry and thirsty as they were from the walking, how could they hold back when it was right in front of them? Each drank a bowl right off. Then suddenly the two guards' eyes were popping out of their heads, saliva began to dribble from the corners of their mouths. After swaying first this way, then that, they pitched over. Song Jiang jumped up, exclaiming: "How can you be so drunk with just one bowl?" He took a step forward to help them up, but then without warning his own head began to spin and his vision blurred, and he crashed to the floor. They stared at each other helplessly, unable to move hand or foot.

"Bloody hell!" the innkeeper said. "No business for days, but now heaven's sent me three nice pieces of stuff!" He dragged

Song Jiang out first and got him into the work room under the cliff and onto the bench. Then he went back and got the other two. He returned for the packs and took them to the back. When he opened them and saw that they were full of money, he said: "I've been running this place for a good many years now, but I never came across a convict like this one. I wonder how a criminal like this comes to have so much loot? I guess he must have dropped down from heaven as my reward!" He tied the bundles again and went to the door to await the return of his assistants to help him with the cutting up.

He stood there at the door quite a while, but he didn't see a soul until three men appeared at the bottom of the hill and began to climb steadily towards him. He recognized them and greeted them hurriedly: "Where are you off to, then?" One of the three, a large man, said: "We've come up here to meet someone, we reckon he ought to have reached here by now. We've been looking out for him down there every day but we haven't seen him, he must have got held up somewhere."

"Who exactly is it you're expecting?"

"Someone pretty remarkable."

"But who is this remarkable person?"

"Prepare for a surprise then. It's the Yuncheng registrar, Song Jiang!"

"You don't mean the one who's known among the rivers and lakes as the Opportune Rain?"

"The very same."

"But what's he doing in these parts?"

"I don't exactly know myself. The other day a friend from Jizhou turned up and he said, 'For some reasons Registrar Song Jiang of Yuncheng has been tried in Jizhou and sentenced to exile in the Jiangzhou prison camp.' I worked it out that he's got to pass here, there's no other road. I often meant to go and see him in Yuncheng, but now he's coming here I don't want to miss such an opportunity to make his acquaintance, that's why I've been waiting down there for several days. Today these two friends and I thought we'd stroll up the mountain to buy a bowl of wine from you and have a little chat. How's business at the moment?"

Chapter 36

"To tell the truth, the last few months there's scarcely been any business at all. Today, though, heaven smiled on me and I've got my hands on three nice pieces of stuff, and a bit of loot thrown in."

"What sort of people were they, these three?"

"Two policemen and a convict."

"You haven't started on them yet, have you?"

"I just took them into the workshop and I'm waiting for the lads to come back and help me with the cutting up."

"Would you let me have a look at them first?"

The four of them went into the operating room under the cliff. There on the work bench Song Jiang and the two guards were laid out with their heads hanging over the edge. The big stranger looked at Song Jiang carefully, but he didn't know him of course. Nor did the golden seals on his cheeks provide a clue. But after a moment's consideration he had an idea: "Get the policemen's packs. We can look at the official order. That should tell us something."

"Right!" The innkeeper went and got the packs from the back. When they opened them they found a great deal of silver inside. On top was the money they'd been given recently. They opened the document pouch and looked at the order. "Bloody hell!" they exclaimed.

"Heaven must have ordained it, that we should come up here today," the big man exclaimed. Think if you'd started work a little sooner! You came so close to a terrible accident that would have ended our brother's life!"

It was a case of:

When anger or revenge must strike you cannot run away.
What chance will bring or fate ordain you cannot ever say.
You cannot wear out iron shoes, however hard you try,
What comes will come without your help, no use to reason why.

"Quick, go and get the antidote," the big man urged. "You've got to revive our friend straight away."

The innkeeper was equally horrified. He hurriedly mixed the antidote and returned with the big man to the workshop. First

揭陽嶺宋江逢李俊

they removed the cangue. Then, holding Song Jiang upright, they poured the mixture down his throat. After that the four of them carried him out into the front saloon. With the big man supporting him, Song Jiang gradually came round. He looked at all the people in front of him with a blank expression, failing to recognize any of them. The big man asked his two friends to take his place while he pressed his knuckles to his forehead and prostrated himself.

"But who are you?" Song Jiang asked. "Am I still dreaming?"

The innkeeper now prostrated himself also. Song Jiang acknowledged the courtesy and said: "Please get up, both of you. Where in fact am I? May I be so bold as to ask your names?"

"My name is Li Jun," the big man answered. "I'm from Luzhou. I work as a pilot on the Yangtze river. Being as I am a river expert, they call me the White-Water Dragon. The publican here is from these parts, from Jieyang Hill. He's a smuggler by trade, name of Li Li, but people also call him Hell's Executioner. The other two are from the banks of the river Yangtze, near here. They're salt smugglers and they're here now on business, they've been staying with me. They're also experienced at swimming and handling river boats. They're brothers; this one is Tong Wei, alias the Cave Dragon, and the other is Tong Meng, alias the River Rider."

The two brothers prostrated themselves before Song Jiang four times.

"I was unconscious until just now, how do you know my name?" said Song Jiang.

"I've got this friend," the White-Water Dragon began, "he's a businessman and he's just returned from Jizhou. He mentioned your name and said you'd been sentenced to exile in Jiangzhou prison camp. Well, so many times I'd thought of going to pay my respects to you in your home town, only my fate never permitted it. When I heard you were going to Jiangzhou and had to pass by here, I went and waited for you at the bottom of the hill. Five or six days I waited but I didn't see you. Today on a lucky impulse these two friends and I came up here to get ourselves a cup of wine. We fell into conversation with the Executioner and what he said gave me a start, I can tell you! We rushed into the workshop right away, but I didn't know you, see, so after giving it some pretty hard thought I suggested we take a look at the official order, and then we knew it was you. Do you mind if I ask you a question? I heard you were arrested in Yuncheng. But why have you been banished to Jiangzhou?"

Song Jiang duly gave them a full account of the killing of Yan Poxi, and everything up to the time Shi Yong gave him the letter at the inn and he went home and was sentenced and banished to Jiangzhou. The four men kept sighing in sympathy.

"Why don't you stay here instead of going off to suffer hardship in Jiangzhou prison?" the Executioner asked.

"The people on Mount Liang kept on begging me to stay there, but I wouldn't because I didn't want to disgrace my old father," Song Jiang said. "So how can you think I would stay here?"

The White-Water Dragon said to the Executioner: "You see? A man of honour can't be made to bend the rules. You'd better go and revive those guards."

The Executioner called his assistants, who had returned by now, and they carried the two guards out into the front room and administered the antidote. When they came round, they stared at each other and said: "It must have been weariness from all that travelling. How else could we have got drunk so quickly?" Everyone laughed.

That evening the Executioner provided wine for everyone and they stayed at his house. Next day there was more wine and food, and Song Jiang and the guards were given back their baggage. Having said goodbye, Song Jiang, the White-Water Dragon and the Tong brothers went down the hill together as far as the White-Water Dragon's house, where they stayed. Wine and food were brought out and they were entertained royally. The White-Water Dragon treated Song Jiang like a brother and begged him to stay a few days longer. But Song Jiang was determined to go. When he saw it was impossible to persuade him, the White-Water Dragon presented the guards with silver. Song Jiang was fitted with the cangue again, the bags were packed and they said goodbye to the White-Water Dragon and his two friends. Turning their backs on Jieyang Hill they took the road for Jiangzhou.

The three had marched without pause for the first part of the day when around noon they came to a place full of people and noise, a bustling market town. When they reached the centre, they found a crowd gathered round in a circle to watch something. Song Jiang pushed through the crowd to get closer to whatever was going on and found it was a practitioner of martial arts and peddler of patent medicine. They stood and watched him as he performed with the staff. After a while the artist laid aside his staff and gave a demonstration with his fists. Song Jiang applauded: "Great staff play, and great boxing!" The man took up a plate and said: "I've come a long way to bring my art to you good people. My skill is nothing special, of course, but I trust in your bounty. True, I have received praise in many quarters, but to your discerning eyes I probably seem a common mountebank. Still, if you want an efficacious ointment, I have some here. If you've no need of ointments, then I would ask you to donate a few ounces of silver or a copper coin or two, just so my visit will not have been altogether in vain."

He went among the crowd with the plate, but not one cent did he receive. "Good sirs," he began again, "pardon me, I pray, if I trouble your generosity!" He passed round again with the plate, but the people just stared blankly, not one coin did they give him.

Song Jiang, seeing his embarrassment when he had passed the plate twice to absolutely no effect, told his guards to take out five taels of silver. To the performer, he said: "Master, I'm just a convict, I haven't got much to give you. These five taels of silver are just a token of my good will, please do not despise them."

The man took the silver and after weighing it in his hand pronounced: "In the whole of Jieyang City, it seems, a great place like this, there's not a single connoisseur who can show his appreciation. Only this kind gentleman, quite contrary to the nature of things since he himself is subject to a judicial sentence and merely in transit here, presents me with five taels of good silver. It puts me in mind of the verse:

They said that the poet had got it all wrong
Who went to the brothel to peddle a song.

But many rich men with their riches won't part;
It isn't fine clothes that show a big heart!

These five taels are truly equal to fifty from someone else. I humbly bow down to you, sir, and beg to inquire your name, that I may proclaim it wherever I go."

Song Jiang replied: "Master, even if this paltry sum were worth so much, there wouldn't be any need to thank me."

But while they were speaking, a big stranger thrust his way through the crowd, bellowing: "Who the bloody hell is this? Where've you come from and where are you bloody going? What d'you mean by coming here and trying to ruin my reputation in Jieyang?" Then up went his fists and he took a swing at Song Jiang.

If this fight had not taken place, things might well have been different. We might never have seen how:

In the river Yangtze dragons churn the waves;
In the Marshes of Mount Liang, tigers rush the slopes.

If you want to know why this stranger wanted to beat Song Jiang up, you must read the next chapter.

Chapter 37

Song Jiang is chased by Mu Hong, the Unstoppable; The Pilot acts up on the river at night!

Now when Song Jiang made the mistake of giving five taels of silver to that martial arts master, a big man suddenly appeared among the Jieyang crowd and bellowed: "That scoundrel has no business barging in here with his bloody staff tricks and whatnot, I've already warned everybody to ignore him. And now you, you little shit, just because you want to show off how much money you've got, you go and pay him for it and cause me to lose face in my own home town!"

Song Jiang answered: "If I choose to give him money, what business is it of yours?"

The big stranger grabbed Song Jiang and shouted: "You dare to answer me back, you bloody convict?"

"Why shouldn't I answer you?" Song Jiang said.

The other raised his fists and swung at Song Jiang's jaw, but Song Jiang ducked. The man closed again and Song Jiang was about to retaliate when the martial arts master fell on the man from behind. He grasped his topknot in one hand while with the other he grabbed his waist and with a sudden twist sent him sprawling. When his opponent tried to struggle to his feet he felled him again with a kick. The two policemen had to restrain the martial arts artist while the other crawled to his feet. He gave them a black look and said: "Come what may, I'll get even with you two!" With that he left, heading south.

"May I ask your name and where you're from?" Song Jiang said to the martial arts man.

"I'm from Luoyang in Henan," the other replied. "My name is Xue Yong. My grandfather was on old field-marshal Zhong's staff, but he got on the wrong side of some officials and was never promoted. That's why his descendants have to earn their living giving demonstrations and selling medicines. Among the rivers and lakes I'm known as the Pill Monger. Will you now permit me to make so bold as to ask your name?"

"My name is Song Jiang and I'm from Yuncheng."

"You don't mean to say you're Song Jiang the Just of Shandong, the Opportune Rain?"

"Yes, at your service."

The Pill Monger prostrated himself at once and Song Jiang raised him up, saying: "How about having a cup of wine together?"

"Good idea, I've been longing to make your acquaintance, but I just didn't have the opportunity." He quickly gathered together the articles of his trade and they went off together to a neighbouring hostelry to order a drink. But the host said: "I've got plenty of wine and food, certainly, but I daren't sell you any."

"Why not?" Song Jiang asked.

"It's that big chap you fellows were fighting, it's his orders. If I sell you wine he'll come and smash this place up. I live here and I can't afford to offend him. He's the big boss here in Jieyang, everyone does as he says."

"In that case we'd better just go and find somewhere else to stay," Song Jiang said. "Obviously that man likes to make trouble."

The Pill Monger said: "I'll go back to my inn and pay for the room. We can meet again in a couple of days time in Jiangzhou. You go on ahead."

Song Jiang took out twenty taels of silver which he gave to the Pill Monger and then said goodbye and left.

Song Jiang and the two guards had to leave that inn. But when they went into the next place for a drink, the landlord said: "We all know the young master's orders, how can we sell you anything? You're just wasting your time and energy, it won't do you any good." There was nothing they could say to this, so they went on, and kept on going, because in every establishment they tried the answer was the same. Eventually they reached the very edge of town, where there were a few meagre little eating-places in one

Chapter 37

of which they hoped to find a room for the night. Even here they were rejected. When Song Jiang asked, the answer was always: "We've already received the young master's orders, we can't provide you with shelter." Song Jiang could see it was no use discussing it, so they set off resolutely down the main road. The sun was a red disk setting towards the horizon and the light was fading fast:

> *Mist swathes the distant peaks; cold vapours envelop the tall sky. Troops of stars pay homage to the pale moon, vying with her in splendour; green waters bow to blue mountains in a contest of jade hues. From the old temple, deep in the woods, the bell's gentle tolling fades away; from the fishermen's boats dots of light begin to wink. On the branch the nightjar cries to the evening moon; in the garden the butterfly comes to rest amid flowers.*

They began to be worried when they realized it was getting late. "We should never have stopped to watch that fellow with the staves and got the big man annoyed," they said to themselves. "Now it turns out that we're caught with no village ahead of us and no inn behind. Where are we going to spend the night?"

At that moment they saw lights far away along a track on the edge of a wood. Song Jiang said: "Hey, see that light? There must be a house there. Why not go there and ask them politely to let us stay the night? We'll leave early in the morning."

"But those lights are not on our route," said the guards.

"That doesn't matter. It's not on our way, but even if that means walking another mile or two tomorrow, it won't make a lot of difference."

So they left the main road and before they had gone a mile a big manor house appeared beyond the wood. They went up to the door and knocked. In response to their knock a servant opened the door and asked: "Who are you? And why do you come knocking on doors and disturbing people in the middle of the night?"

"I'm a convict travelling to my place of exile in Jiangzhou," Song Jiang explained somewhat nervously. "We missed the right moment to stop for the night and now we can't find anywhere. I'd like to ask if we can stay here. Of course we'd pay whatever is appropriate."

"In that case just wait here a moment," said the servant. "I'll go and tell the Squire, and if he's agreeable you can stay."

The man disappeared inside and quickly returned to say: "The Squire asks you to come in."

They were received in the thatched hall by the Squire, who told the servants to show them to their room and invited them to partake of some supper. A servant led them down the steps to a room at the side. He lit a lamp and invited them to make themselves comfortable, while he brought three portions of rice, together with soup and various dishes. Later he collected the bowls and plates and vanished inside.

"Well, Registrar," the guards said, "seeing there aren't any strangers present, we might as well take off that cangue, so you'll sleep more comfortable. Then tomorrow we can be off early."

"Good," said Song Jiang.

When the cangue was off, they all went outside to wash. The sky was filled with stars. Song Jiang noticed that there was a building beside the threshing floor and behind it was a narrow road leading off into nowhere. They went in again, closed the door and prepared for sleep. "It's really lucky that this old gentleman is letting us sleep here tonight," they said. Just as they were speaking, they noticed there were people with lighted torches milling about on the threshing floor. Song Jiang put his eye to a crack in the wall and saw the Squire accompanied by three servants with torches going around inspecting everything. "This old gentleman is just like my father," he thought. "He wants to see to everything himself. Even at this time of day he won't just go to bed, he has to see everything is all right first."

As Song Jiang was speaking, a great clamour arose outside, with voices shouting for the gates to be opened quickly. Several men rushed in, the foremost of them carrying a halberd and the rest equipped with pitchforks and staves. By the light of the torches Song Jiang could make out that the leader was the same big man who had wanted to beat him up earlier at the inn in Jieyang. He also heard the Squire say: "Where've you been, my

Chapter 37

son? And who've you been fighting with? What do you need all these weapons for at this time of night?"

"Listen father, is my brother at home?" the big man asked.

"Your brother was drunk tonight," the Squire replied. "He took himself off to sleep at the back."

"I'll go and wake him up. We're going on a manhunt."

"I don't know who you've been quarrelling with, but waking your brother up isn't going to settle it. You'd better tell me what it's all about."

"You've no idea, father, there was a mountebank, a peddler of quack remedies, in town today, the blighter had the cheek not to come and get our permission first. He went straight to the marketplace and started selling his medicines without a licence and performing with his staves, so I told everyone not to give him a single penny. And then this convict pops up, heaven knows where from, and wants to pretend he's the great gentleman, and get everyone's attention, so he gives him five taels of silver, just to make me a laughing-stock in Jieyang. I was just on the point of beating him up when that bloody peddler hit me from behind and knocked me down. He punched me and kicked me so hard my ribs are still hurting. I told all the innkeepers not to let them in, either to drink or to stay, so the three of them won't have a roof over their heads tonight, and I got a bunch of thugs from the gambling houses to go to that peddler's inn and haul him out and give him a good thrashing. They've hung him up now in the sheriff's. Tomorrow we'll take him down to the river, tie him in a sack and chuck him in. That should take the wind out of the bugger's sails. But now I can't find where the convict and the two policemen have got to. There's no inn further down the highway, I just can't think where they're spending the night. I want to get my brother so we can split forces to give us a better chance of catching the bugger."

"You really shouldn't be so hasty, my son," said the Squire. "What business is it of yours if he decides to give the peddler some money? Why do you have to beat him up? All right, so you got a beating, but you're not seriously hurt. You just listen to me. Don't tell your brother about this. If you get beaten up, what's he supposed to do about it? And you're liable to kill someone. Now you listen to what I say. Go to your room now and go to bed. It's after midnight. Don't go making a row and waking people up, disturbing the whole neighbourhood. Gain some merit by exercising a little restraint."

The big man paid no attention to his father's words. He took his halberd and rushed inside. The Squire hurried after him.

"Now we're in a real mess," Song Jiang said to the guards. "What are we going to do? It turns out we've picked his home to stay in. The only thing to do is to get out. If he discovers we're here he's going to kill us. Even if the Squire doesn't tell him, is it likely the servants will keep quiet about it?"

"You're right," the guards said. "We shouldn't waste any time, we must leave at once."

"We'd better not take the main road," Song Jiang said. "We'll leave from the back."

The guards shouldered their bags and Song Jiang was fitted with the cangue again. They forced a gap in the fence at the back of the house and by the light of the moon and the stars pushed ahead down a small track leading into the heart of the woods. In their haste they paid no heed to where they were going. After walking for about two hours, they came to a place that was full of rushes, with a big river sweeping past. They had reached the banks of the river Yangtze.

Just then they heard shouts behind them and saw a flurry of torches chasing after them amid a general hue and cry. "Merciful Heaven, we're done for!" exclaimed Song Jiang. They plunged on into the thick of the reeds, but when they looked back the torches seemed to be getting nearer. With mounting alarm they waded on through reedbeds which seemed to stretch ahead of them to the very limits of the earth, if not of the sky too. But then there was a broad river blocking their path, with wide inlets on each side. Song Jiang's sighs ascended to heaven: "If I'd known this was going to happen, I should have stopped with them on Mount Liang. Who would have thought that I would come to end my days here?"

At this critical juncture, the reeds suddenly parted and a boat glided stealthily out. Song Jiang immediately hailed the helmsman

Chapter 37

没遮拦追赶及时雨

and offered to give him silver if he brought his boat over and rescued them. The boatman asked: "Who are you and how did you get here?"

"We're being pursued by robbers, and they've driven us into this corner," Song Jiang said. "Quickly bring your boat here and ferry us over the water. I'll give you more even than you ask for."

At this mention of more silver, the boatman drove his boat across to them. They leapt in at once. One of the guards dropped the bundles into the boat's hold, while the other shoved the boat off with his staff of office. The boatman leant on his oar, at the same time listening to the satisfying sound the bundles made as they fell on the deck and secretly rejoicing. Driven by the boatman's oar the boat was soon out in midstream. Meanwhile, their pursuers had reached the river bank. A dozen torches could be seen. Each of the two leaders carried a halberd and the score or so of followers were each equipped with spears or staves. "Ahoy there, boatman!" they shouted. "Bring your boat over here, quickly!"

Song Jiang and the two guards huddled in the bottom of the boat and said: "Don't do it, boatman! We'll give you a bit extra if you don't."

The boatman nodded and ignoring the people on the bank rowed the boat with a creaking oar towards the middle of the river. Those on the bank shouted: "You there, boatman, don't go away! We'll kill you for this!" The boatman gave a few contemptuous snorts but vouchsafed no answer. Again the men on the bank called out: "Who are you? How can you have such a nerve? Come back here!"

"Zhang's my name," the boatman shouted back scornfully. "And you'd better keep a civil tongue in your heads!"

"Of course, it's old Zhang," said the tall man on the bank. "Can't you see it's me and my brother?"

"'Course I can see you. I'm not blind, am I?"

"If you can see us, why don't you come over here? We want to talk to you."

"If you want to talk you can wait till tomorrow. My passengers are in a hurry."

"Your passengers are what we're after!"

"My passengers are my relatives, my meat and drink, my all. I've invited them on board for a bowl of knife noodles."

"If you'll come back here we can come to an agreement."

"You think I'm going to hand over my meat and drink? That's a laugh!"

"Friend Zhang, that's not what we mean. We only want that convict. Just bring him here, there's a good fellow!"

Continuing to row, the Boatman said: "I haven't had something like this for days, I'm certainly not coming back just to have you take them away from me. You'll just have to put up with it. We can talk another day."

Song Jiang had not caught the boatman's meaning. He and the two guards in the bottom of the boat were quietly saying: "What a bit of luck that this boatman has saved our lives. We'd better let him know we won't forget his kindness. It's just as well this boat was here to ferry us across."

Eventually the boatman was far enough away from the shore. Looking back towards the shore, they saw the lights moving away through the reeds. "Bloody hell!" Song Jiang said. "It's really like they say, 'Meet a good man and the evil flee.' This has got us out of a pretty tight corner."

But as he rowed on, the boatman now broke into song — a Huzhou ditty:

On the bank of the river born I was,
Don't fear no law, neither man's nor God's.
The King of Hell said he wanted a ride,
When I got his gold he went over the side.

When Song Jiang and his guards heard this song, their legs felt a bit wobbly. But Song Jiang decided he must be joking. However, before they could give the matter more thought, the boatman threw down his oar and said: "Now then, you lot, it seems you've a taste for getting smugglers into trouble, but today it's me you're up against! Which do you prefer, knife noodles or wontan soup?"

"Don't make fun of us, my good man," said Song Jiang. "What do you mean by knife noodles and wontan soup?"

The boatman glared at him and answered: "Who says I'm bloody joking? If it's the noodles you want, I got a knife in the hold there keen as the March wind, it'll cut you into ribbons in a jiffy — and there won't be no seconds, one go'll do it! If it's the soup, then strip off and over the side with you, you got the whole river to die in."

"Heaven have mercy!" Song Jiang lamented. "It's like they say, 'troubles never come singly, happiness never returns'."

"Think it over if you must, but let me know quick," the boatman growled.

"Boatman, let me explain. I'm a convict, banished to Jiangzhou, can't you find it in your heart to pity me and spare the three of us?"

"Spare the three of us!" the boatman mimicked. "You make me sick! I won't spare one half of one of you. Don't you know my reputation? Dogface Uncle Zhang, they call me, an' if it was me own mother and father it wouldn't cut no ice with me! So shut your fucking mouth and get in the water!"

Song Jiang tried again. "We'll give you everything that's in our bundles, all the money and valuables and clothes and stuff, if only you'll spare our lives!"

"You can all three get your clothes off double-quick and jump in the river," the boatman shouted. "Jump, if you're going to, if not I'll shove you in!"

So there were Song Jiang and the guards clutching each other and on the point of throwing themselves in the river, when, creak, creak, creak, the sound of oars came over the water. Song Jiang quickly looked around. A fast boat was flying downstream towards them. There were three men in the boat: a big man holding a forked spear standing in the bow and two youths in the stern plying oars. Under the starlight it rapidly approached. The big man in the bows hailed them: "You there in the boat, identify yourselves. What are you doing in these waters? Any goods you may be carrying, who sees them has part."

The boatman turned to see who it was and hurriedly replied: "Oh, it's Mr. Li! I was wondering who it could be. Been out on business too, have you sir? Why didn't you let me in on it?"

Chapter 37

299

"You've been operating round here too, have you Zhang? What've you got in the boat? Anything of substance?"

"I tell you, it'll make you laugh. I hadn't been doing much, not for days. I lost a bit gambling too, hadn't a cent left. So there I was sitting on the bank, feeling pretty low I can tell you, when I was approached by these three pieces of goods being chased along by a bunch of men. Turned out to be two fucking policemen, with a little dark-faced shit of a prisoner, where from I couldn't rightly say. According to him he's been banished to Jiangzhou, but he doesn't have no cangue. The crowd that was chasing after them was the two Mu brothers from town. They were dead keen to get their hands on them. But I'd already seen there was something substantial there, so I didn't give them up."

"Wait a minute! I suppose it couldn't be my friend Song Jiang?"

The voice sounded familiar to Song Jiang, so he called out: "Who's that on the other boat? Please rescue Song Jiang!"

It gave the other quite a shock. "It is, it's my friend. Why ever did you not speak out before?"

Song Jiang crawled out onto the deck to see who it was. The stars were bright and he could make out the man standing in the bows of the other boat quite clearly:

> On the banks of the Yangtze he makes his home, this hero of universal fame. His brows are thick, his eyes large and his complexion ruddy, his beard and whiskers are stiff as iron filaments. He has a voice like a gong and his stature's immense. He knows well how to wield a frosty blade, and he'll surge through the waters and leap o'er the waves with amazing effect. Such is Li Jun, native of Luzhou, known to all as the White-Water Dragon.

It was indeed Li Jun, the White-Water Dragon, and the two rowing in the stern were the two Tong brothers, the River Rider and the Cave Dragon.

As soon as he knew it was Song Jiang, the White-Water Dragon leapt aboard. "What a close shave!" he exclaimed in horror. "If I'd come a minute or two later, you could have perished. It must be heaven was directing my steps today, because when I was sitting at home I suddenly felt restless, so I decided to row out into the channel and smuggle a little salt. I had no idea I was going to find you here in such a predicament!"

The boatman meanwhile had been pondering all this, not daring to open his mouth. Now at last he said: "Mr. Li, is this dark gentleman really Song Jiang of Shandong, the Opportune Rain?"

"Who else?" said the White-Water Dragon.

The boatman prostrated himself and said: "Oh sir, why didn't you tell me your name? You'd have saved me from doing something terrible! I was near to finishing you off!"

"What is our friend's name?" Song Jiang asked the White-Water Dragon.

"Let me introduce him. This gentleman is my adopted brother, a native of Little Mount Solo, named Zhang Heng, nicknamed the Pilot. He works here on the Yangtze river at a fine safe trade!" Song Jiang and the two guards laughed at this.

The two boats now rowed over to the landing. When the boats had been tied up, Song Jiang and his guards were helped out onto the bank. The White-Water Dragon said to the Pilot: "I've often told you there there's never a gentleman like Registrar Song of Yuncheng for uprightness. Now you can really get to know him."

The Pilot struck a flint and lit a lamp so he could take a good look at Song Jiang, then flung himself down on the sand in respectful greeting, saying: "Please forgive me for what I did!" Song Jiang also took a good look at the Pilot:

> *Immensely tall, and with slanting eyes, he is famous up and down this stretch of the Yangtze. He surges through the water like a water sprite, he leaps o'er the waves like a flying whale. He doesn't fear dangerous waters and wild winds. The sight of him fills the flood dragon with dread. He is yet another of the stars sent down by heaven to stir things up on earth. He lives at Little Mount Solo and they call him the Pilot.*

"Why are you under arrest, sir?" the Pilot asked.

The White-Water Dragon explained about Song Jiang's sentence and banishing to Jiangzhou. The Pilot listened and then said: "I'd like to tell you something, in my family there were two of us, myself and this younger brother of mine, born of the same mother, and would you believe it? He's completely white, white as snow. Not only can he swim ten to fifteen miles, but he can keep going under water for seven days and seven nights, he can live in the water just like a fish! And on top of that he's a martial arts expert. People call him the White Eel. We used to make our living on the banks of the Yangtze, with a scheme of our own devising."

"I'd like to hear about it," Song Jiang said.

"When we lost money gambling, we'd take a boat to a clear place on the river bank and offer to ferry people across privately. There was always a few takers who wanted to save a penny or two or was in a hurry. As soon as the boat was full I'd get my brother to dress up as a merchant with a big sack who wanted to be ferried across. I'd row out into midstream, put down the oar, cast anchor and pull out a big knife. Then I'd ask for the money. Originally I might have asked just five hundred coppers, but now I'd change it to three thousand. I'd ask my brother to pay up first. As we'd arranged, he would refuse, so I'd grab him by the scruff of the neck and the seat of his pants and chuck him in the river, splash! Then I'd ask the others in turn. They'd all be terrified by now and they'd fork out without a murmur. When they'd paid up I'd deliver them to a remote spot on the other bank, then I'd pick up my brother from the river and we'd go over the other side, divide up the spoils and go off to gamble. We made a good living like that."

"I suppose there were plenty of customers along the river who wanted a service of that kind," said Song Jiang, and the others all laughed.

The Pilot said: "We've changed our trade now. I do a little private business on the river here, smuggling, that is, while my brother's working at present in the fish trade in Jiangzhou. I'd give you a letter for him when you go there, only I don't know how to write, so I can't."

"We'll go into the village and hire a scribe to write it for you," said the White-Water Dragon. Leaving the Tong brothers to look after the boats and carrying lanterns they set off for the village.

They'd barely gone a few hundred yards when they saw

Chapter 37

torches were still flickering along the bank. The Pilot said: "Those two brothers haven't given up and gone home yet."

"What two brothers?" said the White-Water Dragon.

"The two Mu brothers from town."

"Let's call 'em over to pay their respects to our friend here," said the White-Water Dragon.

Song Jiang protested at once: "That's not at all a good idea. They've been trying to catch me!"

"Don't worry about that," the White-Water Dragon reassured him. "It's just that they didn't know it was you. They're in the same line of business as us."

The White-Water Dragon waved and let off a piercing whistle and immediately the torches and the little band of men began to approach at speed. When they came close and saw the Pilot and the White-Water Dragon conversing politely with Song Jiang, the Mu brothers had a shock. "Are you acquainted with these three then?" they said. The White-Water Dragon grinned. "Don't you know who this is?" he said.

"We've no idea. We only know he gave money to that mountebank in the town and made us lose face. We can't wait to get our hands on him."

"Well he's the one I've told you about so many times, Registrar Song Jiang of Yuncheng, otherwise known as the Opportue Rain. You'd better show your respect at once."

Throwing away their halberds they flung themselves on the ground. "We've heard of you so often," they said, "but we never thought to meet you here like this. We fear we have been appallingly rash and done you great injury. We implore you to forgive us."

Song Jiang helped them up and said: "Please tell me your names, gentlemen."

The White-Water Dragon spoke for them. "They're brothers and they're from a rich family. They're from hereabouts. Their names are Mu Hong, the Unstoppable and Mu Chun, the Irrepressible. They control the city of Jieyang. There's three of us here, you see. Let me explain. On Jieyang Hill and its environs, I'm the boss, together with the Executioner. In Jieyang City it's those two.

The smuggling on this stretch of the Yangtze is controlled by the Pilot, Zhang Heng and his brother Zhang Shun, the White Eel. Together we're known as the Three Bosses."

Song Jiang said: "We didn't know anything about that. But if we are all brothers, let me beg you to release the Pill Monger."

"You mean the mountebank? Don't worry, I'll tell my brother to go and get him and bring him here. Allow us to invite you to our house to make up for our rudeness."

The White-Water Dragon said: "That's great. We'll all go to your house then."

Mu Hong sent two servants to watch the boats and ask the Tong brothers to join them. He also sent men on ahead to give advance warning and order wine and food, have sheep and pigs killed and get ready a great feast.

They waited till the Tongs arrived and then all went back to the manor together. It was around dawn. At the manor Squire Mu was invited to come out and meet them and they all sat down in the thatched hall, Mu Hong and Song Jiang opposite each other. They talked for a while and it soon became fully light. Mu Chun arrived with Xue Yong, the Pill Monger, and joined them. Mu Hong entertained Song Jiang and the rest royally at the feast he had organized. They stayed at the manor that night. Next morning Song Jiang wanted to leave at once but Mu Hong wouldn't hear of it. He insisted they all stay on at the manor and took Song Jiang off to stroll in town and see the sights of Jieyang. Three days he kept him. Song Jiang became anxious that he was exceeding the limit and insisted he must leave. No matter how much Mu Hong and the others insisted they couldn't get him to stay longer. So they arranged a farewell feast.

Next day Song Jiang was up at dawn, bade farewell to his hosts and before leaving told the Pill Monger to stay on a few days at the manor and then come on to Jiangzhou so they could meet again. Mu Hong said: "Don't worry, we'll look after him here." He then had a tray of silver brought, which he presented to Song Jiang and made a further gift of silver to the two guards. Before they actually got going the Pilot found someone at the manor to write him a personal letter to his brother which Song Jiang packed in his bag.

Chapter 37

The company saw them off as far as the bank of the river. There a boat was summoned. The luggage was taken aboard first, whilst the people waited on the bank. Song Jiang's cangue was fitted for the journey and they all came on board to offer him a farewell drink. Everyone was weeping at the prospect of parting. The White-Water Dragon, the Pilot, the two Mu brothers, the Pill Monger and the Tong brothers all went their separate ways. Of them no more.

We shall now follow Song Jiang and his guards as they travelled by boat to Jiangzhou. This boatman was nothing like the first one. He hoisted a sail and in no time was able to set them ashore at Jiangzhou. With Song Jiang wearing his cangue as usual and the guards carrying the official order and the baggage, they presented themselves at the government offices. The court happened to be in session. The governor of Jiangzhou was called Cai Dezhang, and he was the ninth son of Cai Jing, the Grand Preceptor at court — Jiangzhou people referred to him as Cai the Ninth. He was greedy and extravagant and extremely haughty in all his dealings. His father had got him appointed to Jiangzhou because it was a region of rich revenues, populous and rich in produce.

The guards presented their papers and escorted Song Jiang into the courtroom. The governor looked Song Jiang over and noticing something irregular about him said: "Why does the cangue not bear the provincial seal?"

"There was heavy spring rain along the way," the guards explained, "and the seals were ruined."

"Write out your report immediately," the governor said, "and send him to the prison camp outside the city. This court will appoint its own guards to accompany you."

Accordingly the two guards escorted Song Jiang to the prison camp and handed him over. The Jiangzhou guards received the report, and inspected Song Jiang and his escort. But first they all went to a wineshop and had a drink. Song Jiang took out several taels of silver and gave them to the Jiangzhou guards. An official receipt for the prisoner was made out and he was taken to a cell to wait. The Jiangzhou guards went to the warder's room to put in a word for him to be reasonably treated and to complete the procedures for handing him over and getting a receipt, before returning to the city. The two original guards handed over all Song Jiang's luggage amid many protestations of gratitude before bidding him farewell and returning. They said to themselves: "Although we've had some rough times, we've made a good bit of money out of it." After waiting a while at the government offices for the report they had to take back, they set out on the return journey to Jizhou.

Song Jiang meanwhile intended to buy himself some favourable treatment, and when the warder came to his cell he gave him ten taels of silver. He sent another ten taels to the warden's office, together with other gifts. Amongst the officers of the camp and the regular soldiers detailed to serve there he distributed silver so they could buy some extra food. For this reason his presence was welcome to all and sundry.

In a little while he was taken to the inspection room, where the cangue was removed and he was interviewed by the warden. The latter, having received the bribes, said: "New prisoner Song Jiang, hear this: in accordance with the regulation laid down by Emperor Wu De every new prisoner must receive a hundred disciplinary lashes. Guards, secure the prisoner." Whereupon Song Jiang said: "I became infected with a bad cold on the way here and am not yet recovered."

"The man certainly appears to be sick," said the warden. "His colour is yellow and his body emaciated, these are symptoms of sickness. Just credit him with the punishment. Since he has served in a government office, let him work as a copying clerk in the office of this camp."

An order to this effect was drawn up and Song Jiang was told to report to the office. He expressed his thanks and went back to his cell to pick up his things and transfer them to the office. When the other convicts saw Song Jiang had been given such status, they bought wine to honour him. Next day Song Jiang bought provisions himself to return the compliment. Shortly after he invited the head gaoler and other guards, and he regularly sent gifts to the warden. Since he was well provided with gold, silver and other valuables it was no problem for him to make friends. As they say: "The world's favour goes with fortune, men's kindness is linked to rank."

One day when Song Jiang was drinking with the head gaoler in the office, the latter said to him: "Do you remember, friend, how a little while back I told you how our prison superintendent always expects a present? How come you haven't sent him anything yet? It's been more than ten days. He's coming here tomorrow, and it's going to look quite bad."

"Don't worry about that," said Song Jiang. "If the fellow asks for money he won't get any. If you need any yourself, all you have to do is ask for it, but that superintendent isn't going to get a penny out of me. Let him come: I've got something to say to him."

"Registrar, this man's got a hell of a temper. And besides, he really knows how to use his fists and his feet. If there's trouble and he comes down on you hard, don't say I didn't warn you."

"He must do as he pleases. But don't worry. I've got my own methods. Maybe I'll give him something, maybe I won't. Maybe he'll ask me for it, maybe he won't."

But even before he'd finished speaking, a guard came in and announced: "The superintendent's come. He's in the main hall, kicking up a horrible row, wants to know where the new prisoner is and why he hasn't sent the customary gift."

"What did I say?" said the head gaoler. "Now he's going to take it out on all of us."

Song Jiang only laughed. "You'll have to excuse me now," he said. "We'll continue our conversation another time. I'll go and have it out with him at once."

The gaoler stood up, saying: "As for us, we'd better keep out of his way."

Song Jiang left the office and went straight to the inspection room to find the superintendent. Now if Song Jiang had not see that man, it would not have happened that:

Jiangzhou is changed into a den of wolves and tigers;
Bodies are heaped at the crossroads, the streets awash with blood.

And as a result:

Heaven's snare is broken, they return to the Marshes;
The world's trap is sprung, they return to Mount Liang.

But if you want to know what happened when Song Jiang met the prison superintendent, you must read the next chapter.

Chapter 38

Song Jiang and the Magic Messenger get together; Iron Ox and White Eel have a set-to in the river!

So Song Jiang took leave of the head gaoler, left the office and made his way to the inspection room. Here he found the prison superintendent sitting on a stool in front of the door.

"Where's this new prisoner?" he growled.

One of the prison guards pointed out Song Jiang and said: "That's him."

"You black-faced little runt," the superintendent roared. "Who said you could skip the customary gift of cash?"

"'A gift is that which is freely given, it comes from the heart.' How can you demand a gift by force?" Song Jiang said. "That just shows how low you are."

The onlookers felt their hands grow clammy with sweat. The superintendent exploded. "You prison scum, you dare to speak like that to me? You've really got it back to front, calling me low! 'Oy, guards, take the bugger off and give him a hundred strokes."

But all the prison officers were sympathetic to Song Jiang and when they heard the order to beat him they made themselves scarce. The superintendent now found himself alone with the prisoner. The fact that everyone had left him in the lurch made him even angrier. He picked up the whip and advanced on Song Jiang, intending to thrash him within an inch of his life.

Song Jiang said: "If you're going to beat me, you'd better tell me what my crime is!"

"You're in my hands, you scum, if you so much as cough, that's crime enough!"

"You want to find fault with me, but you'll find nothing that's a capital offence."

The man was furious: "You think you don't deserve death, but I tell you, if I want to finish you off, I'll do it, easy as killing a fly."

"If I deserve death just for not giving you money, what about someone who's a friend of the leader on Mount Liang, a friend of 'Professor' Wu Yong's, what would that crime deserve?" said Song Jiang smiling ironically.

When the superintendent heard this, he hurriedly dropped the stick he was holding. "What's that you said?" he stammered.

"I merely asked what would happen to someone who knows the bandit leader, 'Professor' Wu Yong. Why are you so surprised?"

Flabbergasted, the superintendent grabbed Song Jiang's arm and said: "Who exactly are you? Where do you get your information from?"

"I am from Yuncheng district in Shandong. My name is Song Jiang."

The man could hardly believe his ears. He hurriedly saluted Song Jiang with joined hands and said: "You mean you're the famous Song Jiang, known as the Opportune Rain?"

"Yes indeed, for what it's worth," said Song Jiang.

"This is not somewhere we can talk properly," said the other. "I daren't even show you the proper courtesy here. Let's go somewhere in town where we can speak our hearts."

"By all means, but do me the favour of waiting a moment while I go and lock my door."

Song Jiang quickly went to his room, collected the Professor's letter and took some silver. He locked his door and asked the prison guard to keep an eye on things. Then in the company of the superintendent he left the prison camp. They hurried into Jiangzhou where they immediately repaired to a tavern, one that was a little off the street, and found themselves a place upstairs.

"Tell me, I beg you, how did you come to meet the Professor?" the superintendent asked.

Song Jiang took the letter from his pocket and handed it to the superintendent. The latter broke the seal, read it through and then, having tucked it away in his sleeve, stood up and prostrated

Chapter 38

及時雨會神行太保

himself at Song Jiang's feet. Song Jiang immediately returned the courtesy and said: "I am afraid just now I used language that must have been hurtful to you, please forgive me."

"I had only heard that someone called Song had arrived in the prison. It is the custom for prisoners to give me five taels of silver. Over ten days had passed and I saw no sign of it. Since today was a holiday, I decided to come and get it. I had no idea that the prisoner was yourself. The language I used just now was highly offensive. I sincerely beg you to forgive me."

"The head gaoler mentioned your name to me many a time," said Song Jiang. "I resolved to pay my respects to you, but I didn't know where you lived. Also I had no excuse to go into the city, so I had to wait for you to come to me. It was in order to have the chance of a meeting that I withheld the silver, not because I begrudged it you. I was sure you would come if I delayed the payment. And now you see it has come to pass and my dearest wish is fulfilled."

But who do you suppose this person is with whom Song Jiang is talking? It is the very man whom the Professor recommended, that is to say, Dai Zong, chief superintendent of the two prisons in Jiangzhou. At that time, during the Song Dynasty, all the chief prison officers in the area of Jinling were called "officers of the court." In Hunan the heads of gaols were all called "superintendent." This Dai Zong, by the way, had an amazing Taoist power: when he travelled, bearing important military intelligence for example, he would bind two special amulets onto his legs and initiate a special "walking mode." With two amulets he could travel two hundred miles in one day, with four he could cover four hundred. For this reason he was known as Dai Zong the Magic Messenger. As the poet testifies:

His face is broad, his lips well formed, his eyes bright and prominent. He is tall and thin in build and elegant in bearing. Jewel-like flowers adorn his headgear. Yellow insignia indicate his office of messenger; a red braid marks him as an emissary. The power in his legs enables him to outstrip a thoroughbred; seldom is his silk robe free of dust. Amazing the ability of this Magic

Messenger: ask him to do three hundred miles, it's off in the morning, back at dusk.

So Song Jiang and the Magic Messenger talked away to their hearts' content. They sat themselves down in the tavern and told the waiter to prepare wine and side dishes, while they settled down to enjoy themselves in their little upstairs nook. Song Jiang recounted tales of the brave men he had met, the people and events he had encountered on his travels. The Magic Messenger likewise opened his heart and told all about how he had come to know the Professor.

As they were thus engaged, talking of their affairs, and after they had downed two or three cups, a commotion arose downstairs. The waiter rushed into the room and said to the Magic Messenger: "Please, superintendent, you're the only one who can deal with him, no one else can! Please may I trouble you to come and talk some sense into him?"

"Who is it kicking up such a row down there?" the Magic Messenger asked.

"It's that fellow who is often with you, that Mr. Li, the one they call Iron Ox. He's downstairs asking for the owner because he wants to borrow money from him."

"Oh, so it's that devil who's making all the fuss, is it? I wondered who it could be." Turning to Song Jiang, the Magic Messenger said: "Please stay here while I go and fetch him up." He disappeared downstairs and a moment later returned with a big black-faced individual, whose appearance Song Jiang found quite startling. "Who is the big fellow?" he asked.

"He's one of the warders at the prison. His name is Li Kui. He originates from Five Furlongs village in the Yishui district of Yizhou. He is nicknamed the Black Whirlwind, and his friends all call him Iron Ox. He killed a man and had to flee from justice. Although he received a pardon, he ended up here in Jiangzhou and never went back home. His temper is ugly when he's had a few too many, and the people in the town are terrified of him. He's a pretty skilful fighter with two axes, but he's also good with his fists or the staff. At the moment he's employed here at the prison."

There is a poem which describes him:

His home is in Yizhou, east of the Jade Hills,
Killing, arson and violence give him his thrills.
No need to blacken his face, he's black as a whole,
His eyes are as red as a burning coal.
Down by the river bank he grinds his great axe;
At a tall pine on the cliff edge he idly hacks.
He is strong as a wild bull, rigid as steel;
The name of Iron Ox strikes universal chill.

Iron Ox meanwhile had been observing Song Jiang and said: "Superintendent, who is the dark chap?"

The Magic Messenger turned to Song Jiang with a laugh and said: "You see what a monster he is? Absolutely no manners!"

"I asked a question, what's wrong with that?" said Iron Ox.

"Why couldn't you say 'Who is that gentleman?' instead of 'Who's the dark chap?' If that isn't rude I don't know what is. Anyway, I'll tell you. This gentleman is a very famous person, someone whose protection you have often said you would like to have."

"You mean Song Jiang the Black of Shandong, known as the Opportune Rain?"

"Really, what a brute you are! The way you say it — without any of the respect due to position. Well, why aren't you prostrating yourself? How much longer are you going to wait?"

"If it really is Song Jiang, of course I'll prostrate myself. But if it's just a nobody, why the hell should I show him respect? How do I know you aren't having me on?"

Then Song Jiang spoke. "I can assure you I am Song Jiang," he said.

Iron Ox clapped his hands. "Why didn't you say so in the first place?" he said. "That's real good news to me!" With this he flung himself down before Song Jiang, who immediately returned the courtesy and said: "My muscular friend, please be seated."

"Come and sit by me," said the Magic Messenger, "and have some wine."

"I can't stand these piddling little cups," said Iron Ox. "Let's have some big bowls."

"What were you so upset about downstairs?" Song Jiang inquired.

"I've got this big lump of silver which I gave as security for ten smaller sums that I needed for ordinary use. I asked the landlord here to lend me ten taels, I was going to redeem the lump sum and then pay him back and I needed some small change too. The bugger refused me! I was just going to teach him a lesson, smash the place up for him, when you called me up here."

"Is ten taels all you need?" Song Jiang asked. "Isn't there interest to pay?"

"I've already paid the interest. I just need ten taels to get my capital back."

Song Jiang took out ten taels of silver and offered them to Iron Ox, saying: "Here, go and redeem your funds."

Iron Ox accepted. "That's great!" he cried. "Now you two please wait for me here. I'll go and get the silver and then come to repay you. Afterwards I want to invite Song Jiang to drink a cup or two with me, somewhere out of town."

"Why not sit down and drink a cup or two first?" said Song Jiang.

"I'll go first and then come back," said Iron Ox. He thrust aside the curtain and went downstairs.

"You really shouldn't have lent him money," the Magic Messenger said. "I wanted to stop you, but you'd already let him get his hands on it."

"Why, what's wrong?" said Song Jiang.

"He's honest and big-hearted enough, but he's got a terrible weakness for drinking and gambling. When did he ever have a big lump of silver in hock? I'm afraid you've been had. He was in such a hurry to get out of the door, he must have gone to gamble. If he wins, then you'll get your money back, but if he loses, how's he going to find the ten taels to return to you? And I shall feel bad because I'm responsible."

"Stop treating me like an outsider," Song Jiang said. "Why make such a fuss about a little bit of money? Let him go and lose it if he likes. I'd say he's got the look of a proper hero."

"It's true he's got good qualities, but he's far too rough and too reckless. When he gets drunk up at the prison he doesn't bother the inmates, but he always picks a fight with the strongest of the warders. I've had all sorts of problems with him. He thinks he's got a flair for searching out injustices and beating up bullies. That's why everyone in Jiangzhou is so scared of him."

The poem says:

Bribery makes the law an ass.
Many a prisoner's paid the price.
Revenge for the suffering of the weak,
Heaven has lodged in Li Kui's fist.

"Well, let's drink up," said Song Jiang, "and then let's go and take a stroll in Jiangzhou."

"Of course, I was forgetting," the Magic Messenger said. "I ought to take you to see the river."

"The sights of Jiangzhou, that's just what I would like."

Let us leave the two of them drinking their wine, and follow Iron Ox, who after getting the silver said to himself: "Just imagine! Song Jiang hardly knows me and he's ready to lend me ten taels of silver! That's real thoughtfulness for you, they certainly tell no lies about his generosity! The trouble is, he had to arrive here when I've just been losing continuously at the tables. I haven't a sou. How can I do the proper thing and invite him? Well, since I've got the silver I'd better go and try my luck again. If I can win a few taels I'll be able to invite him and put up a reasonable show."

So Iron Ox hurried off to Zhang's gambling house, somewhere outside the city limits. He went straight to the table and flung down the ten taels of silver. "Pass me the cup, I want to throw," he shouted.

Zhang, who knew that Iron Ox always played fair, said: "You'd better sit this one out. You can come in on the next throw."

"I want to bet on this one!"

"Why don't you just stay on the sidelines and try guessing what's going to come up?"

"I don't want to, I want to bet on this throw. I shall put five taels on." One of the players was just about to throw, but Iron Ox

Chapter 38

swept the cup out of his hands and shouted: "Who is betting against me?"

"All right then, I am," Zhang said. "For five taels."

Iron Ox shouted: "Heads!" and threw, clunk. It was tails.

Zhang scooped up the silver.

"Wait a minute," Iron Ox shouted. "That's ten taels I put down."

"All right," said Zhang. "I'll put another five on. If it's heads this time I'll give you back all your silver."

So Iron Ox took the cup and shouted "Heads!" and again it came out tails.

Zhang grinned and said: "I told you not to bet this time, I said wait. You wouldn't listen to me and now tails have come up twice."

"This silver isn't my own," said Iron Ox.

"What difference does it make whose it is? You've lost, what more is there to say?"

"Well, there's nothing for it," said Iron Ox, "you'll have to lend me some money, I'll pay you back tomorrow."

"Are you crazy? You know the proverb, 'There's no father or son at the gaming table.' You lost, fair and square, so what are you whinging about?"

Iron Ox pulled up his tunic and shouted: "Are you or aren't you going to give me back my money?"

"Mr. Li," Zhang said, "you're usually such a good loser, why're you so churlish today?"

Iron Ox said nothing. He simply seized the silver, grabbing another ten taels or so of other people's, and stuffed it all down the front of his shirt. Then he glared at them and said: "I'm usually a good loser, am I? Well, just for the moment I'm tired of being a good loser."

Zhang rushed forward to wrest the silver from him but Iron Ox sent him flying with a little push. A dozen or more gamesters now converged on Li Kui but he lashed out left and right; he beat them till they didn't know where to hide themselves. He then made for the door. "Hey, where do you think you're going?" the doorman said, but Iron Ox shoved him aside, kicked open the door and left. The other gamblers pursued him as far as the door, shouting: "Mr.

Li, that's not fair! You've taken our money!" They contented themselves however with standing at the door and shouting; no one dared approach any nearer.

Iron Ox was already on his way when he felt a hand on his shoulder, and a voice saying: "What the devil do you mean by stealing the punters' money?"

"You fuck off!" Iron Ox shouted. But when he turned round to look, he saw it was the Magic Messenger, and behind him was Song Jiang. His face fell. "Forgive me, forgive me," he said. "I'm usually a good loser, but today I didn't want to lose your money. And now I haven't even the means to invite you. It made me so sick I just didn't know what I was doing. I'm afraid I was a little hasty."

This made Song Jiang laugh out loud. "If it's just silver you need, for your expenses," he said, "why don't you ask me? Given that there's no doubt you've lost to him, you'd better give him back the money, and quickly."

Li Kui had no alternative but to take out the money and hand it over to Song Jiang who called Zhang over and gave it to him.

"Saving your honours, I shall only take what is mine," Zhang said, "we'll forget about the ten taels Mr. Li lost to me in two throws, for the sake of avoiding recriminations."

"Just go ahead and take it," said Song Jiang, "have no scruples about it."

But Zhang could not be persuaded.

"Well at least no one has been hurt, I hope," Song Jiang said.

"There's the cashier, the croupier and the doorman, he knocked them all out," Zhang said.

"Then let them divide this money between them," Song Jiang said. "I don't suppose Mr. Li will want to show his face here again, so I will give it to you on his behalf."

Zhang accepted the money, saluted and withdrew.

"Now," said Song Jiang, "let us all go and drink a few cups together."

"Down by the river," said the Magic Messenger, "there's a wineshop called the Inn of the Lute. It dates from the days of the poet Bai Juyi, in the Tang Dynasty. Let's go there. We can enjoy the view of the river while we're drinking."

"What about some dishes to go with the wine? Should we get them here in the town first?" said Song Jiang.

"No need, nowadays they've got everything there."

The three of them made their way to the Inn of the Lute. This turned out to have the river Yangtze on one side and the innkeeper's house on the other. There were a dozen or so tables inside. The Magic Messenger chose a nice clean one and asked Song Jiang to take the place of honour. He himself sat down opposite, with Iron Ox beside him. When they were seated they told the innkeeper to send up some dishes of vegetables, fruit and fish.

The waiter brought two jugs of a wine known as "Spring in a jade bottle," which is a famous Jiangzhou brew, and removed the clay stopper. Song Jiang gazed out at the river. It was really a first-class prospect:

Distant peaks rise blue above the clouds; far reaches of the river flash like silver. Flocks of gulls and egrets swirl above the shoreline; a few fishing boats thread their way home through the reeds. White wavelets lap against the skyline; the cool wind breathes soughingly across the face of the water. Amid sunset clouds mountains approach the empyrean; the Inn of the Lute lies half open to the water. The eye is taken by such spaciousness and exquisite decoration: the railing's reflection cased in liquid crystal, jade waters sparkling outside the window. Here sat in days gone by the poet Bai Juyi who rose to literary fame and Sima who achieved high rank after bitter trials.

Iron Ox said: "This wine should be drunk in big bowls. It's nonsense to drink it by the thimbleful."

"Don't be so uncouth," said the Magic Messenger. "Just drink your wine and shut up."

But Song Jiang called the waiter over: "Serve the two of us in the small cups, and bring a big bowl for our big friend here."

The waiter got the extra bowl and then poured the wine and served the dishes.

Iron Ox said: "Song Jiang really is a great man, everything they say about him is absolutely true. How well he understands my tastes. To have him as a sworn brother is really worth something!"

The waiter who served them poured six or seven rounds and then Song Jiang, elated with the company and the wine, suddenly felt a desire for hot fish soup. "Do they have good fish here?" he asked the Magic Messenger.

"Can't you see the river is packed with fishing boats?" the Magic Messenger said. "How could there not be good fish?"

"After all this wine I could really do with some fish soup," Song Jiang said.

The Magic Messenger called the waiter and ordered three bowls of fish soup with chillies and spring onions. They came at once, and when Song Jiang saw them he said: "Good food is nothing to fine china, as the saying is. This is only a simple tavern but look what beautiful china they've served us in!" He picked up his chopsticks and invited the Magic Messenger and Iron Ox to start eating. He himself took some fish and a few mouthfuls of soup.

Iron Ox did not use his chopsticks. He merely plunged his hand into the bowl and pulled out a fish, which he consumed whole, bones and all. Song Jiang couldn't help laughing. He drank another two mouthfuls of soup and then put down his chopsticks and stopped eating.

"I'm afraid the fish is too salty for you," said the Magic Messenger.

"No, I just like to drink the soup, after so much wine. Though actually I have to agree that the fish is not especially good."

"I can't eat it either. Far too salty, quite inedible."

Iron Ox, who had finished the fish in his own bowl, said: "If you both don't want it, I'll eat it for you." He reached over and fished out what was in Song Jiang's bowl and ate it, and then treated the Magic Messenger's bowl the same way. Drops of soup flew all over the place and spattered the table.

When Song Jiang saw that Iron Ox had gobbled up three bowls of fish soup and the bones as well, he called the waiter and said: "I think our big friend here is hungry. Could you get a big piece of meat and cut him a couple of pounds in slices? I'll pay you in just a moment."

"I'm afraid we only have mutton," the man said. "We've no beef. We could give you some good fat mutton, if you like, but that's all there is."

Hearing this Iron Ox flung the remains of his soup in the waiter's face, drenching him from head to foot.

"Whatever are you doing?" the Magic Messenger cried.

"I won't stand for it," Iron Ox answered. "The bugger wants to suggest I only eat beef, to avoid selling me any mutton!"

"I was only asking, that was all," the waiter protested.

"Just go and cut some," said Song Jiang. "I'll pay for it."

The waiter swallowed his anger and went to cut two pounds of meat, which he put on a plate and placed on the table. Iron Ox did not hold back. He grabbed the meat with both hands and commenced to stuff himself. It was all gone in a flash.

"Heavens, what a fellow you are!" Song Jiang exclaimed.

"What a great man this Song Jiang is," said Iron Ox. "How he understands my tastes, damn it. Meat is better to eat than fish any day."

The Magic Messenger called the waiter again. "That fish soup you just gave us — the bowls it was served in are magnificent, but the fish itself is salty and quite inedible. If you've got any other fresh fish, make us another bowl of hot soup, the gentleman here needs something to clear his head after the wine."

"I'll be honest with you," the waiter said. "That fish was yesterday's. Today's live fish is still in the boats. They can't start selling until the factor comes, that's why we haven't got any really fresh fish."

Iron Ox jumped up, saying: "I'll go and get you some myself."

"No, stay where you are," said the Magic Messenger. "We can send the waiter for it."

"The fishermen on the boats won't refuse me," said Iron Ox. "So it had better be me." And before the Magic Messenger could stop him he was off.

The Magic Messenger turned to Song Jiang and said: "I have to ask you to forgive me for bringing that individual along. He's so rude, it's enough to make one die of shame."

"It's his nature," Song Jiang said. "What's the point of trying to change him? I admire his honesty and directness."

Thus the two of them sat talking and laughing together. Here's a poem:

> *Mist on the Pen river, miraculous scene;*
> *Mountains cluster above the banks,*
> *Moonlight, a silver flute and solitude;*
> *Withered sedge, stripped bamboo*
> *And the dew falling.*

Meanwhile Iron Ox had arrived at the riverside, where he found the boats drawn up in a straight line, about eighty or ninety of them, made fast under the green willows. Some of the fishermen lay in the stern, asleep, others were mending their nets in the bows, and still others were bathing in the river. It was the middle of the fifth month, and the sun's red disk was just sinking in the west. But there was no sign of the factor, who was supposed to come to the boats to sell the fish. Iron Ox went and stood near the boats and shouted: "Hey, there! You on the boats, get me two live fish!"

The fishermen replied: "We have to wait. We can't start trading till the boss comes. Can't you see the buyers are all sitting on the bank there?"

"I'm not waiting for your fucking boss. Just give me two fish."

"We haven't even burnt the paper sacrifice, we can't start selling yet. What makes you think we'd sell any to you?"

Seeing that none of them was disposed to get him the fish, Iron Ox leapt onto one of the boats and none of the fishermen dared to stop him. But Iron Ox knew nothing of boats. The first thing he did was to start pulling up the bamboo gate. The fishermen on the bank yelled at him to stop. Next he started rummaging around under the planks of the deck. But how could there be any fish there? You see, the boats on this river have part of the stern cut away, to about half way up the hull, to let the river water flow through, which is how they keep the fish alive. The opening is closed off by a bamboo gate, which allows fresh water to enter but stops the fish escaping. This is why Jiangzhou has such good

Chapter 38

fish. Iron Ox knew nothing about all this. By pulling up the bamboo gate he had let all the fish escape. When he jumped onto another boat and began to do the same thing, all seventy or eighty fishermen rushed onto the boat in order to beat him with their bamboo poles.

Iron Ox waxed furious. He wasn't going to stand for this. He stripped off his cotton tunic leaving only a simple cloth tied about his loins. Seeing a confusion of bamboo poles coming at him he raised both arms and caught four or five of them in his hands, snapping them like someone breaking off chives. The fishermen were horrified. They cast off quickly and poled their boats out into midstream. Iron Ox, half naked, his rage waxing still greater, seized a broken punt pole and leapt onto the bank, where he proceeded to lay into the buyers, who panicked and took to their heels, complete with their carrying-poles.

In the midst of all this confusion, a man appeared, emerging from a little side-alley. "Boss, boss!" they shouted, as they saw him and all gave tongue to their complaints: "That ugly great thug came to steal our fish. He's chased all the boats away."

"What thug?" the newcomer asked. "Who dares to commit such an outrage?"

"The bugger's still there by the river," they said, "looking for people to beat up."

The newcomer advanced towards Iron Ox, saying: "Listen here, you! Even supposing you've eaten a leopard's heart or a tiger's gall, you ought to be afraid of crossing me!"

Iron Ox examined the speaker. He was very tall and about thirty-two years old. He had a full set of whiskers, moustache and beard, he wore a green gauze turban folded in the form of a swastika, and under it a red skull cap; he was dressed in a tunic of white cloth, bound by a belt and had white gaiters and canvas shoes with many buckles and eyes. He was holding a portable scales, and had indeed come to sell the fish. When he saw Iron Ox creating such a commotion, he handed his scales to one of the merchants and advanced on Iron Ox, shouting: "So you want a fight, do you, you swine?" Without even replying, Iron Ox whirled his pole and struck at the other man. But the other darted in and snatched the pole. So Iron Ox grabbed him by the hair, while the other went for the legs, trying to trip him. But how could he have had the strength to match Iron Ox, whose strength was like a water buffalo's? Strain as he might, he couldn't budge him. He essayed several jabs to the ribs but Iron Ox barely noticed them. He tried a flying kick, but Iron Ox merely pressed his head down towards the ground and began hammering his back with iron fists. Struggle as he might he could not get free.

As Iron Ox continued to beat his victim, someone encircled him with his arms from behind while another person assisted, shouting: "Disgraceful! Absolutely disgraceful!"

Iron Ox turned and saw it was Song Jiang and the Magic Messenger. He stopped at once and his adversary escaped from his grip and vanished like smoke.

The Magic Messenger berated Iron Ox. "I told you not to go for the fish, and here you are fighting with these people! If you happened to kill someone, who'd save you from prison or execution?"

"You're afraid I might involve you in something, but if I killed someone, I'd take the responsibility myself," said Iron Ox.

Song Jiang now spoke. "My friend," he said, "don't argue! Just put your tunic on and let us go and drink wine."

Iron Ox picked up his tunic, which was lying at the foot of a willow, and threw it over his shoulders. Then he followed Song Jiang and the Magic Messenger. They hadn't gone ten paces when they heard someone shouting behind them: "You black assassin! We'll see who wins this time!"

Turning to see who it was, Iron Ox saw that it was the same man. But he had stripped naked, except for a pair of bathing trunks, revealing a body white as snow. He had taken off his turban but retained the red skull cap. He was not far from the bank, standing alone in a little fishing boat, which he manoeuvred with a pole, and hurling taunts at Iron Ox. "Come on, you black traitor! Call me a coward if I'm afraid of you! The first to break off is no man!"

Iron Ox went wild when he heard the taunts. He gave a tremendous roar and then, throwing off his tunic, turned and

Chapter 38

黑旋風鬧浪裡白跳

charged. The other manoeuvred his boat so that it was near the bank and held it steady with one hand on the pole, shouting insults all the while. Iron Ox replied in kind. "Come up here on the bank then, if you're not afraid!" The other man struck Iron Ox a blow on the legs with his pole, to infuriate him still further and tempt him to jump onto the boat. The telling is slow, it happens in a flash. All the man wanted was to lure Iron Ox onto the boat. When he succeeded, he pushed his pole into the bank and shoved with both feet so that the boat shot out into midstream, like a leaf whirled away by a sudden gust of wind. Now, although Iron Ox was not completely unfamiliar with the water, his experience of it was not extensive, and he felt a certain trepidation. His opponent, meanwhile, had ceased his insults and thrown down his pole. "Come on, then!" he shouted. "Now we're really going to see who's the best man." He gripped Iron Ox's shoulders and said: "But first of all we're not going to fight, I'm going to teach you how to drink water." He rocked the boat so violently that it capsized and the two heroes were catapulted head over heels into the river, disappearing with a resounding splash. Song Jiang and the Magic Messenger rushed to the bank, but the boat was out in the river and they could only look on helplessly. A crowd had gathered by now and there were four or five hundred people watching under the willow trees. "That black thug is going to learn a lesson," they were saying. "If he comes out of it with his life, he'll at least have got a bellyful of water!" Song Jiang and the Magic Messenger watched the surface of the river break as Iron Ox's opponent dragged him up, only to thrust him under again. The struggle was proceeding out in midstream, where the water rippled by in emerald waves; one body showed as completely black, the other seemed white as frost. They gripped and twined about each other so tightly they seemed welded into one. Every one of the four or five hundred onlookers on the bank was cheering them on.

One is the prodigy of Yishui district; the other is the strange devil of Little Mount Solo. One has a skin that's supple and smooth, the other a hide that might be composed of charcoal dust. One is a metamorphosis of the celestial white serpent, the other a reincarnation of the great black tiger. One is hammered out of sterling silver, the other wrought of tempered steel. One is the white-tusked elephant of Mount Wutai, the other is the iron-scaled dragon of Hell's River. One is a painted Lohan showing off miraculous powers; the other a stone door-god displaying ferocious strength. One writhes and turns until his whole body is soaked in sweat and he exudes real pearls; the other strains till moisture steeps his whole body and black ink floods forth. One resembles the God of Fire, whose form is glimpsed in still clear depths; the other is like the black fiend, whose face appears amid surging white waves. The white dragon obscures the sun in the sky, the black fiend blots out the sky's reflection in the water.

Iron Ox's friends saw that he was helpless in the other's grip and had swallowed water till only the whites of his eyes showed. He was being repeatedly dragged up and submerged. He had gone under more than a dozen times:

*Sail a boat on dry land, such a hard task he craves;
But a bout under water, for that he don't qualify.
Black Whirlwind should never have whipped up the waves.
From Iron Ox, we might say, he has turned water buffalo.*

Seeing Iron Ox was definitely getting the worst of it, Song Jiang asked the Magic Messenger to get someone to help him. "Who is that big white fellow?" the Magic Messenger asked the fishermen. Those who knew replied: "That's the factor, who controls the local sale of fish; his name is Zhang Shun and he's a brave man." At this point Song Jiang remembered something. "Would that be the person they also call White Eel?"

"That's him!" they all cried.

"I've got a letter for him from his brother, Zhang Heng, the Pilot," he told the Magic Messenger. "It's back at the prison."

The Magic Messenger immediately gave a shout in the direction of the river: "Mr. Zhang, stop fighting! We've got a letter for you from your brother. That black fellow is our friend, please let him go, and come up here to talk to us." Out in the river White Eel recognized the Magic Messenger, whom he had seen many times. He let go of Iron Ox, swam to the bank and dragged himself out. He saluted the Magic Messenger and said: "Superintendent, please forgive me if I've done wrong."

"If you want to do something for me, please go and help my friend there. When you bring him back I'll introduce you to someone," the Magic Messenger said.

White Eel dived in again and swam to Iron Ox, who by now was having the greatest difficulty in keeping his head above water. In a moment White Eel was beside him and had grabbed one of his arms. He swam as easily as if he was walking on dry land, his body half out of the water, kicking up big waves with his legs and striking out with his free arm, as he towed Iron Ox to the bank. The onlookers all cheered. Song Jiang was amazed. Finally, when Iron Ox and White Eel were both on the bank, Iron Ox panting for breath and vomiting out water, the Magic Messenger said: "Now we shall all go to the Inn of the Lute to talk."

White Eel put on his tunic again and Iron Ox did likewise and the four of them went back to the inn.

"Do you know who I am?" the Magic Messenger said to White Eel.

"Of course I know the Superintendent, but until now I had not had the opportunity to pay my respects."

Pointing to Iron Ox, the Magic Messenger asked: "And do you know him? I am afraid he attacked you today."

"How could I not know Iron Ox? Only we had not actually been introduced till now."

"That was quite a ducking you gave me!" said Iron Ox.

"And what a drubbing you gave me!" said the other.

"Well now it's made you sworn brothers," said the Magic Messenger. "As the saying is, 'You only really know someone when you've fought with him.'"

"But don't provoke me on dry land," Iron Ox said.

"I shall wait for you in the water," White Eel replied.

They all laughed at this and the two former enemies asked each other's forgiveness. Then the Magic Messenger pointed to

Song Jiang and said to White Eel: "And do you know who this gentleman is?"

White Eel looked him up and down and said: "I don't. I've never seen him before."

Iron Ox jumped to his feet and said: "This gentleman is Song Jiang the Black!"

White Eel said: "Can it really be Registrar Song from Shandong, the Opportune Rain?"

"It is indeed my friend," said the Magic Messenger.

Immediately White Eel prostrated himself before Song Jiang, saying: "I have long heard of your renown, but I didn't expect to meet you here today. I have often heard the folk of the rivers and lakes speak of your great virtue, your kindness to all who need help and your generosity."

"Enough, I don't deserve such praise," said Song Jiang. "A little while back I spent a few days with Li Jun, the White-Water Dragon, near Jieyang. Afterwards I encountered Mu Hong near the Yangtze river and met your brother Zhang Heng, who wrote a letter which he asked me to give you. It's back at the prison, I didn't bring it with me. I came here with Superintendent Dai and our friend Iron Ox just to drink a few cups at the Inn of the Lute and enjoy the scenery. When I happened to say I would like some fresh fish soup to clear my head, Iron Ox insisted on coming to get the fish, nothing we could say would stop him. Then we heard a commotion down by the river. We asked the waiter to go and see what was happening, and he told us it was a big black fellow fighting with someone. So we rushed here to stop it. I had no idea I should meet you. In one day I have made the acquaintance of three great heroes. I must really say fortune has smiled on me. Let me ask you all to sit down and join me in a few more cups."

So the waiter was employed again bringing wine and dishes and preparing another feast. White Eel said: "Since you want fresh fish, I shall go myself to get you some."

"Thank you very much," Song Jiang said.

"I'll go with you," Iron Ox said.

"Oh no, not again!" said the Magic Messenger. "Haven't you drunk enough water already?"

White Eel guffawed and then taking Iron Ox by the hand, said: "This time we'll both go. Let's see what they say to that!" Indeed it can be said that:

He scraps like a tiger on land;
In water he fights like a dragon.
Yet his friendship he'll always extend.
In his home town he's truly a paragon!

Together they left the inn and went down to the river. White Eel gave a whistle and the boats all came rushing towards the bank. "Who's got golden carp?" White Eel asked.

"I have," one answered, and "I've got some," said another. In a moment a dozen fine carp were being presented. White Eel chose the four biggest, threaded them on a willow branch and sent Iron Ox back first to the inn to have them cooked. Meanwhile he organized the buyers and instructed his deputies to start weighing and selling the fish. Then he too returned to the inn and to the company of Song Jiang, who thanked him for the fish. "But why so many?" Song Jiang asked. "If you had given me just one it would have been more than sufficient!"

"A little thing like that! It's not something to make a fuss about," White Eel said. "If you can't eat it all now, you can take it back to your temporary residence for dinner."

They sat in order of seniority. Since Iron Ox was older than White Eel, he took the third place and the latter the fourth. The waiter was called again and two bottles of their best wine, "Spring in a jade bottle," were brought, together with fish, and side dishes. White Eel told the waiter to use one of the fish for soup, steam another in wine, and to cut one into small pieces. As they enjoyed their wine, each of the four men told of something close to his heart, and everything was going swimmingly, when a young girl of about fifteen in a gauze dress suddenly appeared and, having softly wished them all a thousand happinesses, opened her mouth and proceeded to sing. Iron Ox was just on the point of telling them boastfully about various feats of daring when this singing burst out. Since the other three all started listening to the song, he had lost his audience. A fury seized him and jumping up

Chapter 38

he thrust his parted fingers into the girl's face. With a scream she collapsed on the floor. Everyone gathered around the girl. Her face was the colour of earth and no sound issued from her lips. The proprietor of the inn now prevented the four from leaving and said the affair must be referred to the police. It was really a case of "Boil an egret, burn a lute, earn yourself a fine dispute."

If you want to know how finally Song Jiang and his friends escaped from the inn, read the next chapter.

Chapter 39

Song Jiang writes a poem, he should have known better;
The Magic Messenger carries a forged letter!

Now when Iron Ox stuck his fist in that girl's face and knocked her down, the innkeeper thrust himself between them, saying: "Gentlemen, please what are you trying to do?" Anxiously he called his waiters and assistants over to give the girl first aid. When they sprayed water over her face she came to and they helped her to her feet. She had lost a chunk of skin from her temple, which was the cause of her fainting. Now they had brought her round there was general relief.

The girl's parents had heard the name Black Whirlwind, Iron Ox's other name; they were struck dumb and for a long time stood there not daring to open their mouths. Once the girl had regained her speech, her mother took out a handkerchief and bound up her head and then began gathering up her hairpins.

"What is your name, where do you live?" Song Jiang asked them.

"Our name is Song, sir, I'll tell you no lies," the old woman said. "We're from the capital. This is our only daughter, her name's Yulian. Her father has taught her a few songs, and nothing would satisfy him but that she should come to this restaurant and sing to people, to earn a bit of money, you know. But she's so flighty, she has no sense of what's proper. She took no heed that you were talking, she just had to go and sing. Then this gentleman gets impatient and gives her a bit of a knock. We certainly don't want to make a complaint and give you gentlemen a lot of bother."

Seeing that she spoke so circumspectly, Song Jiang said: "If you send someone with me to the camp, I will give you twenty taels of silver. Let her rest and later you can find her a good husband so she won't have to come here and sing for her living."

The old couple prostrated themselves in gratitude, saying: "We don't deserve so much!"

"A promise is a promise," Song Jiang said. "I never go back on my word. Let your husband come with me and I'll settle up with him."

The old people thanked him again. "We are deeply grateful, Your Honour," they said.

"Now look at you," the Magic Messenger said to Iron Ox. "Just in order to shut someone up you've made our friend spend all that money!"

Iron Ox said: "I only meant to touch her with my finger. She fell down by herself. How was I to know the bloody girl was so fragile? You could punch me in the face a hundred times and it wouldn't do anything to me!"

Song Jiang and the others all laughed. White Eel called the waiter over and said to him: "I'm paying."

"Don't worry about that," the man said. "I just want you to leave."

Song Jiang didn't want to accept the offer. "I invited you," he said. "Why should you pay?"

But White Eel was adamant. "When you were in Shandong we were even planning to join you. Now I've got the luck to be here with you face to face, you've got to let me do this little thing."

The Magic Messenger said: "Song Jiang, my friend, it seems Mr. Zhang has set his heart on inviting you, I think you should give way."

"All right, then," said Song Jiang. "On condition that you allow me to invite you another time."

White Eel was satisfied. Carrying the two carp he, the Magic Messenger and Iron Ox, and also old Song, accompanied Song Jiang from the inn back to the prison camp. Arriving there, they went and sat in the inspection room while Song Jiang fetched two bars of silver amounting to twenty taels for the old man, who thanked him and departed. Of him no more.

It was getting dark by now. White Eel gave Song Jiang the fish and the latter handed over his brother's letter. White Eel now left. Song Jiang also gave Iron Ox a fifty ounce silver bar, saying: "This is for you." After which the Magic Messenger and Iron Ox said goodbye and returned to the town.

Song Jiang presented one of the fish to the warden and kept the other himself. The fish was temptingly fresh and tasty, and Song Jiang ate too much of it. That night he had such a pain it felt as if his guts were being tied in knots. By daybreak he had been to the bathroom twenty times. He was so giddy he collapsed on his bed and slept. Since everyone liked him in the camp, they all brought him rice porridge and soup and looked after him and fed him. Next day White Eel came with two more big golden carp, since he knew Song Jiang liked fish, to thank him for bringing the letter. He found him in bed with diarrhoea, attended by the inmates of the camp. White Eel wanted to call the doctor, but Song Jiang said: "It's my own fault for being greedy. I ate too much fish. Just get me some of that special mixture for diarrhoea and I'll be fine." He told White Eel to give the fish away, one to the warden and the other to the Magic Messenger. White Eel did so, and got him the medicine, then left. Of this no more.

The inmates of the camp continued to look after Song Jiang. Next day the Magic Messenger and Iron Ox came to see him in the office, bringing wine and meat, but they found him still sick and unable to face any food, so they consumed it themselves in the front room. They stayed till evening. Of this no more.

Song Jiang continued to rest in the camp for another week or so, after which he felt well much better, quite recovered from the sickness, and began to think about going to see the Magic Messenger in the town. Another day passed and the Magic Messenger did not turn up, so next day after breakfast somewhat before nine o'clock he took some silver, locked his room and left the camp. He strolled easily down the road till he reached the town. In front of the government offices he asked where he could find Superintendent Dai. Someone said: "He has no family, he stays at the monastery of the Goddess of Mercy next door to the Temple of the City God." Thither he directed his steps, but found the door locked and no one in.

Next he inquired about Iron Ox. "He's a restless soul, he doesn't have any fixed place," everyone told him. "He tends to sleep at the gaol, but he doesn't have a regular routine. He'll spend a couple of nights here and a few more there, you can never really say where he lives." Song Jiang also asked about the factor, White Eel. "He lives in a village outside the city," they said. "At the time of the fish auction he's always down by the river. He only comes into town to collect money."

After hearing all this Song Jiang decided to go and look for White Eel in the country. Hoping to meet someone of whom he could ask the way, he strolled along gloomily by himself. When he had left the town behind the river scenery was beautiful, he felt he would never tire of it. He found himself in front of an inn. Raising his eyes he saw the inn sign, a pole from which hung a blue inn pennant bearing the words "Famous wines of the Yangtze River." Attached to the carved eaves was a sign with three characters in the calligraphy of Su Dongpo: "The Yangtze Pavilion." He thought: "At home in Yuncheng I often heard about the wonderful Yangtze Pavilion in Jiangzhou. So this is it! Although I'm on my own here, it would be a pity to miss it. Why not go in by myself and have a drink or two?"

Beside the door were two red carved pillars and on them two white signs each with five characters: "Finest wine in the world, at the world's finest inn." He went upstairs and found himself a seat in an alcove beside the river. Leaning on the rail he looked around. It was indeed a fine inn, with a view that Song Jiang felt no amount of praise could do justice to. The waiter came upstairs and asked: "Are you waiting for someone sir, or are you by yourself?"

Song Jiang said: "I was expecting two people but they haven't come yet, so bring me a jug of good wine first. You can give me some side dishes and some meat too, but I don't want any fish. The waiter went downstairs with the order. Soon he returned with a tray and a jug of Blue Bridge Wind and Rain wine. He set out the dishes of vegetables and fresh fruit of the season, poured the wine, arranged some plates of fat mutton, tender chicken, marinated goose and prime beef all served on handsome red

Chapter 39 337

china. Song Jiang quietly appreciated all this, congratulating himself on his good fortune: "This kind of well-presented food and clean china is typical of all that's best in Jiangzhou. Although I'm sent here as a banished man, I have the opportunity to see some really fine scenery. We've got several famous mountains and ancient monuments at home, but nothing to compare with the prospect here."

Being all on his own, Song Jiang drank one cup after another, leaning on the rail and taking his ease, and he gradually became somewhat tipsy. Suddenly he was filled with melancholy: "I was born in Shandong, I grew up in Yuncheng, I come from an educated family, I have known many heroes of the rivers and lakes, but although I've gained a certain undeserved reputation, I am past thirty and have still achieved no lasting fame and gained no real profit, my cheeks are lined by care, and here I am now, a banished man. My father and younger brother remain at home, what chance have I of ever seeing them again?" Imperceptibly the wine mounted to his head, tears welled up in his eyes, as an overwhelming emotion took hold of him. Suddenly he felt inspired to write a poem. He asked the waiter for a brush and inkstone. After getting up and looking around him, he saw a whitewashed wall covered in previous customers' compositions. "Why not write it here?" he thought to himself. "If later I prosper, and if I pass this way and see it again, it will remind me of former times and today's bitterness." While the euphoria of drunkenness was still upon him, he ground some ink, loaded his brush and going over to the whitewashed wall wrote with a flourish:

I passed a studious youth,
But later learned discretion's worth.
Like a tiger lying in wait on the hill
With sheathed claws I bide my time.
At present I mourn my branded cheeks,
My banished state, here in Jiangzhou.
But the day of my revenge will come
And the banks of the Yangtze swim in blood.

When he'd finished and looked at what he'd written he was

潯陽樓未
江吟反詩

filled with pleasure and he drank several more cups, growing merrier by the moment. He became so excited that his hands began to dance and his feet to tap. He took up the brush again and went and wrote four more lines after the first poem:

> *My heart's in the north, my body in the south,*
> *By this river I wander, wallowing in sighs.*
> *My ambition's lofty as the clouds; if it succeeds,*
> *I can scorn the most famous outlaws' deeds.*

At the end of this he also wrote in big letters: "Song Jiang of Yuncheng wrote this." Then he threw the pen down on the table and recited it to himself. After drinking a few more cups he became really drunk. The wine had completely vanquished him. He called the waiter and asked for the bill. Taking out some silver he gave the waiter more than he owed and told him to keep the change. Then he marched out. Stumbling and swaying he made his way back to the camp. He opened the door of his room and collapsed on the bed, falling asleep at once and not waking till morning. When he awoke he had a hangover and remembered nothing of his poetic efforts at the Yangtze Pavilion the night before.

Now on the other bank of the river opposite Jiangzhou there was a town called Wuweijun, a somewhat desolate place. Here lived a retired official by the name of Huang Wenbing. This individual, although a scholar, was also a great proponent of flattery and servility; he was narrow-minded and prone to envy and spite. Those who were better than himself he would destroy, those who were inferior he ridiculed, and he delighted in offending the local people, who often referred to him as Bee Sting Huang or Bee Huang, for short. He knew that Governor Cai was the son of Grand Preceptor Cai at court and took every opportunity of buttering him up, crossing the river with great frequency to pay him visits, all in the hope of being recommended for a post, since he wanted to serve as an official again. Evidently Song Jiang was destined to be unfortunate, because he came up against this adversary.

One day this Huang Wenbing was sitting at home feeling

bored. He decided to take two servants and go and buy some seasonal gifts. Next he took a fast boat across the river from his house and directed his steps towards the government offices, intending to pay Governor Cai a visit. Unfortunately an official dinner was in progress and he didn't like to go in. Returning to the boat, he found his people had moored it outside the Yangtze Pavilion. Since it was a warm day he decided to go and pass some time inside. He strolled in, and after looking around, took himself upstairs, where he remained leaning happily on the rail. There were a good many poems on the whitewashed wall, he observed. Some were quite good, but others were irregular and confused enough to arouse his contempt. When he came to Song Jiang's poem with the four additional lines, he received a shock: "This is seditious, if I'm not mistaken. Who could have written it?"

Then he saw Song Jiang's name at the end. He read the poem through again: "*I passed a studious youth, But later I learned discretion's worth.* This fellow has a pretty high opinion of his own value," he said to himself. "*Like a tiger lying in wait on the hill, With sheathed claws I bide my time.* The villain evidently has no regard for what is befitting his status. *At present I mourn my branded cheeks, My banished state, here in Jiangzhou.* But this is not some person of rank, it is evidently a convict! *But the day of my revenge will come And the banks of the Yangtze swim in blood.* On whom does the villain desire vengeance? He plans to stir up trouble here. What does he think he can achieve, if he's only a convict? *My heart's in the north, my body in the south, By this river I wander, wallowing in sighs.* These two lines at least are reasonable." When he came to "*My ambition's lofty as the clouds; if it succeeds, I can scorn the most famous outlaws' deeds,*" he nodded to himself and said: "This is an unconscionable villain, he wants to outdo all the great outlaws. If that isn't sedition I don't know what is!" He read the name, "Song Jiang," again, and said: "I've heard that name somewhere. I believe it's some minor official or other."

He called the landlord over and asked: "Who exactly was the author of these two poems?"

"A geezer who came last night all on his own. He drank a

whole bottle of wine and got roaring drunk and went and wrote all that."

"What was he like?"

"He had the golden seals on his cheeks, reckon he was one of them convicts from the prison."

"No doubt of it," said Huang Wenbing. He asked for a brush and inkstone, and copied the poems down on a piece of paper, which he put away. He told the landlord not to rub it out.

When he left the restaurant Huang Wenbing took the boat and went home to sleep. Next day after breakfast accompanied by a servant carrying a box with gifts he made his way to the government office. The governor had just adjourned the court and was in his residence. The servant went in to announce him and after a certain time Governor Cai sent a servant to take Huang into the inner hall. The governor now entered and after an exchange of small talk and the presentation of the gifts they both sat down. "I came across to see you yesterday, Your Excellency, but I found there was an official reception so I didn't like to intrude," Huang Wenbing respectfully explained. "I have come again today to pay my respects and assure you of my gratitude for all the favours you have shown me."

Governor Cai said: "But you're a friend and a colleague, there was nothing whatsoever to stop you coming in. I am afraid I have failed in hospitality."

The Governor's servants now brought tea. Huang Wenbing said: "May I make so bold as to ask, Your Excellency, if you have been vouchsafed any news of your gracious father?"

The Governor replied: "We did receive a letter from home the other day."

Huang Wenbing said: "And what is the news of the noble preceptor, if I may be permitted to inquire?"

"In his letter my papa writes that recently the court astrologers have reported to the Emperor that intensive study of the heavens has revealed an evil star, which is shining on the kingdoms of Wu and Chu. It appears that troublemakers are active in the region, and it is essential to investigate and suppress them. In addition children in the market-place have been heard singing a certain rhyme: 'The bane of our land are home and wood; water and work will do us no good. Thirty-six stand in a row, in Shandong rebellions grow.' My good papa accordingly warns me of the need to keep a tight rein on my province."

Huang Wenbing turned this over in his mind for a while and then said with satisfaction: "Your Excellency, this is not news to me." He took from his sleeve the poem that he had copied and presented it to the Governor, saying: "See what I have here!"

"This is seditious!" the Governor said when he had read it. "Where did you get hold of it?"

"Yesterday afternoon, when I did not want to intrude on you, I went back to the river and having nothing better to do I entered the Yangtze Pavilion to relax and escape the heat. I was looking at the poems customers had written when I saw this, which had been recently written on the whitewashed wall."

"Who do you think could have written it?"

"Your Excellency, the name is clearly written underneath. It says 'Song Jiang of Yuncheng wrote this'."

"I wonder who this Song Jiang is then?"

"He's written plainly enough, '*At present I mourn my branded cheeks, My banished state, here in Jiangzhou.* He's obviously a prison inmate, one of the convicted criminals in the prison camp."

"I wonder what he's up to!"

"You must not neglect this. It's exactly as it said in your gracious father's letter. That rhyme the children were singing corresponds precisely to this man."

"How do you make that out?"

"'The bane of our land are home and wood.' The one who would lay waste our country's wealth and goods must have a name composed of the character for 'home' and the character for 'wood.' That's 'Song,' what could be clearer? The second line, 'water and work do us no good' points to one whose name has 'water' next to 'work,' obviously 'Jiang.' This fellow whose family name is Song, given name Jiang, writes seditious poems. As they say, 'Hear heaven's voice, let the people rejoice!'"

"But what do you make of 'Thirty-six stand in a row, in Shandong rebellions grow'?

"Either it's the year of the Emperor's reign, or it's some kind of magic number. As for 'in Shandong rebellions grow,' well, Yuncheng is in Shandong. This rhyme fits the facts in every particular."

"But is there such a person here?"

"When I asked the innkeeper yesterday he said this person had written the poem only the day before. It's a simple matter, we just need to check the list of prisoners, we'll soon see if he's on it or not."

"You think of everything, my friend," said the Governor, and ordered a servant to tell the prison registrar to bring him the prison records. When the records were brought from the registry, the Governor examined them himself and saw that the name Song Jiang of Yuncheng did indeed appear at the end, as a prisoner who arrived in the fifth month.

"It's our man in the rhyme!" Huang Wenbing cried. "This is serious! If you delay I fear the news will leak out. Better seize him at once and shove him in the lock-up. You can think what to do with him afterwards."

"You're absolutely right." said the Governor. He went into session at once and told an official to summon the prison superintendent immediately.

When the Magic Messenger had saluted, the Governor said: "Take some guards and go at once to the prison camp and arrest the criminal who has been writing seditious poems in the Yangtze Pavilion, a fellow called Song Jiang of Yuncheng, and bring him here. Do not lose a moment."

The Magic Messenger was horrified and lamented in his heart. As soon as he left the courtroom he went and sent all the gaolers home to fetch their weapons and told them to come to a meeting at his house next to the Temple of the City God. They all went off in different directions, while the Magic Messenger sped to the prison camp, using his magic walking, and burst into the copying room. Song Jiang was there when he pushed open the door, and seeing who it was hurriedly greeted him, saying: "The other day I went into town but I couldn't find you anywhere. Since you weren't in and I was bored, I went to the Yangtze Pavilion and drank a bottle of wine. I've been feeling dizzy for the last two days, I've still got the hangover."

"Brother, what's this you wrote on the wall there the other day?"

"Who remembers everything he does when he gets drunk?"

"The Governor just called me into the courtroom and told me to get plenty of guards and go and fetch Song Jiang, accused of writing a seditious poem at the Yangtze Pavilion. I'm to bring you before the court. It gave me quite a shock, I can tell you. For the moment I've got all the guards waiting at the Temple of the City God, so I could come and let you know first. What are we going to do? How are we going to get you out of this?"

Song Jiang hearing this scratched his head but could think of nothing. He could only lament. "This time I'm really done for!" he said.

"I'll tell you one possible way out dear brother, but I don't know if you'll like it. I daren't delay now, but before I come back with the others to arrest you, you must mess up your hair and smear excrement on the floor and fall down in it. You must pretend to be mad. When we come for you, rave and gibber as if you've gone clean out of your mind. I'll go back and tell the Governor about it."

"I'll gratefully follow your suggestion, brother, I just hope it works."

The Magic Messenger hurried off. He went to his house beside the Temple of the City God and told all the guards to hurry with him to the prison camp. Arriving there he shouted with deliberate fierceness: "Where is the new prisoner Song Jiang?"

What the chief of militia saw when he led his men into the copying room was Song Jiang with his hair in total disorder, rolling about in his own filth.

When he saw the Magic Messenger and the guards Song Jiang said: "Who the bloody hell are you?"

The Magic Messenger gave a calculated roar: "Seize the bastard!"

Rolling his eyes and wildly waving his arms, Song Jiang babbled: "I am the Jade Emperor's son-in-law. His Majesty has sent me here with a hundred thousand men to kill all of you Jiangzhou people, the King of Hell is in the vanguard and the Demon General in the rear. They gave me a silver seal weighing more than eight hundred catties to kill you scum."

The guards all said: "This is obviously a lunatic. What's the use of arresting him?"

"You're quite right," said the Magic Messenger. "We'd better go and report this. If they really want him we can always come back."

They all went with the Magic Messenger to the government offices where the Governor was awaiting them in the courtroom. They reported to the Governor as follows: "Evidently this Song Jiang is mad. He's covered in excrement and he doesn't even care, he's ranting and raving and he stinks to high heaven. We didn't like to bring him here."

Before the Governor had time to inquire further, Huang Wenbing slipped out from behind the screen and said to him: "Don't believe it. The one who wrote the poems did not write like a madman. There's some deception here. Arrest him anyway. If he can't walk, then have him carried here."

"You're right," said the Governor. "Don't argue," he told the Magic Messenger, "just bring him!"

The Magic Messenger having received this order could only lament and return with the guards to the prison camp. He told Song Jiang: "Dear brother, things do not look good. I'm afraid you'll have to go." A bamboo cage was brought and in it Song Jiang was taken to the district court.

"Bring the felon here," the Governor ordered.

The guards forced Song Jiang in front of the bench, but he refused to kneel. He glared at Governor Cai and said: "Who the hell are you? How can you dare to question me! I am the son-in-law of the Jade Emperor and I have orders from His Majesty to bring an army of a hundred thousand troops to kill all you Jiangzhou people. The King of Hell is in the vanguard, the Demon General in the rear, and they've given me a silver seal weighing eight hundred catties. Let me go at once or you shall die for it!"

The Governor could not make head or tail of all this. But Huang Wenbing said: "Call the prison warders and ask them if this man was mad when he arrived, or whether he only recently became mad. If he was mad when he came, then it's genuine. But if he only recently became mad, he's a fake."

"That's a very good idea," said the Governor. He sent people to the prison camp, where the warders did not dare deceive him and had to say: "When this man arrived he did not seem to be mad, this madness seems to have appeared only recently."

The Governor was outraged. He ordered the gaolers to tie Song Jiang up and give him fifty lashes on the spot without pause. Song Jiang was beaten till he lost consciousness and was half way to nirvana. The skin was broken, wounds opened and the blood poured out. The Magic Messenger could only watch and lament and could think of no way to help him. At first Song Jiang continued to rave, but finally under the torment of the beating he confessed: "It was a mistake, I was drunk, the poem was a piece of foolishness, it has no meaning."

Having obtained this confession, the Governor imposed the twenty-five catty cangue of a condemned man and ordered Song Jiang to be locked up in the prison. He had been beaten till he could no longer walk. After the cangue was fitted he was thrown into a cell for condemned prisoners. The Magic Messenger did what he could to help by telling the gaolers to take great care of this prisoner. He also arranged food for Song Jiang. Of this no more.

When the court adjourned Governor Cai invited Huang Wenbing into the residence to thank him. "If not for your perspicacity and far-sightedness," he said, "I was close to being deceived by that scoundrel."

Huang said: "Your Excellency, this business is still pressing. Quickly write a letter, to be delivered with all possible speed to the Grand Preceptor, informing him of everything, and pointing out how you are dealing with a matter of national import. And tell him at once that if he wants the prisoner alive a prison cart will be used to transfer him to the capital; but if he does not want him alive, given the very real danger of losing him *en route*, let

Chapter 39

him be beheaded right here, as an example to felons and to deter further disorders. When this is known at court it cannot fail to please."

"What you say makes good sense. When I write home I will commend your efforts and ask my father to petition the Emperor on your behalf for an appointment as governor of some wealthy district, so you may gain wealth and fame."

Huang thanked him. "I am deeply indebted to you, Your Excellency. I shall remain forever your faithful servant."

Having thus persuaded Governor Cai to write a letter home and put his seal on it, Huang Wenbing now asked: "Whom can you send with it that you trust?"

"I have a prison superintendent in my district called Dai Zong who can do what is known as magic walking, he can cover more than two hundred miles a day and still arrive early. If we get him to take it, he'll be there and back in around ten days."

"If he is really so fast, that's splendid, splendid!"

The Governor laid on wine in a back room, and entertained Huang Wenbing. Next day the latter bade the Governor farewell and returned to Wuweijun.

Governor Cai prepared two gift boxes and filled them with gold, pearls, jewels and other such pleasant things and placed his seals upon them. First thing next morning he summoned the Magic Messenger to the residence and said: "I have certain gifts and a letter which I want delivered to the Grand Preceptor's palace in the Eastern Capital to honour my father's birthday on the fifteenth of the sixth month. Since the date is so close, you are the only one who can get there in time. If you spare no effort, going without pause for sleep, and bring back the reply, I shall value your services most highly. Be assured that I have your future very much at heart. I have worked out how long it should take with your magic walking, and I shall await your return. Do not linger on the way or make any mistake."

The Magic Messenger could hardly refuse. He was obliged to take up the letter and the gift boxes and make his farewells. After making arrangements for the journey he went to the prison and said to Song Jiang: "Don't worry, brother, the Governor is sending me to the Grand Preceptor's but I'll be back within ten days. I can make some inquiries at the Preceptor's court and perhaps find a way to resolve your affair. I will leave the matter of your food in Iron Ox's hands. He will arrange for you to get it and won't let you go short. So just stay calm and resist for a few days."

"If you can just save my life that will be quite enough," said Song Jiang.

The Magic Messenger called Iron Ox and gave him his instructions there and then: "Our brother made the mistake of writing a seditious poem and has got a prison sentence for it. How it will end I don't know. I'm under orders from the Governor to go to the Eastern Capital, but I'll be back in a little while. I am making you responsible for bringing him his food, morning and evening. Be sure to look after him properly."

Iron Ox answered: "Why the hell should reciting a bloody poem be such a big deal? People can have led actual rebellions and they get promoted to important posts. But don't worry, you can go off to the Eastern Capital with an easy mind, no one in the prison will dare to interfere with him. If everyone behaves, all well and good. If they don't, I'll get my axe and behead the fuckers."

Before he left, the Magic Messenger again admonished him: "Take care, brother, don't indulge in wine and neglect our brother's meals. Don't go and get drunk and leave him to starve."

"Brother, set your mind at rest. If you're really so worried, I'll promise to give up drinking completely until the day you return. I'll stay in the prison and look after Song Jiang all the time, how's that?"

The Magic Messenger was very pleased with this. "If you're truly resolved to look after him well, that's fine." After the Magic Messenger had said goodbye that day and left, Iron Ox really did give up drinking and stayed all the time in the prison to look after Song Jiang, not straying by so much as a footstep from his post.

We will leave Iron Ox to look after Song Jiang and follow the Magic Messenger as he returns home, puts on new leggings and hemp shoes and an apricot yellow tunic, adjusts his belt and attaches his name tablet to it, dons a new headdress, puts the letter and travelling expenses away in the bag, slings the two gift boxes on a pole and leaves town. He has with him four of the special amulets for magic walking, two for each leg. He has only to intone the magic formula and magic walking will commence:

> *Like riding on mist he goes, like walking on air. Feet skimming the ground he soars over the mountains. One minute he's leaving a country town, the next he's passing a great city. Truly miraculous are the priceless magic amulets, with them a hundred leagues is as an inch before one's nose.*

The day the Magic Messenger left Jiangzhou he travelled till nightfall before stopping at an inn to rest. He removed the amulets and burnt a quantity of paper gold as an offering. After a night's rest he was up early, partook of food and drink and left. He had tied on the four amulets again and was carrying the boxes on a pole. He set off at a grand pace, flying along with the sound of wind and rain in his ears, his feet not touching the ground. He planned to stop only for some vegetarian food and plain wine, or a few snacks. When night fell, he stopped at once and found an inn to rest in. Next day he was up at dawn to profit from the morning cool. On he went with his four amulets and the boxes on a pole. When he had done nearly a hundred miles, quite early in the morning, he looked about for a clean inn, but not one did he see. It was the beginning of the sixth month and so hot the sweat was pouring off him, he was completely drenched, and he was afraid of getting sunstroke. Also he was extremely hungry and thirsty. Then he saw in front of him, by the edge of a little wood, a most inviting inn, situated beside the water on the edge of a lake. He lost no time in approaching. It looked spotlessly clean and had places for twenty; the tables and benches were painted red and lined up along the windows. He entered with his carrying-pole and found a secluded seat. He put down the boxes, took off the shoulder strap, and sprinkled his yellow tunic with water and hung it up to dry on the window rail. As soon as he sat down the waiter approached and said: "How much wine can I serve you, sir? And what would you like to eat with it? We've got pork, mutton or beef."

The Magic Messenger said: "I don't want a lot of wine, but bring me a spot of rice."

"As well as wine and rice we've got fresh bread and noodle soup."

"I won't eat meat. Have you got any vegetarian food?"

"I can find you some chilli tofu, how about that?"

"That'll do fine."

In no time at all the waiter had produced a bowl of tofu, served some dishes of vegetables and poured three big bowls of wine. Since the Magic Messenger was hungry and thirsty, he scoffed the wine and the tofu in one go and was about to ask for more rice when suddenly the whole world started to spin. His brain began to cloud, stars danced before his eyes, and he collapsed in a heap beside the bench. "He's gone!" the waiter cried, and a man immediately appeared from inside. This is what he was like:

> *His frame is big, his waist is small,*
> *For guests he always has a smile.*
> *This hero on Mount Liang they call*
> *Zhu Gui the Dry Land Crocodile.*

When the Crocodile entered, he said: "Take the boxes in, but first search him and see if he's carrying anything."

Two rascals hastened to do his bidding. When they searched the Magic Messenger they drew from an inner pocket a roll of paper containing a letter which they handed to the Crocodile. The Crocodile tore it open and saw that it was a personal letter because the envelope bore this message: "Hoping it finds you in peace, this letter carries respectful greetings, dear father, from your most obedient son Cai Dezhang." The Crocodile broke open the envelope and began to read. The letter began: "Having captured a certain Song Jiang of Shandong, author, as the popular rhyme foretells, of a seditious poem, and having closely confined him in prison for the time being, I now await your instructions ..."

For quite a while the Crocodile was struck dumb by the gravity of what he read. His assistants picked the Magic Messenger up and lugged him into the butcher shop to cut him up. But his belt was left beside the bench, with the red and green name tablet still

Chapter 39

attached to it. The Crocodile picked this up and examined it. Engraved on it in silver letters was: "Dai Zong, Chief Superintendent of the two prisons of Jiangzhou."

"Stop!" the Crocodile shouted to the assistants, "don't begin yet. I often heard the military leader say that in Jiangzhou there is a 'magic messenger' named Dai Zong who is his dearest friend. I wonder if this can be he? But why would he be carrying a letter so injurious to Song Jiang? Thank heavens this letter has fallen into our hands! Let's get the antidote and bring him round. There's a few answers I'd like to get from him."

His assistants mixed the antidote in some water. They supported the Magic Messenger's head and poured it into him. In a little while his eyebrows began to twitch and his eyes to flutter. Then with an effort he sat up. When he saw the Crocodile was holding the opened letter in his hand, he shouted: "Who the hell are you? How dare you knock me out with drugs! And how could you take it on yourself to break open a private letter to the Grand Preceptor? That is a most fearful crime!"

The Crocodile only laughed: "What does the fucking letter matter? So what if it's a letter to the Preceptor I've opened? As far as I'm concerned, a letter like this gives me a bone to pick with the Emperor himself."

The horrified Dai Zong asked: "Who are you, my friend? May I ask your name?"

"I've no call to hide or conceal it," he replied. "Zhu Gui, the Dry Land Crocodile, from the band of heroes on Mount Liang, that's me."

"Then if you are one of the leaders of Mount Liang, you must know 'Professor' Wu Yong?"

"'Professor' Wu Yong is our military leader, in charge of our army. How do you know him?"

"We are close friends."

"I suppose you're not by any chance the Magic Messenger of Jiangzhou, Superintendent Dai Zong, of whom our military leader has so often spoken?"

"I am he."

"But before Song Jiang went to his place of exile in Jiangzhou, he passed through our mountain stronghold and the Professor gave him a letter for you. So why do you now seek to undo Mr. Song and take his life?"

"Song Jiang and I are also close friends. Recently because he composed a seditious poem I was unable to save him from prosecution. Now I am on my way to the Preceptor's court where I hope to find some way of saving him. How could I possibly want to harm him?"

"If you don't believe me, take a look at this letter of Governor Cai's."

The Magic Messenger looked and got a shock. He told the Crocodile everything about the letter from the Professor and his first meeting with Song Jiang and how Song Jiang had got drunk in the Yangtze Pavilion and written that poem, with such unfortunate results. The Crocodile said: "In that case, you must please come to the mountain retreat and discuss with the leaders what to do, how we can save Song Jiang's life."

Having hurriedly ordered wine and food to be served in the Magic Messenger's honour, the Crocodile went to the water pavilion and loosed a signal arrow towards the opposite shore. In response to the signal, some soldiers quickly rowed over in a boat. The Crocodile and the Magic Messenger got into the boat with the boxes and were rowed across to Golden Sands Landing. When the Professor was informed at the camp he rushed down to receive them. Greeting the Magic Messenger, he courteously said: "It is long since we parted, what wind has blown you here? Please come up to our stronghold and meet all the leaders."

The Crocodile explained why the Magic Messenger had come and how Song Jiang had recently been sentenced. On hearing this, Chao Gai anxiously asked the Magic Messenger to take a seat and tell them what exactly Song Jiang had received such a sentence for. The Magic Messenger told them all about the affair of the seditious poem. Chao Gai was so upset by this that he wanted everyone immediately to saddle their horses and muster their men and go down to attack Jiangzhou and bring Song Jiang back.

But the Professor objected: "Not so fast, brother. Jiangzhou's a long way from here. With all those troops on the move we'd be certain to make a big stir and raise the alarm, with the gravest consequences for Song Jiang. We can't use just force in this matter, we must use our brains. Now I'm not very clever, and all I can devise is a simple plan, but with Superintendent Dai's assistance I think we can certainly save Song Jiang's life."

Chao Gai said: "Please tell us your plan, it's sure to be good."

"Governor Cai has sent Superintendent Dai with a letter to the capital. He is expected to bring back the Grand Preceptor's answer. Now this answer is our opportunity. We must forge an answer for the Superintendent to take back. The letter will say, 'On no account are you to take action against the criminal Song Jiang yourself. He must be sent under close guard to the capital. We will interrogate him to uncover all the facts, then execute him publicly in order to scotch the rumours.' When they bring him past here we will send troops down the mountain to seize him. How's that?"

"But suppose they don't pass this way? It could all go disastrously wrong!" Chao Gai objected.

Taoist Gongsun Sheng said: "That's all right. We can send out scouts far and wide, so that whichever route they take, we've only to wait and in the end we'll get him. I'm only afraid they might not send him."

Chao Gai said: "Very well then. But there isn't anyone who can write the letter in Preceptor Cai's calligraphy."

"I've already thought of that," said the Professor. "Nowadays four schools of calligraphy are flourishing: Su Dongpo's, Huang Luzhi's, Mi Yuanzhang's, and the Grand Preceptor Cai Jing's. These four, Su, Huang, Mi and Cai are the four greats of the Song Dynasty. Now I am acquainted with a certain bachelor in Jizhou, by name Xiao Rang, whom everyone calls Magic Hand, because he is able to reproduce all the famous calligraphers' styles. He is in addition quite adept with the spear and the staff, and knows how to thrust and parry with a blade. I am sure he can do the Grand Preceptor's writing. Why don't we send Superintendent Dai to speak to him and say, 'The Temple of the Peaks in Tai'an wants an inscription done, they're sending you this payment in advance of fifty taels of silver for your family's expenses,' and then get him to come. Afterwards we can send people to bring all his family up the mountain so we can persuade him to join our company. How about that?"

Chao Gai said: "He can write the letter, that's all right, but we'll need a seal as well, to stamp it."

"There's another friend of mine, I've got it all worked out. This one is also a native of central China, living in Jizhou. His name is Jin Dajian, he's a great stone-carver and he makes beautiful seals and jade carvings. He also knows how to use a staff. He's such a wonderful carver of jade that everyone knows him simply as the Craftsman. We'll send another fifty taels to persuade him to come and do the carving. While he's on the way, we'll carry out the same plan. We can use both of these men in the stronghold."

Chao Gai said: "That's brilliant!"

After a banquet that day in honour of the Magic Messenger they all went to bed.

Next day after breakfast the Magic Messenger was asked to dress up as the abbot of a monastery. Carrying a few hundred tales of silver, he tied on his amulets and descended the mountain. He was ferried across from Golden Sands Landing to the other bank and set off at speed for Jizhou. In under four hours he reached the city and began asking for Magic Hand Xiao Rang. Someone told him: "His house is by the Confucian temple to the east of the government offices."

When the Magic Messenger arrived at the door, he gave a cough and asked: "Is Master Xiao at home?" A scholarly-looking gentleman emerged. Not knowing who the Magic Messenger was, he asked: "What is it, father? What can I do for you?"

After a courteous greeting, the Magic Messenger said: "I am abbot of the monastery of the Temple of the Peaks in Tai'an. We are engaged in repairing the Five Peaks Tower and the rich men of our district want to have a tablet inscribed. They have entrusted me with the mission of presenting this silver to you, fifty taels in remuneration for your services, and asking you to be so good as to accompany me to the temple to carry out the work. The day is chosen, it brooks no delay."

Chapter 39

Magic Hand said: "All I can do is to write the pattern, nothing else. If you want to set up a tablet you need an engraver as well."

"I have another fifty taels of silver here and it is my intention to ask Jin Dajian, the Craftsman, to do the engraving. We have found an excellent day for it, I do hope you will agree. If you can help me find the Craftsman, we will all go together."

Magic Hand took the silver and went with the Magic Messenger to seek the Craftsman. When they arrived at the Confucian temple, Magic Hand suddenly pointed: "That fellow coming towards us is the Craftsman, Jin Dajian." Magic Hand stopped him and introduced him to the Magic Messenger, explaining about the Tai'an temple and the repair of the Five Peaks Tower, and the rich people wanting a tablet, and how the abbot had fifty taels of silver for each of them if they went along with him. Jin Dajian was impressed by the silver. The two of them invited the Magic Messenger to have a cup of wine and some side dishes with them in a local hostelry. The Magic Messenger handed over the silver to the Craftsman and said: "The fortune-teller has fixed the day, I would like you to get going right away."

"The weather's very hot," said Magic Hand. "If we start now we won't get very far and we may not even find somewhere to spend the night. It would be better to get up at dawn tomorrow and take ourselves off then."

"I'll second that," said the Craftsman.

So they agreed to get an early start next day and went home to pack their things in readiness. Magic Hand invited the Magic Messenger to spend the night with him.

Next day at dawn the Craftsman appeared with his luggage and the three of them set off together. When they had gone less than three miles, the Magic Messenger said: "You keep going at your own pace, I don't want to hurry you. I'll go on ahead to tell the leaders so they'll be ready to receive you." With this he quickened his pace and raced on in front. The other two, with their luggage, proceeded quite slowly. In the early afternoon, when they had done some twenty miles or so, they suddenly heard a wild whistle and a band of men came leaping down the hillside. There were around fifty of them and they were led by Short-Arse Wang of

Windy Mountain, who roared out: "You two, who are you and where are you heading? Catch 'em boys, we'll have their hearts to eat with our wine."

"We're only two craftsmen going to engrave a tablet for the Tai'an temple, we haven't a penny of our own, all we've got is some clothes."

"I don't want your money or your clothes," said Short-Arse. "All I want from a pair of clever dicks like you is your hearts and livers to eat with wine."

Thus beset, Magic Hand and the Craftsman had to summon up their courage, raise their staves and charge him. Short-Arse likewise raised his halberd and attacked. Wielding their various weapons they had fought out half a dozen bouts when Short-Arse suddenly turned about and left. They were about to give chase when they heard a sound of gongs on the mountain and from the left appeared the Door-God in the Clouds, Song Wan, and from the right Skyscraper Du Qian, followed by Whitey Zheng. Each was accompanied by thirty troops. They immediately seized Magic Hand and the Craftsman and dragged them into the forest.

"Don't be afraid," they said. "We are under orders from Leader Chao to invite you to come and join our band on the mountain."

Magic Hand said: "What does the mountain stronghold want us for? We haven't the strength to tie up a chicken, all we're good for is eating up rice."

The Skyscraper said: "General Wu knows you. Also he knows about your valour and martial skills. The Magic Messenger was sent specially to get you."

They looked at each other in amazement, uncertain what to say. But by now they had reached the Crocodile's inn, where everyone was provided with wine and food, and the same night a boat was summoned and they were taken up the mountain. When they reached the stronghold they met Chao Gai, the Professor and all the other leaders. A banquet was held and they were told about the forging of Cai Jing's reply — "That's why we invited you to come and join our company."

When they heard this they each put a restraining hand on the

Professor's sleeve and said: "We could stay here, that's no problem, but we've both got our families at home to think of, when the authorities find out they'll make them suffer."

The Professor said: "There's no need for you to worry about that. Tomorrow you'll see why." The rest of the evening was given up to eating and drinking.

First thing next morning a soldier came and announced: "They're all here."

The Professor said to Magic Hand and the Craftsman: "Please come and personally receive your families." They didn't know whether to believe him or not. Halfway down the mountain they met a number of sedan chairs carrying their families up — everyone was there, young and old. Magic Hand and the Craftsman were amazed and asked them what exactly had happened. They all said: "After you left yesterday, these people came with the sedan chairs and said you were at an inn outside the city and had caught a fever. They wanted us to come with the whole family to save you. Once we left the city they wouldn't let us get out of the chairs. They just brought us straight here." Both families told exactly the same story. Magic Hand and the Craftsman kept quiet after that and resolved to return up the mountain and join the band. Two dwellings were prepared for their families. The Professor then asked them to join him and discussed with Magic Hand the writing of the reply in Cai Jing's handwriting which was going to save Song Jiang's life. The Craftsman said: "I have carved every seal of the Grand Preceptor's, both with his official name and his personal name." The two of them set to work and produced the letter. After this there was a banquet, and then the Magic Messenger was sent off on his journey, having been told exactly what to do. The Magic Messenger said his farewells and went down the mountain. The soldiers rowed him across from Golden Sands Landing to the Crocodile's inn. There he tied on his four amulets, said goodbye to the Crocodile and set off.

After the Professor had seen the Magic Messenger off at the ferry, he returned with the others and they had a big dinner. But just as they were drinking, he suddenly uttered a loud despairing cry. The other leaders asked: "What ever is the matter, general?"

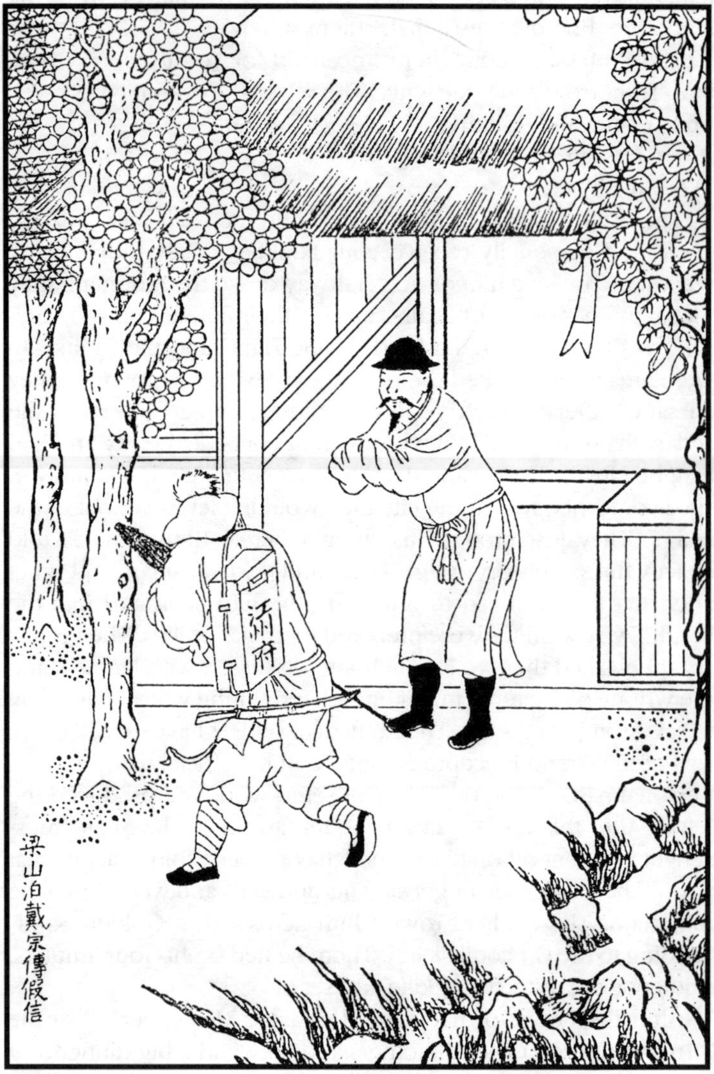
梁山泊戴宗傳假信
濟州府

Chapter 39

"You just can't imagine! That letter of mine has signed the Magic Messenger's and Song Jiang's death warrants!"

Horrified, they asked: "But what is wrong with your letter?"

"I couldn't see the wood for the trees! It contains a fatal flaw!" Magic Hand said: "I copied the Grand Preceptor's hand perfectly, not a word was wrong. Where is the fault?"

The Craftsman also said: "I'm sure my carving was perfect, not a single slip, so what's this fatal flaw you're talking about?"

The Professor joined his fingers and explained the mistake. Without this mistake, how would we have seen that:

In Jiangzhou town, the heroes create turmoil,
In White Dragon temple, the pot starts to boil.

Nor would it have been the case that:

Amid a storm of arrows men flee for their lives,
From the midst of a forest of weapons a hero is saved.

But if you want to know what mistake the military leader, "Professor" Wu Yong had made, you must read the next chapter.

Chapter 40

The heroes of Mount Liang raid the execution ground;
Twenty-nine leaders at White Dragon temple assemble!

When Chao Gai and the others asked the Professor: "What is the error contained in your letter?" the latter replied: "When I wrote that answer which Superintendent Dai has just taken I had a lapse of concentration, I completely overlooked something. The letter was stamped with the four characters, 'Hanlin Academician Cai Jing,' was it not? It's that stamp which is going to betray the Magic Messenger."

"But I've seen Preceptor Cai's writings and compositions many, many times," said the Craftsman. "They always bear that stamp. I carved it perfectly, there's not a single error, how can there be something wrong?"

"Don't you see?" the Professor said. "Governor Cai, present governor of Jiangzhou, is the Grand Preceptor's son. How can a father use his own name on the stamp when he writes to his son? It's simply not done! That's the mistake I made. I completely overlooked it. When the Magic Messenger reaches Jiangzhou they'll put him to the torture and demand the true facts. It's a disaster."

"Quickly, send some one to catch him and bring him back," said Chao Gai. "Then we can write it again, can't we?"

"How could anyone catch him? He'll be doing his magic walking. He'll have done at least a hundred and fifty miles by now. But there's not a moment to be lost. There's just one way for us to save them."

"How can we save them, what's your plan?" said Chao Gai.

The Professor leant forward and whispered in Chao Gai's ear: "We must do this, and this ... and so, and so.... You must pass the word round quietly, let everyone know. This is our only chance, we must not let it slip."

When they had all received their orders, each made his preparations for travel and that same night they went down the mountain and headed for Jiangzhou. Of this no more. You may ask why I do not tell you what the plan was, but just be patient and you shall see.

By this time the Magic Messenger had arrived back in Jiangzhou exactly on time and gone to deliver the letter. Governor Cai was delighted to find him so punctual and entertained him for three whole hours. On receiving the letter, he asked: "Did you see my father?"

"I only stayed one night and left the next day," the Magic Messenger replied. "I was not able to see His Excellency."

The Governor broke open the letter and read first of all that the various items in the boxes had all been safely received. Further on his father said that he wished personally to question the dangerous criminal, Song Jiang, who was to be sent immediately to the capital in a secure prison cart closely guarded and with an appropriate escort. Every precaution was to be taken to prevent his escaping along the way. The letter ended by saying that Huang Wenbing would be recommended in due course to the Emperor and would undoubtedly receive an appointment. When he read all this, Governor Cai's joy knew no bounds. He had a silver ingot weighing twenty-five catties brought and presented it to the Magic Messenger. He also ordered a prison cart and discussed whom to send with it as escort. The Magic Messenger thanked him and went home. He bought some wine and meat and went to the prison to see Song Jiang. Of this no more.

Governor Cai did all he could to expedite the construction of the prison cart and within a day or two it was on the point of setting off, when the porter suddenly announced: "Huang Wenbing of Wuweijun is asking to see you." Governor Cai invited Huang into the residence. Huang presented several gifts, new wine and seasonal fruit, for which the Governor thanked him, saying: "This is too much, you really shouldn't."

"Just local stuff, barely worth your trouble," Huang replied.

Governor Cai said: "I have to congratulate you on a prestigious appointment."

"Has Your Excellency heard something then?" Huang responded.

"The messenger returned yesterday. The malefactor Song Jiang is to be sent to the capital. And in due course you will be recommended to the Emperor and you will receive an important post. It's all in my father's letter."

"Then I am most deeply grateful for Your Excellency's interest. And that messenger of yours is indeed miraculous."

"If you don't believe me, take a look at the letter and see for yourself."

"I fear it is taking too much on myself to read your personal letter. But if you insist, I would like to take just a glance at it."

"We are the closest of friends, of course you can see it." He told a servant to bring the letter and then handed it to Huang Wenbing.

Once he got it in his hands, Huang Wenbing examined that letter from head to tail. He turned it around and looked at the envelope and observed that the stamp was new. He nodded to himself and said: "This letter is not authentic."

"You must be mistaken. It is written by my father himself, it is in his own hand. How can it not be authentic?"

"Your Excellency, when a letter comes from home does it usually bear this stamp?"

"Indeed, in the general run of things the letters do not have this stamp, they are usually addressed informally. In this case the chop must just have been lying to hand, so he stamped the envelope with it".

"Your Excellency, please do not count it an impertinence on my part! But this letter has been written to deceive you. At present there are four famous styles of calligraphy, Su, Huang, Mi and Cai, and everyone has studied them. In addition, this stamp came out when your father was appointed a member of the Hanlin Academy, it appeared on official documents and there are many who have seen it. But now he has been promoted to Grand Preceptor. Why would he go back to the Hanlin Academy stamp? And what is more, this is a father writing to his son, he could not use his own name on the seal. Your worthy father is a man of great knowledge and understanding. How could he make a careless mistake like this? If you do not believe me, question the messenger carefully about the people he saw at your father's palace. If he gets it wrong, the letter is forged. Please do not think ill of me for saying all this. It is only because you have shown me such favour that I so presume."

"Well, it's easy enough," the Governor said. "The fellow has never been to the capital before, we've only to question him and the truth will out."

Governor Cai had Huang Wenbing sit behind the screen while he went into session and announced that he had business with the Magic Messenger. Officers were accordingly sent out in all directions to look for him. There is a poem which says:

> *After the poem, the forged letter;*
> *The bandits were trying to make things better.*
> *But for the sting in Bee Huang's tail,*
> *The governor, poor fool, had fallen for it all.*

When the Magic Messenger got back to Jiangzhou he had gone first to the gaol to see Song Jiang, in whose ear he whispered all that had happened. Song Jiang was overjoyed. After that someone invited the Magic Messenger to drink with him. So he was drinking in a tavern when he heard that the officers were looking for him. When he reached the court, the Governor said: "I gave you a hard mission and I have not yet sufficiently shown my appreciation of your efficiency."

"I went as a special messenger in your service, of course I wouldn't waste any time," the Magic Messenger replied.

"I've been very busy lately, I didn't have time to ask you more. When you went to the Grand Preceptor's palace for me the other day, which gate did you enter by?"

"When I reached the capital it was already dark, I couldn't tell which gate it was."

"Who was it who received you in our residence? And where did you stay?"

"When I got to the palace I found a gate and went in with the letter. Almost immediately a porter appeared. He took the boxes and then told me to go and find an inn to sleep. Next morning I got up at dawn and went to wait at the gate. They brought the answer out right away and since I didn't want to be late I naturally didn't ask any questions but just got going at once."

"Which porter did you see? How old was he? Was he a thin dark man, or a fat man with a pale complexion? Was he tall or short? Did he have a beard and whiskers or was he clean-shaven?"

"It was quite dark when I arrived, and I left next morning in the fifth watch, so it still wasn't properly light, you couldn't make anything out clearly. As far as I could tell he was getting on, he was about medium height, and I think he had something of a beard."

The Governor exploded. "Arrest this man!" he screamed. A dozen guards rushed forward and threw the Magic Messenger to the ground.

"But I haven't done anything!" the Magic Messenger protested.

"You deserve to die, you bastard!" the Governor shouted. "Our old gatekeeper, Wang Gong, has been dead for years. There's only Young Wang now to keep the gate, how can you say he's old and has a beard? And in any case the porter, Young Wang, isn't allowed to enter the house. If any missive or package arrives the procedure involves first Zhang, the major-domo, then the secretary, Li, who reports within, and only then is it received. And for a reply there's always a wait of three days. I sent those two boxes of things, how could they be received just like that, instead of some confidential person coming and asking you to give a complete account? I was in a hurry yesterday and for a moment you fooled me. Now you'd better confess right away where you got that letter from!"

"I was just so worried about getting back in time, I didn't give it much thought," the Magic Messenger said.

"Bollocks!" screamed the Governor. "The only way to get the truth out of this lying bastard is to beat him. Guards, beat this man till he squeals!"

The prison guards could see there was nothing for it. Without regard for the superintendent's dignity they tied him up and beat him till cuts opened, the flesh split and the blood flowed freely. Unable to stand any more, the Magic Messenger confessed: "It's true, the letter's a fake!"

"And how did this forged letter come into your hands?" the Governor yelled.

"On my way I had to pass the Marshes of Mount Liang. A band of robbers set upon me, tied me up and took me up the mountain. They were about to cut my heart out, but then they found the letter on me. They took all the things in the boxes but they left me alive. Thinking it was impossible for me to return, I begged them to kill me there on the mountain; but instead they wrote this letter so that I could return safely. I deceived you because I was too afraid of being held responsible."

"It sounds plausible, but there's still something wrong," the Governor said. "It's obvious you were hand in glove with those robbers in the Marshes of Mount Liang. The plan was to get your hands on my goods, so why all these lies? Beat him again!"

Under further torture the Magic Messenger confessed his connection with the Mount Liang band. The Governor continued the beating and interrogation for a while, but since he was only getting the same story he said: "There's no point in going on with this. Put a heavy cangue on him and throw him into prison." With that he adjourned the session and went to thank Bee Sting Huang. "But for your perceptiveness, I might have made a serious blunder."

"It's obvious this villain was in league with the Marshes of Mount Liang, it is a conspiracy, and if we do not repress it there will be dire consequences."

"When we have obtained confessions from these two, and drawn up a case, we will have them beheaded in the marketplace. Then, when it is done, we will send a full report to the Emperor."

"Your Excellency's judgement is indeed clear and incisive. Firstly it will be most pleasing to the Emperor, who will see how successfully you have brought this business to a conclusion. And secondly, it will forestall any attempt by the outlaws on Mount Liang to raid the gaol."

Chapter 40

"My friend, your understanding is remarkable, you think of everything. I shall mention you in my report and I shall personally interest myself in your advancement."

After lavish hospitality that day, Bee Sting Huang was seen off in style and returned to Wuweijun. When he convened the court next day, Governor Cai summoned the court secretary and said: "Get the case copied out quickly and append the confessions of Song Jiang and Dai Zong to it. Have a crime sheet written out and fix the day for a beheading at the execution ground. With planned and premeditated crimes of this nature no time should be lost. By executing Dai and Song we will prevent much trouble later."

Now the court secretary who was dealing with the case, also called Huang, was on good terms with Dai Zong, but he could think of no excuse that would get him off. He could but pity him. However he did say: "Tomorrow is an imperial remembrance day; and the day after is the full moon of the seventh month, both these are days on which executions are not permitted. And after that it's a national holiday. The execution really cannot be carried out for the next five days." Well, the first step to save Song Jiang had come from Heaven, the next was up to the heroes of Mount Liang.

Governor Cai needs must follow Secretary Huang's advice. So it was only on the morning of the sixth day that he sent men to the crossroads to sweep the execution site. After breakfast, a guard was selected, together with the headsmen and their assistants, over five hundred men in all, and sent over to wait outside the main prison. After nine o'clock the prison guards asked the Governor if he would come himself to supervise the execution. Secretary Huang now displayed the crime sheet in the courtroom, the sentence of beheading was duly announced, and rush mats were laid down. All the prison officers of Jiangzhou, knowing there was nothing they could do to help Song Jiang and the Magic Messenger despite their friendly feelings towards them, grieved for their fate. When these preliminaries were completed, back in the main prison the Magic Messenger and Song Jiang had their hands tied behind their backs and their hair washed with starch and made into an oval bun to which an artificial red flower was added. They were then driven to an altar with a black-faced god and given the bowl of eternity rice and the cup of farewell wine. They bowed to the god when they finished, and mounted the wooden donkey. Some sixty prison officers now herded them through the prison gate. The two men looked at each other, but found nothing to say. Song Jiang merely stumbled a little and the Magic Messenger lowered his eyes and sighed. Several thousand citizens of Jiangzhou were there to watch, jostling and craning their necks:

> *Hatred hangs like a cloud, the atmosphere is dense with resentment. No gleam lightens the air above, all around a sad wind howls. Tasselled spears threaten; the low note of drums saddens all hearts. Staves and cudgels thickly cluster; the monotonous gong subdues the spirit. The crime sheet waves on high; after this going, men say, how can there be a return? White paper flowers flutter; life is but a passing moment, all aver. Eternity rice is hard to stomach, the wine of everlasting farewell sticks in the gullet. Now the hideous executioner grips his knife; the fell minister of justice grasps his axe. Under black banners the sprites are gathered, ghosts linger at the crossroads. The presiding officer prepares to give the signal, the coroner is ready and waiting, to cart away the corpse.*

The executioner had summoned a group of ruffians to harry the prisoners along to the execution ground at the crossroads, surrounding them with a forest of spears and staves. Song Jiang's face was to the south, the Magic Messenger's to the north. They were obliged to sit now and wait till the presiding officer arrived and gave the signal at twelve forty-five.

Raising their eyes, the people read the crime sheet, which said:

> *Jiangzhou prisoner, Song Jiang, author of a seditious poem containing wild and felonious language. Guilty of collusion with the robbers of Mount Liang and conspiracy against the state. Sentence: death by decapitation. Criminal, Dai Zong, convicted of illegally purveying to Song Jiang a private letter and of complicity*

Chapter 40

with the robbers of Mount Liang and conspiracy against the state. Sentence: death by decapitation. Presiding officer: Governor Cai of Jiangzhou.

The Governor reined in his horse. Everyone was waiting for the signal.

Then suddenly on the eastern side of the execution ground a group of snake charmers were seen trying to force their way forward to have a closer view of the proceedings. The guards attempted to push them back but without success. While all this was going on, on the west of the execution ground a group of martial arts merchants and medicine peddlers began trying to force their way in. The guards shouted: "'Oy there, you lot, where's your manners? Who do you think you are, to come pushing in like this?"

The martial arts merchants responded: "You provincial louts, we've travelled the world, we been everywhere, we have, do you think we haven't seen a man killed before? If the Emperor himself executes someone in the capital, everyone's allowed in to see it. What's so earth-shattering about the execution of two men in this God-forsaken dump? Why the hell shouldn't we come and have a look?"

As this lot were arguing with the guards, the presiding officer shouted: "Move back, you can't come through!"

While the row continued unabated, there appeared on the south side of the execution ground a group of porters with carrying-poles who also wanted to get in to watch. The guards shouted: "You there, where are you trying to take those loads?"

"We're carrying goods for the Governor, you can't stop us!" they replied.

"If you're working for the Governor, you'd better find yourselves another route," the guards said.

The porters set down their loads and grasping the poles settled down among the crowd to watch. At this point on the north of the execution ground a group of merchants pushing two carts appeared, also bent on forcing their way through. "Where do you think you're going?" the guards shouted.

"We're just passing, please let us through," the merchants replied.

"How d'you think you're going to get through here?" the guards said. "If you want to get on with your journey you'd better find another route."

"That's no bloody good," they said. "We're from the capital, we don't know your blasted streets, we've got to stick to the main route."

Since the guards would not let them pass, the merchants became jammed in a tight mass so they could not move anywhere. On all sides now the noise was incessant. The Governor could see there was no remedy. He could only watch as the merchants climbed onto the carts and settled down to view the spectacle.

In a short while the crowd in the square parted a little, and a voice rang out: "The time is twelve forty-five!" The Governor as presiding officer then ordered: "Let the decapitation take place!" Two assistant executioners removed the cangues and the ministers of justice took up their axes — it's slow in the telling — everyone wanted to get a clear view — it happens in a flash. A deafening tumult arose. Suddenly, as the word "decapitation" reached the ears of the merchants on their carts, one of them took out a little gong and struck it several times: dong, dong, dong! Everywhere things began to happen. But first there's a poem:

> On impulse he enters the tavern's door,
> By waters that smoke in the autumn air.
> With wine he seeks to ease his grief,
> With verse to purge his heart of care.
> But the exile's song fails of its aim,
> And he lands in a dismal dungeon again,
> Till the heroes of Mount Liang, provoked,
> Descend like a storm on the town for his sake.

Then from the upper floor of a teahouse at the crossroads a great black tiger of a man, stark naked and brandishing a pair of broad-edged axes, leapt down like a bolt from the blue, letting out a wild whoop that echoed round the heavens like a thunderclap. His axes rose and fell and the two executioners fell to the ground.

Chapter 40

In a moment he had hacked a path to where the supervising officer sat on his horse. The guards hurriedly readied their spears, but they were powerless to stop him. Everyone fled in a bunch, pressing round the Governor.

At this moment the snake charmers on the east produced swords, and began killing the guards. The martial arts merchants on the west raised a great cry and also started a general massacre, killing prison officers and guards. The porters on the south began whirling their poles in all directions, knocking down guards and spectators. The merchants on the north jumped down off their carts and pushed them forward to block the road. Two of these merchants dived into the mêlée and emerged, one carrying Song Jiang, the other carrying the Magic Messenger. Some of them took out bows and started shooting arrows, others took out stones and set up a bombardment and still others took out iron-tipped spears which they began to wield.

Now these supposed merchants were of course Chao Gai, Colonel Hua, the Tamer, the Little Duke, and the Halberdier. The fake martial arts merchants were the Dandy, the Red-Haired Devil, the Door-God in the Clouds and Skyscraper. The fake porters were the Crocodile, Short-Arse, Whitey and Shi Yong. The snake charmers were the three Ruan brothers and the Daytime Rat. Seventeen leaders of Mount Liang had come on this expedition, with over a hundred men, and they were all now hard at it, mowing people down on all sides.

And in the thick of it was the big swarthy fellow, tirelessly whirling his axes and felling opponents. Chao Gai and the others did not know who he was, but it was easy to see he was in the forefront and had accounted for the greatest number of the enemy. Then Chao Gai suddenly remembered something. The Magic Messenger had spoken of a certain Black Whirlwind, officially called Li Kui, who was dear to Song Jiang: a wild, rough sort of fellow, he had said. So Chao Gai called out: "You there, in front, are you by any chance the Black Whirlwind?" But the one he addressed paid him no heed and went on furiously whirling his axes and killing people. So Chao Gai instructed the soldiers carrying Song Jiang and the Magic Messenger to stick close behind the black fellow. The latter simply went on killing, there in the market-place, making no distinction between military and civilian, until the corpses lay all about in heaps and the gutters ran with blood. The number of those who were overthrown was countless.

The leaders of Mount Liang had abandoned their carts or their loads and were all following the big black fellow, fighting their way out of the city. Bringing up the rear were Colonel Hua, the Tamer, the Little Duke and the Halberdier, four famous bowmen who shot off their arrows behind them like a cloud of locusts. Who of the soldiers and people of Jiangzhou dared come forward? By now the big black fellow had hacked his way to the banks of the river. He stood alone on the bank slaughtering people, his body drenched in their blood. Chao Gai now rested his halberd and said: "This is no fault of the ordinary people, stop killing them!" But the other paid no attention. He went on wielding his axes, a single blow to each one, felling them in rows.

When they had progressed along the bank about two miles from the town, they were confronted by a broad river, with no way across it. Chao Gai lamented when he saw this, but the big man cried: "Don't worry, just take our brothers into the temple."

There was indeed a big temple, close to the river bank, but its gates were tight shut. The big fellow heaved his axes and burst it open. Inside they found a screen of ancient junipers and dark green pines, providing deep shade. In front of them the monastery sign said in gold letters: "Temple of the White Dragon." The soldiers carried Song Jiang and the Magic Messenger inside and laid them down. Only then did Song Jiang trust himself to look around. When he saw Chao Gai and the others tears came to his eyes. "Is this a dream, brother?" he asked.

Chao Gai chided him: "You wouldn't stay with us on the mountain, and now just look at the result! But tell me, who is that big dark fellow who is wreaking such havoc?"

"He's Li Kui, whom they call 'the Black Whirlwind.' Many times he suggested helping me to escape from the main gaol, but I was afraid we would be caught and didn't let him."

Chao Gai said: "His energy is amazing, and his courage unflinching."

Colonel Hua said: "Bring clothes for our two brothers here."

During this conversation, Iron Ox was suddenly seen rushing off waving his two axes. Song Jiang called to him to stop. "Where are you off to?" he asked.

"I'm going to find that blasted monk and kill him, the unthinkable swine didn't receive us, he even shut the bloody gates. I'm bloody well going to make a sacrifice of him, if I can only find the bugger."

Song Jiang said: "Come here and meet the leaders first."

Accordingly Iron Ox threw down his two axes and knelt right down in front of Chao Gai, saying: "Elder brother, forgive Iron Ox for being so uncouth."

When he was introduced to everyone, he and the Crocodile were delighted to learn that they were countrymen.

Colonel Hua now said to Chao Gai: "You told everyone just to follow Iron Ox and now look where we are! There's a big river in front of us blocking our way. We're cut off and there's no boat to take us across. If the army in the city decide to pursue us, what can we do against them? How can we save ourselves?"

Iron Ox said: "Don't worry. We'll all go back and attack the city first, and finish off that bloody Governor Cai once and for all. We won't leave till we've done that."

At this point the Magic Messenger had just regained consciousness and he cried: "Brother, why must you always be so foolhardy? There are five or six thousand troops in the city, if we go and attack them we're bound to be destroyed!"

Ruan the Seventh said: "Over there on the other side of the river I can see some boats tied up. Why don't I and my brothers swim over and fetch boats to ferry us all across?"

"That's by far the best plan," said Chao Gai.

So the Ruan brothers stripped off their clothes and dived into the water, each equipped with a sharp knife. But when they had only gone about three hundred yards, three rowing boats appeared upstream and came flying towards the others, with a whistling sound like the wind. To their considerable dismay they saw there were about ten men in each, all fully armed. When they told Song Jiang, he said: "Then I must be doomed!" and rushed out of the temple to see. On the first boat sat a big man holding a five-pronged fork which flashed bravely in the sunlight. His hair was tied on top of his head with a red cord and he wore white silk trousers for swimming. He was whistling. And who do you think this was?

East runs the River for many a league,
Follow its course and a hero you'll meet.
His face is like chalk and his body's like whey,
He travels in water as if on his feet.
In the gorges no rapids can cause him to fear,
To snatch from the dragon his ball he would dare;
He masters the flood like a fish in the sea,
His name is White Eel, world-famous is he.

When the White Eel in the first boat saw them, he shouted: "Who are you? How do you dare to hold a meeting at the White Dragon temple?"

Song Jiang dashed out of the temple and said: "Brother come and help us!" When he saw it was Song Jiang, White Eel gave a great shout of "Right away" and the three boats flew towards the bank. Seeing this the Ruan brothers turned back. The whole company was now assembled on the bank in front of the temple.

White Eel had a dozen sturdy fellows with him in the boat. His brother the Pilot was in the second boat with Mu Hong, Mu Chun and the Pill Monger, and a dozen retainers. In the third boat were the White-Water Dragon, the Executioner, the two Tong brothers and a dozen smugglers. All were now standing on the bank, fully armed. White Eel was elated when he saw Song Jiang. He prostrated himself and said: "Ever since you were sentenced I have been unable to rest. But I could think of no way to rescue you. Recently I heard that Superintendent Dai was taken and elder brother Li had disappeared, so I went and got my brother and went to Squire Mu's to ask for news. We were just on our way now to attack Jiangzhou. We planned to free you from gaol, of course we had no idea they had already rescued you and brought you here. Dare I ask if this great company has something to do with the famous leader of the Marshes of Mount Liang, Chao Gai?" Song Jiang indicated the foremost figure of the group and said: "This is indeed elder Brother Chao Gai. Please come into the temple everyone so you can be introduced."

So all of these leaders, that is, the nine from the boats, and Chao Gai's party of seventeen, together with Song Jiang, the Magic Messenger and Iron Ox, making altogether twenty-nine, met together in the White Dragon temple. This is what became known as the Lesser Gathering in the White Dragon temple.

When the introduction ceremonies between each of the twenty-nine heroes were just completed, one of the men burst into the temple and breathlessly announced: "In Jiangzhou town there's drums and gongs and a huge army's on the move, they're coming for us! You can see the banners blocking out the sun and swords as thick as grass! There's armoured foot and horse in front, and spearmen behind that and they're pouring down this road to the White Dragon temple!"

Iron Ox immediately let out a great roar of "Kill 'em!", grabbed his axes and charged out of the door. Chao Gai shouted: "It's all or nothing now! Rally round me, men, and we'll smash the might of Jiangzhou before we go home to Mount Liang!" The others all cried in unison: "Let's go!" And a hundred and fifty men all shouting together raced along the river bank towards Jiangzhou.

But for this, how would we have seen:

The river flowing with blood, the corpses heaped in mounds;
The green river dragon spitting deadly fire,
The mountain tiger raging like a storm through the heavens.

But if you want to know how Chao Gai and the rest of the company fared, you must read the next chapter.

Chapter 41

Song Jiang plans the capture of Wuweijun; White Eel takes Bee Sting Huang alive!

Now these heroes from Mount Liang assembled in the White Dragon temple outside Jiangzhou, having just stormed the execution ground and rescued Song Jiang and the Magic Messenger, were seventeen in all, namely Chao Gai, Colonel Hua, the Tamer, the Little Duke, the Halberdier, the Red-Haired Devil, the Dandy, the Door-God in the Clouds, the Skyscraper, the Crocodile, Short-Arse, Whitey Zheng, Shi Yong, the three Ruan brothers, and the Daytime Rat. Under their command were eighty or ninety seasoned troops. Those who had joined them on the Yangtze river amounted to nine more leaders, namely the White Eel, his brother the Pilot, the White-Water Dragon, the Executioner, the two Mu brothers, the two Tong brothers and the Pill Monger. They had more than forty men, all of them smugglers. They had arrived in three big boats. In addition there was Iron Ox, who had led the charge out of the city along the banks of the river. So altogether that meeting in the White Dragon temple numbered about a hundred and fifty.

And now they heard the soldier say: "There's a great beating of drums in Jiangzhou city, and waving of banners and sounding of gongs. They're heading this way, shouting and cheering."

When he heard this, Iron Ox gave a roar, seized his axes and bounded out of the door. The others too raised a shout, and brandishing their weapons sallied forth to encounter the enemy. But first the Red-Haired Devil and the Crocodile transferred Song Jiang and the Magic Messenger onto one of the boats for safety. The White-Water Dragon, White Eel and the Ruan brothers took charge of the boats. Along the bank they could see the forces streaming out of the city, some five or six thousand horsemen, the first ranks all in full armour, equipped with bows and arrows and wielding long lances. Behind them thronged the infantry, charging to the attack with waving banners and loud cries.

At this point Iron Ox was well in advance of the others. Waving his axes and stripped for action, he was rushing to the attack. Behind him were Colonel Hua, the Tamer, the Little Duke and the Halberdier, all backing him up. Colonel Hua seeing how the enemy cavalry that faced them were steadying their lances feared for Iron Ox's safety and surreptitiously reached for his bow, fitted an arrow to it, bent it to the full and let fly at the leader of the cavalrymen. The very first arrow sent him tumbling headlong from his horse. This gave the rest of the cavalry such a fright that thinking only of saving themselves, they jerked their horse's heads round and fled, trampling half of their own infantry as they did so. At this point all the heroes charged, cutting down the enemy till the bodies lay piled in heaps and the river ran red with blood. They went on killing till they were at the gates of Jiangzhou. By then the troops defending the city had prepared ballista missiles and stones which they rained down on the attackers. All the government troops now beat a hasty retreat inside the walls and closed the gates. It would be days before they dared venture forth again. The heroes, dragging a reluctant Iron Ox with them, returned to the White Dragon temple and prepared to board the boats. Chao Gai drew them up in good order, and one by one they went down into the boats, which shoved off and left.

The wind was directly behind them so they hoisted sail, the three bigger boats carrying the troops and the leaders setting their course for Squire Mu's. With a following wind they were at the jetty in no time and all disembarked. Mu Hong invited them all into the inner hall where Squire Mu came out to receive them and Song Jiang was able to meet all the other leaders. The Squire said: "You've been hard at it all afternoon, please go and rest in the guest quarters to restore your strength." So they all retired for a while and rested or repaired their clothes and arms. Meanwhile Mu Hong had the servants slaughter an ox, a dozen pigs and sheep, and provide chickens, geese, fish and ducks for a magnificent banquet in honour of the leaders. Later while they were drinking, many incidents were recalled. Chao Gai said: "If you hadn't come with those boats to save us we would have been in serious trouble."

Squire Mu asked: "What made you try and leave the city by that road?"

Iron Ox said: "I was just looking for where there were most people to kill. It was they who chose to follow me, I didn't tell them to." This made everyone laugh.

Song Jiang now rose to his feet and said: "We would both have lost our lives, Superintendent Dai and myself, if all of you had not come to the rescue. Our debt to you is deep as the ocean, how can it ever be repaid? But I still can't get over the way that bastard Huang Wenbing just kept on and on, repeatedly finding ways to express his malice and engineer our downfall. How can I leave this injustice unavenged? I hesitate to ask you this, but would you all do me one more enormous favour? Would you go with me to attack Wuweijun and kill that swine Huang Wenbing, in order to take from me this inexhaustible anger of mine, before we go back home? What say you?"

"But to enter the enemy camp secretly, to raid their very headquarters, that's something that can only work once, how can it be repeated?" Chao Gai objected. "They will be ready for us now. Wouldn't it be better to go back to the mountain fortress and recruit a big force, together with 'Professor' Wu and Taoist Gongsun, Leopard's Head Lin Chong and Thunderclap? There'd still be time enough to avenge you."

Song Jiang said: "If we go back to the mountain first, we can't come out again. In the first place it's a long way. And then Jiangzhou must have reported it to the court and they'll be on the alert everywhere. We mustn't do something foolish. No, we have to take advantage of this opportunity, strike while the iron is hot, there's no point in waiting till they're fully prepared."

Colonel Hua said: "He's right. But all the same, we've nobody who knows the roads, or exactly where he lives. We should send someone first to spy out the land and find out as much as possible, to see exactly what there is there in Wuweijun and pinpoint Bee Sting Huang's house. Then we can get to work."

The Pill Monger now jumped up and said: "I've travelled a lot in the rivers and lakes and I know this place called Wuweijun pretty well. Suppose I go and take a look?"

"That would be great," Song Jiang said.

That same day the Pill Monger said goodbye and left. Song Jiang and the others, meanwhile, remained behind at Squire Mu's and considered the attack on Wuweijun. Swords and spears and bows and arrows were got ready and also a number of large and small boats and suchlike. These preparations were complete when, having been gone two days, the Pill Monger returned, bringing with him another man.

When the Pill Monger greeted Song Jiang, the latter asked: "Who is this good fellow?"

"This is Hou Jian. He's from Hongdu. He's a master tailor. He can make the needle simply fly and his thread just races along. But he's also pretty handy with spear and staff, as I know because he was my student. Because he's small, dark and wiry they call him the Long-Armed Ape. I found him working at Bee Sting Huang's house so I brought him along."

Song Jiang was very pleased with this and asked Hou Jian to sit and join their discussions. The latter was in fact one of the original baleful stars, or demon princes, so of course he was a kindred spirit.

When Song Jiang asked about Jiangzhou, and about the roads in Wuweijun, the Pill Monger said: "Governor Cai has now counted their losses. More than five hundred government troops and civilians were killed. The number wounded by arrows is beyond reckoning. He has sent messengers to ride night and day to report it to the court. The city gates are closed at midday and anyone wanting to get in or out is questioned closely. Of course the persecution you suffered is not the fault of Governor Cai, it's all because of that Huang Wenbing, who repeatedly incited him against both of you. Now since the raid on the execution ground there is great alarm in the city, and they're on the alert night and day. When I went to Wuweijun to gain intelligence I bumped into

Chapter 41

my friend Hou Jian, when he was leaving the house to eat, that's how I got all this information."

"And how did you know about all this, Mr. Hou?" Song Jiang asked.

The Ape replied: "From childhood I have always loved practising with spear and staff. My master here taught me such a lot, I shall always be grateful to him. Recently Bee Sting Huang called me to his house to make him some clothes. When I was leaving I happened to meet my master; he mentioned your name and told me about this business. I very much wanted to meet you so I came personally to make this report. This Huang Wenbing has an elder brother called Huang Wenye, another son of the same mother. Huang Wenye devotes himself to good works: mending bridges and repairing roads, paying for Buddha images and feeding monks, rescuing the oppressed, succouring the needy. In Wuweijun they call him Buddha Huang. His younger brother, on the other hand, although he's a retired official, has a malicious spirit and spends his time doing evil. Everyone in Wuweijun calls him Bee Sting Huang. The two brothers live apart, though they are in the same street close to the north gate of the town. Bee Sting Huang is nearer to the town wall and Buddha Huang is towards the main street. One time when I was working there Bee Sting Huang came home and I heard him say, 'Governor Cai has been cheated and I have advised him to execute the offenders first and report to the Emperor afterwards.' Buddha Huang was angry when he heard this, and said, 'Why do always have to stick your nose into everything? It's nothing to do with you, why do you always want to make life difficult for other people? If there's justice in heaven and present retribution, all you're doing is heaping coals of fire on your own head.' Then in the last couple of days, news of the raid on the execution ground reached us, and Bee Sting Huang was scared stiff. He rushed off to Jiangzhou to see the Governor and discuss things with him and he still hasn't returned."

"What is the distance between Bee Sting Huang's house and his brother's?" Song Jiang asked.

"It used to be a single house, before they were divided. There's just a vegetable garden in between."

"How many people are there in the house, and how many separate households?"

"About forty or fifty, counting both men and women."

"Heaven favours my revenge, this person must have been sent to help me," Song Jiang said. "All the same, I shall need the support of all of you."

They all said with one voice: "Even if we have to die in the attempt, we are determined to rid the world of that evil scheming bastard, in order to avenge your wrongs and wipe out your hatred."

"My quarrel is only with this scoundrel Huang Wenbing, it's nothing to do with the people of Wuweijun. And since his brother is an honest fellow he must not be harmed either. We do not want posterity to say we acted dishonourably. When we attack we must avoid doing the least harm to any of the people. But I've a plan for this attack. All I ask of you is a little help."

"We will do whatever you ask," they replied in unison.

Song Jiang said: "I would like to ask Squire Mu to provide eighty or ninety sacks and we shall also need over a hundred bundles of reeds for burning. We'll use five big boats and two small ones. I'd like White Eel and the White-Water Dragon to take charge of the two small boats and I'll explain how to manoeuvre them; on the big boats we'll have the Pilot, the three Ruans and Tong Wei, the Cave Dragon, with all the others who are experienced on water manning them. This should enable my plan to succeed."

Mu Hong said: "We've got dry reeds, fuel and sacks, our people on this estate all know the water and can handle boats, so just go ahead, please, and tell us what to do."

Song Jiang said: "First I want Mr. Hou to take the Pill Monger and the Daytime Rat into Wuweijun and hide there. In a few days' time a pigeon with a bell attached to it will be released outside the gates at midnight. Then the Daytime Rat is to go up on the city wall and stick out a white silk pennant near Bee Sting Huang's house, as a signal to show which part of the wall is nearest to it. And Shi Yong and Skyscraper are to dress up as beggars and go to the city gates and wait there. When they see the fire it will be their signal to kill the guards on the gate. The White-Water Dragon and White Eel will approach on the river and lie there in readiness." When Song Jiang had allotted these duties, the Pill Monger, the Daytime Rat and the Ape set off. Next it was the turn of Shi Yong and Skyscraper, dressed as beggars and each carrying a concealed dagger. The sacks filled with sand and mud were brought and together with the reeds and the fuel loaded onto the boats. The other leaders stood in readiness, well provided with arms, and the fighting men hid under the decks of the boats. The leaders now boarded their boats. Chao Gai, Song Jiang, and Colonel Hua were on the Cave Dragon's boat; the Dandy, Short-Arse and Whitey were with the Pilot; the Magic Messenger, the Red-Haired Devil and the Tamer were with Ruan the Second; the Little Duke, the Halberdier and the Executioner were with Ruan the Fifth; Mu Hong, Mu Chun and Iron Ox were with Ruan the Seventh. That left the Crocodile and the Door-God in the Clouds, who remained at Squire Mu's to listen for the news from Jiangzhou. Tong Meng, the River Rider, was sent ahead in a fast fishing boat to reconnoitre. The brigands and other fighting men were hidden under the decks, while the farm-hands and boatmen manned the boats. They came secretly the same night to Wuweijun. It was seasonal weather for the seventh month, cold nights and a fresh breeze, the water glistening under the moonlight, with the river in shadow and brightness flooding the hills, as if all were fashioned in jade.

It was about the first watch when all the boats arrived at Wuweijun where they chose a place where the reeds were thick and moored in a long line. The River Rider returned and reported: "All's quiet in the town." Song Jiang ordered the men under his command to unload the sandbags, reeds and dry firewood and move them to beside the town wall. They heard the drum beat the hour: it was exactly nine o'clock. Song Jiang told the soldiers to take the sandbags and firewood and pile them up beside the wall. The leaders now took up their arms, leaving only the Pilot, the Ruans and the Tongs to guard the boats and hold themselves in reserve, while the rest charged towards the town. When they were just a few hundred yards from the north gate, Song Jiang gave orders for the pigeon with the bell to be released and on top of the

The Marshes of Mount Liang

town wall a bamboo pole appeared with the white signal tied to it, fluttering in the breeze. Song Jiang immediately ordered his troops to pile up the sandbags at this spot and then told the assault party to carry their loads of reeds and firewood up onto the wall. The Daytime Rat was waiting for them there. He pointed and said: "Bee Sting Huang's house is in that street."

"Where are the Pill Monger and the Ape?" Song Jiang asked.

"They've entered Bee Sting Huang's house, they're waiting for you," was the reply.

"And have you seen Shi Yong and Skyscraper?"

"They're in position near the town gate."

Song Jiang now ordered his men to descend from the wall and proceed to Bee Sting Huang's door. The Ape suddenly materialized under the eaves of the house. "Go and open the garden gate and let them in," Song Jiang whispered urgently. "Tell them to make a bonfire of the reeds and the primed firewood and tell the Pill Monger to fetch fire and light it. Then go and knock on Bee Sting Huang's door and shout, 'The official's house next door is on fire, bring out any boxes and trunks for safekeeping.' After they open the door I'll take care of them."

Song Jiang told everyone to line up on both sides while the Ape went and opened the garden door. The troops carried the reeds and firewood inside and piled it up there. The Ape had found the tinder and handed it to the Pill Monger. The fire was lit. The Ape slipped out and went to knock on the door of the house, shouting: "The official's house next door is on fire, we've got to move all the chests and boxes out for safekeeping, come on, open the door quickly!" When those inside awoke they saw the flames next door and hurriedly opened the door and rushed out. With wild shouts, Chao Gai, Song Jiang and the others fell on them. Each hero went to work on his own account: if they saw one, it was one dead; if they saw two, it was a pair. The members of Bee Sting Huang's household, family and others, young or old, some forty or fifty all told, were slain one and all. There was not one survivor. Only Bee Sting Huang himself was missing. The company collected up all of the very considerable quantity of family possessions in gold and silver that he had long been extorting from honest citizens. Then when a whistle was heard they shouldered these goods and rushed to the wall. Meanwhile Shi Yong and Skyscraper after seeing the fire had each drawn his sharp knife and killed the soldiers on the gates. When they saw a group of neighbours approaching down the street carrying buckets and ladders to fight the fire, they shouted: "Stop where you are! We are the company from the Marshes of Mount Liang. There's thousands of us here and we've come to kill Bee Sting Huang and his thieving clan and to avenge Song Jiang and Dai Zong. We intend no harm to the people. Go home quickly and shut your doors. Don't meddle with what does not concern you." Some of the neighbours were still not convinced and simply stood there gaping, but when Iron Ox suddenly charged out, whirling his axes, there was a terrified shout and they picked up their ladders and buckets and fled in disorder. Some guards also issued from a backstreet with some men who were dragging fire-fighting equipment, ropes and hooks, aiming to fight the fire. But Colonel Hua quickly armed his bow and shot the first one through, crying: "If you want to die, then come and try to put the fire out." The others beat a hasty retreat. Finally, the Pill Monger took a torch and set fire to Bee Sting Huang's house front and back and the flames began to rage. Here's how it was:

> Black clouds enfold the earth, red flames fly toward heaven. A myriad golden snakes march irresistibly forward, the writhing flames scatter a thousand embers. A fierce breeze fans the flames, carved beams and painted pillars last but an instant; leaping flames fill the sky, mansion and hall are gone in a flash.

It was not just an ordinary fire, for

> Bee Huang had an evil nature,
> He roused the god of fire.
> His malice raised an evil flame,
> He made the fire that burnt him.

Shi Yong and Skyscraper had already killed the guards on the gate and Iron Ox destroyed the lock with a blow of the axe. When the gate was open, half the band left the town through the gate

Chapter 41

below while the other half departed over the wall above. The Pilot, the Ruans and the Tongs came to help them carry the booty aboard the boats. The people of Wuweijun had already heard about the raid on Jiangzhou execution ground, in which countless people were killed, so no one dared interfere. They simply went back home and hid. For Song Jiang and his friends the only thing missing was that they had failed to capture Bee Sting Huang himself. They embarked, shoved off and returned to Squire Mu's. Of this no more.

Now in the city of Jiangzhou, when they saw the fire in Wuweijun painting the sky red, everyone began to talk about it, and naturally the Governor was informed. It so happened that Bee Sting Huang was with the Governor just then discussing some business. When he heard the news he hurriedly said to the Governor: "There is a fire in my district, I must hurry back home to see what's going on." Governor Cai immediately ordered the gates to be opened and arranged for him to go on an official boat. Bee Sting Huang thanked him and left at once, found his servants and boarded the boat with all haste. They rowed out into the stream and headed for Wuweijun. The fire was now seen to be raging fiercely and the reflection painted the surface of the river red. The helmsman said: "It's somewhere near the north gate which is on fire." This did nothing to reassure Bee Sting Huang. When they reached the middle of the river, a small boat was seen rowing in the opposite direction. Before long another boat appeared, rowing towards them. But instead of passing them by, it came straight at them. "Ahoy there! Who are you?" Bee Sting Huang's servants shouted. "What are you doing rowing straight towards us?" Suddenly in the other boat a large man jumped up with a grappling iron in his hand and shouted in reply: "This boat is heading for Jiangzhou with a report on the fire!" So Bee Sting Huang emerged and asked: "Where is the fire?"

"Near the north gate in Mr. Huang's house," the other replied. "His family have all been killed and his goods stolen by the robbers of Mount Liang. Now they've set fire to the house."

Bee Sting Huang began wildly cursing his fate, he nearly went out of his mind. When he heard him, the other man grappled their boat with his hook and leapt aboard. Bee Sting Huang was no dim-wit, he guessed what was about to happen and he rushed to the stern and dived into the river. But someone from the second boat was already lurking under the water. He seized Bee Sting Huang round the waist and supporting his head dragged him aboard the boat. The big man on board assisted. They tied him with rope. The one who grabbed Bee Sting Huang from the bottom of the river was White Eel; the one in the boat with the grappling hook was the White-Water Dragon. With these two now aboard, the official boat's helmsman saw no better policy than to prostrate himself. The White-Water Dragon said: "I'm not going to harm you. I only want this bastard Bee Sting Huang. Go back and tell that ass, Governor Cai, that we of the Mount Liang band will let him keep his donkey's head for the time being, but sooner or later we'll return and take it."

Shaking like a leaf, the helmsman stammered: "I will tell him."

Now they had Bee Sting Huang in their boat, the White-Water Dragon and White Eel were content to let the official boat go.

The two men in their fast boats raced back to Mu Hong's. When they got there they found all the company on the bank waiting for them. The boxes had been unloaded. When he heard that they had captured Bee Sting Huang, Song Jiang could scarcely contain his joy, which was shared by the whole company. "I'm looking forward to meeting this person," he said. The White-Water Dragon and White Eel duly bundled Bee Sting Huang out onto the bank. When everyone had had a good look at him, he was locked up and they all left the river and returned to Squire Mu's house. The Crocodile and the Door-God in the Clouds joined them here and everyone went to the thatched hall. Song Jiang had Bee Sting Huang's wet clothing removed and he was tied to a willow tree. The leaders were asked to sit in groups. Song Jiang ordered a pot of wine and everyone raised their cups. Beginning with Chao Gai and going right down to the Daytime Rat, thirty of them in all were present.

Song Jiang began to berate Bee Sting Huang: "You scoundrel! I had no quarrel with you, neither past nor present, why did you try to ruin me, not once but five times, telling Governor Cai to

Chapter 41

have us both killed? You're supposed to have read the classics, how could you behave so viciously? There's no personal vendetta between us, why did you have to plot against me? Your brother Huang Wenye was born of the same mother, how is it that he spends his days doing good? I'm told that in your town they call him Buddha Huang. I was most careful not to do him the least harm yesterday. But you, all you do is attack people and suck up to the powerful. You toady to government officials, you oppress good citizens. I have heard that in Wuweijun they call you Bee Sting Huang. Well today I'm going to pluck your sting out."

Bee Sting Huang said: "I recognize my faults, please let me die."

Chao Gai shouted: "You bloody fool, do you think you're not going to die? Today you're going to learn to regret not having acted better from the beginning."

Song Jiang asked: "Which of you will do it for me?"

Iron Ox jumped to his feet at once and said: "I'll do it for you, I'll settle this villain. He's good and fat, I see, he'll make good eating when he's roasted."

Chao Gai said: "That's right, get a sharp knife and a basin of charcoal, we'll cut the bugger into little pieces and have him with the wine. That's the cure for our brother's anger!"

Iron Ox took a knife and said to Bee Sting Huang with a smile: "Now, you bastard, while you were sitting in Governor Cai's back room you could argue the hind leg off a donkey, if it was for the sake of ruining others and getting the Governor excited with pure fabrications. Now you want to die quickly, but I say you shall die slowly." Then with the sharp knife he began cutting pieces from the legs, choosing them carefully, and roasting them on the charcoal to serve with wine. Cut a piece, roast a piece. It wasn't long before Bee Sting Huang expired. Then Iron Ox slit open the chest and took out the heart and liver and handed it to them to make a soup. When the company had seen Bee Sting Huang carved up they all went to the thatched hall to celebrate with Song Jiang. There is a poem about this:

Bee Sting Huang was a toady and a schemer,

Toward better men he harboured jealous hate.
But what he got for scheming was slow death,
To be carved and roasted was his awful fate.

Suddenly Song Jiang knelt on the ground. All the others hurriedly knelt too and said: "Dear brother what is the matter? Please tell us what it is, of course we will listen."

Song Jiang said: "I have no skills. From childhood I studied the classics. When I grew up I tried to make the acquaintance of the world's heroes. But because my strength is slight and my talent weak, I have never been able to entertain them fittingly, as is my life-long wish. After I was banished to Jiangzhou, I have to thank Chao Gai and all of you who tried so hard to make me stay, but I was determined to see my father, that's why I couldn't. Then, since heaven so ordained it, my way took me to the Yangtze river and I ran into a number of other heroes. But fool that I am, I got drunk and in a moment of madness wrote something which put Superintendent Dai's life at risk. I owe my life to your fearlessness, when you braved the tiger's lair, the dragons' pool, to rescue me by force. You even put yourselves out to help me achieve my revenge. Now we have committed a great crime and caused an uproar in two cities, all of which will be reported to the Emperor. So I have no alternative but to seek refuge with our brothers in the Marshes of Mount Liang. I would like to know the views of everyone on this. If you are agreeable, let us pack up and leave at once."

Almost before he had finished, Iron Ox jumped up and cried: "We'll all go, we'll all go. If anyone says he won't, he'll get a fucking taste of my axes, I'll chop him in two!"

Song Jiang said: "You express yourself too violently, we will only go if it is truly and honestly what everyone wants."

Everyone gave their opinion: "We have killed hundreds of officers and troops, we've turned two places upside down, the court is bound to be informed and a force will be sent to take us. Where can we go, if we don't go with you, live or die together?"

Song Jiang thanked them with joy in his heart. The Crocodile and the Door-God in the Clouds were sent on in advance to

Chapter 41

advise those guarding the stronghold, and the others left afterwards in five parties. The first group to leave consisted of Chao Gai, Song Jiang, Colonel Hua, the Magic Messenger and Iron Ox, the second of the Red-Haired Devil, Skyscraper, Shi Yong, the Pill Monger and the Ape, and the third of the White-Water Dragon, the Executioner, the Little Duke, the Halberdier and the two Tongs. The fourth group comprised the Tamer, White Eel, the Pilot and the Ruan brothers, and the fifth the Dandy, Short-Arse, the two Mu brothers, Whitey and the Daytime Rat. The twenty-eight leaders in their five groups commanded a thousand men. Each man received a share of the booty from Bee Sting Huang's house and loaded it onto the carts. Mu Hong took along the old squire and the household retainers, and also loaded suitable amounts of goods and valuables onto carts. Amongst the retainers there were some who did not want to go. They were all given silver and went their own ways. Some of the servants wanted to go. They were taken along. After the first four parties had left one after another, Mu Hong collected up everything in the house, then got a dozen torches and set fire to the manor. This done, he abandoned his estate and set his course for the Marshes of Mount Liang.

No need to tell of how each of the five contingents fared on their journey, setting off in succession, separated by some seven miles or so. Rather we shall tell how the first of them, that is to say, Chao Gai, Song Jiang, Colonel Hua, the Magic Messenger and Iron Ox, rode forward, accompanied by carts and their company of soldiers, and travelled for three days till they came to a place known as Yellow Mountain. Song Jiang said to Chao Gai as they rode towards it: "This mountain has a wild aspect, do you suppose there are troops waiting in ambush there? Do you think we should wait till the others catch up so that we can all pass at the same time?" He had hardly finished speaking when the sound of gongs and drums broke out in the pass up ahead. "What did I say?" said Song Jiang. "Stay where you are, we must wait for our friends behind to catch up, so we can confront the villains." Colonel Hua meanwhile fitted an arrow to his bow, Chao Gai and the Magic Messenger grasped their halberds, Iron Ox took up his axes and closely surrounding Song Jiang they all spurred their horses forward. Immediately on the hillside four or five hundred troops materialized. From the front ranks four big fellows, all armed, rode out and shouted loudly: "You lot have raised an uproar in Jiangzhou and plundered Wuweijun, you have killed many government troops and civilians, and now you are planning to retreat to the Marshes of Mount Liang. Well, we four have been waiting for you a long time. If you want to get back safely you must leave Song Jiang here and we'll spare your lives."

When he heard this, Song Jiang rode out in front, dismounted and knelt and said: "Song Jiang was caught in a trap, then rescued by all these heroes. He does not know in what way he has offended you, but hopes you will condescend to spare him."

When they saw Song Jiang kneeling before them, the four men hurriedly reined in their horses, threw down their weapons, rushed forward and threw themselves on the ground, saying: "We four brothers had only heard the famous name of Song Jiang of Shandong, the Opportune Rain, we never thought we would live to see the day when we would meet him. We heard how you had been sentenced for something in Jiangzhou and we decided we would come to raid the gaol, only we didn't have accurate information. The day before yesterday we sent some of our men to Jiangzhou to find out more. When they came back they told us a group of brave men had already devastated Jiangzhou and carried out a daring raid on the execution ground to rescue you. They told us you had set off towards Jieyang, but afterwards returned to burn Wuweijun and plunder the residence of Bee Sting Huang. We guessed you would be coming this way. We repeatedly sent out scouts to watch this road. But we feared the report might be false, that is why we tested you with these questions. Please do not hold it against us, now that we have truly found you. To celebrate this good fortune we have prepared a humble feast in our camp, as a most inadequate welcome. We beg you all to come to our humble camp for entertainment."

Song Jiang was delighted and raised them up and politely asked to know their names. The first one was called Ou Peng and was from Huangzhou. He had been a guard on the Yangzi but he

Chapter 41

had offended his superior officer and had been forced to take refuge in the rivers and lakes and become an outlaw. He had given up his name and changed it to Golden Wings. The second was called Jiang Jing, and he was from Tanzhou in Hunan. He was a failed scholar, who when he did not pass the state examination gave up the pen for the sword. Since he was quite clever and fairly expert in calligraphy and numbers — he could manage six figure sums without the slightest error — and was also adept with spear and staff and good at marshalling and deploying troops, everyone called him the Magic Calculator. The third was called Ma Lin and he was from Jinling in Jiankang. He had once been an insignificant idler, but he could play the flute and was also so quick with a knife that even a hundred attackers could not penetrate his defence. They called him the Magic Flautist. The fourth was Tao Zongwang from Guangzhou. He was from the class of tenant farmers. He was handy with a spade and had great strength. He could also handle a spear and a knife and they called him the Nine-Tailed Turtle. There is a poem about these four:

Sturdy and powerful beyond all compare
He covers the ground as if walking on air,
Golden Wings is exactly the name for Ou Peng,
Head of the Yellow Mountain gang.

In youth he wasted his days with the pen
As an adult in tactics he sought to excel.
A soldier of worth and a demon with figures,
Jiang Jing is both gifted in fighting and letters.

His flute in the mountains rings loud as a bell,
With a couple of knives he can weave quite a spell.
Ma Lin's appearance is ugly as sin,
But he's first of them all when a battle he's in.

Zongwang is like a fierce tiger made,
He lays about him with a spade.
This Nine-Tailed Turtle has tricks beyond count.
These are the leaders of the Yellow Mount.

Such were the four worthies who had detained Song Jiang. Soon their men brought boxes of fruit, a big pitcher of wine and two big plates of meat, and cups were provided for everyone. Chao Gai and Song Jiang were served first, then Colonel Hua, the Magic Messenger and Iron Ox. Introductions were made all round and everyone was given wine. A few hours later the next party arrived, and all got handed cups and were introduced. When they had all raised their cups they were invited up the mountain. So the first two groups, consisting of ten leaders, went up to the Yellow Mountain stronghold where the four incumbents had oxen and horses slaughtered for them, and sent a succession of men down the mountain to invite the leaders of the three remaining groups up to join in the feasting. They all arrived within the day and attended the celebrations in the assembly hall.

Whilst he was drinking, Song Jiang spoke thus: "I am at present on my way to take refuge with Leader Chao Gai in the Marshes of Mount Liang and become one of their company. I wonder if you four would be interested in leaving this place and going with us to the great fortress on Mount Liang, to become members of the band?"

The four replied in unison: "If the two noble leaders do not reject us, we would like nothing better than to serve them in whatever they command."

Song Jiang and Chao Gai were delighted with the reply: "In that case, please prepare everything for the journey."

This decision was pleasing to everyone. They stayed for the rest of the day and the following night, and the next morning Song Jiang and Chao Gai still sharing the command went down the mountain and set off first. The rest all set out in due order, the distance between them being only some seven miles. The Yellow Mountain four got together their valuables and other things, collected three or four hundred men, burnt down the fortress palisades and followed behind as a sixth party.

Song Jiang was pleased to have added these four from Yellow Mountain, and he said to Chao Gai as they rode along: "During these wanderings in the rivers and lakes, although I've had some big frights, I've also got to know a good many fine fellows. Here

Chapter 41

I am now on my way to the mountain retreat with you, and this time I am resolute, together we shall live or die, you and I." They chatted thus as they pursued their way, and without noticing it arrived at the Crocodile's inn.

Now the four leaders who had stayed behind to guard the Mount Liang stronghold, namely the Professor, Taoist Gongsun Sheng, Leopard's Head Lin Chong and Thunderclap, with the two new arrivals, Xiao Rang the calligrapher, alias Magic Hand, and Jin Dajian the engraver, alias the Craftsman, had already been informed of events by the Crocodile and the Door-God in the Clouds, and every day they had been sending a welcoming party of the lesser chiefs over to the inn. They now all went together across to Golden Sands Landing and with much beating of drums and blowing of flutes began the journey on horseback or in sedans up to the stronghold. When they reached the pass, the Professor and the other five welcomed them with wine, and they all went to the assembly hall, where joss-sticks were lit.

Chao Gai now invited Song Jiang to become lord of the mountain retreat and asked him to take the highest place. Song Jiang, of course, refused. "You are absolutely wrong," he said. "It is only thanks to your courageous intervention that I am still among the living. You, my friend, were always the chief of the mountain stronghold, how can you resign that position to someone of no talent? If you insist on this I would prefer to die."

Chao Gai said: "Why do you talk like this? If you hadn't risked everything to rescue me and the other seven in the first place, enabling us to escape to the mountain, this company today would not exist. You are truly the stronghold's patron. If you do not take the seat, who deserves to?"

Song Jiang said: "As far as age is concerned, you are my senior by ten years. How can I take precedence? It would be most dishonourable of me!"

Only at the third instance was Chao Gai prevailed upon to take the seat, with Song Jiang in second place, the Professor in third, and Taoist Gongsun Sheng in fourth.

Song Jiang said: "We shouldn't make distinctions of merit. The original leaders of Mount Liang should all sit in the hosts' places on the left, and the new arrivals should take the guests' places on the right. Later when people's contribution can be judged they can be classified individually."

Everyone responded with one voice: "This is absolutely right."

In a line on the left were Leopard's Head Lin Chong, Liu Tang the Red-Haired Devil, the Ruans, Skyscraper, the Door-God in the Clouds, the Crocodile and the Daytime Rat. On the right according to age, all deferring to each other, Colonel Hua, Thunderclap, the Tamer, the Magic Messenger, Iron Ox, the White-Water Dragon, Mu Hong, the Pilot, White Eel, the Dandy, the Little Duke, the Halberdier, Magic Hand, Short-Arse, the Pill Monger, the Craftsman, Mu Chun, the Executioner, Golden Wings, the Magic Calculator, the Tong brothers, the Magic Flautist, Shi Yong, the Ape, Whitey and the Nine-Tailed Turtle. Altogether forty leaders sat down together at that banquet, amid much tootling of flutes and rattling of drums.

Song Jiang began to speak of the business of Governor Cai and the children's rhyme. "I tell you, that unspeakable bastard Bee Sting Huang, it was absolutely nothing to do with him! Yet he had to go to the Governor with this insane rigmarole! According to him, 'The bane of our land are home and wood' meant that someone who would lay waste the country and its wealth must have in his name the character for wood added to the character for home, that's 'Song,' of course. 'Water and work do us no good' meant that someone with the character for work added to the three dots that stand for water would do great harm — in other words 'Jiang.' So Song Jiang was clearly implied. The following lines 'Thirty-six stand in a row, in Shandong rebellions grow' meant Song Jiang would create an uprising in Shandong. That's why they arrested me. Then the Magic Messenger unluckily delivered the forged letter and that made Bee Sting Huang urge the Governor to carry out the execution first and report it later. If you hadn't come to the rescue I certainly wouldn't be here now."

Iron Ox now jumped up and said: "Dear brother, I think we can see heaven's will in all this. Although you had to put up with a lot from him, he's been repaid by our cutting him up alive. We've plenty of troops, so if we do rise up what have we to fear?

Chapter 41

Chao Gai will be our emperor, Song Jiang the prince, the Professor will be chief minister, and Taoist Gongsun the senior counsellor. The rest of us will be the army. We'll plunder the capital and capture the bloody throne, and then we can all live a life of ease up there, won't it be grand? Better than staying here in these bloody marshes, surely?"

The Magic Messenger hurriedly shouted: "Iron Ox, you're talking bloody nonsense! Remember where you are, you can't go on behaving like you did in Jiangzhou. You've got to pay attention to our two leaders' wishes and commands. If you go shooting your mouth off again, I'm going to make an example of you and bash your brains out!"

Everyone laughed when Iron Ox answered: "Aiya! If you bash my brains out I don't suppose I'm likely to grow some more in a hurry. I'd better just drink my wine."

Song Jiang also spoke of the first battle when the Mount Liang forces had to repel the government troops. "When I first heard that news I truly feared for you. I little thought that one day I myself would also be in the same situation."

"And yet if you'd listened to us before and remained comfortably in the mountain stronghold, instead of going on to Jiangzhou, wouldn't you have saved yourself a lot of trouble?" the Professor said. "But it was your fate, that's the only way to explain it."

Song Jiang said: "By the way, where is Brigadier Huang An who led that attack on Mount Liang?"

Chao Gai said: "He didn't last more than a couple of months. He fell ill and died."

Song Jiang responded with a sigh.

Everyone seemed very happy feasting that day. Chao Gai first made arrangements for housing Squire Mu's family. Then he ordered Bee Sting Huang's possessions to be brought and distributed to the men as a reward for their efforts. He also called for the original treasure boxes and offered them to the Magic Messenger. The latter refused and asked for them to be taken to the treasury for general use. Chao Gai asked the troops now to come and pay their respects to the White-Water Dragon and others and there were general introductions. Oxen and sheep were slaughtered and the feasting continued in the camp for days on end. Of this no more.

Chao Gai now assigned lodgings for everyone on the mountain and the construction of houses and repairing of walls recommenced. At dinner on the third day, Song Jiang stood up and addressed the company as follows: "I still have one important matter on which I would like to crave your indulgence. I wish to go down the mountain again and request a few days' leave of absence, if this is agreeable to you all."

Chao Gai said: "Where do you want to go, and what is this important matter?"

Song Jiang calmly explained where he was planning to go. And this was to have important consequences:

Amid a forest of spears and blades, another narrow escape;
Surrounded by wild cliffs, the hero is granted a vision.

Indeed, the Mystic Lady was to give him three books, and he was to write some pages of history.

But if you want to hear where Song Jiang wanted to go, you must read the next chapter.

Chapter 42

The mystic books received in Dead-End Village; Song Jiang meets the Mystic Lady!

Now when Song Jiang at the feast told everyone that he wanted leave of absence to go down the mountain, he explained: "Here we are, we've been feasting for days and we're having a fine time, but I have no idea how things are going with my old father at home. Since Jiangzhou have informed the Grand Preceptor, in my home district of Jizhou they will be obliged to take action and get the Yuncheng authorities to persecute my family and hold them responsible for my capture. I am afraid my father's life is at risk. I long to see him and, with your approval, I would like to go home to fetch him and bring him here to the mountain, to put an end to my anxieties."

Chao Gai said: "My dear brother, this is an important question of moral obligation. Certainly it is not right for us to be enjoying great pleasures while at home your father is suffering. How could I do other than agree with you? The only thing is, since we've all been celebrating for some days now, none of the troops here are prepared. Why not wait a couple of days till we can equip a detachment and go together with you to fetch him?"

"In itself, waiting a few days is nothing," Song Jiang said, "but I fear that the Jiangzhou authorities will send orders to Jizhou to persecute my family, that's why the matter brooks no delay. However, there's no need to send a big force, I shall go alone in secret, and my younger brother, Iron Fan, will help me bring my father here with the utmost haste. That way, not a soul need know in the village. If we took a big troop of men the whole district would certainly be alerted, which could defeat our purpose."

Chao Gai said: "But supposing you should meet with some mishap along the way, there'd be no one to help you out."

Song Jiang said: "For the sake of one's father, even death is worth risking." Nothing they could do would persuade him to stay, he was determined to leave at once. He chose a broad-brimmed hat, picked up a short staff, buckled on a sword, and went down the mountain. The other leaders accompanied him as far as Golden Sands Landing before returning.

After crossing and landing at the Crocodile's inn, Song Jiang took the highway to Yuncheng. On the way he stopped only for food when he was hungry, for drink when he was thirsty, resting late and starting early. Finally he found himself approaching the Song village. Since it was late in the day he went to stay the night at an inn. Next day he hurried on to the Song village, but then it was too early, so he lay low in a wood till evening. When he went and knocked on the back door, Iron Fan came to open it. The sight of his brother appeared to give Iron Fan quite a shock. "Why have you come home?" he said in consternation.

Song Jiang replied: "I have come to fetch father and you."

"But everyone here knows now about that business of yours in Jiangzhou. The district authorities have sent two inspectors, they come looking for you every day. We are under house arrest, we can't move anywhere. They're only waiting for the official order from Jiangzhou in order to arrest us both and throw us into prison until they catch you. There are several hundred soldiers on patrol, night and day. You mustn't waste any time. Go back to Mount Liang and ask all the leaders to come to rescue us."

Song Jiang was so upset by this that he broke out in an icy sweat. Not daring even to enter the house, he simply turned around and left. He raced back along the road towards Mount Liang. It was dark and the moon was misty, so it was hard to find his way. He deliberately chose the smallest and most isolated of roads to travel on. When he had been going almost two hours, he heard shouting behind him. He turned and listened. The pursuit was only about half a mile behind. He could see a forest of torches blazing in the night and could hear shouts of "Don't let Song Jiang get away!"

"If I'd only listened to Chao Gai, this would never have happened!" he thought as he hurried on. "May heaven pity me and come to my aid!"

He could see a place of some kind ahead of him; it was still distant, so he just kept doggedly on. In a little while the wind swept away the thin clouds and the moon emerged fully. Then he knew exactly where he was. It made him cry out in dismay and he nearly fainted. The place where he found himself was known as "Dead-End Village." It was surrounded in fact by high mountains and steep perpendicular cliffs; a deep river ran along the bottom of the valley and there was only the one road. Once you were in this place, search as you might on one side or the other you'd find nothing but the one road, with no other way in or out. When Song Jiang realized where he was, he would have liked to turn back, but escape was blocked by his pursuers. The torches blazing behind him made it almost like broad daylight and he had no choice now but to keep on towards the village and hope to find somewhere to hide. After skirting the edge of a wood he saw an old temple. Here's what he saw:

> *The walls are in ruins, the roof sags; green moss decks the painted walls of the two galleries, rank grass fills the flower beds. The arms are broken off the demons at the gate and their ugliness no longer impresses; in the main hall the god sits bareheaded in defiance of etiquette. The spider has spun his web on the altar, the mole and ant makes their nest in the incense burner. The fox sleeps nightly in the urn for burning paper offerings, the bat rests undisturbed on the screen before the image.*

Song Jiang pushed open the door of the temple and aided by the moonlight entered and looked for a place to hide. He examined the main hall, front and back, but it afforded no hiding-place. He was beginning to panic. Just then he heard voices outside: "Why not have a look inside this temple, chief?" He recognized one of the voices as Zhao Neng's. Desperate for somewhere to conceal himself, his eye fell on a niche or shrine intended for an image. He drew back the curtain, crouched down and hopped inside. He found a place for his cudgel and then huddled on the floor, scarce daring to breathe. As he did so, the light of the torches came inside the building.

When he managed to peep out, he saw Zhao Neng and Zhao De with a troop of fifty men holding torches which they shone about to illuminate every corner of the temple. "This time I have reached a dead end," he thought to himself. "All I can do is pray for the protection of the spirits and the gods' compassion."

When after a while they started to leave, one after another, and no one had looked in the shrine, Song Jiang said to himself: "It's a miracle!" But at that very moment, Zhao De approached the shrine with his torch and shone it inside. "Now they've got me for sure!" Song Jiang thought. Using the handle of his halberd in the other hand Zhao De lifted the curtain. As he moved the torch to illuminate the shrine from top to bottom, the smoke swirled about and a speck of black soot fell in Zhao De's eye, blinding him. He threw the torch down and extinguished it with his foot. He left the building, saying to the soldiers: "He's not in the temple — there's no other road, where the devil can he have got to?"

"He's probably hiding in the trees by the village," they said. "But there's no fear he'll get away. This place is called 'Dead-End Village,' the only way out is back along this road. There are high mountains and woods all around, and there's no way up. All you've got to do, sergeant, is block the approach to the village. Then he can grow wings and fly up into the sky, if he likes, but he can't escape. When it gets light we can search the village real good and we'll have him."

"Right!" said Zhao De, and began to depart with his troops.

"Really the gods must be on my side," Song Jiang was just thinking. "If I get out of this alive, I must repair this temple and build a new ancestral hall, it can only be that the spirits protected me."

He had hardly finished this thought when a soldier in front of the temple door shouted: "Sergeant, he's here!"

The Zhaos and their men came racing back.

"What cursed luck!" Song Jiang thought, "Now I'm bound to be caught!"

"Where is he?" Zhao Neng demanded, arriving at the door.

Chapter 42

"Take a look at these two handprints in the dust on the temple door, sergeant," said the soldier. "He must have shoved it open just now and dodged inside."

"You're right, we'd better go over it again real thorough."

The whole lot came in again and started searching. Song Jiang was thinking: "What a stupid fate mine is, this must mean I'm finished!"

They searched the place from top to bottom, they did everything but turn over the bricks. After a period of searching and shining the torches around, Zhao Neng said to his brother: "He must be in that shrine there. You didn't search it carefully enough just now. I'm going to have a good look." A soldier held up a torch, while Zhao Neng raised the curtain with one hand and half a dozen heads peered in. But before they could focus properly on everything inside, a gust of foul air burst from within and blew out all the torches, swirling about and obscuring the whole temple, so they even couldn't see one another. "My God!" said Zhao Neng. "Usually when you get a foul wind like this it means there's a god in there, who wants to rebuke us for shining the light around, that's the reason why this kind of foul wind arises. We'd better go. We'll simply set up a block on the road and wait for daylight before searching any more."

Zhao De said: "But we still haven't searched properly inside the shrine. We'd better give it a poke with a halberd."

"You're right," said Zhao Neng.

But as the two of them were about to proceed, the mysterious wind began to blow again from the back of the temple, and it blew till the sand flew up and stones began to move, it came surging forth, causing the roof of the temple to creak to and fro and a black cloud to descend enveloping everyone. The cold draught froze them and their hair stood on end. Zhao Neng didn't at all like this turn of events. "Let's get out brother, the god is angry," he yelled to Zhao De. Everyone fled from the temple in confusion. They didn't stop running till they were outside the gate. Some fell head over heels, others sprained their ankles, but they all scrambled up again and fled for their lives. Someone could still be heard inside the temple compound screaming for mercy. Zhao Neng went back in to look and found one or two soldiers had fallen inside the entrance courtyard and got their clothing caught in the roots of a tree, so that struggle as they might they could not break free. They had thrown away their pikes and were tugging at their clothing and screaming for help. Song Jiang listening in his hiding-place could barely restrain his laughter.

Zhao Neng freed the men's clothing and hustled them out of the door. Several of the soldiers in front said: "We said this god was too powerful, but you lot would stick around in there and you only set those demons off. We'd best go and set up the road block so he can't get away." Zhao Neng and Zhao De both agreed: "That's right, we only need to guard the road securely on every side." With this they all went off to the entrance to the village.

Meanwhile Song Jiang in his hiding-place was assessing his fortunes: "It's true I haven't been caught, but how am I ever going to get out of here?" Just at that moment, as he was vainly racking his brains for a solution, he heard someone moving about outside. "Oh, no! Trouble again!" he thought. "Why didn't I get out before?" However, it turned out to be only two young acolytes in green who stopped beside the shrine and said: "We have instructions from Holy Mother to invite the Heavenly Prince to speak with her." Song Jiang was much too wary to make the slightest sound in answer. So the acolytes repeated: "Holy Mother invites you, Heavenly Prince, please to come with us." Song Jiang still did not dare speak. Again the acolytes said: "Prince Song, please do not delay, Holy Mother has been waiting a long time for you." From the fluting tones Song Jiang knew that these were not men speaking, so he raised himself from the floor of the shrine and looked out. What he saw was two young female disciples dressed in green standing beside the altar. He had quite a shock, because they looked so much like ceramic images.

When they said again: "Prince Song, Holy Mother invites you," he drew aside the curtain and stepped right out. The two acolytes, each with her hair tied in the shape of a shell at the back, bobbed up and down and made him a kowtow. Here is what he saw:

Their skin is like pearls, their hair green, they have white teeth and

Chapter 42

shining eyes. As they flutter about, not a speck of dust sullies their purity, they radiate heavenly grace and harmony. Styled like a conch shell, their hair rises up like a mountain peak. The phoenix slippers are elegant as lotus petals. Their robes are of dark green, interwoven with silver thread, they are girt with purple sashes and gold clasps. Such perfection of elegance and refinement suggests messengers from heaven.

Then Song Jiang asked: "What is the reason for this heavenly visitation?"

"We come at Holy Mother's behest to invite the Heavenly Prince to her palace."

"You must be mistaken," Song Jiang said. "My name is Song and my given name is Jiang, but I'm not a heavenly prince."

"How can we be mistaken? Please come now, Holy Mother has long awaited you."

Song Jiang said: "Who is this Holy Mother? I've never even met her, how can I presume to visit her?"

"If you come, then you will meet her. Don't ask so many questions."

"Where is she?"

"In her residence at the back."

With the disciples in green leading the way, Song Jiang left the temple. They passed through a gate in the corner of a wall that extended behind and to one side of the temple, and the acolytes said: "Prince Song, this is the entrance." Song Jiang followed them through the gate and looked about him. The sky was bright with stars and the moon shone, a soft breeze whispered and all around were luxuriant groves and bamboo thickets. "So this is what there is behind the temple," Song Jiang thought. "If I'd only known, I wouldn't have hidden in the temple and had to suffer all those shocks."

Where he was walking there were banks on either side planted with great pine trees, so large a man could not encircle them with his arms. In the flat space between was a broad avenue curved like the back of a tortoise. Song Jiang kept thinking to himself: "I had no idea there was such a fine road behind the temple." When he'd followed the acolytes for less than half a mile, he heard the tinkling of a running stream. Ahead was a bridge of black stone with a red rail on either side. The banks were enlivened with exotic flowers and rare grasses, dark green pines, luxuriant bamboos, jade-green willows, and delicate apricots, whilst under the bridge the water tumbled like scattered silver or billowing snow, gushing from the mouth of a stone grotto. After passing the bridge, two rows of unusual trees appeared and in the middle a tall red star gate. He passed through and lifting his eyes beheld a palace:

> *The red door is studded with gold nails, there are green tiles and carved eaves. Winged dragons twisting round the pillars play with a bright pearl; paired phoenixes on the screen outshine the sun. The surrounding walls of clay are stained vermilion, and all around the palace flowers bloom among stately willows. The hall is of great splendour, and within it the light from an auspicious lantern casts lovely shadows. Wafted through windows arched like a turtle's back sweet breezes lightly stir the yellow gauze; beyond the curtains tied back with delicate ribbons, the pale moon hangs silently in a sky like purple velvet. If this is not the abode of some heavenly being, it must be at least the dwelling of an earthly queen.*

"I was born in Yuncheng," Song Jiang thought, "yet I never knew this was here." He stood there nervously, not daring to go on. The acolytes urged him forward. They led him on through the gates of the palace into the wide forecourt. The two side galleries had vermilion pillars, hung about with embroidered curtains, the great hall in the centre was bedecked with lanterns and candles. The acolytes led him step by step from the courtyard to the platform. Before the steps leading up into the hall were more acolytes in green who said: "Holy Mother welcomes you, please enter." When he arrived at the main hall Song Jiang was trembling all over and his hair was standing on end. He stopped on a brick stairway depicting dragon and phoenix. The acolytes passed through the curtains and the order was given out: "Heavenly Prince Song please approach the throne." On reaching the screen before the throne, Song Jiang bowed low and prostrated himself, saying: "Your humble servant is not worthy. I can only pray for mercy and beg you to favour me with your graciousness."

From behind the screen came the order: "Be seated, Heavenly Prince."

But Song Jiang dared not so much as lift his head. So four of the acolytes raised him and placed for him a seat of fine porcelain, and he was obliged to sit. Order was given for the screen to be rolled back. Several acolytes rushed to roll up the spangled curtain, securing it with golden hooks.

Holy Mother now asked: "I trust you have been well since we parted?"

Song Jiang rose to his feet and bowing said: "Your humble servant dares not look at Your Holiness."

"Now that you are here there is no need for further ceremony."

Now at last Song Jiang ventured to raise his eyes. He saw the throne all glittering and bright, adorned with lanterns and candles. On either side were young green-clad girl acolytes holding sceptres and tablets and servant girls with flags and fans. In the centre, on a throne embellished with precious stones and dragons, sat Holy Mother.

Holy Mother spoke again: "Please approach, Heavenly Prince." She ordered the acolytes to bring wine. Two junior acolytes filled jade cups from a bottle of "Rare Flower" wine. A senior acolyte offered a cup of wine to Song Jiang. Not daring to refuse, he rose to his feet, took the jade cup in his hands and, fixing his eyes on Holy Mother, knelt and drained it. The wine tasted superb and seemed to suffuse his being with a glow of understanding, as if he were bathed in heavenly dew. Another acolyte now appeared with a plate of celestial dates which she offered to Song Jiang. He was terrified of committing a breech of decorum, so he took one with the very tips of his fingers and then having eaten it kept the stone in his hand. The acolyte poured another cup of wine and presented it to him, and again he was obliged to drink. Holy Mother ordered another cup after this, so another was poured and offered and again he drank. The dates were offered again and he ate two. Altogether now he had drunk three cups of wine and

宋公明遇九天玄女

eaten three dates. He began to feel the slight flush of intoxication. He was terrified of getting drunk and losing his composure, so he bowed and said: "Your humble servant has no strong head for wine and begs to be excused."

"If the Heavenly Prince cannot take wine, he may desist," was the reply from above. "Fetch me the three mystic books. I shall give them to the Heavenly Prince."

An acolyte slipped behind the screen and returned bearing a jade tray with a package wrapped in yellow silk and containing the three mystic books. They were presented to Song Jiang. When he looked at them, they were as though five inches long, three inches wide and three inches high. He did not dare open them but bowed and took them reverently and bestowed them in his sleeves.

Holy Mother spoke: "Heavenly Prince, I give you these three books that you may always perform heaven's will. Be ever a steadfast proponent of righteousness, preserve your land and people, shun evil and pursue justice. I have a four-line mystic verse for you. Commit it to memory and have it always with you, do not ever forget it."

Song Jiang bowed again and expressed his eagerness to receive the mystic verse. Holy Mother intoned:

Chance lodgings will bring many joys,
Scaling the heights will hold no fears.
'Gainst foes without, bandits within
Many a valiant deed is done.

When he had heard it, Song Jiang again bowed reverentially. Holy Mother spoke again: "Because evil desires are not entirely eradicated from your heart, and your journey is yet unfinished, the Jade Emperor has sentenced you to remain here below for a space. But in a while you will mount again to the Purple Mansions. Meanwhile you must not be in any way remiss. If for some further transgression you are again sent down to the underworld, I shall be unable to save you. These three books you must study attentively and with profit. This knowledge is to be shared only with the Occult Star, it is not for the eyes of others. After your success you must burn them, they must not remain in the world. Commit their injunctions to memory. At present there is a gulf between heaven and earth. It would not be right for you to tarry here long, you must return quickly." So saying, she ordered the acolytes to take him back with all speed. "We will again meet here in the jade halls of the golden palace on another occasion."

Song Jiang thanked Holy Mother and followed the disciples who led him out of the palace and through the star gate as far as the stone bridge. There they said: "The Heavenly Prince has just had a fright. But for the Holy Mother's protection you would have been caught. But when daylight comes you will undoubtedly be delivered from your predicament. Do you see the two dragons playing in the water beneath the bridge?"

Song Jiang leant on the rail and looked over. He did indeed see two dragons playing in the water, but just then the acolytes gave him a push and with a loud cry he fell ... and found himself in the shrine. It had all been a magic dream.

He pulled himself to his feet and looked around. The moon was high, he guessed it to be around midnight. When he felt in his sleeves, he found three date stones and the package, which he took out and examined. It contained indeed the three volumes of the sacred books. And he could still taste the wine on his tongue, too. "This is a very strange dream," he thought. "It is like a dream and not a dream. If it was a dream, how do the sacred books come to be here in my sleeve? And the taste of wine in my mouth and the date stones in my hand? And I remember exactly what was spoken, I haven't forgotten a word. So perhaps I wasn't dreaming. Certainly I am here in the shrine now, it's as if I was catapulted here. The explanation must be quite simple. It must be that this goddess is so potent she can manifest her divine power in this manner. Only I wonder which goddess it was?" He pulled aside the curtain in order to see. On the carved throne sat a beautiful lady, exactly like the one in the dream. Song Jiang thought: "This Holy Mother insisted I was a heavenly prince. It looks as if in a previous life I must have been someone of some importance. These three tomes will surely be useful. I still remember the mystic four-line verse she gave me. The acolyte said, 'When

Chapter 42

遁道村玄三卷天書

daylight comes you will undoubtedly be delivered from your predicament.' It's getting light already, I'd better be going."

He felt about him till he laid hands on his cudgel, brushed the dust off his clothes, carefully descended from the shrine and made his way via the left-hand gallery to the front of the temple. When he looked up he saw an ancient sign with four gold characters inscribed on it: "Temple of the Mystic Lady." Song Jiang joined his palms and prayed: "Heaven be praised. Of course it was the Mystic Lady of the Ninth Heaven who gave me the three books and preserved me from death. If ever again I am allowed to see the sun, I shall certainly return and restore the temple. I entreat her divine mercy to defend and protect me." After giving thanks, he set off cautiously, heading for the entrance to the village.

He was only a little way from the temple when he heard a tremendous hullabaloo occurring some way ahead of him. "This is no good," he said to himself. "I'd better wait for a bit, I obviously can't get out now. If I go forward I'm bound to be caught. The best thing will be to hide behind this tree at the side of the road."

When he'd slipped behind the tree, he saw a bunch of soldiers approaching in a disorderly rout, out of breath and trailing their swords and spears, all frantically shouting: "Heaven save us!"

Watching from behind his tree, Song Jiang thought: "Strange. They were supposed to be blocking the way out of the village, waiting to catch me. Where are they charging off to?" The next minute Zhao Neng also appeared, shouting as he ran: "We're done for!"

"What is it that's scared him like that?" Song Jiang wondered.

Then he saw a huge fellow chasing behind. On the top half of his body there was not a stitch of clothing, his immense physique was totally exposed. He was waving a pair of double-edged axes and shouting: "Don't let the bastard get away!" If it was not clear in the distance, there was no doubt when he got nearer: it was Iron Ox.

"Am I dreaming?" Song Jiang wondered, still not daring to come out of hiding.

When Zhao Neng reached the temple he tripped over the root of a pine tree and crashed to the ground. Iron Ox caught up with

Chapter 42

him, planted a foot on his back and raised his axe. He was already about to strike when two more pursuers appeared behind him, their felt hats resting on their shoulders, each wielding a halberd. The senior of these two was Golden Wings, the junior was the Nine-Tailed Turtle. When he saw them Iron Ox, fearing that in defiance of all the rules of brotherhood they might rob him of his glory, chopped Zhao Neng in half with one tremendous blow down the middle that opened up his whole chest, and then raced away to massacre more of the fleeing troops, who were running in all directions.

Behind these, three more heroes could now be seen, doing great destruction: in front the Red-Haired Devil, second Shi Yong, and third the Executioner. All six now paused to confer: "Well, we've routed those bastards, but we still haven't found our brother Song Jiang. What can we do now?" Suddenly Shi Yong shouted: "Who the devil is that, hiding behind that bloody pine tree?"

Song Jiang at last saw fit to reveal himself: "You have just saved my life," he said. "How can I ever repay you?"

They were immensely relieved to see him. "There you are!" they said. "We must go and tell leader Chao at once!" Shi Yong and the Executioner both rushed off.

"How did you know to come here to rescue me?" Song Jiang asked the Red-Haired Devil.

The latter replied: "When you first went down the mountain, Leader Chao and the Professor were anxious. So they told the Magic Messenger to follow you and find out where you were. But Leader Chao still could not rest easy, so he asked me and the others to come and back you up, as he feared something might go wrong for you. On the way we ran into the Magic Messenger, who said, 'Two bloody fools are chasing our brother.' Leader Chao was furious. He sent the Magic Messenger back to the mountain to tell the lot who stayed behind, that's to say the Professor, Taoist Gongsun Sheng, the Ruan brothers, the Little Duke, the Halberdier, the Crocodile and the Daytime Rat, to look after the defence of the stronghold, and told everyone else to come and help look for you. Some one said they'd followed you to Dead-End Village.

We killed all the blighters who were blocking the approach to the village, there's no one left there. There was only these few who fled into the village. Iron Ox went after them and we followed. We were afraid you weren't here....."

Before he could finish, Shi Yong arrived with Chao Gai, Colonel Hua, Thunderclap, the Tamer, the Pill Monger, the Magic Calculator, and the Magic Flautist. The Executioner also arrived with the White-Water Dragon, Mu Hong, the Pilot, White Eèl, Mu Chun, the Ape, Magic Hand and the Craftsman. This great band of heroes all converged. Song Jiang thanked all the leaders. Chao Gai said: "I implore you brother not to go down the mountain on your own again. You refused to listen to me once more and look what troubles resulted."

Song Jiang said: "My friends, this was all on account of my father. I was intensely worried, I simply could not sit still. It would have been quite impossible for me not to come and fetch him."

"I have news that will make you happy, then," Chao Gai said. "I already told the Magic Messenger to take Skyscraper, the Door-God in the Clouds, Short-Arse, Whitey, and the two Tong brothers and fetch your father and the rest of your family. They should be in the mountain retreat by now."

Song Jiang was overjoyed to hear this and thanked Chao Gai, saying: "After this great favour you have done me, I could die now without regret!"

Chao Gai and Song Jiang, both equally happy with the turn of events, now mounted horses and rode with the others out of Dead-End Village. Song Jiang put his hand respectfully on his forehead as he rode and turning his eyes heavenwards, gave thanks to the gods for their protective power and prayed that he might come again some other day to fulfil his vow. There is an old song which directly describes how Song Jiang's righteousness and honour obtained heaven's grace:

When chaos reigns and fortune's overthrown
Heroes establish an order of their own.
In Shandong now a hopeful dawning pricks;
The four great stars are grown to thirty-six.

Chapter 42

Above Yuncheng an auspicious air's observed;
This was the spot for Song Jiang's birth reserved.
In youth the annals and classics are his passion;
Grown up, he turns to charity and compassion:
His are all the virtues of the righteous;
The Mystic Lady adds to them her scriptures.
Roaming the world, with heroes he oft converses,
And suffers many an ill ere his luck reverses.
To the Marshes of Mount Liang he'll then retire,
And raise a host that will expiate Heaven's ire.

So now the whole company left Dead-End Village and returned to the Marshes of Mount Liang. The Professor led the defenders of the camp out to Golden Sands Landing to meet them. They all then went to the assembly hall and formally greeted each other. Song Jiang anxiously inquired: "Where is my father?" Chao Gai requested Squire Song to come out, and in a little while Iron Fan appeared, resting one hand on a mountain sedan which was carrying Squire Song. Everyone helped the Squire down from the sedan and escorted him into the hall. Song Jiang's heart leapt at the sight and he broke into a delighted smile. "You have had too many shocks, father, I have not been a good son to you, I should never have allowed you to suffer these things."

Squire Song said: "It's all the fault of those two dreadful Zhao brothers. They sent people to watch us every day, waiting for the order from Jiangzhou so they could arrest us and clap us into prison. When we heard you knocking on the back door there were already eighty or ninety soldiers in the thatched hall in front. Then they disappeared and we didn't know what had frightened them away! In the third watch two hundred or more men opened the gate and bundled me into that sedan and carried me off. They told your brother to pack our belongings and set fire to the manor. Naturally I couldn't wait to know what was going on. They brought me here."

Song Jiang said: "The fact that our family is reunited here today is entirely due to the valour of our friends here." He told his young brother to express thanks formally to all the leaders. When Chao

Gai and the others had all paid their respects to Squire Song, cattle and horses were slaughtered and a grand feast was organized in honour of Song Jiang's reunion with his father. They were all quite drunk when they parted that night. The celebrations continued next day and everyone, great and small, had a good time.

On the third day, Chao Gai had also prepared a feast in honour of Song Jiang's father, when Taoist Gongsun Sheng was suddenly reminded of something which stirred him deeply. His thoughts had turned to his old mother in Jizhou. It was long since he left home and he had no idea how she was. So whilst they were all busy drinking, Gongsun Sheng suddenly stood up and addressed the leaders as follows: "I have to express my deep gratitude to all this brave company for having so long looked after me and shown me such great kindness. But since the day this poor Taoist came with our leader Chao Gai to the mountain, a time filled indeed with feasting and pleasure, not once has he been back home to visit his old mother. My religious teacher will also, I fear, be anxiously awaiting me. I would like therefore to make a visit to my home town, bidding you all farewell for some three or four months, after which I shall return and be with you again. This would fulfil my dearest wish and ensure that my poor mother does not have to wait in vain."

Chao Gai said: "I always listen to what you say, father. Your mother up there in the north has no one to look after her. Now that you tell me this, how can I refuse you? Only it's so hard to part with you. If go you must, just wait till tomorrow so we can send you off properly."

Gongsun Sheng thanked him. They got drunk again that day before the evening ended and everyone went to bed. Early next morning a feast was arranged below the pass to bid Gongsun Sheng farewell.

Gongsun Sheng had dressed in his previous fashion as a wandering Taoist, with a pouch attached to his belt and a bag tied at the waist, a pair of fine swords slung on his back, a hat of palm bark hanging on his shoulders and a fan shaped like a tortoise shell which he held in his hand. Thus equipped he went down the mountain. All the leaders accompanied him and there was

Chapter 42

a farewell celebration below the pass where everyone raised a cup in his honour. After the first round Chao Gai said: "If we cannot persuade you to stay, father, please do not break faith with us. I part with you most unwillingly, but for the sake of your respected mother we cannot prevent you. After a hundred days I hope the crane will deign to return to this humble abode. Please do not fail to keep your word."

Gongsun Sheng said: "After you have all treated me so kindly for so long, how could I ever break my word to you? I will go home and visit my religious teacher and make proper arrangements for my poor mother, then I will return to the mountain retreat."

Song Jiang said: "Why not take someone with you, father? Then you could bring your mother here to the mountain, so you could look after her all the time."

Gongsun Sheng said: "All her life my mother has loved peace and quiet, she cannot stand shocks. That's why I wouldn't like to bring her. At home we've a little farm on the hillside, my mother manages it well enough by herself. I just want to go and visit her, then I'll be back with you again."

Song Jiang said: "In that case, look after yourself. I just hope you will soon make us happy with your return."

Chao Gai brought out a tray of gold and silver as parting gift and Gongsun Sheng said: "That's far too much. All I need is a little for travelling expenses."

Chao Gai persuaded him to take half. He tied it in his pouch, bowed low, said farewell, crossed from Golden Sands Landing and set off for Jizhou.

The rest were dispersing and were about to return up the mountain when suddenly Iron Ox let out a great cry and burst into tears. "What ever is the matter?" Song Jiang hurriedly asked him. "Fuck it all!" he said between sobs. "This one goes to fetch his dad, that one goes to see his mum, but you'd think Iron Ox simply came out of a hole in the ground!"

Chao Gai asked: "But what do you want?"

"I've got an old mother who's alone, too. My elder brother works on someone else's farm, how can he keep her and make her happy? If I could go and get her and bring her here so she can be happy for a while, that would be really good."

Chao Gai said: "Then let it be so. I'll send some others with you to help bring her back, it's entirely reasonable."

"Impossible!" Song Jiang said. "Our friend Li has a most difficult character. If you let him go home he's sure to get into trouble. If you send anyone with him that won't do either. Since his temper's like a blazing fire, he's bound to clash with someone along the way. He killed lots of people in Jiangzhou. It's not for nothing you know that they call him the Black Whirlwind. Anyway, is it likely the authorities haven't acted already and sent the order for his arrest there? Just look at you, Iron Ox! Your very appearance is wild and dangerous. If something goes wrong, it's a long way off, how can we know about it? You'd better wait a while and when you know everything is quiet you can go, that'll be time enough."

But Iron Ox said impatiently: "You're not such a patient man either. When you wanted to fetch your father you went dashing off down the mountain. If my mother is suffering there in the village because of me, it breaks my heart to think."

Song Jiang said: "Don't be so hasty. If you really want to go and fetch your mother, then you should accept three conditions. If you do, we'll let you go."

Iron Ox said: "Tell me what they are then."

On his fingers Song Jiang listed the three conditions. And it was from this that Iron Ox …

Put forth the hand that shook heaven and earth;
And fought the fearsome tiger in the mountains.

But if you want to know the three conditions that Song Jiang told Iron Ox, you must read the next chapter.

Chapter 43

The false Li Kui robs travellers on the highway; Iron Ox kills four tigers on Yiling Heights!

"Just tell me what those three conditions are, brother," Iron Ox said. And Song Jiang told him: "If you want to go back home to fetch your mother, the first condition is that you do not drink on the journey. Second, given that you're so hot-tempered, we can't send anyone with you, so you must just go quietly by yourself and bring your mother straight back. Third, don't take those two axes with you. Control yourself during the journey, go quickly and come back soon."

Iron Ox said: "There's nothing I can't keep to in that. Don't worry, I'll leave today, and I won't waste any time."

On this occasion Iron Ox's preparations were quickly made. He just stuck a dagger in his belt, shouldered a halberd, provided himself with one large silver ingot and three or four small ones, drank a few cups of wine, shouted out a salute, bade everyone farewell, went down the mountain and across the water from Golden Sands Landing, and was gone.

After they had seen him off, Chao Gai, Song Jiang and the others went back and sat down in the assembly hall. But Song Jiang was still uneasy. "This Iron Ox," he said, "if he's on his own he's sure to get into some trouble. Is there anyone of the company who comes from the same part of the world? Someone who could go there and get news of him?"

Skyscraper said: "There's the Crocodile, he's from Yishui in Yizhou, he's Iron Ox's countryman."

"Of course, I had forgotten," Song Jiang said. "Iron Ox said so himself the other day in the assembly at the White Dragon temple."

So Song Jiang sent for the Crocodile. One of the men raced down the mountain with the message; he arrived at the inn and asked the Crocodile to go up to the fortress. "Our friend Iron Ox has just gone off home to fetch his mother," Song Jiang said to the Crocodile. "I didn't want to send anyone with him, because he gets so aggressive when he's been drinking. But I'm really afraid he may get into trouble on the way. I've just heard that you are his compatriot. Would you mind going there to his district to keep an eye on him?"

The Crocodile replied: "Yes, I am from Yishui district in Yizhou and I've a brother called Zhu Fu who has opened an inn outside the west gate of the city. This Iron Ox lives in the same area, at East Dongdian outside Baizhang village. He's got an elder brother called Li Da, who works on someone else's land — a pretty wild character, who killed a man once and fled to the rivers and lakes and has never gone back home. If you want me to go back there and make some inquiries it's no problem. The only trouble is there won't be anyone to look after the inn. Still, I haven't been home for a long time and I'd very much like to go back and pay my brother a visit."

"There's no need to worry about the inn," Song Jiang said. "I'll get the Ape and Shi Yong to look after it for you for a while."

The Crocodile was satisfied with this. He said goodbye and went back down the mountain to the inn, where he packed his bags, handed over the establishment to the Ape and Shi Yong, and set off for home.

Back at the mountain retreat Song Jiang passed the days feasting and drinking quite contentedly with Chao Gai, and studying the mystic books with "Professor" Wu Yong, the Occult Star. Of this no more.

Meanwhile Iron Ox all on his own left the Marshes of Mount Liang and took the road to Yishui. He diligently abstained from wine on the road, so he did not provoke any incidents and the journey was uneventful. When he reached the west gate of Yishui, he saw a knot of people studying a notice. He placed himself in their midst and heard someone read out: "The first name on the notice is the chief bandit Song Jiang, he is from Yuncheng. The second name is the lesser bandit Dai Zong, he is superintendent of the two prisons in Jiangzhou. The third name is the lesser bandit Li Kui, he is from Yishui in Yizhou." Iron Ox, listening at the back, was on the point of making some totally inappropriate and uncalled-for remark, when someone came thrusting through the crowd, seized him by the waist and cried: "Brother Zhang, what are you doing here?"

When Iron Ox twisted round to see who it was he recognized the Crocodile. "What are you doing here?" he asked.

"I want a word with you," the other said.

They went together to an inn in a district just outside the west gate. They found a clean room at the back and sat down. The Crocodile pointed at Iron Ox and said: "What a foolhardy fellow you are! That notice says clearly that there's a reward of a hundred thousand for the capture of Song Jiang, five thousand for the Magic Messenger, and three thousand for Iron Ox. So why were you standing there looking at it? Suppose someone had been sharp-sighted and quick-handed enough to catch you and hand you over to the police, what would you have done then? Our brother Song Jiang was afraid you would cause a disturbance, so he didn't want to send anyone with you. But he still feared you would do something silly here, and he sent me along to find out how you were getting on. I was a day behind you leaving the mountain, but I got here a day ahead, why's it taken you so long?"

Iron Ox answered: "He told me I wasn't to drink on the way, that slowed me down. How did you know about this inn? You're from here, aren't you, where is your house?"

"This inn belongs to my younger brother, Zhu Fu," said the Crocodile. "Yes, I do come from these parts. I used to do business in the rivers and lakes but I lost all my money, that's why I joined the company on Mount Liang and became an outlaw. So now I'm visiting my home." He called his brother Zhu Fu over and introduced him to Iron Ox. Zhu Fu ordered wine for Iron Ox. "Our brother told me not to drink," Iron Ox said, "but I'm home now, so what's bloody wrong with drinking a bowl of wine?" Not daring to try and stop him, the Crocodile let him drink.

They sat there drinking into the small hours. Some food was

ordered and Iron Ox ate. Around dawn, when the moon and stars were fading and a rosy glow was spreading in the east, he set off for his village. "Don't take the short cut," the Crocodile told him. "When you pass the big tree take the highway heading east and go straight to Baizhang. That'll take you to East Dongdian. Find your mother and bring her at once and we'll go back to Mount Liang together."

Iron Ox said: "I most certainly will take the short cut. It's a long way, who wants to waste time taking the highway?"

The Crocodile said: "There's lots of tigers along that small track. And there's robbers too."

Iron Ox replied: "Do you think I'm afraid of them?" He put on his hat, took up his halberd, buckled on a sword, bade farewell to the Crocodile and his brother and set off for Baizhang.

When he'd gone a couple of miles it began to grow lighter. As he was walking through the wet grass, a white rabbit suddenly appeared, hopping along ahead of him. Iron Ox chased after it for a while. Then he laughed and said: "This creature has led me a merry dance." There is a poem which says:

Quiet reigns on the mountain path,
The west wind shakes yellow leaves from the trees.
Chancing upon a hare he chases it too far,
And quite forgets that his journey is urgent.

As he was proceeding on his way, Iron Ox saw in front of him a small mixed wood of big trees. The season was early autumn and the leaves had all turned. When he reached a hut on the edge of this wood, a big man emerged and shouted: "You'd better pay the toll here, if you can. If not, I'll have your baggage."

Iron Ox looked at him. His hair was tied in a red silk bandanna and he wore a robe of rough cloth. He carried a pair of axes and he had blackened his face. Iron Ox shouted back: "Who the fuck are you? And what makes you think you can rob highways here?"

The other said: "Want to know my name do you? Well, it'll frighten you out of your wits! I am the Black Whirlwind, that's who I am! Now, if you put down the money for the toll, and your baggage, I'll spare your life and you can go!"

Chapter 43

Iron Ox roared with laughter. "You fucking son of a bitch! What are you, and where have you sprung from? You've even pinched my goddamn name, so you can stand here talking bloody nonsense!" So saying he levelled his halberd and charged. The other offered no resistance whatsoever. Instead he tried to flee, but was brought down by a blow to the thigh from Iron Ox's weapon. Planting one foot on the man's chest Iron Ox shouted: "Do you know who I am?"

The other cried: "Please sir, spare the life of this stupid fool!"

"I am the real Black Whirlwind, famous throughout the rivers and lakes! I am Li Kui and you have abused my name!"

"My name really is Li, but I'm not the real Black Whirlwind. It was because you're so famous in the rivers and lakes that I took your name, which even the spirits are scared of. By purloining your name I was able to rob as I liked on the highway here. If a merchant comes through on his own, just hearing the name Black Whirlwind is enough, he throws down his baggage and runs for his life. I've been able to scrape a living like this. But I haven't really hurt anyone. I gave myself the professional name of Li Gui. I live in the village just down the road."

"The insolence of the bastard! Robbing folk of their bags and baggage on the highway and ruining my reputation! You even copied my trick of using two axes! Well you'd better be prepared for one of my axe blows now." He stretched out his arm and snatched one of the axes and prepared to strike. But the panic-stricken Li Gui cried: "Sir, if you kill me you're killing two people at once!"

Iron Ox arrested his stroke. "If I kill you I'm killing two people? How's that?"

"I would never have had the courage to rob on the highway, if I hadn't got a ninety-year-old mother at home with no one else to look after her. That's why I made bold with your name, sir, to scare people, so I could lay hands on a few goods to support my poor mother. But God's truth, I really never hurt anyone. So now you see, if you kill me, my old mother is going to starve to death."

Now although Iron Ox was a violent character who could murder someone without blinking an eyelid, when he heard this

假李逵遨前徑
劫單身

story he thought to himself: "Here's me going home specially to fetch my mother, and if I then go and kill someone who's his mother's sole support, heaven will not look kindly on it. No, I mustn't, I must spare the bugger." So he let him go, and Li Gui, after taking back the axe, bowed deeply and prostrated himself.

Iron Ox said: "But remember, I'm the only true Black Whirlwind, so from now on don't go taking my name in vain."

"I shall change my name at once and go home and change my profession," the other said. "I'll never again take advantage of your name to rob highways."

Iron Ox said: "You have a filial heart. I will give you ten taels of silver as capital to help you change your profession." He gave him an ingot and Li Gui bowed in thanks and departed.

Iron Ox laughed about it afterwards. "The poor sod fell slap into my hands. Anyway, he's a filial son and he's going to change his ways, if I'd killed him it would not have been pleasing to heaven. But now I'd better get going." He took his halberd and trudged on along the small mountain path. There is a poem here:

One seeks his mother: his intention misfires.
One claims a like virtue, but the tale is a liar's.
When sons thus their love for a mother proclaim,
Just ask if the words and the deeds are the same.

Iron Ox had walked till well into the morning, by which time his stomach told him he was hungry and thirsty. There was nothing around him except a proliferation of mountain paths; there was no inn or eating-house in sight. But as he went on he began to catch glimpses in the distance of a couple of thatched cottages nestling in a hollow on the hillside. He headed for one of the houses and was able to observe a woman coming out of the back. A bunch of wild flowers was stuck in her hairdo, and her face was plastered with rouge and make-up. Iron Ox put down his halberd and called out: "Hey, Auntie, I'm a traveller and I'm starving, I can't find any sort of inn anywhere. I'll pay you a good price if you'll get me something to eat and drink."

When she looked at Iron Ox and saw his physique, the woman

dared not refuse him. Reluctantly she replied: "There isn't anywhere to buy wine but I can cook you some rice."

"All right. But do plenty. I'm bloody starving."

"Will a litre be enough?"

"Make it three."

The woman went to the kitchen to light the stove and then after washing the rice beside the stream came back to cook it. When Iron Ox went out the back to wash his hands, he saw a man limping down the hill. After he'd gone back into the house he heard the woman open the back door — she was about to go up the hill to get vegetables. Meeting the man, she asked: "What's the matter with your leg, dear? Have you twisted your ankle?"

"I was that close to never seeing you again!" he replied. "Can you imagine how bloody unlucky I was? I went out looking for a lone traveller. I'd been waiting two whole weeks without doing any good. Today, I thought I'd just found myself something, and who do you think it turned out to be? Only the real Black Whirlwind! Well, since it was that fucker I'd bumped into, I naturally hadn't a hope against him. He clobbered me in the leg, in fact. Then he knocked me down, and was just about to do me in, when I got the idea of shouting, 'If you kill me you're killing two!' He asked me why and I told him, 'I got this ninety-year-old mum at home with no one to look after her and she's sure to starve!' The silly bugger actually believed me! He let me go and gave me some silver to start a business with and told me to change my way of life and look after my mother well. I was afraid he might be watching and follow me, so I got out of that wood and found a very lonely spot and slept there a while, before coming back here round the other side of the mountain."

The woman said: "Keep your voice down. Just now a big dark fellow came up and told me to cook him food, I think it might be him. He was sitting out there by the door, you'd better go and take a look. If it is him, go and get the drug to put in his food. When he eats it, it'll knock him out and the two of us can deal with him. If we can make some money out of him, we'll be able to move into town and start a business; we won't have to stay here robbing highways."

Chapter 43

When he heard this, Iron Ox said to himself: "The bastard! I just gave him some silver, and spared his life, and now he wants to kill me! That's really a bit too much!" He strolled over to the back door. As luck would have it, the wretched Li Gui was just coming out. Iron Ox grabbed him by the hair. The woman fled through the front door. Iron Ox pinned Li Gui's arms and forced him to the ground. He pulled out his knife and speedily severed his neck. Knife in hand he rushed to the front door to find the woman, but he couldn't discover where she had gone to. He went inside again and searched the house. He found two wicker baskets full of old clothes, and at the bottom he found some loose change in silver and some jewellery. He took it all. He also went and retrieved the silver ingot from Li Gui's body and tied it all up in his bundle. Then he went and looked at the pot. The three litres of rice were about done: all that was missing was some dishes to eat with it. He helped himself to rice and ate it plain for a while. Then he suddenly laughed and said to himself: "I'm an idiot! There's good meat staring me in the face but I didn't think of eating it!" He took out his knife and went and carved two good hunks of meat from Li Gui's leg, washed them in water, put some more charcoal in the stove and proceeded to roast them. Thus cooking and eating as he went along, he ate till he was full. Then he dragged the body back into the house and set fire to it. Shouldering his halberd he departed.

By the time he reached East Dongdian the sun was already setting in the west. He hurried to his home, pushed open the door and entered. His mother was sitting on the bed. "Who is it?" she cried out. He looked and saw that she was blind in both eyes. She was sitting on the bed praying. "Mother, Iron Ox has come home," he said.

"My son, you've been gone such a long time!" she said. "Where have you been all these years? Your brother works on someone else's estate, he just scrapes a living and there's not really enough to feed me. I cried my eyes out, thinking about you, I went blind in both eyes. How have things been with you?"

Iron Ox thought: "If I tell her I'm an outlaw in the Marshes of Mount Liang, she'll never agree to go with me. I'd better make something up." So he said to her: "I've become an official now and I've come to take you back with me."

"That's wonderful," she said. "But how will you be able to take me?"

"I'll carry you on my back for the first part. Later we'll look for a cart."

"Wait till your brother comes, then we can see about it."

"Why wait? We'll go now."

But just as they were about to leave, Li Da appeared with a pot of rice.

When Iron Ox saw him walk in, he prostrated himself and said: "It's been a long time, brother!"

His brother responded angrily: "What the bloody hell have you come here for? I suppose you want to get us into trouble again."

The mother said: "Iron Ox is an official now. He's come to take me with him."

"Mother! Don't believe that shit! The first time when he killed that chap I had to wear a cangue and fetters and suffer a thousand indignities. Now I hear that he's mixed up with that crowd from the Marshes of Mount Liang. They raided the execution ground recently and turned Jiangzhou upside down. He's joined a gang of robbers, do you hear? The other day orders arrived from Jiangzhou, with a warrant for his arrest, and the court wanted to detain me until he's caught. Luckily the chap I work for spoke up for me. He said my younger brother had disappeared more than ten years ago and never returned, and that it might be someone using the same name who had falsified his particulars. My boss paid everyone money on my behalf, that's how I managed to get out of it, otherwise they'd have held me hostage and beaten me. Now there's a notice up offering a reward of three thousand for his capture. You'd better have died, instead of coming back here to tell us a pack of lies!"

"Don't be angry, brother," Iron Ox said. "If you'd just come back with me to Mount Liang, where we can have a fine life, wouldn't it be great?"

Li Da was furious. He would have liked to attack his brother,

Chapter 43

but he knew he couldn't handle him, so he hurled the pot of rice on the floor and left.

Iron Ox said to himself: "If he's gone like that, he'll go and tell people where I am and they'll come to get me. If I want to get out of this we'd better leave as soon as possible. My brother has never seen a lot of money, so what I'll do is, I'll leave him this big fifty-tael ingot. I'll put it on the bed. When he comes back he'll find it and he'll give up the idea of chasing me." He felt around in his pouch and took out the ingot and placed it on the bed. Then he said: "Mother, I'm going to carry you on my back now."

"Where are you taking me?" she asked.

"Don't ask questions, just remember you're going to be happy. I can easily carry you." So saying, he picked up his mother, took his halberd and left. He chose the remotest of paths.

Li Da, meanwhile, had gone rushing off to his master's house to report the matter. He raced back with a dozen farm-hands, but when he reached home he could see no sign of his mother. But he did see the ingot on the bed. This caused him to reflect: "Iron Ox has left me the silver and taken mother off somewhere. There must be some of his friends from Mount Liang with him. If I follow, they'll kill me. No doubt he's taken mother off to join their idle life in the stronghold on the mountain." The others saw no sign of Iron Ox and had no idea what was going on. Li Da told them: "Iron Ox has carried my mother off. But I don't know which way they've gone. There are so many different paths round here, how can we hope to find them?" Seeing that Li Da didn't know what to do, they hung around for a while and then all went home separately. Of this no more.

We must return to Iron Ox. Fearing that his brother would send people after him, he carried his mother deep into the mountains by narrow, lonely paths. It was getting late:

> *Evening mist floats across distant hills; the smoke of fires obscures fantastic peaks. Rooks in ragged flocks seek the wood. A hundred bird calls fill the trees. Wild geese in their orderly formations drop and disappear among the reeds. The fireflies' points of light hover over country paths and settle in the rank grass that is their home.*

The autumn wind sweeps through the trees scattering dead leaves.
Frosty air is wafted into the deepest corners of the mountains.

As daylight was fading, Iron Ox and his mother arrived at the foot of a steep ascent. The mother's sight was so bad she knew no difference between night and day. Iron Ox recognized the spot. It was called Yiling Heights. Once past it, they would find human habitations. By the light of the stars and the moon, the two of them, mother and son, slowly proceeded up the mountain, until the mother said: "My son, if you could find me a drink of water it would be so nice."

Iron Ox said: "Wait till we're past this mountain, mother. We'll find someone to give us lodging and something to eat."

"I ate some dry food for lunch, I'm terribly thirsty." she said.

"My throat feels as if it's on fire, too," Iron Ox said. "Just wait till we're at the top and then I'll find you some water."

"My son, I implore you, I'm dying of thirst."

"And I'm completely exhausted, too," Iron Ox said. Near the top he saw there was a big black rock beside a pine tree. He set his mother down on this, stuck his halberd in the ground and said: "Be patient, mother, and sit here for a moment, while I go and find some water." He could hear the sound of water, coming from the bottom of a ravine somewhere, so he followed his ears and after skirting several cliffs, came upon a gully down which a goodly stream of water was running. There's a poem that describes what he saw:

> *It winds 'twixt the cliffs with such boisterous zest,*
> *You know that its birthplace is up on the peak;*
> *The river runs ever, and never finds rest,*
> *Till it runs to the ocean, great billows to make.*

When he reached the bank of the stream he scooped water up in his hands and drank a few mouthfuls. Then he thought: "How am I going to carry this water to my mother?" He stood up and looked around in all directions. Far up the slope he saw a building. "That's it!" he thought. Grasping vines and creepers he hauled himself up the steep incline. He pushed open the gate and looked

Chapter 43

inside. It was in fact a shrine dedicated to a local god. In front of the main hall there was a stone incense burner. Iron Ox tried to lift this, but it was a solid block and tug as he might it wouldn't budge. Suddenly he lost patience and wrenched the base right out and smashed it against the stone steps in front of the hall. The bowl broke off and he picked it up and went back down to the stream, where he plunged it in the water and got a bunch of grass and scrubbed it clean. He filled it half full with water, raised it in both hands and returning by the way he had come staggered off up the hillside.

But when he reached the pine tree his mother was not on the stone. Only his halberd was there. He called out that he'd brought her water. But still she did not appear or answer his call. He began to get worried. He put down the incense burner and looked around in all directions: still no sign of her. About thirty paces away, however, he found traces of blood. When he saw this his heart misgave him. Following the trail of blood, he came to the mouth of a big cave, where two tiger cubs were toying with a human leg. Truly, we can say that:

The false Black Whirlwind felt the heat:
In life a fake, in death ... roast meat.
Now it's the mother's leg that's savaged:
To man or beast by hunger ravaged
All that's flesh is good to eat.

Iron Ox pondered: "I came back from Mount Liang to get my mother. With enormous effort I carried her this far, and all for you to go and eat her! For if that human leg the fucking tigers have brought here is not my mother's, whose could it be?" He was filled with a great rage, his light-coloured hair stood on end, he raised his halberd and ran at the tiger cubs. Startled by this, the tiger cubs, one big, one small, snarled and lunged at him with all their teeth and claws. He killed one of them at once. The other fled inside the cave. He followed it inside and dispatched it there. From this vantage point, squatting inside the tiger's lair, he saw a big tigress charging towards him, snarling and showing her claws. "You're the monster that ate my mother!" he said to himself. He put down his halberd and took the knife from his belt. When she reached the mouth of the cave the tigress first swept the entrance with her tail, then began to enter backwards. When he saw what she was doing, Iron Ox, employing every ounce of his strength stabbed desperately at the base of the tail, burying the knife in her anus. Such was the strength of his blow that the blade and hilt penetrated right through to her belly. With a deafening roar the tigress sprang away from the cave taking the knife with her, and bounded down the sheer side of a ravine. Iron Ox picked up his halberd and left the cave. The tigress maddened by the pain went on crashing down the rocky incline. Iron Ox was just about to go after her when from behind the trees a sudden gale arose. It blew so furiously the leaves were shaken from the trees like rain. According to the old saying: "Clouds originate from dragons, and wind is produced by tigers." At that moment, amid a storm of wind and by the light of the stars and the moon, a great roar burst out and a huge tiger with sad eyes and a white forehead appeared. This beast sprang furiously at Iron Ox. Calmly taking advantage of the animal's own momentum, Iron Ox held his blade firm and struck under the throat. The tiger never attempted a second spring. Firstly it was only concerned to escape the pain. And in the second place, its windpipe was pierced. It fled no more than half a dozen paces before it collapsed on the mountainside with a sound like half the mountain falling, and expired on the spot.

So Iron Ox had killed a whole family of tigers. But he still went back into the cave with his weapon in hand to have a look, in case there was another tiger. There was no sign of one. Exhausted, he returned to the temple and slept there till dawn. Early next morning he collected up his mother's remains, two legs and some other bones, and wrapped them in a shirt. Then he dug a grave at the back of the temple and buried the bones. He wept for a long while. There is a poem about this:

> *At Yiling, with the wind in the west, the season autumn,*
> *The tigers, male and female, gather in the forest on the heights.*
> *Soon the sight of his old mother's sparse remains,*

Chapter 43

黑旋風沂嶺殺四虎

Causes the hero to lament her fate.
Oblivious to danger he visits the tiger's den,
And four tigers pay with their lives for his revenge!
Behind the local temple he inters his mother's bones.
This hero's name? Li Kui, the famous Iron Ox!

By now Iron Ox was exceedingly hungry and thirsty. He was obliged to collect his luggage, take up his halberd and slowly make his way down the mountain. Suddenly half a dozen tiger hunters appeared, equipped with traps and bows and arrows. When they saw Iron Ox, strolling down the mountain all spattered with blood, they had quite a shock. "Are you the god of the mountain or something?" they asked. "How do you dare to cross this mountain alone?"

Iron Ox considered his reply carefully. "Recently that notice has gone up in Yishui, there's a reward of three thousand for my capture," he thought. "I daren't tell them my real name. I'd better invent a story." To the hunters he said: "I am a merchant. Yesterday afternoon I was crossing the pass with my mother. Because my mother wanted a drink I went down to the stream to get some water. A big tiger dragged my mother off and ate her. I tracked it to its lair and killed first two cubs and then two big tigers. I slept in the temple till it got light and then came down the mountain."

"Don't believe you!" the hunters shouted in unison. "How could one man kill four tigers? After all, the famous tiger killers in history are each only said to have killed one. Two tiger cubs, that's possible, but the two big tigers, that's really beyond a joke! Goodness knows how many beatings we've all received on account of those two beasts. Ever since that den of tigers has been here on Yiling Heights, which is nearly six months now, no one has cared to venture there. We just don't believe you. Who do you think you're going to fool?"

Iron Ox replied: "I'm not from these parts, why should I want to lie to you? If you don't believe me, we'd better go back up the mountain together and I'll try to show you. You can bring some porters along to help carry the tigers down."

Chapter 43

The hunters said: "If it's really true, we shan't be able to thank you enough, it will be great news."

The hunters whistled and in a moment thirty or forty men had gathered, all carrying long hooks and staves. They followed Iron Ox back up the mountain. Dawn had broken by now and when they reached the top the two dead tiger cubs by the den were clearly visible — one outside and one in the entrance — and then also the tigress dead on the mountainside, and a big male tiger lying dead in front of the shrine. The sight of four dead tigers sent the hunters into raptures. They got rope and tied them up to carry them down the mountain. They offered to go with Iron Ox to collect the reward, but first they sent someone on ahead to inform the village headman and other notables, who all came out to meet them. The tigers were carried to the house of a rich man, Squire Cao by name. This individual was a retired government official, who devoted himself to mischief and debauchery in the district. He had recently used some kind of skulduggery to add considerably to his fortune. This Squire Cao now came to see for himself and invited Iron Ox to sit in the thatched hall and tell him how he came to kill the tigers. Iron Ox told the story of how he had come to the mountain the night before with his mother and how she wanted a drink and how this led to the killing of the tigers. Everyone was amazed. Squire Cao wanted to know the great hero's name. Iron Ox replied: "Zhang is my name. I have no given name, people just call me Big Zhang."

There's a poem about this:

Everyone knows of the bogus Li Kui;
Nobody speaks of how Li Kui pretended.
But with Li Kui becoming Big Zhang for the day,
Who's true and who's false? It's quite a conundrum!

Squire Cao said: "Big indeed! Only a very big man could kill four monsters like that!" He ordered a feast to be laid in a sideroom. Of this no more.

Now when it became known in the neighbourhood that four tigers had been killed on Yiling Heights and taken to Squire Cao's it became a topic of conversation in every local establishment and everyone living in the village or on the surrounding slopes, man, woman or child, flocked to see the tigers and to get a glimpse of Squire Cao entertaining the hero who had killed them, drinking with him in the main hall. Amongst them all was Li Gui's wife who had taken refuge with her parents in her old home in the village. She came with everyone else to see the tigers. When she recognized Iron Ox, she hurried home to tell her mother and father: "That big black fellow who killed the tigers is the one who killed my old man and burnt my house down. He's the Black Whirlwind, alias Iron Ox, one of the robbers of Mount Liang." Her parents went at once and told the headman. The headman said: "If he's the Black Whirlwind, then he's the one who's wanted for the murder of a man in Baizhang, the one that fled to Jiangzhou and got involved in some other business too, and we received an official order for his detention. Recently the authorities announced a reward of three thousand for his capture. So now he's here, is he!" He secretly sent someone to ask Squire Cao to come and see him. Squire Cao excused himself from the company, saying he wanted to wash his hands, and hurried round to see the headman, from whom he learnt that the killer of the tigers was Li Kui, who had killed a man in Baizhang on the other side of the mountain and whose arrest had been ordered by the authorities. Squire Cao said: "Listen carefully. In case we've got this wrong, it wouldn't be a good idea to annoy him. If we're right then there's no problem. We can easily capture him. I'm just afraid it might not be him, in which case we'd be in trouble."

The headman said: "Apparently Li Gui's wife recognized him. He went to their house asking for food, and then killed Li Gui."

Squire Cao said: "In that case all we need do is give him plenty of wine and ask him if he wants to go to the government office to collect the reward for killing the tigers or if he'd rather collect it in the village. If he doesn't want to go to the government office, then he's our man. I'll get someone to change the cups around, we'll get him drunk and then send someone to the magistracy to ask them to send a sergeant to arrest him, it can hardly go wrong." There is a poem about this:

Chapter 43

> *The tiny mustard seed, they say,*
>   *Will go through the needle's eye,*
> *And it's always on a narrow road*
>   *You meet an enemy.*
> *Li Gui's jealous ghost has not*
>   *Yet taken its departure;*
> *And the Whirlwind truly stands*
>   *In an unpropitious quarter.*
> *For killing the tigers on the hill*
>   *He's earned the official fee;*
> *For the killing of a man he deserves*
>   *To be placed under lock and key.*
> *Remember the man that watched the bird*
>   *That watched the praying mantis.*
> *Now the best policy it seems is*
>   *Don't advertise your prowess.*

When the headman and the others had accepted this proposal, Squire Cao went back home. He detained Iron Ox, plying him with wine and saying: "I'm sorry I had to leave you for a moment just now. Let me ask you to undo your belt and put down your halberd, please make yourself comfortable."

Iron Ox said: "Very well, but I'm afraid I lost my knife in the tiger's belly, I've only got the sheath now. If I need to cut anything I shall have to ask someone to lend me a knife."

"Don't you worry about that," said Squire Cao. "I've got plenty of good blades. I shall be happy to give you one."

Iron Ox took off his sword and his belt and gave them to a retainer to put away for him. He leant his halberd against the wall. Squire Cao called for a big platter of meat and a big jug of wine. The rich men and the headman, the hunters and all the rest drank many toasts with Iron Ox taking it in turns and using large bowls and cups. Squire Cao asked: "I wonder, would you prefer to deliver the tigers to the authorities and claim the reward personally, or would you rather just seek some form of recompense from us here?"

"I am just a traveller, passing through," Iron Ox said. "My time is valuable and just because I happened to kill this family of tigers there's no need to go to the government and ask for a reward. If you feel inclined to offer me something here, that will be quite all right; if not, I shall just continue my journey."

Squire Cao said: "We certainly don't want to hold you up. Just wait a little while, and we'll make a collection here in the village towards your travel expenses. We can take the tigers to the authorities ourselves."

"I would be grateful if you could provide me with some clothes, though, so I can change."

"Of course, of course," said Squire Cao. He produced a padded robe of fine black cloth so Iron Ox could change his blood-stained clothing. Then to the sound of drums and flutes, wine was brought. They all pressed Iron Ox to drink, a cup of warm wine, followed by one of cold. Not realizing that it was a plot, Iron Ox drank to his heart's content. He had completely forgotten Song Jiang's instructions. Within a few hours he was drunk as a lord and couldn't even stand on his feet. They carried him into an empty room at the back and tipped him onto a wooden bench. Then they took two ropes and tied him down. The headman was told to send messengers flying to the district office to report the matter. Li Gui's wife was sent along too to make an official statement from which an indictment could be drawn up.

There was great excitement in Yishui. The Governor, greatly concerned, went into session at once. "What have you done with this Black Whirlwind?" he asked. "This is a dangerous conspirator, we must not let him get away."

The plaintiff and the hunters said: "We've got him tied up at the house of Squire Cao, of this district. Since there's no one capable of subduing him, we were afraid something might go wrong and we might lose him on the way, that's the reason we didn't bring him with us."

The Governor sent for his sergeant of police. When the latter presented himself before the bench he barked out a salute. Who this was you can learn from the poem:

His face is broad, his eyebrows thick,

Chapter 43

Thick as you've ever seen.
His beard and whiskers red, his eyes
Like a foreigner's jade green.
This is the famous Green-Eyed Tiger,
This is sergeant Li Yun.

The Governor sent for this Li Yun and told him: "They've got the notorious Black Whirlwind, alias Iron Ox, tied up in the house of Squire Cao at the bottom of Yiling Heights. Take plenty of men and bring him here secretly, but don't alarm the public or let him escape."

Green-Eyes left with his orders. He selected thirty experienced men, all well-armed, and hastened off to Yiling.

Now Yishui was only a small place. Nothing could long remain hidden there. Already the rumour was going round the market: "They've caught that Black Whirlwind who created such havoc in Jiangzhou. Green-Eyes has been sent to pick him up."

The Crocodile, who was staying with Zhu Fu's family outside the east gate heard this and rushed to the back room to tell his brother: "This black fellow has got himself into trouble again, how can we rescue him? It's precisely because Song Jiang feared he might get into trouble that he sent me to keep an eye on him. Now he's been caught how can I go back to the mountain fortress and face our leader if I don't rescue him? What are we going to do?"

Zhu Fu said: "Don't worry brother. But I tell you, this sergeant Li is a good fellow. He can hold his own against forty or fifty at once. Even you and I, supposing we made a concerted effort together, could not handle him. No, we've got to use our brains, not just brute force. Green-Eyes and I are normally good friends, he has taught me some useful tricks in martial arts. So I know pretty well how we can deal with him, only I won't be able to stay here afterwards. Tonight we must get twenty or thirty catties of meat cooked, and order a dozen bottles of wine. The meat must be cut in big pieces and then we'll mix a drug in with it. Before daybreak we and some of the inn servants will carry it to a quiet place along the road and wait for them when they're bringing Iron

Ox, to offer them wine. When the drug takes them we can rescue Iron Ox. How about that?"

"Great plan," said the Crocodile. "We mustn't waste any time. We must get it all set up and then be off."

Zhu Fu said: "The problem is, Green-Eyes doesn't drink. So even if we can drug him, he'll come round pretty quickly. And one more thing: when this business gets out, I won't be able to remain here."

The Crocodile said: "Listen brother, this inn of yours, you don't make much out of it, do you? Wouldn't it be better for you to get your family and go with me to the mountain? If you join the band you'll have gold and silver galore and as many clothes as you like, it's a great life! Tonight, get a couple of your chaps to look for a cart to take your wife and valuables off with instructions to wait by the tenth milestone so we can all meet up and go to the mountain. Now, I happen to have some of the drug here in my pack. If Green-Eyes doesn't drink, we'll drug his meat and get him to eat a lot. When he passes out we'll rescue Iron Ox and take him back, what's difficult about that?"

Zhu Fu said: "You're right." He gave orders for a cart to be found, made up several bundles and loaded them on the cart, abandoning the rest of his household goods, told his wife and children to get onto the carts and told two of his people to take them on ahead.

That night the Crocodile and Zhu Fu cooked the meat, cut it into big pieces and mixed in the drug. Together with the wine they made two loads of it, and also took along twenty or thirty cups. They even took a quantity of vegetables, also drugged. This was in case there were any who did not eat meat, in order to take care of them too. There were two inn servants carrying a load each. The two brothers took some fruit and nuts and they all set off well before dawn and stopped in a very quiet part of the road. When it was just beginning to get light they heard gongs in the distance. The Crocodile posted himself beside the road.

Now around the fourth watch a party of thirty or forty soldiers, who had been drinking in the village half the evening, brought Iron Ox out with his hands tied behind his back. They set off with

Green-Eyes riding at the back. When he saw them coming, Zhu Fu stepped forward and barred the way, saying: "Greetings, Master! I want to invite you to take a break." He ladled out a jug of wine, poured some into a big cup and offered it to Green-Eyes. The Crocodile brought out the meat and the servants offered the fruit and nuts. Green-Eyes hurriedly dismounted, rushed forward and said: "My dear friend, you should not have gone to all this trouble."

Zhu Fu said: "It's just a little token of my respect."

Green-Eyes took the cup but did not drink.

Zhu Fu knelt and said: "I know you do not drink, Master. But this wine is in your honour, so please just this once taste half a cup."

Green-Eyes could scarcely refuse this invitation, so he made a show of taking two sips.

Zhu Fu said: "Since you do not drink, let me invite you to have some meat."

"I am still full from last night," Green-Eyes said. "I couldn't eat anything."

"You have travelled quite some way, you must be hungry. Even if you don't want to eat, please take just a little something, in order not to shame me." He selected two good pieces and proffered them. Seeing him so attentive, Green-Eyes reluctantly ate two pieces of meat. Zhu Fu now offered wine to the local magnates, the headman, the hunters and the rest, whilst the Crocodile went and invited all the soldiers and retainers. This lot didn't care whether it was hot or cold, good or not good, they simply guzzled all that was to hand. Like the wind sweeping away the scattered clouds or the river bearing off fallen blossoms, they made a clean sweep of it.

Iron Ox was watching all this. Seeing the Crocodile and his brother, he knew that there must be some plan, so he said: "Aren't you going to offer me any?"

"You're a criminal!" the Crocodile shouted. "Who'd give anything to you? A murderer like you, you'd do better just to shut your mouth!"

Green-Eyes looked at his men and was about to give the order to move off again, when he saw they were all gaping at each other, quite unable to move. Their lips trembled, their legs had gone numb. They stumbled and fell. "It's a trap," Green-Eyes started to shout, but when he tried to move he too felt his head sinking and his legs floating, and he crashed to the ground. He fell in a flaccid heap and lay there unconscious. The Crocodile and Zhu Fu each took a halberd, and shouting: "You're not getting away!" set upon those who had not yet eaten or drunk and other bystanders. The quickest escaped, those who were slow were killed on the spot.

Iron Ox now gave a great shout. He burst his bonds, grabbed a halberd, and was on the point of killing Green-Eyes. Zhu Fu hurriedly intervened, saying: "Don't harm him, he's my teacher, we're good friends. Just get out of here, quick!"

Iron Ox replied: "If I don't kill that old ass Squire Cao I shall never calm down." He rushed off, brandishing his halberd, and killed Squire Cao and Li Gui's wife. Then for good measure he killed the headman, and since he was now really aroused he slaughtered a crowd of hunters and the thirty or so soldiers. The others, retainers and onlookers, only wished their parents had given them more than two legs. They ran for their lives, fleeing down the remotest paths.

Iron Ox was still busy looking for people to kill. "It's nothing to do with innocent bystanders, stop killing them!" the Crocodile shouted, standing in his way. Only then did Iron Ox desist. From the bodies of soldiers he stripped off two pieces of clothing which he put on.

The three were now preparing to set off, halberds in hand, down the smallest paths. But suddenly Zhu Fu said: "This is not right. I have sentenced my teacher to death. What's he going to say to the Governor, when he recovers? He'll have to follow us. You two go on ahead, I'll wait for him. I can't forget the great kindness he's shown to me. He's always been fair and honest with me. I'll wait and ask him if he'll join us and go to the mountain to join the outlaws. It's my duty to do this. I don't want him to have to go back and face the music."

The Crocodile said: "You're quite right. Now, I'll go on ahead with the cart, but I'll leave Iron Ox here with you to assist you. Only remember, Green-Eyes didn't eat a lot, so he'll come round in less than a couple of hours. If he doesn't appear by then, don't insist on waiting for him."

"Of course we won't," Zhu Fu said.

So the Crocodile went on ahead. Zhu Fu and Iron Ox sat down by the roadside and waited. And of course in under two hours they saw Green-Eyes racing towards them, brandishing his halberd and shouting: "Stop, you scoundrels!"

Iron Ox seeing him so furious, leapt to his feet, raised his halberd and charged him, much to Zhu Fu's distress. Well, as a result of this, two more tigers were eventually added to the Marshes of Mount Liang and four heroes were honoured before the great assembly hall.

But if you want to know who prevailed in that fight between Iron Ox and Green-Eyes, you must read the next chapter.